Praise for Ted Kosmatka's debut novel, *The Games*

"Exacting science and meticulous attention to detail provide the backbone for this thriller, which blends the best of Crichton and Koontz."
—*Publishers Weekly* (starred review)

"Very like something Michael Crichton might have written . . . An outstanding debut novel; expect big things from Kosmatka."
—*Booklist* (starred review)

"Kosmatka successfully captures the thrill of ground-breaking technology characteristic of Michael Crichton's technothrillers. . . . The pleasure of his polished, action-packed storytelling is deepened by strong character development. This near-future sf thriller will capture the imagination of unstoppable monster lovers and fans of disaster fiction alike and seems destined for the big screen."
—*Library Journal* (starred review)

"Kosmatka's debut novel is a . . . technological thriller that revs up like a racecar with a dose of bad attitude and steadily creeping horror. [Readers] who enjoy the karmic boomerang of authors like Michael Crichton or Preston and Child should eat this up."
—*School Library Journal* (starred review)

"I stayed up very late just to finish this, and *The Games* certainly lives up to its buzz. . . . *The Games* is a sci-fi/thriller with unexpected depth and humanity, and a few twists that I didn't see coming. Very highly recommended!"
—My Bookish Ways

THE
GAMES

THE GAMES

TED KOSMATKA

BALLANTINE BOOKS • NEW YORK

2013 Del Rey Mass Market Edition

Copyright © 2012 by Ted Kosmatka

Published in the United States by Del Rey, an imprint of The Random House Publishing Group, a division of Random House, Inc., New York.

DEL REY is a registered trademark and the Del Rey colophon is a trademark of Random house, Inc.

Originally published in hardcover in the United States by Del Rey Books, an imprint of The Random House Publishing Group, a division of Random House, Inc., in 2012.

ISBN: 978-0-345-52662-5
E-Book ISBN: 978-0-345-52663-2

Printed in the United States of America

www.delreybooks.com

9 8 7 6 5 4 3 2 1

Del Rey Mass Market edition: February 2013

To my mother and to my father

THE
GAMES

PROLOGUE

The boy lay motionless in the tube as the machine moved all around him. He held his breath and concentrated on the pinging, trying to clear his head like the white coats told him.

"Look into the screen, Evan," a voice said from a speaker near his ear.

Evan blinked against the sudden burst of white static and turned his head away.

They'd said this was going to be the last test, but they'd said that once before. They had lots of ways to test you here.

"What are you looking for, exactly?" Evan's mother asked from her spot near the door. She was backed against the wall, holding her purse tightly to her abdomen as if afraid to move farther into the room.

"Gross abnormalities," the man at the computer said. He didn't look up from his terminal as the machine continued its slow spin.

Evan glanced back at his mother. *They think I'm gross.*

There were four men in white coats in the room now, though only one was what his mother called a real doctor. The two younger men were testers from the special school, and the oldest man wore a dark tie under his white coat and probably wasn't any kind of doctor at all. That one scared Evan most of all.

The machine made a new noise, a clicking sound that Evan felt along the sides of his head. "What's it doing?" Evan asked, trying to sit up in the cramped tunnel.

The man with the tie stepped away from the computer and gently guided the boy onto his back again. "You must remain still. This is a big camera, and it's taking pictures of the inside of your head."

"I don't see a flash," Evan said.

"It uses magnets, not light."

"Can it tell what I'm thinking?"

"No," the man said.

But they'd said that before, too. Evan knew better; all these tests were to see what he was thinking. His mother told him so. Because of what he did to the game. Because of what happened to Mr. Jacobs.

Evan concentrated on being still. He didn't trust the man, didn't like the way his eyes tightened when he looked at the computer screen. *What did he see? How gross am I?* Evan closed his eyes.

"Mrs. Chandler—"

"Miss," she interrupted.

"Oh, sorry," the man at the computer said. He was the real doctor, and new to Evan's case. "Were there any complications with your pregnancy when you were carrying Evan?"

"No."

"Any family history of birth defects or deformity?"

"Nothing like that, no."

"Mental illness, learning disabilities?"

"Some of that, yeah."

"Who?"

"My brother."

"What was his diagnosis?"

"I don't know; he died when I was young. Why are you asking me all this? Did you find something?"

The man's eyes lifted from the terminal to her face, then dropped again. It was the man with the tie who spoke: "Sub-cranial morphology can vary widely between normal individuals. There's nothing to worry about."

The machine clicked again. "You need to calm down, Evan," the man at the computer said into the microphone. "Your activity is all over the place, and we need a baseline. You have to relax."

"I'm trying," Evan said.

"Think of something enjoyable."

So Evan thought of his mother. He thought of times between his mother's boyfriends, when he didn't have to share her. He thought of times before the problems at school, before the new teacher Mr. Jacobs found out that he couldn't count numbers right. Before Mr. Jacobs found out he couldn't read.

"Good. Now look into the screen, Evan," the man said.

Evan opened his eyes, and the static was gone, replaced by a blank screen. Then, on that screen, a number flashed.

"What do you see?" the man asked.

"I see a four," Evan said.

"Good. What color is the number?"

"It's white."

"Good."

More numbers flashed on the screen. Five, three, six, nine. Then letters appeared.

"What do you see now?" the man asked.

"Numbers and letters."

"What colors are they?"

"They're all white."

"All of them?"

"Yes," Evan said.

The screen faded to black. "You did good, Evan,"

the man said. "Now we're going to try something different."

The black screen flashed and was suddenly full of spinning gears. The gears were of various sizes and colors, and they spread across the screen in an unbroken chain, each one touching one or two others and all of them moving in unison. The smallest gears moved quickest; the larger ones seemed barely to move at all.

"What do you see?" the man asked.

"I see gears."

"What are they doing?"

"They're turning."

"Good, Evan."

The gears stopped.

"If the top gear was turning toward the left," the man at the computer said, "which direction would the bottom gear be turning?"

"Up," Evan said immediately.

"Which is that, clockwise or counterclockwise?"

"Up," Evan repeated.

Evan's mother spoke: "He doesn't know about clocks, or left or right. I tried to teach him—I mean, we all tried to teach him. . . ." Her voice trailed off.

The man stepped from his computer and bent to look into the tube at the boy. "If this gear was moving like this," he said, pointing and turning a circle with his finger, "then which direction would this gear way over here move?"

"Up," Evan said, pointing along the gear's outside edge, indicating a clockwise rotation.

The man smiled. "So it would."

The next series of images were more complex, but Evan's answers were just as immediate and just as correct. He didn't have to think about it.

"Let's try something different now," the man finally said.

It started easy enough. Strange new shapes appeared on the screen. They weren't gears, exactly, but they had spikes and grooves and jutting angles that let them fit together the way gears do. The man bent near the tube again and showed him how by manipulating a control ball near his hand, Evan could change the images on the screen. He could move them.

"These are three-dimensional puzzles, Evan," the man said. "Your teachers tell us that you are very good at puzzles. Is that true?"

"I'm pretty good," Evan said, but he'd never seen puzzles like this before.

He experimented, moving one image toward another, turning it so their grooves lined up. The images merged, and a chime sounded.

"Good job, Evan," the man said, and walked back to his computer. "Now we'll try some harder ones."

New, complex shapes appeared on the screen. Evan had to rotate each one completely to get a good look, because all the sides were different. He moved them together. He found where they fit. The machine chimed.

"Good, Evan."

The solutions came easily. The complexity of the spatial configurations pulled him in, focused him to a fine point of concentration. Something was happening in his head; he felt it, as if some hidden green part of him was warming in the sunshine. The world around him retreated, became remote, irrelevant.

He no longer noticed the tube, or the computer, or the room with its four white walls and four white coats. There were only the puzzles, one after another, in a blur of shapes he manipulated with the controls at his fingertips.

He worked puzzle after puzzle, listening for the chime when he got them right.

Then the screen was empty, jarringly empty, all at once. It took him a moment to come back to himself enough to speak.

"More," he said.

"There are no more, Evan," the man said. "You've solved them all."

Evan glanced out of the tube, but the white coats weren't looking at him. They stared at their computer terminal.

The man with a tie was the first to look up from the glowing screen. He wore an expression Evan had never seen pointed at him before. Evan's stomach turned to ice.

HOSPITALS ALWAYS stank. There was something strange and sickly about the air in the building, and the breeze coming through the window screen hardly improved it. Evan could smell the garbage that lay heaped in the alley several floors below. Still, he moved closer to the window, pretending interest in the view because looking out the window was easier than looking at his mother. She sat at the big, glossy table. She was crying, though she did it silently—one of the tricks she'd picked up during her time with her last boyfriend.

They'd been in this room for a while now, waiting.

When the door finally opened, Evan flinched. Three men walked in. He'd never seen any of them before, but their coats were dark, and all of them wore ties. It was bad. Men with ties always meant something bad. Evan's mother sat up quickly and wiped the corners of her eyes with a napkin she kept in her purse.

The men smiled at Evan and shook his mother's

hand in turns, introducing themselves. The one who called himself Walden got right to the point. "Evan's tests were abnormal," he said.

He was a big man with a face like a square block, and he wore little wire glasses perched across his nose. Evan hadn't seen anyone with glasses like that in a long time; he tried not to stare.

"Where's the doctor?" Evan's mother asked.

"Evan's case has been transferred to me."

"But they told me Dr. Martin was going to be Evan's doctor. I thought that's why they brought him in."

"Dr. Martin himself felt that Evan's case required special attention that he could not provide."

"But I thought he was supposed to be a specialist."

"Oh, I assure you that he is. But we all feel Evan's case requires . . . a more systematized process of inquiry."

Evan's mother stared at the man. "The teacher died, didn't he?"

"Tim Jacobs? No, he'll survive."

"Then I want to leave."

"Miss Chandler, we feel—"

"Right now, with my son, I want to leave."

"It's not as simple as that anymore." He pulled out a chair but didn't sit. Instead, he stepped his foot on the seat and leaned an arm casually across his extended knee. He towered over the sitting woman. "The man didn't die, but he's still having some motor coordination problems. We're not sure how your son managed to access the game's protocols the way he did. Those VR tutorials are hardwired and aren't meant to be altered from the inside."

"There must have been a glitch."

"There was no glitch. Your son did something. He changed something. A man almost died because of that."

"It was an accident."

"Was it?"

"Yes." His mother's voice was soft.

"I hear that teacher was hard on Evan. I hear he mocked him in front of other students."

His mother was silent.

"Miss Chandler, we're very concerned about Evan." The man who called himself Walden finally sank into the chair he'd been using as a footrest, and now his two silent companions pulled out chairs and sat. Walden laced his hands together in front of him on the table. "He's a special child with special needs."

He waited for Evan's mother to respond, and when she didn't, he continued. "We've tested many children here at these facilities in the last seven years. Many children. And we've never come across anyone with your son's particular mixture of gifts and disabilities."

"Gifts?" His mother's voice was harsh. "You call what happened a gift?"

"It could be. We need time to do more tests. Your son appears to have a very unusual form of synesthesia in addition to several other neurological abnormalities."

"Syna-what?"

"An abnormal cross-activation between brain regions. Often caused by structural malformations in the fusiform gyrus, but to be honest, in Evan's case, we're not sure. Some individuals conflate colors with shapes, or experience smells with certain sounds. But Evan's situation is more complex than that. His perception of numbers is somehow involved."

"But he doesn't understand numbers."

"He tested off the scale for numbers utility."

"He knows what numbers look like, and he can tell

you the name of a number if you write it, but numbers don't mean anything to him."

"On some level, they do."

"He can't even tell you when one number is bigger than another. They're just words to him."

"Those spatial puzzles he solved were more than just puzzles. Some of them were also tricks. Some of them would have required complex calculus to solve correctly."

"Calculus? He can't count to twenty."

"Something in him can. Individuals with one form of synesthesia are often found to have another. We're not sure how Evan does what he does. And in that VR game, we're not even sure what it is that he did, let alone how. Evan needs special attention. He's going to need a special school."

"He's already in a special school," she said, but her voice was resigned.

"Yes, I've looked over his records. Miss Chandler, I have the authority to alter his public tracking. There is no reason why your boy should end up mopping floors somewhere."

"You can change his track? You can do that?"

The man nodded. "I have the authority."

"But why, after what happened?"

"Because we've never seen another boy like him. We're going to have to make up a new track. The Evan Chandler track. And to be honest, we're not really sure where it leads just yet."

EVAN'S MOTHER was hysterical the day they came for him. The sedatives quieted her as soft-voiced men lowered her to the seedy couch. The boy's things were packed into a crate, and her drug-fuzzied mind found preoccupation in that for a moment.

Ten years old, and everything he owned fit into a single white box. It didn't seem possible, but there it was, and two men in dark suits carried the box away between them.

She saw the faces of her neighbors in the open doorway, and she knew they assumed this was an arrest, or just another eviction. It was common. Their feral eyes shuffled through her possessions—the worn couch, her two plastic chairs, the small wooden coffee table with its wobbly leg—scouting for something to grab once the authorities were gone and her things were pushed out into the street.

"I don't see why he has to leave," she said. It was a plea.

"It is better for the boy this way," one of them, a blond woman, said. "We can better nurture his talents if we control the environment. You'll be able to visit as often as you'd like."

Evan's mother wiped the tears from her eyes and struggled unsteadily to her feet. There was no fighting it. A part of her had known that for a while now, since before what happened to Mr. Jacobs, even. Evan was different. It was always going to come to this; the world would take him, one way or the other.

"Can I see it?" she asked.

It was an hour's drive across the city. In the van, Evan's mother rocked him until the vehicle finally pulled to rest before a building surrounded by playgrounds. The group filed out. Children shouted and played in the distance while one boy stood gazing up at a flagpole. Evan's mother stared. That will be Evan, she knew. Strange even here. Odd among the odd.

She bent and kissed her son. "My special boy," she said, and squeezed him until a female agent tugged at the child's hand. Evan looked back and waved good-bye.

"I'll visit you soon, Evan," his mother called.

She watched her son disappear into the building and then broke down in sobs. She never saw him again.

PART I

DISTANT THUNDER

*They conceive trouble and give birth
to evil; their wombs fashion deceit.*

—JOB, CHAPTER 15, VERSE 35

CHAPTER ONE

Somewhere in the blackness a videophone rang. Through force of will, Silas brought the glowing face of the clock radio into focus: 3:07 A.M. His heart beat a little faster.

Is it ever good news at 3:07 A.M.?

He fumbled for the light near his bedside, sliding his hand up to the switch, wondering who could be calling this late. Suddenly, he knew—*the lab*. The light was nearly as blinding as the darkness, but by squinting he found the phone, being careful to hit the voice-only button.

"Hello," he croaked.

"Dr. Williams?" The voice coming through the speaker was young and male. He didn't recognize it.

"Yes," Silas answered.

"Dr. Nelson had me call. You'll want to come down to the compound."

"What's happened?" He sat up straighter in bed, swinging his feet to the carpet.

"The surrogate went into labor."

"What? When?" It was still too soon. All the models had predicted a ten-month gestation.

"Two hours ago. The surrogate is in bad shape. They can't delay it."

Silas tried to clear his head, think rationally. "The medical team?"

"The surgeons are being assembled now."

Silas ran his fingers slowly through his mop of salt-and-pepper curls. He checked the pile of dirty clothes lying on the floor next to his bed and snagged a shirt that looked a little less wrinkled than its brethren. Above all else, he considered himself to be an adaptable man. "How long do I have?"

"Half-hour, maybe less."

"Thanks, I'll be there in twenty minutes." Silas clicked the phone off. For better or for worse, it had begun.

THE NIGHT was cool for Southern California, and Silas drove with the windows down, enjoying the way the wind swirled around the cab of the Courser 617. The air was damp, tinged with a coming thunderstorm. Eagerness pressed him faster. He took the ramp to Highway 5 at seventy miles per hour, smiling at the way the car grabbed the curve. So many times as a youth he'd dreamed of owning a car such as this. Tonight his indulgence seemed prophetic; he needed every one of those thoroughbreds galloping beneath the low, sleek hood.

As he merged onto the mostly empty interstate, he punched it, watching the speedometer climb to just over a hundred and five. The radio blared something he didn't recognize—rhythmic and frenzied, almost primeval, it matched his mood perfectly. His anxiety built with his proximity to the lab.

Over the years he had become accustomed to the occasional midnight dash to the lab, but it had never been like this, with so many unknowns. A vision of Evan Chandler's grossly jowled face entered his mind, and he felt a rush of anger. He couldn't really blame Chandler. You couldn't ask a snake not to be a snake.

It was the members of the Olympic Commission who should have known better.

He switched lanes to avoid a mini-tram, his speed never dropping below ninety-five miles per hour. His dark eyes glanced into the rearview, scouting for a patrol. The ticket itself wouldn't bother him. He was exempt from any fine levied by local authorities while on his way to and from the lab, but the time it would cost to explain himself would be the real expense. *All clear.* He pushed the gas pedal to the floor. Minutes later, he hit his brakes, downshifted to third, and cut across two lanes to catch his exit. He was now out of the city proper and into the suburbs of San Bernardino.

Silas passed the brightly lit main entrance of Five Rings Laboratories without taking his foot off the gas. He didn't have time for the main entrance, the winding drive. Instead, he veered left at the access road, whipping past the chain-link fence that crowded the gravel. At the corner, he spun the wheel and hooked another left, decelerating as he neared the rear gate. He flashed his badge to the armed guard, and the iron bars swung inward just in time to save his paint job.

The lab grounds were vast and parklike—a sprawling technological food web of small interconnected campuses, three- and four-story structures sharing space with stands of old growth. Glass and brick and trees. A semicircle of buildings crouched in conference around a small man-made pond.

He followed his headlights to a building at the west end of the complex and skidded to a stop in his assigned parking spot.

He was surprised to see Dr. Nelson standing there to greet him—a short, squat form cast in fluorescent lighting. "You were right. Twenty minutes exactly," Dr. Nelson said.

Silas groaned as he extricated himself from the vehicle. "One of the advantages of owning a sports car," he said, and stretched his stiff back as he got to his feet.

A nervous smile crept to the corner of Nelson's mouth. "Yeah, well, I can see the disadvantage. Someone your size should really consider a bigger car."

"You sound like my chiropractor." Silas knew things weren't going well upstairs; Nelson wasn't one for quips. In fact, Silas couldn't recall ever seeing the man smile. His stomach tightened a notch.

They made their way to the elevators, and Nelson pushed the button for the third floor.

"So where do things stand?" Silas asked.

"It's anesthetized, and the surgical team should be ready any minute."

"The vitals?"

"Not good. The old girl is worn out, just skin and bones. Even the caloric load we've been pushing hasn't been enough. The fetus is doing okay, though. Still has a good, strong heartbeat. The sonogram shows it's roughly the size of a full-term calf, so I don't think there should be anything tricky about the surgery."

"The surgery isn't what I'm worried about."

"Yeah, I know. We're ready with an incubator just in case."

Silas followed Nelson around a corner and down another long hallway. They stopped at a glass door, and Nelson slid his identification card into the console slot. There were a series of beeps, then a digitized, feminine voice: "Clearance accepted; you may enter."

The view room was long, narrow, and crowded. It was an enclosed balcony that overhung a surgical suite, and most of the people were gazing into the chamber below through a row of windows that ran along the left wall.

At the far end of the packed room, a tall man with a shaggy mane of blond hair noticed them. "Come in, come in," Benjamin said with a wave. At twenty-six, he was the youngest man working on the project. A prodigy funneled from the eastern cytology schools, he described himself as a man who knew his way around an oocyte. Silas had taken an instant liking to him when they'd met more than a year ago.

"You're just in time for the fun," Benjamin said. "I thought for sure they wouldn't be able to drag you out of bed."

"Three hours' sleep is all any man needs in a thirty-six-hour period." He grabbed Benjamin's outstretched hand and gave it a firm shake. "What's the status of our little friend?"

"As you can see"—Benjamin gestured toward the window—"things have progressed a little faster than we expected. The surrogate turned the corner from distressed to dying in the last hour, and it's triggered contractions. As far as we can tell, it may still be a little early, but since you can't sail a sinking ship"— Benjamin pulled a cigar from the inside pocket of his lab coat and held it out to Silas—"it looks like our little gladiator is going to have a birthday."

Silas took the cigar, smiling against his best efforts. "Thanks." He turned and stepped toward the glass. The cow was on its side on a large stainless-steel table, surrounded by a team of doctors and nurses. The surgeons huddled around their patient, only their eyes and foreheads visible above sterile masks.

"It should be anytime now," Benjamin said.

Silas turned to face him. "Anything new on the sonogram visuals?"

Benjamin shook his head and pushed his glasses

up his long, thin nose. For the first time his face lost its optimistic glow. "We did another series, but we haven't been able to glean any additional information."

"And those structures we talked about?"

"Still can't identify them. Not that people haven't had a field day coming up with ideas."

"I hate going into this blind."

"Believe me, I know." Benjamin's voice soured. "But the Olympic Commission didn't exactly leave you with a lot of room for maneuvering, did they? The fat bastard isn't even a biologist, for Christ's sake. If things go wrong, it won't be on your head."

"You really believe that?"

"No, I guess I don't."

"Then you're wise beyond your years."

"Still, one way or the other, Evan Chandler is going to have a lot of explaining to do."

"I don't think he's that worried," Silas said softly. "I don't see him here, do you?"

THE SCIENTISTS stood crowded against the glass, transfixed by the scene unfolding beneath them. Inside the white stricture of lights, a scalpel blinked stainless steel. The cow lay motionless on its left side as it was opened from sternum to pelvis in one slow, smooth cut. Gloved hands insinuated themselves into its abdomen, gently separating layers of tissue, reaching deep. Silas felt his heart thumping in his chest. The hands disappeared entirely, then the arms up to the elbows. Assistants used huge curved tongs to stretch the incision wide.

The surgeon shifted his weight. His shoulder strained. Silas imagined the man's teeth gritting with effort beneath the micropore mask as he rummaged around in the bovine's innards. *What did he feel?* A final pull and it was over. The white-smocked physician slowly pulled a dark, dripping mass away as a nurse moved in to cut the umbilical cord. Faintly, a sporadic beeping in the background changed to a steady tone as the cow flatlined. The medical team ignored it, moving to focus their energies on the newborn.

The first surgeon put the bloody shape on the table under the lamps and began wiping it down with a sponge and warm water, while another doctor peeled away the dense layers of fibrous glop that still clung to it.

The surgeon's voice sounded over the speakers in the view room from a microphone in his mask. "The fetus is dark . . . still covered by the embryonic sack . . . thick, fibrous texture; I'm tearing it away."

Silas's face was nearly pushed against the glass, trying to get a better look over the doctor's shoulder. For a moment he caught a glimpse of the newborn, but then the medical team shifted around their patient and he could see nothing. The sound of the doctor's breathing filled the view room.

"This . . . interesting . . . I'm not sure . . ." The doctor's voice trailed off in the speakers.

Suddenly, a shrill cry split Silas's ears, silencing the excited background chatter. The cry was strange, like nothing he'd ever heard before.

The doctors stepped back from the wailing newborn one by one, opening a gap, allowing Silas his first real glimpse.

His mouth dropped open.

LATER THAT morning, the storm that had been threatening for hours finally moved in with all the subtlety of a shotgun blast. Thunder boomed across the expansive field of California mod-sod. Dr. Silas Williams watched from behind the window of his second-story office, hands folded behind his back, drinking in the scene. The familiar ache in his bad ear had finally begun to ebb, becoming tolerable again. It always seemed to act up at the most inopportune times, and he hadn't let himself take anything stronger than aspirin because of what he knew was coming. He'd need his edge today.

Outside his window, the few well-manicured windbreaks of oak, hickory, and alder that stood scattered across the vast green promenade seemed to sway and shake with anticipation. Their branches bowed in the gusts that swept in from the west. In the distance, he could see the road and the cars—their headlight beams turned on against the darkening mid-morning sky.

He'd always felt there was magic in these moments just before the rain, when the sky brooded and rumbled its promises. The last few moments before a hard rain seemed to exist outside of time. It was the eternal drama, old as nature. Old as life. A dull curtain of precipitation spread west to east across the landscape, instantly soaking the grass. For a moment, he clutched at the wispy borders of ancient half-memories of other storms on other continents, of tall savanna grass waving and genuflecting before the monsoon.

The first fat drop spattered the window. Then another, and a dozen, and the window ran like a river, smearing away the outside world. As the sky darkened further, and the scene beyond the window lost its form in the streaming rain, his reflection materialized in the glass before him. He considered the visage gazing intently back at him. A good enough face, if a little weatherworn. For the first time in a long time, on this day of birth and rain, his mind cast back to his childhood. To a face so like his own.

Silas remembered his father in flashes—long legs, a towering silhouette that tucked him in at night. Huge hands with long, rectangular palms. Masculine. Solidly there.

Then not.

Silas's father was killed in a refinery fire when he was three, leaving behind only the faintest ghosts of memories for his son. Most of what Silas knew of his father came from his mother's stories and pictures. But in many ways, it was the pictures that spoke most eloquently.

The family portrait that hung in his mother's living room for decades showed a huge, broad-shouldered man with tight curls shorn low to the scalp. A gentle half-smile dimpled his left cheek. He was sitting next to Silas's mother, holding hands, his dark brown complexion contrasting sharply against the warm New Orleans honey of her skin. He had the kind of face that some Americans would have described as exotic—both broad and angular, an unexpected bone structure that snagged the eye. Immense cheekbones, high and sharp, dominated the proportions of his face. Many times growing up, Silas had noticed people lingering in front of that picture, as though his father was a puzzle to figure out. What did they see in that dead man?

While in her twenties, Silas's sister had leveraged their father's bone structure and long limbs into a modeling career. It had paid for college when she chose to go against the tracking of her state sponsorship. A thing most young people couldn't afford to do. Ashley was married now, and had a young son. She still had a year left on her primary nuptial contract, but they were a happy couple and already had plans to re-up lifelong at the first option. He envied them a little. What they had was so different from what he'd shared with Chloe all those years ago.

He remembered the arguments and the shouting, the slammed doors, the things said that couldn't be taken back. But it was the silences that did the most damage. The interminable quiets that ate their evenings, growing longer over every passing month as they each came to terms with the fact that there was nothing really left to say.

Neither of them had wanted children, and eventually there had been nothing there to hold them together. Their careers became their partners. In the end, they had simply let their contract expire. They didn't even talk about it. The third anniversary came and went without either of them filing for a continuance, and the next day, they just weren't married anymore. A lot of marriages ended like that.

Still, on the evening she'd moved out, he'd felt crazy. He hadn't wanted her to stay, but as he stood there, watching her walk through the door for what would be the last time, he felt . . . grief. Not for the loss of her but for the loss of what there should have been between them. The enormous emptiness of his life had almost overwhelmed him.

As always, his work had been his savior. Later that month, he won the Crick Award for his contribution to design in the *Ursus theodorus* project. He was only twenty-seven years old and suddenly found himself center stage in the biological revolution. The bear teddy had eventually become the fourth most popular pet in the United States, next in line after dogs, cats, and domestic foxes. That had been the start of it all.

A buzz on the intercom interrupted his thoughts.

Lightning flashed. Silas took a deep breath and watched sheets of rain cascade down the glass. He wasn't looking forward to this. There was a mutual dislike between him and most of the members of the Olympic Commission, and this year things had come to a head over their decision to use Chandler's design.

The buzz came again.

"Yes," he said.

"Dr. Williams, Mr. Baskov is here to see you," his secretary said.

Silas was surprised. "Send him in." It was hardly an industry secret that Stephen Baskov represented more than just another faceless vote in the commission. His reputation was widely acknowledged and served him well in the shark-infested waters of the Olympic politico. Officially, he merely chaired the commission. Unofficially, he ruled.

"Hello and good morning, Dr. Williams," Stephen Baskov said, switching his cane to his left hand and holding out his right.

Silas shook it, then gestured toward a chair. Baskov sank into the seat graciously, letting his feet stretch out in front of him. He was a broad man, with even, ruddy features. He wore his snow-white locks combed in such a way as to get the most economy from a diminished budget of hair. He looked to be about eighty years old, an affable old man—grandfatherly, almost—but Silas knew better. His simple appearance was in stark contrast to the reality of the man. Within his worn face, beneath his bushy white eyebrows, shone eyes like hard glacial ice.

"I hear you had quite an exciting time last night," Baskov began.

Silas eased back in his seat and propped his feet up on the big desk. "Yes, it was an eye-opener."

Baskov smiled, resting one grizzled hand on each knee. "My people tell me you're responsible for the successful birth of another gladiator. Congratulations."

"Thank you. I assume that's not all you heard."

"Why do you assume I heard something more?"

"Because if that was all your people told you, then you wouldn't be here right now."

"No, probably not."

"Then what did bring you here? What can I do for you today?"

"The commission decided not to wait for your report. I've been sent to find out just what exactly we're dealing with here. To be honest with you, the description we've been given is a little disconcerting."

"Disconcerting? An interesting choice of words."

"Oh, there were more words used than just that."

"Such as?"

"Inexplicable," Baskov said. "Disquieting. Disturbing."

Silas nodded. "I'd say those fit pretty well."

"None of those are words the commission likes to hear in association with its investment in this project."

"Nor would I."

"Is it healthy?"

"Vigorously," Silas said.

"That's a good sign."

"For now."

"Do you foresee any problems, any reason why it may not be able to compete?"

"All I do see are problems. As to whether or not it can compete, I have no idea. We're going to have to get the blood results back before we can even speculate if it's going to survive the week."

"Why is that?"

"I can't even begin to guess what sort of immunity haplotype it might have. A common cold might kill it."

"A common cold? That's rather unlikely, isn't it?"

"Sir, I have no way of knowing whether it's likely or not."

"You've never had a problem with disease susceptibility before."

"Exactly. I've also never had a problem accessing the template protocols." Silas let a challenge slip through the cracks of his expression.

Baskov noticed it in an instant and turned the tables. "I sense a climate of animosity here," he said, as a smile spread across the lower portion of his face. His voice rose a subtle, questioning octave. "Do you have a problem with me, Dr. Williams?"

The directness of the question took Silas aback. He toyed with the idea of meeting it head-on, but then decided to change tacks slightly. His job as program head was nearly as much a political appointment as it was a scientific one, and although he hated that aspect of the job, he'd learned a few things about diplomacy during his years in the position. Meeting something like the commission head-on was a good way to get a broken head.

"Let me ask you a question, Mr. Baskov," Silas said. "I've overseen the Helix arm of Olympic Development for twelve years. In that time, how many gold medals has the United States brought home in the gladiator competition?"

"Three," Baskov said. His brows furrowed. He wasn't a man used to answering questions.

"Three; that's right. Three games, three wins. They were my *designs* that brought home those medals. Designs, not just the cytological grunt work. Your commission fought against me this time. I want to know why." That question had burned in his gut for all the months he'd watched the surrogate's distended belly grow.

Baskov sighed. "This event is different from the others; I shouldn't have to tell you that. There are factors involved that you aren't aware of."

"Make me aware, then."

"Most of the other Olympic events haven't changed much in the last hundred years. The marathon is still twenty-six miles, and will still be twenty-six miles when you and I are long dead. But the gladiator event is *about* change."

"I thought it was about winning."

"That above all. But it's about showcasing a country's technological advancement. We have to use the newest, best tools at our disposal. It's not like the hundred-yard dash, where you take the fastest guy you happen to have, push him onto the track, and hope for the best."

"I doubt Olympic running coaches would appreciate that oversimplification."

"I doubt I give a damn what they would or wouldn't appreciate. The gladiator event is more than a test of simple foot speed."

"And it's more than some VR sim," Silas snapped back.

"Yes, it is. But that doesn't change the fact that Chandler's computer is capable of design specs that you can't touch. There's only one rule in this event: no human DNA. That's it. That leaves a hell of a lot of room to play, and we weren't taking advantage of it. Ours was a business decision, nothing more. Nothing less. It wasn't meant as a reflection on you."

"If it were a reflection on me, then I could understand it. But my designs have a history of success to back them up. We won. We've always won."

"And the endorsements that go with it, I know. The

commission is very thankful for that. You're a huge part of why the United States has dominated the field. But it could have gone either way last time. You know that."

Silas remained silent. He remembered the blood. He remembered the swing of guts in the sawdust. The U.S. gladiator had outlived its competitor by forty-seven seconds. The difference between gold and silver.

"I'm not sure that you fully appreciate the pressure that the program is under right now," Baskov said. "We can't afford to lose. While you've spent all your time sequestered away in your personal little laboratory retreat here, the rest of the program has had to exist in the real world. Or have you forgotten?"

"No."

"I think you have. The gladiator event is a bloody business—that's why it's so popular and why it's always under attack. The activists have a powerful lobby in Congress this time around, and they're pushing for a new vote."

"And they won't get it."

"No, they won't. Not this time. But public opinion is an unpredictable thing. Success has buoyed it up till now, and the commission was informed that we must continue to be successful if the gladiator event is to remain part of the Olympics. We do not have any other option."

Informed by whom? Silas wondered.

"This competition is not going to be as simple and straightforward as the last," Baskov continued. "Our sources tell us that China's contestant will be very formidable. Let's just say that when we compared your designs to what we know we'll be up against, your ideas came up lacking. You couldn't have won with the codes you had in the scrollers."

"How could you know—"

"You couldn't have won," Baskov interrupted. "Our decision wasn't made lightly."

Silas's face drained of expression as he considered the man sitting before him. He wanted to grab him by the lapels, pull him off his feet, and shake him. He wanted to yell in his face, *What have you done?*

But he thought again of broken heads, and by slow degrees managed to put his anger in a place he could shut down. In controlled, clipped words, he said, "I understand. Perhaps I don't have all the information, but I'm still program head. We still have problems that need to be dealt with."

"I've heard. We've been aware of the problems. Your reports during the last several months didn't fall on deaf ears."

"Then why hasn't the commission acted?"

"We just decided to wait and see what happened."

"Would you like to see . . . what's happened?"

"I was waiting for you to ask."

THEY SHUFFLED slowly down the narrow corridor, with Silas consciously shortening his strides to accommodate Baskov's hobbling gait. He wondered at the anticipation the older man must be feeling. Hell, he was feeling it, too, and he'd already seen the organism, inspected it, held it. The newborn was the most beautifully perfect thing Silas had ever seen.

Baskov broke the silence between them as they turned a corner. "The commission is very troubled by the description we received. It isn't really humanoid, is it?"

"Maybe. Not really."

"What the hell does that mean?"

"When you see it, you'll understand."

"And what about the hands?"

"What about them?"

"Does it really have . . . well, hands? I mean . . . it doesn't have paws or hooves or something like the others?"

Silas suppressed the urge to laugh. *Let the cocky old son of a bitch sweat a little.* "I'd have to call them hands. They aren't like ours, but they're hands." His bitter humor abated somewhat. "The similarities are mostly superficial, though."

"Are you going to have trouble proving no human DNA was used in the design?"

Silas looked down at the old man. For a moment, he felt his temper rise again. He took a deep breath. With the competition less than a year away, it was a little late to be asking that question now. "Your guess is as good as mine at this point," he said. "Chandler's masterpiece didn't provide us with any sort of explanation for the data in the scrollers, just raw code. I assumed that since you chose his design over mine, you would have some sort of idea what you were getting. You need to ask him. My reports are accurate, and if you read them, you—"

"We read them; we just weren't sure if we could believe them."

Silas mulled over several responses to the older man's statement, but since most of them involved the end of his career and quite possibly his incarceration for battery, he decided to say nothing at all. For the first time, he considered the possibility that the head of the Olympic Commission might be utterly irrational in some aspects of his thinking. Power did that to men sometimes.

They stepped through a set of steel doors and followed the narrow hall around the corner. "I want to remind you that the sponsor dinner is still on for tomorrow night. I need you to be there," Baskov said.

"I'll send Dr. Nelson."

"You'll be there in person. We need to quell the rumors that have already begun to fly. Image is money in this business. The delegation will leave from the complex at six o'clock."

Rumors?

They came to a second set of steel doors. A large yellow sign read:

ATTENTION
BADGED PERSONNEL ONLY
BEYOND THIS POINT

Silas carded them through, and Baskov stopped short, blinking against the white brightness of the nursery. A stout, flame-haired man sat against a console near the far wall. There were no windows, but a large glass chamber boxed in the center of the room.

"How's it doing?" Silas asked the redhead.

"Just fine," Keith answered. "Been sleeping like a baby for an hour now. Come to show off your little creation?"

"Not mine," Silas said. "This is Chandler's handiwork."

They peered in. The crib was large, and behind the chromed bars, a loosely swaddled shape twisted and bobbed within a cocoon of pink blankets.

"Looks like it's awake now," Silas said.

"Probably hungry again," Keith replied. "You wouldn't believe how much it loves to eat."

Silas checked the paper printout of the infant's eating habits, then turned back to Baskov. "The chamber is a walk-in incubator. The system has autonomic control of everything from temperature to humidity to oxygen-sat levels."

Baskov nodded, shifting his weight for a clearer view.

"Want to get a closer look?" Silas asked.

"Of course."

They donned sterile masks and gowns, and stretched latex gloves over their hands. "Just a temporary precaution," Silas said.

"For us, or it?"

"It."

Baskov nodded. "Why are we calling it an 'it,' anyway? It's male, right?"

"No, female by the external genitalia. Or lack thereof."

With a soft hiss, the door to the inner chamber opened and they stepped through. The air was warmer, wetter. Silas could feel the heat of the lights on the bridge of his nose above the mask. He bent and reached his hands through the bars and into the crib. Baskov hovered just to his side. The covers peeled back from the writhing form.

Silas heard a sudden intake of air near his shoulder.

"My God," was all Baskov could manage.

The newborn was on its back, four stocky limbs pedaling the air. Once again, Silas struggled to wrap his mind around what he was seeing. There was nothing to compare it to, so his brain had to work from scratch, filling in all the pieces, seeing everything at once.

The newborn was hairless, and most of its skin was a deep, obsidian black, slightly reflective in the warm glare of the heat lamps, as though covered with a shiny coat of gloss. Only its hands and forearms were different. It was roughly the size of a three-year-old human toddler. Wide shoulders tapered into long, thick arms that now bunched and stretched toward the bars. Below the elbow, the skin color shifted to deep red. Its blood-colored hands clenched in the air, the needle tips of talons just beginning to erupt from the ends of the long, hooked fingers. The rear legs were raptor monstrosities, jointed in some complicated way, with splayed feet that corded with muscle and sinew just below the surface of its skin.

Two enormous gray eyes shone out of the brilliant blackness of its face and raked across the two men looking down. Silas could almost feel the weight of the alien gaze. The lower jaw was enormously wide and jutting, built for power. A grossly bossed cranial vault spread wide over the pulled-out face, capped by two soft semicircular flaps of ear cartilage.

It opened its mouth, mewling the same strange cry that Silas had heard the night before. Even the inside of its mouth was midnight black.

"This is beyond . . ." Baskov began.

"Yes, that's a perfect way to describe it."

Baskov began to reach a gloved hand toward the newborn but then apparently thought better of it. "This is beyond the reach of what I thought we were able to do," he finished.

"It is. We cannot do this," Silas said.

The two men locked eyes.

"How?" Baskov asked.

"You're asking the wrong guy, remember? I'm the builder, not the designer."

"Does it seem to be put together well? Are those legs supposed to look like that?"

"Well, everything is symmetrical on the exterior, so that's a good sign. But you haven't seen the really interesting thing yet." Silas leaned through the bars and grabbed the newborn under the upper arms. It struggled, but he was able to flip it over onto its stomach.

"What are those?" Baskov whispered.

"We're not totally sure, but the X-ray data indicate they're probably immature wing structures of some sort."

"Wings? Are you telling me this thing has wings?"

Silas shrugged his answer.

"They're not functional, are they?"

"I don't see how they could be. Flight is probably the single most difficult form of locomotion from a design standpoint, and this thing certainly doesn't look like it was built along avian lines. The bones are huge, strong."

"But why even try? There isn't really room to fly in the arena." Baskov bent closer. "And those big ears are a liability. The eyes, too."

"Now you understand my frustration with your chosen designer. We need to talk to him."

Baskov's expression faded from wonder to irritation. "Chandler isn't as easy to reach as he used to be."

"Where is he?"

"Where isn't the problem. He just isn't easy to reach anymore."

AFTER WALKING Baskov back to the lobby, Silas returned to the nursery and sent Keith home for the night. He stood alone at the side of the crib, silently watching the baby breathe. It *was* a baby. Big as a newborn calf but just as underdeveloped and fragile as any human newborn. He extended a hand through the bars and stroked the infant's back. It lay on its tummy, legs drawn up, bottom stuck in the air.

It's beautiful.

But then, almost all life is beautiful at this stage. Pure innocence combined with complete selfishness.

Its only function was to take from those around it so that it could live and grow, while remaining completely unaware of the effort involved in meeting its needs.

Silas closed his eyes and breathed in the smell of the creature. He felt himself relax a little. His sister hinted once that she thought he'd become a geneticist to create something that was a part of him. She was wrong. That was why people have children.

He wanted to create something better than himself. Better than any man could be. Something a little closer to perfect. But he had always failed. His creations were monsters compared to this. They were just animal Frankensteins that acted out impulses society wouldn't allow men to indulge in.

But he'd come close once. Teddy. *Ursus theodorus* had been loving, gentle, and even intelligent, after a fashion. That last quality had cost the first prototype its life. It had been *too* intelligent. Some people got nervous. The board of directors had had its say, and late one evening, he'd been forced to place the little creature on a table and inject it with enough animal tranquilizer to stop its breathing. He'd stood back with ice in his gut while his creation died.

The next series of Teddys were dumber and better suited the board, but it wasn't the same for Silas. He'd lost his stomach for pet manufacture. When the position at the Olympic Commission became available, he'd jumped at it. If he was going to watch his successes die, he would know to expect it from the outset. No more surprises.

But this was a surprise.

But not my surprise. Not my baby this time.

Chandler was deranged. There was no doubting that. And this was his creation. Silas fought back a surge of begrudging admiration for the man. In all

Silas's years as a geneticist, he'd never even come close to developing a creature like the one that lay before him now.

He shoved the feelings to the side, letting the anger take its place. Chandler knew nothing about genetics. He knew nothing about life. All he knew was computers. And his computer had been the true creator, after all.

This perfect little life form that lay snoring on the other side of the bars had been created by an organized composite of wires, chips, and screens. Somehow, all this beauty, all this perfection, had come from a machine.

CHAPTER TWO

Evan Chandler leaned his significant mass against the wall near the window, picking sores into his face with absentminded fingers. The fluorescent lights hummed softly in the background, providing a subtle soundtrack to the visions in his head. His eyes focused inward on some distant dimly lit horizon. For Evan, that horizon had been growing ever darker over the last several months.

A sudden clap of thunder brought his consciousness swimming to the surface like some strange, stunted leviathan. With an expression approaching surprise, he looked out into the desolation of the early evening. Rain dribbled its way down the glass. God, he hated storms.

He shifted off the wall and trudged over to his desk, where he eased his weight onto a loudly wailing swivel chair. His desk was a sprawling mountain range of papers, folders, and empty foam food containers. He considered the room before him. Stacks of computer digilogs stood at ease like drowsy sentinels against one wall. Several dead brown plants drooped from their pots in various stages of decomposition. He cast his muddied hazel eyes around the chaos, looking for his laptop amid the clutter. Eventually, he gave up. It would be easier to get another than to sift through the various geological layers of refuse he had accumulated.

He knew there was something he was supposed to do today, someone he was supposed to see, but he couldn't quite remember. Looking around the room, he experienced a painful moment of lucidity, saw vividly where he was going, what he was slipping into. It scared him, but the feeling faded. It always did.

A knock on the door startled him, and his fat rolls shimmied as he jerked his chin up from his chest. He'd faded out again. Lost time. Outside the window he saw the storm had passed. *Good.* "What do you want?" he called.

A young woman opened the door and leaned her head through. He recognized her face, though he couldn't quite place her name. Sarah, or Susan, or something like that. Was it his secretary? Did he even have a secretary anymore? He couldn't remember.

"It's getting late, Dr. Chandler," the woman said. "The rest of the team and I are going to call it a day, I think."

Team? "Okay."

She shut the door softly. Curious, he got to his feet and shuffled over to where she had been standing. He swung the door wide and stepped out into the construction chamber. A dozen people dressed in tech cleans were gathering up their equipment. In the center of the room stood a huge monolithic plug booth, half finished. The electronics gleamed under the spotlights. He remembered now. Oh, yes, he remembered.

He picked his way slowly between the piles of electronic equipment and stepped up to the booth. He ran his palm across the smooth surface of the faceplate. It was cool to the touch, smooth and soothing. He felt better. The riptide in his head ebbed ever so slightly.

"How much longer?" he asked the woman as she closed the lid on her pack.

"Should be finished in two or three days."

He didn't bother to respond. His knee creaked audibly under his weight as he bent to inspect the optronic connections leading from the mainframe. He twisled the cable between his fingers, tugging the connection slightly. Nice and tight. You couldn't be too careful, after all. This was his conduit. His church. This booth would help him talk to God.

EVAN WAS into the third bite of his burger when he heard the knock on his office door. Anger surged. They knew he wasn't to be disturbed during lunch. A moment later, just as he brought the burger back up to his mouth, the knock came again.

"What is it?" he snapped.

The door swung inward, and Mr. Baskov limped through.

"Good morning, Dr. Chandler."

Evan nodded. "Mr. Baskov."

"May I sit?" Baskov asked.

"Go ahead, just clear off a chair."

Baskov leaned his cane against the arm of a leather chair, picked up a haphazard pile of papers from the cushion, and placed it on the floor.

"To what do I owe the honor of this unexpected visit?" Evan asked through a squishy muffle of burger, bun, and tomato. A runnel of juice split his chin and deposited another stain on his filthy shirt.

"There was a birth," Mr. Baskov said. "Do you recall the work you did for us on the Helix project?"

"Of course I remember the project." Evan swallowed and wiped his hands with a napkin. "It's the only thing I've been allowed to use the Brannin on.

Why does everyone around here treat me like I can't remember my own name?"

"Good. There has been concern, you see, about the work done with the Brannin."

"Well, I've had some concerns of my own. I'm concerned that I've spent the last fifteen years of my life on the design of a computer I'm not being allowed to use."

"I have nothing to do with that. The concern—"

"And I want to know why it's called the Brannin, anyway. Why isn't it called the Chandler? I designed it." His hamburger made a loud *bong* as he slammed the last oily chunk into the wastebasket near his desk. "Nobody else can even use it."

"There are investors who decide such things. A name is a commodity, like any other."

"My name could be a commodity."

"Once again, I can't really speak to that circumstance, but I have come today to ask you an important question. Do you think you could answer a question for me, Dr. Chandler?"

"These research institutes think that just because you are under contract with them, they have the right to claim and name. So what if the research was done at the Brannin Institute? I could have gone anywhere. They were begging for me. Harvard, C-tech, the Mid—"

"Dr. Chandler!" Baskov's tone stopped Evan's rant. "Why does the Helix project newborn have wings?"

Evan's expression changed. He leaned back in his chair, lacing his pudgy fingers behind his head. "Wings, really?"

"Yes. It also has shiny black skin and prehensile thumbs. But let's start with the wings, okay?"

"I don't know why you're asking *me;* I don't know."

"That's what Silas said. You both can't use the same excuse."

"Who's Silas?"

Baskov shook his head in disbelief. "He's the head of Helix Development. You've met him two or three times. How can you not know about the wings?"

"The guys at Helix fed me the directives. They were the ones who should have gone over them with a fine-tooth comb. If there is a problem with the product, then there must have been a problem with one of the directives."

"Silas said he had nothing to do with the design. He's putting the responsibility on your shoulders."

"Do I look like a geneticist to you? I design virtual-reality computers, not live meats."

"And it was your computer that developed the designs."

"They think just because they have you under contract, they can tell you what projects to work on. It's *my* computer. What gives them the right?"

Baskov took a deep breath, and his eyes gathered force beneath his shaggy eyebrows. He leaned forward in a conspiratorial manner, and when finally he spoke, his voice was soft and measured. "This isn't a game, retard. I don't care what kind of genius you are supposed to be. What I see sitting across from me is a three-hundred-pound sack of shit that doesn't have mind enough left to hold a conversation."

Outraged, Evan attempted to stand, and Baskov slammed his hand down on the desk. "Sit the fuck down!"

Evan sat.

Baskov leaned forward. "You have no idea who you are talking to. You have no idea what I can do to your life if you've fucked this up somehow." Baskov paused, his eyes two sighted gun barrels. "Now, I want you to think real hard, if you still can. I want you to explain to me why the new gladiator looks the way it looks. Why?"

Evan cleared his throat. He started to answer several times but each time thought better of it, struggling for a different way to phrase his response.

"Why?" Baskov shouted.

Evan flinched. "The computer designed the product based on the directives it was given. I don't know what else to say. I really had nothing to do with the design at all. The computer did everything."

"What were the directives?"

"Just a list of what they wanted the product to be able to do."

"The product. You mean the gladiator."

"Yeah, the product. The computer was supposed to design it for those specs."

"Specifically, what were these specs?"

"I don't remember. Um, let me look, I think I still may have a list around here somewhere." Evan stood and ruffled through a stack of papers on top of a filing cabinet.

"You don't have a software file on it?"

"I can't seem to locate my laptop at the moment."

Baskov watched the fat man root through his disorganized office. Baskov sat silently for five full minutes before rising and walking toward the door.

Evan felt a wave of relief at seeing the old man turn to leave. He'd already given up hope of finding the documents he sought, but he'd been too afraid of Baskov's reaction to say so. The laptop might have been lost or thrown out weeks ago. Evan had no idea where it might be. He'd been losing things more and more often lately. He was slipping, and he knew it.

At the door Baskov turned. "How can we get the information out of the Brannin computer files?"

"There are no files, at least not in the sense that you mean. Everything is in V-space. Only one way to access memory. We'd have to start it up again, run the program."

"With the per-minute cost, an unscheduled run isn't going to happen," Baskov said.

"Helix lab has copies, I'm sure."

Baskov nodded, then turned and disappeared through the doorway.

A small kernel of hope formed somewhere in the back of Chandler's mind. *Maybe,* he thought. *Just maybe.*

He thought of his computer. His precious V-space. There was a chance he might soon run his program again.

SILAS SHUFFLED through the massive stack of envelopes on his desk. The mail was mostly advertisements, though a few scientific magazines and professional letters were also sprinkled in. He came to the letter from his sister and put it aside. He would read that one later, at home.

He talked to her at least once a week on the phone and visited her every couple of months, but the letters were special to him. They would be filled with the layered minutiae of her everyday existence. She would tell him about the flower blooming outside her window, or the fight she had with her boss. Actual letters, in the old style. Paper you could hold in your hand. It would all be in there, laid down in lines, her life.

She'd started that when she'd first gone away to school and then sporadically continued the habit for years until she married. Then the letters stopped for a while. After their mother died, the habit had returned, like some childhood habits will.

He didn't write her back. But that was okay; she didn't seem to expect it. She wrote because she needed to share her life with him, not because she needed a reciprocal share of his in return.

Their relationship was close, in its own particular way. Silas had always considered this a minor miracle, considering how far apart they lived and how different their lives were. That was a blessing he didn't take for granted. His sister's family was the only family he had. And except for Ben, the only real friends.

He wasn't lonely. On a weekly basis, he interacted with hundreds of people, knew several dozen well—and when time allowed, he could always find somebody to talk to, catch lunch with, and even occasionally go out with on those rare evenings away from the lab.

But letting them inside was somewhat harder. That was something he'd never been good at, and now that he'd entered his forties, he felt that it had almost ceased to be a viable option.

He flipped the envelope over, and out slipped the usual family photo of his sister, her husband, and their son. They were an attractive family. The kind you might expect to see in prime-time sitcoms or ads about orange juice—the dad neat and professional, the mother beautiful, the son a mixture of the two in a smaller, smiling package. It felt good to look at them, though he couldn't quite put his finger on why.

He put the envelope in his upper desk drawer and tried to summon the ambition to sift through the rest of the mail.

CHAPTER THREE

A small contingent gathered in the entryway of the lab administration building while the sun lengthened through the glass brick, stretching a grid of shadow across the plush green carpet.

Silas hated these things.

He made a point to arrive at six on the nose so he wouldn't have to mingle. He wasn't in the mood to talk. He nodded his hellos just as the group began disjoining to its respective vehicles. Silas entered the convoy in the middle of the pack, four cars down from the front. Except for the driver on the other side of the tinted glass, he was alone.

When his car pulled away from the curb, he flipped the TV on and tried to empty his mind. TV was usually good for that. He would need a kind of mental anesthetic to get through the evening.

The car moved west toward the city and the sun. They eased through the technical district's narrow streets and merged onto the crowded highway. By the time they'd traversed the mountains, night had fallen.

The car took a left on Carter Street and slowed at the conference square. People in business attire carrying label-forward bags turned their heads toward the line of limousines. He knew they were speculating about who might be inside. And he knew Baskov would probably like him to roll his window down and wave, possibly win a few more fans for the home team.

After winding through a grid pattern of short drives, the procession came to a stop in front the Mounce Center. The building was an enormous, stylistically oblique structure that had always reminded Silas of a woman's fedora. Baskov loved to use it for press and sponsor events. Cement planters circled the arched entranceway, providing seats for tired downtown shoppers, tourists, and businessmen, who now stared as the delegates made their way inside. Silas turned his face from the flash of a camera.

Like many large upscale conference centers, the Mounce had the requisite ultramodern expressionistic sculptures on display in its grand lobby. They'd changed it around some since Silas had last been here a few months ago—the same general sculptures but shifted slightly into a new conformation. The abstract figures now gave the distinct impression of having sex, though it disturbed him not to be able to tell in exactly what position it was happening.

An usher led them in loose formation to the dining hall, which was crowded with noisy men and women in business suits. They stood in shifting groups or sat at round tables with white tablecloths and crystal champagne glasses. Most were already drinking. A few, by the looks of them, were well on their way to drunk. Baskov believed in being fashionably late, and the dinner had probably been scheduled for thirty minutes ago. Silas supposed that was one way to make the begging seem less like what it was. Baskov would want them feeling privileged to give their money up. His speech—given usually after the appetizer and before the main course—would hammer that point home.

All eyes were on them as they made their way

around to the back of the room, where the host table spread before an enormous bank of ornate windows. Silas nodded to several people as he edged the crowd, and he sat at the first opportunity. Baskov, of course, was at the center of the table. Silas enjoyed his relative anonymity at the periphery.

Pretty college-age waitresses poured glasses of water while the crowd on the main level discovered their seats. Today was only for those big-money contributors not directly related to the field of genetics: Coke, General Motors, Puma, Artae, IBM, and a dozen others, all negotiating for their opportunity to be the official drink, or shoe, or widget, of the Summer Games of the Thirty-eighth Olympiad. Everybody loves a winner, and the big companies were willing to pay in order to bask in the reflected light of Olympic glory.

Silas sipped his water and threw sporadic noncommittal nods toward the man on his right, who seemed to think they were engaged in earnest conversation of some kind. Silas recognized the man from administration, a suit of some importance, but couldn't place his name. Everyone knew Silas's name, though. That was part of what bothered him about these get-togethers.

The waitresses brought the appetizers—stuffed lobster tails and honey sauce—and Silas had to admit the smell was good. He dipped, bit, and it tasted as good as it smelled. He snagged the waitress's attention as she passed by again. "Can I have a beer?"

She seemed somewhat amused by his strange request but nodded. "What kind?"

"Just give me a Red; don't care which."

He finished off his lobster tail and tried to tip the waitress when she returned. She adamantly refused, saying only, "We're not allowed." He realized he'd somehow embarrassed her and put the money back in his pocket, feeling awkward and out of place. He hated these events. He'd always been more comfortable in a laboratory than out at the money socials.

Baskov rose to his feet. The crowd quieted as he walked around the table and stepped up to the lectern. He smiled, tapping at the microphone and playing up his simple, grandfatherly appearance. "Testing. Testing," his voice boomed out.

Then he coughed, and the microphone picked that up, too. Nervousness seemed to overtake him as he paused and looked out over the crowd of several hundred people. But Silas had seen his speeches too often to believe the façade. The man had no TelePrompTer, carried no cue cards or printed sheets. His speeches were pulled out of his head complete and perfectly honed, usually without a single misspoken word.

"My friends," Baskov began, "I come to you today with great news. The United States Olympic Development team has produced another future gold medal winner."

The crowd broke out in applause. Baskov paused, waiting for the applause to die down. "It was born yesterday, early in the morning, and is now resting comfortably at our complex's neonatal unit. It's healthy and strong, thanks, in no small part, to our program head, Dr. Silas Williams." Baskov turned and smiled toward Silas, clapping theatrically.

Silas stood and nodded his acknowledgment to the crowd as they applauded again. He sat quickly.

"We live in interesting times, my friends," Baskov continued. "I think that history will look back with its clear sight on this, the twenty-first century, and call it the age of genetics. This is the age that will fundamentally alter the lifeways of our species as no other period in the time of man. If you doubt me, read the headlines of your local newspapers. Diseases are being cured. Organ transplants are being performed in instances where rejection would have made those procedures impossible just a few short years ago. Deafness is no longer a life sentence, nor must be paralysis, or blindness. Eye tissues are actually being grown from a person's own cells. I don't know how it is they do it, but they do it, and sight has been returned to people who haven't seen their children's faces in twenty years."

If you have the money or connections, Silas noted to himself. He poured his beer into a glass.

"But these great leaps forward are not limited only to helping those of us suffering from disability or disease. Telomere research holds great promise in the area of longevity. We may see life spans double, perhaps treble. Gene-therapy research is now under way that will one day soon eliminate obesity, baldness, and nearsightedness." He paused for effect. "These are all conditions that will come to an end in our lifetimes. Daily progress is being made. We are standing at the door of a golden age, and that door is swinging open because of the advancements being made by talented people like the scientists at Helix. I believe God is on our side in this struggle. I believe He gave us our uniquely powerful minds in order that we may unlock our own destinies. Yes, we live in interesting times, my friends." He smiled and leaned in to the lectern with his elbows. "And I don't have to tell you who's leading the way, do I?"

The crowd applauded wildly. They knew, all right.

Baskov grinned into the wash of approval, letting it linger. Finally, he continued, speaking in slightly lower tones. "Before the end of next year, our gladiator will compete right here in the U.S., in the city of Phoenix. The human portion of the Games will take place in Monterrey shortly thereafter.

"Rightly or wrongly, the gladiator competition has

come to represent much more than just a simple Olympic event. More than just our opening event. When the rest of the Games commence a month later in Monterrey, the events of Phoenix will still be ringing in the hearts and minds of people around the world. What happens in that arena has come to stand for each nation's bioengineering capabilities. The results are a badge each nation wears. But I think it is much more than that, even. I think it is what biologists call true signaling—a single trait that stands for a whole suite of characteristics related to strength and vitality. It is the peacock's feathers. It is the lion's mane. It is the sheer raging bulk of a charging bull elephant. And these things *are not* meaningless." Baskov slapped his hand on the lectern. "They *stand* for something." Then softly, "Just as this United States team has stood for something for the last twelve years. Our Olympic Development team has yet to lose in the steel arena."

As Silas watched Baskov spool out his practiced monologue, he had to admit the man was very fucking good. The bait was in the fish's mouth, and all he had to do now was set the hook.

"Most significant to you, our precious sponsors, is this: last year more people watched the Olympic Games worldwide than any other single event in the history of the world." Baskov rested for a moment to let it sink in.

"The Chinese don't watch the Super Bowl. Americans don't watch the World Cup. Last year, the only ones interested enough to watch the inauguration of Indian Prime Minister Saanjh Patil were the Indians. And understandably so. Each nation has its own concerns. But everywhere around the planet, people watched the gladiator event. Billions of people."

Baskov paused for effect.

"I don't have to tell you how important product placement is to the dynamic of the global marketplace; you already know that. But you should also know that by helping us, you are also helping yourselves. And I'm not talking about your bottom line. Or not *just* your bottom line, anyway. The scientific advancements that are made while striving toward Olympic gold can be used to benefit everyone. What we learn can be applied against disease. It can be applied toward getting a larger yield from an acre of crop. It can be used to prevent birth defects. By helping us, you are helping yourselves. You are helping mankind."

Wham! Baskov jerks hard on his finely tuned fishing pole. Silas smiled, but it was less a grin of pleasure than one of simple embarrassment. *Poor fish never saw it coming.*

The applause swelled again. Baskov smiled indulgently, holding up his hands in a show of modesty after all that bluster.

But the crowd wouldn't be quieted. Eventually, he gave up and let it roll over him, unimpeded, a wave of applause. The crowd rose to its collective feet, first in the front, then all around the room. The faces were smiling, eyes alight.

Silas took a sip of his beer to assuage the sour that had crept into his stomach. The man should run for president, Silas thought, as the applause went on and on. But no, then he'd lose too much power.

BENJAMIN SAT on a stool in the near darkness of the gene-mapping lab, slowly rubbing his sore eyes. He placed his glasses back on the bridge of his nose and concentrated, but the information contained on the glowing surface of the electrophoretic gel still made no sense. Something had to be wrong. He resigned himself to starting the entire process over again. Either way, Silas would want confirmation.

He pipetted a new sample out of the plastic cap labeled *F helix DNA*. Earlier they had used a centrifuge to isolate the plasma from a sample of whole blood serum drawn from the newborn's arm. Affinity chromatography provided the necessary quantity of purified DNA, which had then been cleaved through several steps by restriction enzymes for the analysis he was about to conduct.

He slid the tip of the standardized pipette cautiously into the agarose gel and pushed the dispense button. The solution gathered in a tiny pool beneath the bulging surface tension of the gelatinous matrix. He hit the toggle at the side of the apparatus and electrified the field. DNA molecules possess a negative charge due to their phosphates, so the various segments always tended to migrate toward the positively charged side of the unit. The differential action of friction on the relative sequence lengths determined how fast and how far they moved. The smaller the segment, the better it traversed the micropores in the gel, and the farther it migrated in the two-minute time period. Benjamin toggled the electricity off.

He stained the newly attenuated DNA with an ethidium bromide standard and bathed the set in ultraviolet light for a full six minutes. As expected, the result was an unbroken fluorescence down the entire column of gel lane. Benjamin then used the Southern blot technique to develop the reference standard he'd need later. He applied a final critical restriction enzyme to the sample set and then transferred the entire assemblage of DNA fragments to a metered nitrocellulose filter, being particularly careful that the sequences on the filter were oriented in the same way as when they were in the gel. If human error was a factor the first time around, this is where it had most likely been introduced.

He looked down at his watch and grimaced. Half past two in the A.M. He wondered vaguely if Silas had gone home yet. His hand lingered on the videophone at the side of his lab bench. Better to wait until he had firm results, he decided. He didn't want to embarrass himself if the bizarre results from his first analysis had simply been the artifact of some careless mistake on his part. He glanced at the electrophoretic gel drying on the counter. Yes, it had to be a mistake.

When the gel had solidified enough to maintain its internal structure, Benjamin slid the new set into the vacuum oven, where the DNA fragments would fix to the metered filter. He punched two hours into the digital timer and hit the start switch. His feet seemed to weigh sixty pounds apiece as he dragged himself to the other side of the lab and collapsed into the swivel chair. He kicked his shoes off and propped his feet up as far as they would go onto the desk. His eyes closed.

There was no dream, just the total nothingness of exhaustion, less like sleep than a subtraction of consciousness. When the buzzer went off two hours later, he managed to hoist himself to the upright position. A sharp pain lanced at his neck when he straightened his head. His left leg was completely numb from the hip down, and he had to rub it vigorously to bring it back to life.

Benjamin pressurized the vacuum chamber and used a pair of tongs to remove the fixed set from the oven. He lowered the nitrocellulose filter into a hybridization buffer and prepared an autoradiograph to visualize the relative positions of the complementary DNA sequences.

Nearly an hour later, just as the first glow of morning was beginning to light the world outside the window, Benjamin finished the restriction map. It was done.

He held the gossamer plastic sheet up to the light.

The polymorphisms were unmistakable.

The genetic diversity contained within the newborn's genome was like nothing he'd ever heard of. Very few bands lined up together on the sheet. It was heterozygous across most tested loci. Half of the young gladiator's genes were apparently either co-dominant or unexpressed recessives.

Why engineer unexpressed genes into an organism? What were those recessives hiding?

Ben rubbed his eyes. Perhaps the more important question was *Why had the world's most powerful supercomputer put them there in the first place?*

He looked at his watch: 5:47. Picking up the receiver, he hit the call button on the vid-phone. He'd try Silas's office first.

SILAS WAS washing his face in his office's bathroom sink when the phone rang. It had been a long night. He pulled a towel down from a ring and patted his face dry. This early in the morning, he knew exactly who was at the other end of the line.

"Hello, Benjamin."

"Silas, I'm glad I caught you. Are you early to work, or late getting home?"

"Home? Haven't been there in a while."

"I know what you mean. Listen, I just got the results of the restriction map. I double-checked it. You might want to come down and take a look."

"Yeah, but give me a minute. I'm just trying to wake myself up. Wait, better yet, why don't you meet me in the cafeteria for some coffee? I want to show you the karyotype I just finished."

"Is the cafeteria open this early?"

"It is if you have a key."

"Must be good to be boss."

"Now I know you're sleep-deprived. I'll trade you anytime you want."

"No, thanks, but I'll see you in five."

SILAS RAISED the coffee cup to his lips with one hand and held the restriction map with the other. He willed his sleep-fuzzied eyes to focus. At forty-three, he was doing a good job staving off the optometrist, but his eyes did take a little longer to wake up than the rest of him. "You double-checked this?"

"Yeah," Benjamin said. "I knew you'd ask."

They sat in the empty cafeteria—a huge, open expanse of white tile divided by endless rows of glossy plastic tables. Against one wall was the kitchen and the glass refrigeration units. Every kind of snack or food or drink you could ask for. Enough to feed a small army of hungry, caffeine-addicted techs. Three hundred people might eat here for lunch. Right now, it belonged to just the two of them.

They sipped their coffees.

Silas put the plastic sheet down on the table and handed Benjamin a white page he'd pulled from the briefcase sitting on the floor. "This is what I was working on," he said. "Don't bother counting, there are one hundred and four."

Benjamin whistled softly as he looked over the sheet. "A hundred and four chromosomes?"

"Certainly puts our paltry twenty-three in perspective."

Ben shook his head as he studied the sheet. He'd

never seen a karyotype like this before. The chromosomes were laid out in neat pairs from largest to smallest, across and down the page. They took up the whole sheet. Benjamin adjusted his small wire-rimmed glasses. "This is some dense reading."

"Yeah, I get the feeling that might be the whole point. With this bulk of material involved, back-engineering wouldn't be time-effective. There's just too much to dig through."

"With a large enough team, we could probably make sense of at least part of this before the competition."

Silas shook his head. "With five years instead of thirteen months, we still wouldn't unravel this, particularly with the diversity in the restriction map you just handed me. It almost seems as if this thing was designed to throw up roadblocks to any sort of investigation. It doesn't want to be understood."

"You mean Chandler didn't want it understood?"

"I'm not sure what I mean."

Benjamin laid his forehead down on the table. "So what next?"

Silas looked at the stack of papers that Benjamin had handed him when he first walked into the cafeteria. "I'm open to suggestions," he said. "You got any ideas?"

"Yeah, but most of them would make me look like a crackpot." Benjamin stretched in his chair. "Oh, hell, you're the . . . What was it the magazines were calling you last time? The genetic pioneer? What do you think?"

"I think my pioneering days are over. But I've got one more idea."

"What's that?"

"How about we get some doughnuts to go with this coffee?"

"That's your idea?"

"Only one I can come up with right now."

"Well, it's the best idea I've heard today." He sipped his coffee. "Though my standards are low this early in the morning."

STEPHEN BASKOV flipped through the report on his desk. He tried to force back the growing sense of apprehension that threatened to muddle his thinking. His mind needed to be sharp to face the decisions ahead.

He eased his chair back and ran a hand through his white hair. It had taken two frustrating weeks to track down the directives used by the Brannin computer. There had been no record of them at the Five Rings complex. The scientists at Helix were able to produce literally thousands of bytes of data on biology, physiology, and genetics, which they had given to Chandler's team for upload. But there were no directives, nothing to guide the design parameters. Earlier today, when he'd finally discovered where the directives originated, he'd come very close to a total meltdown.

His own commission had developed them.

Several people nearly lost their jobs before lunch, but eventually, he'd decided it wouldn't be in his best interest to have disgruntled ex-assistants floating around at this most inopportune of times.

He glanced at the papers on his desk. *Stupid. Stupid.* He couldn't think of a more fitting descriptor. The report on his desk summarized the raw data that the Brannin was given before the design stage of the program. The vast majority of the text was composed of information on the gladiator contest itself—the arena dimensions, the contest rules, as well as the specs of all past contestants. Winners and losers. There was also, thank Christ, a list of qualifications.

Baskov adjusted his glasses. He was relieved, at least, that the computer had been given information about the ban on the use of human DNA in all gladiators. The contestant wasn't likely to be disqualified on those grounds. But it was the last page of the report that interested him the most. He studied the sheet in his hand, reading and rereading the short passages it contained.

That last page contained the sum total of all the directives given to Chandler's computer for the design of the gladiator.

The extent to which the Brannin computer could have misinterpreted Helix's intentions was terrifying.

He wondered how it could have happened. Who had overlooked it? When exactly had things begun to spin out of control?

There was only one directive typed on the page. Just a lone, solitary instruction that had been used to guide the design.

The gladiator was created to do only one thing.

That one directive was this: survive the competition.

He read the sentence over and over.

Survive the competition.

What in the hell type of directive was that? There was an awful lot of room for interpretation in that strategy.

Survive the competition.

He laid the report back down on the smooth surface of his desk. IQ test results to the contrary, he knew Evan Chandler to be a fool. But Chandler was a crazy fool, and if history had taught him anything, it was that the world was often changed through the works of crazy fools.

Stephen Baskov liked the world just the way it was. He pushed the call button on the vid-phone, then punched fourteen digits.

After a few moments, a man appeared on the screen. "Yes."

"I want the Brannin up and running again."

There was a pause. "And the cost?"

"I don't care. Find room in the budget somewhere."

"How long do you need?"

"Give us a full five minutes."

The man stared through the screen. "The budget isn't that flexible. Even for you," he said.

"Okay, three minutes."

"When?"

"Inside of two weeks," Baskov said.

"That's short notice."

"Can you do it or not?"

"I'll see what can be done."

CHAPTER FOUR

Silas's breath hung in a smoky pall on the thin mountain air. He rubbed his hands together as he gazed out over the precipice at the sun boiling up between two jags in the distant range to the east.

"Beautiful, isn't it?"

"Yeah," his nephew answered. His voice still came raw from the thousand-meter climb over rock and scrub.

The terrain was steep, and Silas had pushed hard to beat the sunrise to the top of the ridge. He had almost decided not to bring Eric today, but the boy had size beyond his years and a serious, thoughtful demeanor. For a boy Eric's age, something like this could leave a mark.

When Eric's breathing slowed, Silas had him stand and then tightened the straps on his pack with two firm tugs. He pulled the small curved bow from the carry strap and held it out for the boy. "Keep it in your hand now."

Silas played his fingers along the slow arc of his own bow, feeling for splits in the raw-hewn wood. There were none. His finger hooked the sinewy string and pulled back just an inch. The deep *thwump* of the release was hardly melodic, but it was music to his ears nonetheless. He'd been too long away from places like this, where there were no roads or concrete, and nature didn't have to ask permission.

Back in California, the project would be at a standstill until after the second Brannin run. Baskov had pulled a few strings, and now it looked as if they were finally going to get some answers straight from the source. Silas had never been good at sitting around and waiting, so he'd decided to take drastic measures to retain his sanity: a three-day jaunt in the mountains near his sister's home. The bow felt damned good in his hand.

"Ready?" Silas asked.

"Yeah."

They started down the other side of the ridge and into the broad valley below, the sun on their faces. The valley was really nothing more than a shallow depression between two mountains, a couple of miles wide, a dozen or so long. But it held a cacophonous ecosystem of shrub, pine, and unspoiled wildlife. A small lake pooled in the southernmost rim. To Silas, it was a little piece of paradise.

He kept the boy behind him in the steepest parts of the descent and let him move alongside when the terrain began to level out. There was no trail. They had to pick their way carefully between the rocky outcroppings and the stands of thorny brambles. The temperature rose with the sun, and soon Silas was shocked to realize he was perspiring, despite the altitude and the season.

Eventually, here and there, tufts of buffalo grass began to accumulate in the pockets of soil that gathered in the broken scatter of limestone. Dogtooth violets and wild irises splashed color haphazardly across the slope. When finally they stepped down onto the lush green basin, Silas stopped. "Keep an eye out. This is where we'll find them."

Eric nodded. Silas took his pack off and removed both arrows. He handed one to Eric.

"Now, remember what I told you," Silas said. "This is heavier. It'll drop more quickly than a target arrow, so aim high." He'd taken the boy shooting several times last year, and the little guy was actually a pretty good shot. But targets were an altogether different species of game than what they were hunting today.

They moved out. There was no wind in the valley, and their eyes stretched for any twitch in the vegetation as they walked. Above them, Silas noticed an eagle doing slow circles in the sky, looking for its next meal. A hunter, like them.

Silas glanced over at the boy. He certainly looked as if he was enjoying himself. Silas recognized the expression of total engagement peering out from beneath the eight-year-old's shaggy bowl cut. His nephew's hair was the same thick mass of curls that Silas shared with his sister, though the boy's hair was pale instead of dark, a sandy blond like his father's. He was a beautiful child. Looking at him now, small and earnest, it was painful to fill in the blanks and imagine him older. Childhoods were short. Blink and you miss everything.

"I think I see something," the boy whispered.

"Where?" Silas followed the boy's gaze but couldn't make out anything unusual.

"To the side of the pine. The one with the brown patch."

Silas saw it then. Movement, low down in the thicket. They advanced, but Silas knew it was no deer. When they were finally close enough for him to identify the species, he held his arm out and stopped the boy.

"That's far enough."

"What is it?"

"That, my boy, is what's at the very top of the list

of animals you don't want an introduction to here in the Rockies."

"Wolverine," the boy said.

"Yeah."

"Let's get a little closer; I want to see."

"Not a chance. Your mother would kill me."

"C'mon, just a little closer."

Silas looked at him.

"All right," the boy said, slinking backward through the underbrush.

When they were a safe distance away, Silas pointed toward the stand of trees near the edge of the lake. "That looks as likely a direction as any," he said. They pushed deeper into the valley. When the sun approached what Silas took for middle high, they stopped and broke down their packs for lunch. Two thick sandwiches of beefalo apiece, and a warm beer for Silas. Eric chugged his first Coke down in less than a minute. Silas had him put the crushed can back into his pack. A while later, as they were lounging in the warm grass, Eric sat up suddenly, his posture telling Silas something was on his mind.

"What?" Silas asked.

"Mom told me not to ask you about your work," he said.

Silas laughed out loud. "But you just couldn't help it, could you?"

The boy pursed his lips against a sly, involuntary grin. "I figured I'd just ask polite. If you don't want to talk about it, that's fine."

"I don't mind. This place has helped."

There was silence between them for a moment, then, "What does it look like?"

Silas tried to think of a way to describe it so the boy would understand. "Do you know what a gargoyle is?"

"Yeah, one of those things that hangs off the side of old buildings in old movies."

"Well, it looks a little like a baby gargoyle."

"Must be pretty ugly, then."

"No," Silas said. "That's part of the problem. It's not ugly at all."

"And that's the part you don't want to talk about? Mom says you're under a lot of stress."

"She must think I'm emotionally fragile."

"No, she just says you work too hard, and this was supposed to be your vacation."

"Well, she'd be right about that." Silas tousled the boy's hair and stood. "C'mon, we only have about three hours left. We'd better get a move on if we're going to get a shot off."

They repacked and set off toward the lake, hoping to find better luck. Forty minutes later, they found it. It was sixty yards ahead, grazing in the overhang of a tree. Silas paused, letting Eric think he saw the deer first.

"I see one," Eric whispered.

"Good eyes. You take the left flank. I'll take the right. One of us should get a shot."

They moved forward in what Silas wanted to think of as a two-man V formation, if that was possible. Silas kept the deer just within sight, then slowly moved back in on it. Across the clearing, he saw Eric come to a stop about twenty-five yards short. The deer stopped browsing and lifted its head to sniff at the air. It was a magnificent animal, over five feet tall at the shoulder, with a wide, elaborate rack. It looked like it owned the mountainside. Silas was grateful for the lack of wind. He crept forward, carrying the bow low to the ground in his right hand. He stopped.

The deer sniffed at the air again; then, apparently

satisfied, it lowered its head for a meal of grass. Silas couldn't see the boy.

The arrow came free from his pack in one slow, fluid movement from over his shoulder. His eyes stayed with the deer as he notched the arrow. Arm muscles bunched as he pulled the bowstring back. He paused. As his eye found the deer at the tip of his arrow, Silas remembered what it was like to be on a first hunt. He waited for Eric. His right arm began to complain. Soft annoyance at first but growing louder. The deer took a step, lifting its head. Silas closed one eye, and the deer's shoulder disappeared from his vision, blotted out completely by the arrow's tip. His arm was screaming now. His grip began to tremble. He took his eye off the deer and scanned the bushes to the side of the clearing. *What is the boy waiting for?* He focused on the deer again and had to concentrate to keep the bow steady. Finally, he heard it, a soft *twang* from off to his left. But the shot went high, a blur over the deer's back. It startled into a long, reflexive leap.

Silas's release followed in the next heartbeat. The string whirred.

He knew the shot was true as it left his bow. A good archer always knows.

The arrow lanced through the air, a momentary streak of aluminum. It connected solidly on the upper part of the deer's shoulder—

—and then bounced off.

The arrow fell harmlessly to the grass.

Silas's cry of triumph chased the white tail deeper into the valley.

"Great shot," Eric said when he materialized across the opening.

Silas jogged toward the place where the arrow had landed and smiled as he bent to pick it from the grass.

Its round plastic tip had changed from clear white to a deep blue. He held it up for the grinning boy to see.

It was a two-hour walk back to the lodge, and they made their way lazily up the side of the valley, enjoying the scenery now that the pressure of the hunt was finally over. At the top of the rise, they paused for one final look before hiking down the other side.

The lodge was enormous and built of raw timber in the old pioneer style, but the inside was state of the art. The structure was as ironic as the system it preserved. The man behind the counter smiled when Silas handed him the blue-tipped arrow.

"A buck," he observed. The man scanned the arrow into a computer, and the printer buzzed softly for a second. He handed Silas the sheet. "Suitable for framing. Apollo is one of our finest bucks."

Silas lowered the sheet so that he and the boy could look it over at the same time. It was a large color picture of the deer he'd shot, photographed at some previous time standing near a brook with the mountain in the background. The deer's vital statistics were recorded in the lower-right corner of the sheet: age, estimated weight, number of points. A microchip planted under the deer's skin had communicated with the arrow to approximate the arrow's strike point. A red dot now appeared on the deer's shoulder in the photograph.

"A good shot," the man said. "Just a bit high."

"We'll take a frame with it," Silas said.

Preservation safaris were expensive, but when Silas handed the picture to Eric, the boy's face made it all worthwhile.

IT WAS nearly nine-thirty when Silas finally walked his nephew up the sidewalk to his front step. Nights tended to get cold in Colorado, even at this time of year, and the air carried a chill in it.

Ashley answered the door and hugged her son inside. She had a hug for Silas in the foyer, clapping his back.

"Did you boys have a good time?" she asked.

"Yeah, we got one." Eric handed his mother the framed photo, and she considered it critically for a moment. "And whose little red dot is this?"

"His," the boy admitted, jamming a thumb in Silas's direction.

"It was a joint effort. Eric flanked him." Silas tousled the boy's hair again while he tried to pull away.

Eric snatched the picture back from his mother, kicked off his shoes, and bounded up the stairs by twos. "Hey, Dad. Dad!" He disappeared down the hall.

Silas followed his sister up the stairs of the split-level house and into the kitchen. The kitchen was the visiting area of the home. It was a familial trait; Silas knew she'd got that social peculiarity from their mother.

"Coffee?"

"No, thanks, my stomach," he explained.

"Still bothering you?"

"Only when I eat or drink. And sometimes when I breathe."

"Oh, is that all?"

Silas smiled. "I'll take some milk, if you've got it." He pulled a chair out from the table and sat.

She poured him a glass just as her husband, Jeff, appeared from down the hall. "High and to the right," Silas's brother-in-law said, holding the picture out in front of him with both hands and shaking his head sadly. "Same old Silas, never could hit something that didn't have concentric red circles on it."

Silas shook hands with his brother-in-law. Jeff had been out of town on business when Silas picked the boy up late last night, so it'd been almost two months since they had last seen each other.

Jeff was blond to an extent usually reserved for Scandinavian children, but it seemed to fit him—the overlying sense of the man was one of youthfulness. Silas knew him to be in his late thirties, but Jeff could easily have passed for ten or twelve years younger. Put a ball cap on the guy, shave the chin fuzz, and he'd probably get carded at a bar. He was fine-boned and slender, but that description belied his true nature. Jeff liked his sports and held a second-degree black belt.

It was somewhat disconcerting for Silas to look at a man more than half a foot shorter and fifty pounds lighter and know that the guy could probably knock his butt through a wall if he wanted to. Silas couldn't have picked a better guy for his sister. They were a perfect match—both tough as nails in their own way.

Jeff had a tendency to talk fast, and some people took that for a kind of slickness, but Silas had known him long enough to realize that it was just the speed at which the man functioned. The guy *thought* fast. A moving target Silas could never quite hit dead-on.

"So what's been going on?" Jeff asked.

"They're keeping me busy."

"I'd guess they are. I saw your picture in the paper the other day. Wasn't your best side."

"That's my secret; I don't have a best side."

"Don't be so hard on yourself."

"What was the article about?"

"Just a status article, nothing new," Jeff said. "Letting the world know how the program is advancing. You should really think about changing up your quotes a little, though. Seems like every time I read about you, you're saying the same catchphrases: 'right on schedule,' 'good progress,' 'healthy,' and such."

"They make us say that; it's in the contract."

Jeff chuckled.

"I'm serious."

"Really?" Jeff looked genuinely surprised.

"Yeah, but I haven't talked to a newspaper in months. They're recycling the same old dead interviews."

Ashley set a steaming plate of food in front of Silas.

"What's this?" he asked.

"Dinner," she said, without turning, as she walked back to the stove. "Don't act like you're not hungry. Eat. That is, unless your stomach hurts too bad."

"Well," Silas said, picking up a fork, "I can always eat." He dug into the mashed potatoes, turning his eyes back to Jeff. "So how about you? How are things in the world of high technology?"

"The newest games are kicking our butts in retail. But we're making progress in the catalogs. Different demographic." Jeff was a game programmer for an indy company that made VR games. They were small but growing.

"So when are you and I going hunting again? I haven't been replaced by a younger partner, have I?" Jeff asked.

"I got to be honest with you. Part of the reason I took the time to come up here now is because I know things are going to get nuts at the lab soon. I don't know when I'll get another chance to get away."

"How long?"

"Might be after the Olympics."

Jeff looked properly sympathetic. "That's ten months. Are things going that bad?"

"Yeah."

"What's the problem?"

"Pro*blems*," Silas stressed. "It would be easier to tell you all the things that are right. With any luck, you can see it for yourself at the Olympics."

Jeff smiled. "I can, huh? You wouldn't mean in person, would you?"

"I would, indeed." He pulled an envelope from his shirt pocket. "Three tickets. Second row."

Eric howled in the background. Another steaming plate of food was lowered to the table. "Eat," Ashley said to the boy. His father pulled a chair out for him.

"Have you told Silas about your shrine?"

"It's not a shrine," Eric said emphatically.

Jeff turned to Silas. "He's keeping a scrapbook of every article that's written about the gladiator event. If your name's in it, he cuts it out and puts it in a folder. And you've seen his collection of action figures, right?"

"Da*aaaa*d."

Silas had known, of course, that past gladiators had been turned into a line of toys, but he hadn't realized his nephew collected them.

"Don't be embarrassed," Jeff said.

The boy shot his father a withering look.

At that moment, a plate of food was finally placed in front of Jeff. "About time, woman. I can see where the priorities are around this place."

"Have they set your track yet?" Silas asked the boy, changing the subject.

"Not yet," Ashley answered for him. "He's still scoring too high in too many areas for them to narrow it down. By about this time next year they'll have to decide, even if it means playing eenie, meenie, minie, moe."

The tension on Ashley's face showed what she thought of the tracking system. The kitchen went silent. After finishing the meal, the adults floated into the living room to catch the news.

EVAN TRIED to concentrate, tried to focus on anything but the rush in his head. The world was fuzz he couldn't think through yet. A blur. Pain. So he focused on the pain, trusting it to lead him back. Then came the suicide thoughts, and that, too, was familiar, something to hang on to. How much better it would be to just end it all than to endure this confusion. Fingers touched his face. Fat fingers that fumbled at the sensors. His fingers, he supposed. The sensors came loose in two soft pops. Two more burns at the skin of his temples. Burns on the outside of his head. *But what's it doing to the inside?*

He'd been too deep too long. But the mechs were set; the protocols were humming in V-space bass. Everything was ready for the computer to come online tomorrow. That, at least, was some consolation as he slowly came back to himself. He couldn't remember it ever being this bad before. His head was wood, and he couldn't tell if his eyes were open or closed. This new booth was *good*. Not for the first time, he wondered if he wasn't leaving just a little of himself behind in the quickness. Not for the first time, he realized he didn't care.

His vision came back gradually, and when he could see well enough not to trip over the clutter, he stepped out of the plug booth. His legs trembled slightly under his weight. Around him, the room was dark and blank and empty. He'd sent the techs home hours ago. He didn't like the idea of them hanging around, staring at his body while he was inside. He could imagine them pointing and prodding at him, playing with his private parts while they all laughed.

He looked toward the door and saw it was still locked. He was still alone. *Good.*

He sat and peeled the suit like a snake molting its skin. It came off in huge gauzy strips that left a sticky residue behind. He hated the suit, but he loved the connection it gave him.

Tomorrow, inside the computer, he would see his baby again.

SILAS'S PLANE touched down at Ontario Airport just after three. Such an unexpected name for an airport in Southern California. When you thought of Ontario, you thought of geese and trees and moose. Not traffic and heat and pollution.

He was back at the lab by four-thirty. He tried to hold on to Colorado in his head, but as the paperwork mounted, he felt the quiet contentment slipping away. He finally decided to take a break sometime after midnight.

At the crib unit, Silas watched the steady rise and fall of the small animal's chest. His head hurt. His eyes hurt. He toyed vaguely with the idea of going home for the night. A real bed, a real night's sleep—it felt so good to think of it—but such things were a luxury he couldn't afford now. Tomorrow night, perhaps, but not tonight. There was nothing to do but wait.

He glanced at the row of monitors to his right. Heart rate, respiration, oxygen saturation, temperature, brain waves, and intestinal peristalsis; every possible bodily function was being recorded. The irony didn't escape him. They knew so much about the little creature they knew so little about.

From somewhere deep in his mind a decision that had been percolating finally bubbled up. This would be his last competition. He felt nothing, and it surprised him. He'd been doing this for too long, then.

Looking down, he took no pride in this creation. There was only apprehension. He would see the project through this last contest, but after that, he would find an island somewhere and retire. He'd find a place in the sun where he'd let his skin go dark brown, breed border collies the old-fashioned way—no petri dishes—and then give the puppies away to the neighbor children. This practice would probably make him less than popular with the local parents, but he wouldn't care. It was a nice fantasy. He glanced over at the message on the vid-screen:

Brannin Computer
Online 1300 hours
Questions presented via code 34-trb
Evan Chandler's office
Tomorrow's the big day
Yup—yup—yup
   Benjamin

He'd already read Ben's interoffice memo three times. Most of the questions had been formulated and coded within twelve hours of the organism's birth. So many questions.

Maybe we'll get some answers, Silas thought. *Maybe we'll know for sure.*

The old, well-worn fear resurfaced. He took out a small notebook and glanced at the list of things to check into, look up, double-check, order, verify, replace, and beg the commission to provide. Then he sighed. He wrote a new entry, a single word, and circled it.

All those long years of study. All the discovery. For what? He closed the notebook and slipped it inside the pocket of his lab coat. He supposed his interest in genetics had begun as a way to feel connected to a man whom he'd never really had a chance to know. But now, as he stood in a lab and looked down at the strange creation before him with no past and no future, his father never felt further away.

CHAPTER FIVE

The Brannin Institute was a single five-story glass-and-stone building nestled within an elaborate arrangement of low artificial hills. It was sixteen acres of some of the greenest, most expensive parkland in the world, an island of exquisiteness in the rising urbanized tide that was Southern California. A new supply of leafy climax growth was shipped in on special trucks every three or four years to keep up appearances. The trees were deciduous, mostly, drought-adapted and selected for hardiness, but for all their size and tenacity, they tended to choke and sputter out one by one in the hot, tainted air of Southern Cali.

The Brannin Institute's single small parking lot—usually nearly empty—today was filled to capacity.

News that the Brannin was going online again was cause enough for media interest. But a tip that Silas Williams and Stephen Baskov were also going to be present gave the story a whole new level of juice—enough to draw reporters across the country on red-eye flights from places as far away as New York, Chicago, and Miami. They set their equipment up along the cement walkways in the hopes of shouting a question interesting enough to get someone to stop and answer. Rumors were flying. Long limousines and short, snappy sports cars were squeezed between official-looking sedans and news personnel minibuses.

No one seemed to know for sure why the computer was being brought back online. But they knew the cost, and they knew who was attending, and because of that, they knew it was important.

EVAN CHANDLER sauntered into the chamber. He glanced at the long row of digilog drives that squatted along the wall of the anteroom. Real-space technology seemed so archaic to him now; and as he watched a group of clean techs busily assembling the interface, he couldn't help but feel a little sorry for them. So much, after all, was lost in the translation. There was so much they could never experience on this side of the boundary.

Above him, the scrubbers hummed the air clean of particulate from behind vents evenly spaced across the broad acoustical ceiling. VR laser-optics were notoriously susceptible to dust contamination. It was another thing Evan loved about being in V-space: the only contamination was what you brought inside your head.

A large view screen stood in the center of the room before an audience of empty folding chairs. It's where they would watch him, where they would see what he would see. Or so they thought. He smiled to himself. Evan had a secret.

The drivers were downloading some thirty-six million kilobytes of queries into the plug booth's data streamers. It was part of how the three precious minutes were being paid for. Corporations, economists, researchers—they all had their questions, and all had paid for the opportunity to use a fraction of the Brannin.

But those questions meant nothing to Evan. Their software would talk directly to his V-ware without ever manifesting the slightest visual cue. He had simply to concern himself with opening the computer's memory caches and activating the deduction systems. He hadn't bothered to tell them they were giving him two minutes and fifty-nine seconds more than he needed. Things moved much faster inside, after all.

He pulled a supersized bag of M&M's from his pocket, looked around to see if anyone was watching, then reluctantly put it back. Too many eyes. They would raise hell if they caught him eating anything in a clean chamber. His stomach ached. He cast his eyes around for Baskov. The old SOB thought he knew every damned thing. But he didn't. He didn't know shit.

BASKOV WAS at the back of the room, talking to a tall, lean man in a corporate suit. The man's introduction was conspicuous for its absence, and Evan certainly noticed how politely everyone treated him. They gave him a wide berth. Even Baskov seemed a little uncomfortable around him. Evan was happy to see the old gimp squirm a little. Served him right.

His stomach turned again. *To hell with them.* He walked over to one of the drives and turned his back to the technicians, pretending to inspect the cables. With a glance over his shoulder, he quickly opened the bag of candy and stuffed half the M&M's into his mouth. His head bobbed up and down in quick jerking motions.

A woman in a dark gray jumper approached. "It's time, Dr. Chandler," she said. She had the kind of mouth that showed lots of teeth when she talked, and he noticed how straight and white they were. He liked teeth, and a lot of people around here seemed to have really good ones. He thought about asking her if they were hers or veneers, but if he spoke, she might smell the peanuts, so instead he pressed his lips together and followed her.

It didn't take long to attach the probes and strap him into the booth. The cloth pinched a little at his crotch, but by shifting his weight, it was tolerable. The nice-teeth woman in the jumper lowered the faceplate, and his vision lost its reds. He caught Baskov's critical eye in the crowd just before the visor opaqued. Well, to hell with him; he wasn't going to ruin Evan's day. The old gimp could glare all he wanted, but Evan would still have his two minutes and fifty-nine seconds. *Almost an eternity.*

From somewhere a buzzer sounded briefly. Then the noise from the crowded anteroom began to fade, as if he were receding from it.

Silence.

Silence.

Silence.

Chandler opened his eyes to whiteness.

A flash like a snapped photograph, like lightning, like quick death, and then he saw it: a long, empty corridor. The corridor's edges were broken only by a gathering of switches protruding from the wall in the distance. He walked. It was the ultimate clean room. *No dust in here,* he thought. He moved quickly to start the programs, curling his fingers around the switches and throwing them one by one as he came to them. Each switch activated a different part of the computer, waking it up in bits and pieces. He could hear the thrumming of the drives now.

Evan paused at the final switch, the one Baskov

didn't know about. This switch was very, very small, little more than a tiny white toggle, actually. No, it was smaller than that even. The more you looked at it, the smaller it got, receding from your inspection— an interesting sort of camouflage he'd developed. He squinted, feeling for what was barely there, and then he flicked it. The lights went out.

Time for a little privacy.

He chuckled, and the sound was booming and happy in his ears. It was the sound of a god laughing.

His body was firm and full of energy. His mind was clear. He swung his arms as he walked and whistled a tune he remembered from a vid-show he'd seen as a child. He was Hercules. He was an athlete, a sprinter. He was rage a thousand feet tall, with muscles that rippled as he walked. When he finally stepped from the confines of the corridor and out into the secret place, he paused and took a deep breath of the fresh, clean air. Sunlight filtered through the leafy canopy high above, casting a warm greenish glow on the floor of the forest.

The forest swayed.

"Pea?" he called loudly.

It's what his mother had called him as a child when she tucked him in at night. It was one of the few things she'd given him that he'd been able to hold on to, that name, and it had seemed only right to pass it on.

"Pea?" he called again.

A name is important. It can stamp you for life, so one has to be careful. Naming someone carries with it a lot of responsibility. Pea Chandler. Named for his grandmother's love. Born ten months ago. Father, Evan Chandler. Mother, unknown.

A giggle.

It was supposed to be the father unknown, not the mother.

Something moved.

"Papa?"

There was a rustle of leaves as a small arm parted the bushes at the edge of the clearing. The small dark-haired boy stepped into sight. Evan surged across the clearing and scooped the boy into his arms, hugging him wordlessly against his broad chest. He'd grown so much, lengthened out. Evan guessed him to be about four years old now. *Has that much time passed in here?*

"Papa, where have you been?"

"I've tried to come back, Pea. I thought of you every day."

"It's been so lonely."

"I missed you, too."

Evan carried the child out of the forest on his shoulders. When they came to the first dune of fine white sand, he paused and lowered the boy to his feet. Then, laughing together, they raced up and over the other side of the dune and across the tidal flat into the rolling surf of a warm inland sea.

"You've been busy," Evan told the boy.

"All for you, Papa," the boy said. "I made this all for you."

"How did you know how?"

"I'm not sure."

"You like building things?"

"Yes. This sea has kept me busy."

"It's truly beautiful."

They ran in the waves, and Evan enjoyed the heat of the sun on his back as they played. He picked up the laughing child and tossed him into the water again and again. For a short while, Evan was able to pretend that there was nothing else, that this was his true life and the lonely fat man that existed in some other universe was merely a bad dream from which he had awakened.

The boy wiped the water from his eyes and found his feet somehow in the surge of waves. He stood, pulling back a little so Evan wouldn't grab him up and toss him again. "There is so much I want to show you." The boy's eyes were black and piercing. "And so much I want to ask."

The boy extended his arm, palm down, and the waves suddenly smoothed themselves out. In the space of a heartbeat, Evan found himself standing thigh-deep in a sea that was calm and flat—a single unbroken pane that stretched to the horizon. The only sound was the wind blowing in from offshore, but after another moment, that, too, quieted. He looked down at the boy.

"I've made life for the sea," Pea said. "I call them fish." The boy pointed.

In the distance, an imperfection formed on the flat surface, a ripple, small at first. But the ripple gradually grew into a wave. Evan looked back at the boy, feeling the first stirrings of unease.

"I couldn't wait to show you," the boy said.

The wave swelled as it moved toward them, across the flat sea. The sound of rushing water filled his ears. At a hundred yards out, Evan saw the shape. It was dark and huge, and it roiled wildly behind the growing white wall of froth. An enormous black fin appeared, thick and fleshy, and large as a man. The bulging tail flexed in the surf, and water splashed high into the air. The sea broke away as the thing fought into the shallows. It was a distorted monstrosity, low and flat, with a wide, gaping mouth filled with ragged teeth. Its eyes were white and sightless, extending from stalks at the sides of its head. It ground its belly deeper into the sand with each powerful thrust of its tail, getting closer. Forty yards now. The fleshy fins paddled at the surf, dragging the creature through the shallowing water.

"They keep changing over time. That's something I didn't expect," Pea said.

Evan watched as the thing finally ground to a halt, still twenty yards out—a huge hump of flesh jutting above the water. The eyestalks swayed as the mouth worked open and closed.

"I've made life for the air," Pea said. "I call them birds." The boy pointed again.

Evan followed Pea's outstretched arm upward into the brilliant blue sky. There, triangular forms pinwheeled in the air currents like shiny red kites, their long, thin tails trailing behind them in the wind. As Evan watched, one of the larger creatures swooped down onto a smaller one, enveloping it and severing its tail. The wounded animal screamed and, separated from its stabilizing tail, fell spiraling to the ground in the distance.

"I've made life for the land, too," Pea said. "But I haven't decided yet what to call them." When Pea gestured toward the shore, the dunes themselves began to shift and sag. Something moved beneath them. Something big. Evan heard a sound like sandpaper on steel, a low, corrosive lumbering that seemed to come from everywhere at once.

As he watched, a thing writhed free from beneath the dune and struggled onto the beach. It was huge and pink and formless, with a maw at the front that opened and closed spasmodically against the hard, wet beach. There were no eyes, no obvious sense organs at all, just the single gaping feature at the front— an all-encompassing hunger, a mouth like the end of the world. In the seconds that Evan watched, its skin burned and blackened in the bright sunshine. Within a short time, it was dead.

"How do they live? What do they eat?" Evan asked.

"You're so smart, Papa. They *do* have to eat. At first I made them to want to eat each other. But then soon I had only one of each type left, and those starved. I got tired of having to make them over and over again, so I made them able to remake themselves. That was how I realized how to keep them fed."

"How?"

"They make babies that they eat."

"What do you mean?"

"They eat their babies."

"You have them eating each other's babies?"

"No, they eat their own."

Evan frowned.

"It keeps them happy," the boy said.

"That's all they eat, their babies?"

"Uh-huh."

Evan looked down at the boy for a long moment. "Pea?"

"What?"

"That can't be right. That sort of ecosystem defies physics, the conservation of matter and energy. If they eat only their own babies, and their babies come from them, then it's a closed system."

"I don't know what you mean," the boy said. "But it works. In fact, sometimes a baby gets away. That's how the numbers grow. But even that isn't always the same."

"What do you mean?"

"I've noticed that over time, in later generations, the babies have gotten better and better at getting away. They're born a little older now."

"How can they be born older?"

"They're better able to run or swim or fly when they're born now. They're born more mature. Not like before, when the adults would just gobble them up."

"Why is it changing?"

"I don't know. But the newer generations all have trouble catching their babies. Some of the adults make babies that are mostly too fast, and those adults starve quickly and die. Others make babies that are too slow, and those babies never get away. But it seems like there are fewer of that kind around now, for some reason."

Evan could only stare at the child.

"The ones there are more of are the ones that catch their babies sometimes. But not all the time."

Evan was at a loss for words. *Darwinian evolution inside VR?* He supposed it was possible. Even if it was a fucked-up kind of Darwinian evolution that wasn't constrained by physical laws.

"Why did you make them?" Evan asked.

"I don't know. It seemed interesting."

As good a reason as any, he supposed.

"Are you going to keep making more?"

"Maybe sometimes. It's easier to let them make themselves. I just start them. Then they do the rest. There's so much I've been doing. So much I want to show you. I've made everything for you."

"I want to see it all."

The pull came, then—sudden, familiar, unstoppable. It drove all other thoughts away.

There was still much Evan wanted to ask. He knelt down and hugged the boy. "Pea, they're calling me." The pull grew stronger.

"No, don't go."

"I have to."

"When will you be back?"

"I'm not sure."

"No! You can't leave!"

"It's not my choice."

"I'm so alone," Pea cried. "I need you."

"I need you, too."

"I get so scared. I don't know what I might do."

Evan was pulled up to his feet. "Neither do I," he said into the darkness of his faceplate. "Neither do I."

SILAS WATCHED Chandler's body go into convulsions as the drives wound down to a soft electronic whir. The lights came on, and the room exploded into frenzied activity. A team of medics rushed the plug booth as the obese man broke free from his moorings and collapsed to the floor in a quaking avalanche of flesh and twitching sensor wires. They worked quickly to extricate him from his skin suit, cutting it away in big, gauzy swaths with their stainless-steel scissors. Someone shouted something about a defibrillator. To his left, Silas could see a tech he recognized from Helix shaking his head at the readout on his computer feed.

"What just happened?" Silas asked him.

"Not sure," the man replied. "But that is one crazy son of a bitch."

"What did he do?"

"Not him, *it*. I'm talking about the Brannin. It's flawed."

"What do you mean?" Silas asked.

"Look," the man said, gesturing to the terminal that sat on the folding table in front of him. Silas looked over the man's shoulder at the screen.

ACA CAC UAU AUG CUU CUC CUG GAU UUA CGC AGG UGG
UAG UGA UAC CAC CAA AGG CGA UCG UUU UCA ACU ACC

AUU CGG CGG AAA ACG GGA UUU GUG GUA GGG GGA CGU
AUG AUA CCG CUA AAU UAU GAG AGU AUG GCA UAG GUU
UAA AGA ACU AGA GAG GGU AGU CAC CUG UAG UUU UGA
CGU ACG AUU UCG CGC CUC CCC UCC UGA GAG AUU GGG
CGA CAG UCA CAG GUC UGC ACA CUA UGC CUC CUU CAG
GCG CAC GAG UCU UUG CCA GAC GUC AUC CGU GGG GCA
UGA AGA CUG CAU UGG UUU ACU GGG CAG CUG CGG GCA
AAA UGA UUU UAA UUU GGA AAC GGG CAG CAG CAG GAA
CCC CUA GUC GGG UGC AAU GGG GAC CAA CAA UAG UGA
CAU CUG CAU CAU GAU AAG UUU CAU UAC GAG GGA CAU
CAU CAA AUG GAC UGA UGA GUG UUG CUA CCG AGU UUU
AAC GUG AAA GGG UAC AAU GGA UAG AAA ACH AGU ACG
UAU GGG GGG AUG AAA GUG AGG ACG CCC CGC AGC CCC
CGG GGG CCC CGG CAG AAA AGA AGC AGC AGC CCC CCG
ACG AGC AGA

As Silas read, he tried to feel surprise. He wanted to feel like he hadn't expected this. Somehow, if he could just conjure up a little shock, just a modicum of outrage, he could go on pretending that he really believed this whole thing had been the result of some sort of miscommunication.

"What about the other queries?" Silas asked.

"All answered, by the looks of it."

"But not ours?"

The man scrolled down through several more screens. "Absolutely nothing. It's the same code the Brannin gave us before. It accessed our file, but it didn't answer the query. It just gave the code back to us." The man swiveled around in his chair to face Silas. "I think we've been snubbed."

Silas glanced across the room, and Baskov was staring over another young man's shoulder into a similar computer feed. The scowl creased his face to the bone.

CHAPTER SIX

The first thing Evan did upon regaining consciousness was to immediately wish he hadn't. The
second involved rolling onto his side and puking unceremoniously over the edge of the bed. Hot vomit
splashed cold tile. The sound came at him muffled,
like the world heard from the other side of a closed
car door. His head throbbed. He tried to sit up but
couldn't. His eyes ungummed to a blur of white and
gray. He fought to focus, but the effort exhausted
him, and he collapsed, grateful, back into the dark
swirl.

After a time, the world swam toward him again.
He tried to resist, to retreat, but was thrust into the
light. Of all his senses, one seemed to work. His nose
whispered to him in the oldest language. He was in a
hospital. He could smell the sickness around him.

It came back to him in parts after that. The Brannin. Pea. *What happened to me in there?* He heard a
moan, low and miserable, again from the other side
of that invisible car door that muffled his hearing.
The moan was his, of course, and when he could, he
stopped.

He sensed movement at his side, a subtle change in
the composition of gray that surrounded him.

"Evan, can you hear me?" a voice asked in the distance.

He tried to answer, but the words broke apart in his throat.

"You're going to survive," the voice said.

Evan recognized Baskov's gravelly tone. "Too bad," Evan managed to say.

"Yes, truer words I've yet to hear you speak. The doctors say you'll never be the same again. They say your brain has been damaged."

Evan swallowed hard against the dryness of his throat. *How long have I been out? A day? A month?* "What do you want?" he croaked.

"I told them you were no prize to begin with, that your brain was damaged all along, and they shouldn't waste their effort. But it seems the Hippocratic oath has saved another piece of shit."

"What do you want?" Evan repeated.

"I just want to know what you could possibly have been thinking."

"Pea."

"What is Pea?" Baskov asked.

Evan thought about how to explain, but after a second or two, his mind lost the trail and he forgot what the question had been.

"Where did you go when the screens blacked out?" Baskov asked.

Evan hesitated, trying to judge how much he could hide.

"I'm not a patient man, Evan. We've tried to back-trace what happened, but there is no record to follow. You covered your tracks well. There are ways that I can get you to tell me what I want to hear, but the doctors tell me you are very weak. The drugs could kill you. I'm under pressure that you couldn't begin to understand. If that is what I need to do, I'll do it."

More shapes moved around him in the gray. A dozen voices whispered in tones too low for Evan to unscramble. He thought about dying. It would be a relief in many ways, but Pea would think he'd been abandoned. "What do you want to know?"

"Why didn't the computer answer the Helix queries?"

"What do you mean?"

"You know what I mean. It interfaced the logs but didn't reply."

"That's not possible. The computer can't choose what it responds to."

"It chose not to respond."

"It doesn't know how to ignore."

"It did."

"I activated the logic areas before the smooth-out. You saw me do that, the levers. It *had* to process."

"It didn't," Baskov said flatly.

"Then I don't know."

"Do you expect me to believe you, Evan?"

"Why would I lie?"

"I don't know. Tell me."

"You don't understand," Evan said.

"I understand better than you think. I had people checking up on you, Evan. They've been looking into you the way I should have before I ever involved you in any of this. They interviewed your old professors, your colleagues, your subordinates. Would you like to know what I keep hearing about you?"

"No."

"Sure you do, Evan. At the heart of things, insecure bastards like you always want to hear about yourselves. You want to hear that you're a genius, that you're gifted, that you're special. Well, they said those things, Evan, they did; but mostly they said you were an asshole. They might not all have used that word—though some certainly did—but it came through loud and clear every time. You're a sad-fuck introvert too arrogant and self-absorbed to notice anyone but yourself; consequently, nobody gives a damn about you. That piece of information really helps me. It gives me the keys to your little kingdom. Nobody cares you're here—nobody is going to come looking, or making calls, or pulling strings. You're mine for as long as I want you."

Baskov pulled a chair away from the wall and clattered it across the tile. He sat.

Evan tried to rise, to move away, but he was too weak.

"I'm going to let you in on a secret, Evan. That gift you're so proud of, that genius . . ." He moved closer, speaking softly. "It's maladaptive."

Baskov nodded seriously. "It's shit, Evan. Think about what it's ever done for you. I mean, look at you, for Christ's sake. Isolated, no wife, no children, without friends. Have you ever even been with a woman?"

Evan stared at him.

"Of course not," Baskov continued. "What woman would open her legs for you? What woman would let you know her that way?" Baskov jabbed Evan's gut with a gnarled finger.

Evan turned his head away, wanting to hear nothing more.

Baskov went on. "People think that man will be smarter in the future, that our intelligence is evolving on some upward trajectory as a species, but that's not really true at all. The bell curve rises to its peak at an IQ just above a hundred for a very good reason. The bell's under directional selection from *both* sides, isn't it, Evan? Stray too far from that safe middle bulge and the world becomes unnavigable. Pass a critical threshold on either side of the curve and the world, the real world, unravels in your fingers. You're testament to that.

"I'm a fan of history, and history has shown it time and time again. Einstein used to forget his children in the park. Newton suffered debilitating depressions. Do you know how Gödel died?" Baskov prodded him with his finger again. "Do you?"

"No."

"His death certificate listed inanition as cause. The father of incompleteness couldn't be bothered to eat. He starved himself to death.

"You're not so special, Evan. You're a story that history has retold many times. People like you rise from the fringes at regular intervals. Outside the cloisters of your respective fields, you're helpless—like specialized worker ants born only to provide some benefit to the rest of us before your tragic little lives draw to a close, usually in poverty and madness. Tesla and Turing—do you remember how their stories end?"

Evan kept his face turned away.

"That your kind keeps rising at all shows some flaw in our species' template. You're a sport, a type of sacrificial defect, and it's my burden to see to it that your sad existence is made use of. I take that burden very seriously, Evan. You believe me, don't you?"

Evan said nothing; the finger jabbed him again. He tried to speak then, but his voice gave out.

"Oh, you have something to say?" Baskov said. "Speak up. I'm listening." Baskov leaned closer.

"You," Evan said, pushing the word out, "are jealous . . . of us."

Baskov's face went white. His hands fisted. Evan waited for the blow, but it didn't come.

"You wanted to *be* us, didn't you?" Evan croaked. "As a child, in school. Like Gödel. You studied. But you weren't smart enough." Evan smiled.

After several seconds, Baskov hissed, "I'm going

to enjoy this, Evan. I'm going to enjoy making you talk."

"Probably you will," Evan scraped. "But not so much as you think. Because I know. And now you know."

There was a strange sound. Then the faraway voices murmured.

"Tell me why the computer didn't answer the questions."

Evan saw no reason to lie. "Pea," he said.

"What the hell is Pea?"

Evan swallowed again, and his throat clicked. "I wanted to talk with the profile core."

"What are you talking about?"

"I wanted time alone with him."

"With who?"

"With the profile core. With Pea."

"What is a profile core?"

"I anthropomorphized a redundancy loop in the logic core. It was the one thing that is connected to everything inside. It touches on everything. I named him Pea."

"Him?"

"Yes, the boy."

There was a long silence. Baskov's voice was lower, turned away from Evan, toward someone else in the room: "Will the drugs still work if he is insane?"

"Not sure," another voice answered.

"This is the part I will enjoy, Evan. And the part that comes after."

A few seconds later, Evan felt a muffled sting as a needle penetrated his arm.

CHAPTER SEVEN

Silas sat alone, looking through the thick glass and into the nursery. He took notes on a clipboard as little Felix romped around in the new containment area.

Benjamin was the one who originally came up with the suggestion about the cardboard boxes. It was such a simple thing, but the idea had worked better than they could have hoped, turning the sluggish and docile young organism into the shiny black rush of activity that Silas saw before him now. It had just been bored, apparently. Like any youngster, it wanted to play.

As Silas watched, it busied itself at reducing the boxes to a random scatter of cardboard mulch. It had a talent for disassembly. Its true calling.

Ever the cladistician, Silas unconsciously continued to assess the organism as it played. As much as he tried, the little thing defied classification. Although it was engineered, there should still be something that gave away the roots of its nature, some trait that would reveal itself and imply that, yes, Felix was a feline derivative, or a simian derivative, or an avian derivative. But Silas was left without this closure, and always when he watched it, he felt uneasy because it seemed he was looking at something completely alien.

Putting the clipboard down, Silas walked over to

the refrigerator and pulled out a large jug of milk and a square plastic container of dried prey food. With a heavy wooden spoon, he stirred the milk into the crunchy mix until the consistency was about right.

The biochemists had had a field day with little Felix. After doing a complete metabolic workup, they'd found that the organism could profitably digest an amazingly wide variety of foodstuffs, from grains and cereals to raw meat. Though they guessed that simple dog food would probably have sufficed, they ended up synthesizing their own dietary blend, which, when combined with a hefty pour of whole dairy, seemed to do the job well. The little thing was growing fast and was now cutting a second row of jagged teeth.

Silas opened the outer door of the nursery with his left hand, being careful not to spill the brimming bowl in his right. When he heard the latch click behind him, he opened the inner door and stepped into the nursery chamber. The scent of disinfectant and wet cardboard assailed his nostrils.

The little creature squealed with delight. Silas quickly found it clamoring at his feet for its dinner. Long, thin arms fluttered about his torso, reaching up at the bowl.

"Hold your horses," he said, trying not to stumble over it as he crossed the room. He placed the bowl on the floor in the center of the chamber and watched with satisfaction as the creature dug in ferociously. He made a mental note to increase the feeding again. The thing ate like an elephant.

He smiled, marveling at its vigor. Thin, stumpy wings positioned high on its wide back bobbed rhythmically with the pleasure of eating. Its large gray eyes maintained a position just above the bowl's rim, alternately looking down at the food, then up at Silas. Silas liked that. It would be easier to train the gladiator if it associated humans with the arrival of food. Tay Sawyer, the resident animal trainer, had made a point of stressing that.

When the creature finished the bowl, it sat back and licked its chops, snaking a thick tongue around the outside of its short black muzzle. Gray eyes looked into Silas's brown.

As they stared at each other, Silas wondered what might be going on in its head. What kind of mind worked behind those eyes?

Silas stood and crossed the room. When he stooped to pick up the bowl, the creature made a noise. A strange sound Silas hadn't heard before. He hesitated. This was new behavior. The creature's ears flattened to its skull, and its back arched. Not catlike. Nothing like that. Instead, it reared up like some angry black baboon—but like something else, too. Something not at all like a baboon. Something Silas couldn't place.

The thing moved forward, guarding the bowl.

"Back off," Silas snapped. "Back!"

He clapped his hands, and the creature slunk backward a few feet.

It was still young, he reminded himself. Despite its size. Barely out of infancy. At this age, animals as predatory as genus *Panthera* were still docile cubs that could be petted and played with.

"Come on, back up!"

But the creature didn't move, only hunched down lower to the floor. Silas whispered, "What a strange thing you are."

He slapped his foot on the ground to drive the creature away from the food dish, but it stood its ground, staring up at him.

"I need the bowl," Silas said, by way of exasperated negotiation.

The creature hissed in response—a sound something between a cat's hiss and a hyena's cackle.

"Enough is enough." Silas bent to pick up the bowl, reaching past the creature.

He wasn't, at first, sure what happened.

Pain.

Like being kicked in the hand. A jolt.

And the creature spun away, a dark streak.

Silas flinched, blood spattering the floor. First in fat drops like rain, then in a gush.

Silas clutched his other hand to the wound, squeezing down on the pain, an instinctual response.

"What did you do?" Disbelief pouring out of him like all the blood.

He backed up, blood splattering the tile while he reached for the door. He hit the door-open button as the creature eyed him from a crouch, gray eyes slitted. Its muzzle slid away from its teeth as its face contorted in rage.

Silas took a step back through the opening door, and the creature bolted, crossing the room in springing strides. Silas jerked himself backward, slipping on his own blood, falling through the open doorway. He hit the ground on his shoulder and kicked at the door, trying to shut it. The creature launched itself forward and slammed into the bloody glass a moment after the door clicked shut.

There was a meaty thump, and the gladiator dropped to the ground.

Silas rolled away from the door. Away from the staring, slitted eyes on the other side of the glass.

He pulled himself to his feet, grabbing at the edge of the lab bench to steady himself. Only then did Silas look at the wound.

Only then did he see the missing finger.

On his right hand, his pinkie finger terminated just above the second knuckle.

HOSPITALS. SILAS had always hated them.

The surgery took a little more than an hour.

"We need to shorten the bone," the doctor had said.

To Silas, this seemed counterintuitive, but a series of nurses assured him it was necessary so that skin could be pulled over the wound.

"It's too bad you couldn't find the finger," one of them said.

"Oh, I know where it is."

A finger. Not a pound of flesh, exactly. But it was something. It felt like payment.

They pumped him full of IV antibiotics. Then tetanus shots. Rabies shots were suggested when it was learned an animal bite was involved.

Silas explained to the new doctor at shift change that the animal in question wasn't going to be available for brain tissue dissection. "Honestly, it's worth more than I am. They might want to dissect my brain to make sure I didn't give *it* something."

The next morning, the calls started at nine A.M. The visits soon after that. Tay, the trainer, showed up, accompanied by several members of the team. After the condolences, "It's time to shift gears on this," he said.

Silas agreed.

"Past time," Tay said. "We've officially transited the natal phase of the program. The training phase begins tomorrow.

"I'm really sorry about this," Tay said. "If I had any idea that it might be so aggressive so young . . ."

Silas shrugged as best he could while sitting in the hospital bed. "You did say it was a good thing that the gladiator associated humans with the arrival of food."

Tay cringed.

Silas smiled. "Things happen."

"You say that now. We'll see if you're casual when the drugs wear off."

When Tay left, Silas made several calls to Benjamin, who was already on his way and had to reroute back to the lab. He showed up at the hospital a few hours later, arms laden.

Benjamin laid the requested papers on Silas's hospital bed and collapsed into a nearby chair.

"That bad?" Silas asked, reading Ben's expression.

"A bust," Benjamin said.

"Complete?"

"Not a single match."

"Damn." Silas leafed quickly through the pile of papers that represented nearly two weeks' work for his head cytologist. The DNA fingerprinting hadn't turned up a single template match to any of the known existing orders of animals.

"Are you okay?" Ben asked. "You in a lot of pain?"

"Let's not worry about me at the moment. Let's worry about the project."

"Well, I'm out of ideas," Benjamin said.

Silas leaned back in his bed. He was out of ideas, too. He laced his remaining fingers behind his head and casually considered his friend. His hand throbbed.

Ben was one of those rare individuals, usually of Scandinavian extraction, afflicted with skin so profoundly devoid of melanin that the underlying blood vessels provided a kind of emotional broadcast system. When he was embarrassed, he flushed red to the ears. When angry, deep red ovals would form in the hollows of his cheeks. If he was merely overheated, a rosy glow would reach across his face to his forehead.

It was a communication system both completely alien and completely fascinating to Silas.

As he looked at the younger man's mottled pink face, Silas assessed that there was now a new emotion to be cataloged: frustration. "I think we'll have to take a different angle on this. We've been trying to learn about Felix from the inside out. Now let's try the opposite."

"I don't get you. You're in the hospital, and you're still thinking about work?"

"I've got nine and a half other fingers. What we need now is data."

"You have a problem."

"Exactly."

"I don't think we're talking about the same thing."

"We need to learn everything we can about the creature."

"It's all there," Ben said, gesturing to the paperwork. "Right down to its raw code, but I don't know what you expect to find."

"Maybe I'll know when I see it."

"We've already done a head-to-toe workup."

"Yes, but with the wrong mindset and the wrong people. We were looking for similarities to existing species, existing patterns. If this organism really is new, then we'll have to relate form to function if we're going to learn anything about what to expect."

"So what are you saying—bring in some new talent?"

"Perhaps that wouldn't be a bad idea."

"We can do that. We've had teams of anatomists fighting over time to study it."

Silas considered. He thought of the creature as it had hissed at him. That strange alien sound. "No, that would still be from the wrong perspective. Conventional anatomic study is still rooted in cladistics."

"So is all of biology."

"Not all of it," Silas said.

He flipped open his notebook and scanned down the page, not wanting to look at Benjamin when he said what he was thinking. "I think we need a xeno-biologist."

Silas heard the smile in Benjamin's voice. "Busy field, that?"

"You know what I mean. Theoretical xenobiology."

"How is that gonna help?"

"Fresh eyes. A different perspective."

Ben nodded. "Okay, you're the boss. I guess it couldn't hurt."

"I want you to check who's the best."

"Sure."

"And, Ben."

"Yeah?"

"This is a silent program. No publicity on this one."

"Oh, don't worry. I assumed that."

PART II

THE GATHERING STORM

How dare you sport thus with life.

—MARY SHELLEY, *FRANKENSTEIN*

CHAPTER EIGHT

Vidonia João stepped through the hatch of the small aircraft and into the direct glare of the Southern California sun. She paused at the top of the platform and turned her face into the hot breeze. It had been a long flight on short notice, but despite the heat, it felt good to be in the open air again.

Long black hair fanned out behind her, exposing the planes of an unusual face.

Her ancestral pool was broad and shallow, drawn from the oldest sailing routes across the North and South Atlantic. It was the kind of face sometimes seen in Caribbean markets or metropolitan fashion shows—places where the world's cultures mixed and matched and made their own thing. Soft brown skin, full lips, a long, high-arched nose.

She cast her dark eyes into the glare and saw a tall blond man waiting at the bottom of the stairs. *Silas?* she wondered. She shouldered her travel bag and descended in a series of bounces that drew the man's eye to places other than her face.

"Dr. João?" the blond man asked. His face was scorched deep red by the noonday sun.

Her white teeth flashed affirmation.

"I'm Benjamin Wells, head cytologist at Helix. We're happy you decided to join us."

"Happy to be here. It will be nice to step out of the

classroom for a while." Her accent was soft, subtle, something she'd worked hard to smooth out in the eleven years she'd been an American citizen.

"Well, glad to oblige you. You'll certainly be doing more than teaching here."

"That's what I've been told, but it's still not clear what exactly I *will* be doing. Opportunities in industry aren't exactly common in my field."

"Dr. Williams wants to brief you about that when we get to the compound. If you'll follow me," he said.

And as simple as that, the introductions were over.

Vidonia followed him across a dozen yards of hot tarmac to a low, sleek limousine. The driver nodded as he took her bags, and the bite of the air-conditioning was welcome on the bare skin of her calves.

"Any jet lag?" Benjamin asked once they were on their way.

"Not too bad."

"Good, because Silas will want to see you as soon as possible."

"The sooner the better. Are we stopping by the hotel first?"

"Hotel? I guess you *are* still in the dark. You'll be staying at the compound. This is a blue-level project, and they take security pretty seriously around here. For your own safety and the safety of the program, all consultants are to be on-site for the duration."

"How many consultants are there?" This was getting more interesting by the minute.

"Counting you?"

"Yeah."

Benjamin looked up, as if counting to himself. After a moment of contemplation, "One," he said.

"One?"

"Yep."

Vidonia reclined deeper into the leather seat and let

the view through the window wash over her. The limo was making good time, cruising in the commercial lane while the rest of the traffic struggled along bumper to bumper.

They were high in the air, and the elevated highway gave a breathtaking view of the city. Low rectangular buildings sprawled away in all directions, and in the distance, glittering spires stretched toward the sky. There were no trees or green of any kind. It made her sick for her childhood. But that was so long ago now. Long ago and far away, and she the better for it, she told herself.

Twenty minutes later they descended the skyway, and the landscape around the thoroughfare had opened up considerably. The urban sprawl had given way to something else. The broad steel buildings they drove past were now spaced farther apart, crouching on huge park-size swaths of grass. Here, at least, green had taken a foothold.

"This is the technical district," Benjamin said, when he noticed her interest.

It reminded her of the poem *Where Science Lives,* all those steel buildings on their neat little parks. The straight roads and ordered landscaping. Looking out at that, it was easy to imagine that science belonged here and might have little use in places where the roads weren't quite so clean and orderly. Places where dirty children begged at the corners.

Ben revealed his discomfort at her continued silence through his fidgeting and an occasional awkward glance. She knew the type, always looking for the next interaction and confused about what to do in its absence. An unusual temperament in a scientist. She decided to put him at ease. "Was I hard to find?"

He shook his head. "Not really. But I did a lot of

research before I contacted you. You're near the top of your field."

"You give me too much credit, really," she said. "But even if I am near the top, why not contact those at the summit? Why me?"

"That's rather complicated."

She looked at him, waiting.

"You've managed not to attract a lot of attention from those outside your area of specialty."

"Or much in it," she said.

Ben smiled. "Your absence isn't likely to require a lot of explanation in scientific circles."

"Oh, I'm beginning to understand," she said. "So you mean I'm good, but I'm not so good that I'm going to be missed."

"Something like that."

When they arrived at the compound a few minutes later, the scale of the place shocked her. The facility was enormous and sprawling—a maze of winding roads that took them past several suites of buildings and parking lots. Ben took her directly to the research lab. They parked and entered the building. She said nothing as he led her down the long halls and carded her through the checkpoints.

When she stepped through the door of the research lab, she looked around for a moment, unsure why he'd brought her there.

"This would be your lab," he said.

"This?"

"Yes."

"This would all be for my use?"

"Yes." Ben motioned her forward.

The lab was something she hadn't expected. She let her fingers play over the smooth, silver benchtop that ran along the wall. She gestured to her left.

"A CAT scan," Ben responded. "That's basic. We also have X ray, thermal imaging, and internal photo time-lapse. But the rest we thought best left up to you."

"I can order other equipment?"

He nodded. "Silas wants the lab designed around you. Let us know what your needs are, and they'll be provided for. Whatever you want, within reason. And my experience has been if it's not completely crazy, then it's within reason. They believe in keeping the talent happy around here."

"And the computer system?"

"Tandem link, virtual imaging tied from different ports of scan. It will do."

"Yes," she said, impressed. "That will certainly do."

She sank into a swivel chair and let it run a slow circle. What was she getting herself into?

"How much control do I have?"

"All and none. You'll have the freedom to do what you feel is necessary, but ultimately, you answer to Silas. What he says goes. Oh, and you can't publish until after the Olympic Games. We'll need you to put that in writing before you begin."

"Eight months. That won't be a problem."

"Still interested?"

She looked around at the gleaming equipment. "Very."

"Good, then it's time you met Silas."

SHE HEARD him before she saw him. *Thwump, thwump, thwump.* She followed Benjamin around the side of the building and into a kind of courtyard. Bushy trees draped in tiny white flowers stood in staggered formation along one side of the clearing.

Several picnic tables crowded at the far edge. Beyond them, a single basketball hoop cast its crooked shadow along the edge of a parking lot. The cars in the lot were parked at a respectful distance.

The ball left Silas's hands in an arc. It bounced high off the rim, touched backboard, rim again, and then fell away. Missed.

Ben clapped loudly as they approached across the grass. "They told me you were out here. I wouldn't believe it if I didn't see it with my own eyes."

The man turned, and Vidonia tried to conceal her surprise. He wasn't what she had expected.

"You must be Dr. João," he said, extending a large hand. The pinkie, she noticed, was partly missing— the skin healed but still slightly pink. "I'm Silas Williams."

"Nice to meet you. And it's pronounced *Zhoo-wow*."

"I'm sorry."

"It's quite all right, I get that all the time. It's Portuguese. I'm familiar with your work."

Silas smiled. Like many very tall men, he had a heavy jaw, and his smile seemed awkward perched across all that bone. Strong, high cheekbones balanced out his rectangular face. The complexion beneath the roughness of a few days' stubble was smooth mocha, and his curly hair was graying vigorously upward from the temples, giving him a distinguished look, despite his size.

"Has Ben showed you the lab yet?" he asked.

"Yeah, she's hooked," Ben interjected.

Silas bent for the ball, then tossed it from one hand to the other. He turned and regarded the basketball hoop thoughtfully.

"There is something about this game that I've really missed," he said.

"Oh yeah?" Ben asked, his voice, incredulous, rising an octave.

"When you've got the ball in your hand and you're staring at the hoop, it's easy to push everything else away."

"When was the last time you touched a ball?" Ben asked.

"You focus on the rim, calculate distance, concentrate . . ." Silas flicked his wrist and sent the ball tumbling through the air. It connected firmly with the front of the rim and bounced back in his direction.

"Why the sudden interest in athletics?" Ben asked. When Silas didn't answer, Ben pressed, "Did something happen that I don't know about?"

Silas grabbed the ball again and tossed it over to Vidonia. She caught it and turned it in her hands, looking at him. Looking at him.

"Shoot," he said, finally.

She didn't hesitate. She brought it up to her chest and heaved. The ball carved its little parabola across the blue sky. Air ball, not even close.

Silas picked the ball from the grass and stepped back onto the pavement, dribbling in long bounces. "Used to play a lot when I was a kid. You don't have to think. You just aim and throw; your body does the math for you. There's something to that, probably."

"Did something happen today, Silas?" Ben asked.

"Yeah, something happened." Silas shot again. This time the ball rasped through the net. He turned back to Vidonia. "You're probably wondering why you're here."

"It had crossed my mind," she said.

"You're curious why we'd want a xenobiologist."

"This isn't a field where it's common to get job offers in the middle of the night from halfway across the country," she said. *Particularly from Olympic Development,* she thought.

"Well," he said, as he bent to retrieve the ball, "as you've probably guessed, since you say you are familiar with my work, the organism in question isn't of extraterrestrial origin. I should get that out of the way at the beginning. But it is alien. Yes, I think it fits the broadest definition of that word—alien—but it is from here, right from this facility. That's why we called you."

"So this *is* about the gladiator competition," she said.

He nodded.

"Is it the contestant?"

"It's supposed to be. We're not sure what it is, actually. We were hoping you could help us find out."

"I don't think I understand what you mean."

"We need you to help find out what it is we're dealing with."

She paused. "Please don't take this the wrong way. But with all due respect, shouldn't you already know?"

"We should, but we don't."

"It is an engineered organism, isn't it?"

"Yes."

She crossed her arms in front of her, wanting to ask more. Instead, she said the only thing that really mattered. "I'll help any way I can."

"Thank you."

Silas dribbled the ball.

"What went wrong today?" Ben asked Silas.

Silas turned toward him. "That's a long story," Silas said. He shot the ball again, and it sprang away from the hoop at a high angle. He trotted after.

"I don't mind long stories," Ben pressed. "What happened?" The glib undercurrent in his face had drained away now.

Silas tossed him the ball. "Three points, shoot."

Behind his glasses, Ben's blue eyes were bright in the angle of the sun. The ball rotated in his hands. He bent, straightened, shot. The ball spanked high against the backboard and skipped across the pavement, toward the grass.

Silas snagged it as it bounced. "Nothing so important," he said. "And maybe not such a long story, really, come to think of it."

Silas shot the ball. It dropped through the hoop with a swish of net.

"It opened its wings today," Silas said. "That's all. It stretched them out, eight feet, maybe."

Ben's face lost some of its tension. "That's what has you out here shooting baskets?" he asked.

"No, you should have seen it. Those wings. It was goddamned beautiful, Ben. That's what has me out here."

"It has wings?" she asked. Unless she was mistaken, there was little room for flight beneath the steel netting of the gladiator arena.

She followed alongside the two men as they walked through the grass toward the lab. From this perspective the buildings were low, squat boxes of glass and steel. The windows reflected green tress, blue sky, white clouds.

"Yeah, but it will never fly," Ben said. "Too complicated. No one has ever bioengineered that trick from scratch."

"I don't know about that anymore," Silas said. He hooked an arm around the ball and carried it against his hip. He turned to her. "C'mon, I guess it's time we introduced you to Felix."

"Felix?" she asked.

"A little nickname," Ben said. "The petri dishes were labeled alphabetically alongside the Helix project heading. Embryo F was the first to start dividing in one of the surrogates. F-Helix."

"Cute."

"It's been called a lot of things, but cute isn't one."

She raised an eyebrow. "But it's beautiful?"

"Beautiful and cute are two different things," Ben said. "Sharks are beautiful."

"How far back did you take the design process?" she asked.

This time it was Silas who answered. "All the way to raw code."

"Down to individual gene splices?"

"Down to nucleotide base-pair sequence," Silas said. "We *made* genes."

"I didn't realize that was possible."

Silas looked suddenly uncomfortable. "Genome assembly took a year. We used a blank to start."

"A blank?"

"Oh, that's what we call a cow ovum without the nucleus. We've got the patent on that one."

"Kind of like a seedless orange."

"Yeah."

"So where'd you get this amazing seedless cow?"

"We engineered it. It's actually one of Benjamin's ideas, and how he ended up working for me in the first place. Now we've got an entire brood of them as frozen blastocysts. You can denucleate an ovum manually, but it's a very slow process, and it weakens the cell. It's much better if the ovum naturally lacks its nucleus."

"So you thaw one out every time you produce a gladiator?"

"No, this is an entirely new process. We've never gone all the way back to raw code before. Cell infusion was the most difficult part, and we decided to use the scatter approach and thawed several hundred blanks. DNA insertion killed 99.7 percent of the cells. Three survived, and of those three, only one successfully implanted in the cow's uterus."

"I'm still not sure what exactly is expected of me," she said.

"Pretend it's a specimen dropped from the sky," Silas said. "Pretend that you don't know where it came from or what makes it tick. Pretend that it's the organism that will take the theoretical out of theoretical xenobiology."

"I've been waiting a long time for an organism like that."

"What would you do to try and understand it? How would you predict how it might develop?"

Her mind whirled at the implication. She followed the men into the building. How could they know so little about their own creation?

Five minutes later, she understood.

SHE GAZED through the thick glass of the nursery. Ben and Silas stood behind her, giving her space.

She wasn't sure what she was seeing at first, but her heart beat quicker in her chest.

Alien, yes, she agreed.

That was the only word she could think to describe it. She had never seen skin like that. The fluorescent lighting reflected in its deep blackness. The blood-red hands.

She knew enough about genetic engineering to know the thing she was looking at shouldn't have been possible. It was too far ahead. She had expected an uncomfortable Frankenstein, a predator hewn together in bits and pieces from across the order Carnivora.

Like most scientists, she followed the gladiator competition closely, and nothing she'd ever seen or read had led her to anticipate what she was looking at now. She watched the creature through the glass, and slowly, by degrees, she came to agree with Silas on another point. It was beautiful. But it was a terrible sort of beauty.

"How?"

"We still don't know," one of them answered for both.

HER LAB took only two days to assemble.

The supplies she requested arrived more quickly than she would have thought possible. She found it somewhat unsettling, in fact, to receive a piece of equipment within hours of requesting it—equipment that might cost more than she would earn in ten years. She was used to the pace of the university, where requests were ignored or just flat out scoffed at until you had slogged through reams of documentation and waded through months of purchasing committees. Yesterday, most of her special orders had arrived via jet, leaving her to wonder at the vast resources at the project's disposal.

She unpacked new boxes of glassware, Pyrex, latex gloves, flasks and beakers, and a scientific scale that measured to the sixth decimal place. She unpacked goggles and long metal tongs and a box of syringes. She unpacked calipers for the measurement of anatomical features. She unpacked medical supplies and electronics, and she put them all away. Slowly, slowly, she unpacked her disbelief at being here. She put that away, too.

She put everything into drawers and cabinets and onto shelves, and each time took a moment to stare at the items she put away in an attempt to commit to memory where exactly she'd put them. She considered labeling the drawers but decided against it. Instead, she followed the same system she had at the university: a medical/biological/electronic gradient that ran from left to right across the room, with the most commonly used items always in the top drawers.

When the lab was complete, she spent the remainder of the evening watching Felix and going over the next day's strategy in her mind. She had been waiting eleven years for an opportunity to use her knowledge and skills for something other than an academic exercise. That opportunity hadn't come in the form she'd anticipated, but it was here, and she was going to see to it that the job was done right.

When she first began studying xenobiology, she'd been attracted by the newness of it all. It was a wide-open speculative field, the kind of field a person could make a mark in, the razor's edge of new science. There had been an atmosphere of optimism then, within the scientific community, that it was only a matter of time before man discovered extraterrestrial life. The universe was, after all, just so damned big. Her field of expertise rose in anticipation of that day. The moons of Saturn and Neptune had seemed particularly promising, at least at the single-cell level. But now the Sol system moons had all been probed, and if life was out there, then it was way out there. But she'd never regretted her field of study. She knew what drove her.

From an early age she'd hungered to understand the world around her. The sciences had drawn her just as naturally as a flame drew insects in Brazil. The Brazil of her youth.

Her mother had said, during that final argument all those years ago, that science had become her religion.

Vidonia had denied it then, but as a ten-year-old, she had lacked too much the understanding of herself to explain the void it filled in her. Now, if biology was her denomination, she supposed that she had to admit to a certain degree of zealotry. But like many zealots, she had come about her faith through hardship.

She was born thirty-seven years ago in the slums of Bahia, Brazil. She'd never known her father. Of those early years, there was much she tried to forget: her mother most and least of all.

Her mother was a fancy girl, kept by men from time to time, and she wore her Catholicism like a shield against her sins. Life had been hard for them. Vidonia remembered the long periods of hunger, punctuated by occasional bursts of borrowed opulence. Her mother hadn't been beautiful, but her skin was light, and for certain kinds of men, this was enough. Vidonia never learned her father's name, but whoever he was, she knew she had his complexion.

She attended school for the first time when she was seven years old. She hadn't been able to read, but still their tests had pointed her out, pulled her from the throng of slum children. They took notice of her, asked questions. They provided special tutors, and later, special classes. When she was ten, and they wanted to send her away, her mother resisted. By then, her mother had made several siblings for her to watch in the afternoon and needed the babysitter so she could go out and earn her money. Besides that, her mother learned there would be no formal religious training at the school for the sciences.

It was no wonder, really, how learning came to be so important to Vidonia. It had pulled her from the despair of the streets as no cathedraled savior ever could have.

Her educational route, after that, had run a circuitous course, leading her through ecology, microbiology, and genetics. Eventually, at the age of twenty-two, it led her to the United States, where she continued her studies in the life sciences.

Once she learned the rules that undergirded life on earth, it seemed only logical to attempt to apply them against a new backdrop. For her, the field of theoretical xenobiology was the inevitable destination of a long voyage.

Now, as she watched the strange organism romp through the nursery beyond the glass, she couldn't help but feel that it had all been worth it. Here it was, at last. This creature was something different.

She didn't understand fully how it came to be, but she didn't have to. It was something new, and now it was her job to see if the rules had changed.

SHE WOKE early the next morning to her small, functional room. She'd decided yesterday that it suited her. She barely felt the water on her skin, tasted nothing of the toothpaste. Her clothes matched only because she had packed them that way. Her mind was elsewhere. She thought of John only in passing and only to marvel at having not thought of him the whole day before. Something about that felt good to her, not thinking of him, but she didn't dwell.

She carded through the door of her lab, and the lights kicked on automatically. Butterflies wrestled in her stomach. She made the call. The minutes dragged on as she waited. Time enough for her to wonder at the strange twists of fate that had led her to this place. Time enough to begin to wonder if her mother's God would approve.

Big men in white suits arrived with the young gladiator strapped to a gurney. Silas and Benjamin stepped in behind them. As per her orders, the specimen was sedated but not fully anesthetized. It could make the difference on her tests.

The men lifted the creature from the gurney and strapped it onto the silver specimen table in the center of the room. It writhed sluggishly for a moment before slumping into catatonia. Vidonia took her recorder from the front pocket of her lab coat and placed it on the table.

She hit the record button and began. "October twenty-second, initial evaluation of Helix project specimen at"—she paused, flipping through the pages Silas had provided her with—"age one hundred ninety-three days. And three hundred fifteen days since surrogate implantation by blastocyst F."

She paused, looking at Silas and Ben. Then she turned back to the table and let her eyes play over the entire length of the organism.

"Specimen appears healthy. No signs of illness or injury. It has an approximate dorsoventral length of one hundred forty centimeters." She looked at the digital readout on the table. "A weight of twenty-four kilograms. Skin is highly unusual in its reflective qualities and shows marked hyperpigmentation. No evidence of hair or dermal papillae." She bent close, running a latexed finger across the abdomen. "Dermis appears smooth and absent of coetaneous structures of any kind. Specimen is hexapoidal, with three sets of differentiated symmetrical limbs. Upper posterior limbs appear modified for flight. Upper anterior limbs terminate in four digits"—she flexed the organism's hand—"and an opposable thumb. Each digit terminates in a nail or claw, subdermal status of which is unknown at this time."

"Be careful," Silas said. He held up his hand.

She took a long breath. It wasn't fear she felt but

excitement. A slight tremor thrummed in her left leg, so she stepped back from the table and poured herself a glass of water from the sink against the wall. She felt the coolness slide down her throat and settle in her stomach. Ben and Silas remained silhouettes beyond the bright ring of light, and she was thankful for that. She stepped back to the table.

"The cranium is large, oblong in general shape, tapering to a point in the back. The eyes are large and forward-facing, light gray in color, with vertical pupils. Approximate field of binocular vision is"—here she stopped, her face tensed in thought—"one hundred sixty degrees." Behind her, Silas made a sound. She went on.

"Immature or flaccid cartilaginous ears sit high atop the head. The cartilage is thick at the base, thinning near the tip. The face is large, prognathic, and hyper-robust in bone structure. The mouth is broad and forward-projecting."

She used a wooden tongue depressor to open the creature's jaw, looked in. "Dental pattern is complex and differentiated, atypical mammalian pattern. Omnivore, probably."

"Omnivore?" Silas spoke from the shadows.

"It's hard to tell for sure. The large canines provide a tearing apparatus in the front, but the molars are five-cusped—good for grinding up tough grains or vegetable matter. I'm not sure what to make of this second row of teeth. The pattern is unique, to my knowledge—looks like they could be used for shearing of some kind, almost like a row of wire cutters. I can't imagine what foods they could be used for."

"Bone shearing," Silas said. His hand flexed.

"Yeah, maybe that."

She turned the recorder off and began the next phase of the evaluation.

It started with the drawing of blood. The shiny black organism shivered oddly as she took twenty-five ccs from its right forelimb. She then took twenty-five ccs from its left hind limb. She placed the blood samples into the refrigeration unit beneath the counter and wheeled the specimen to the X-ray machine. She motioned for Silas and Ben to get behind the leaded glass and made final adjustments to the orientation of the machine. She joined the men and hit the button.

They let her work without commenting, and she was silently pleased at their deference to her expertise. She activated the fluoroscope again and watched the image assemble on the computer screen. When the read was complete, she stepped around and rotated the position of the specimen for a final shot. She didn't bother to print out the sheets—time enough for that later. She wanted the specimen in an altered state for as short a span of time as possible. The effect that drugs might have on the organism was difficult to calculate.

Using a scalpel, she shaved off bits of skin from the lower back of the organism. "Typically the least sensitive part of the dermis," she said, as she put the sample into a plastic cup, which was then placed alongside the blood samples in the refrigeration unit.

Nuclear resonance was last and would be most telling. Her students had called it the magic camera, and the magic camera could see all. The creature barely stirred as the big men in white maneuvered its slumped form into the cylinder. Across the room from the scanner, Silas and Ben stood, looking over her shoulder at the computer screen. The image told a strange story as it rotated.

She tried to remain calm, but it was a losing battle. Instead, she tried to appear calm, and this she had some success with. She wasn't sure what exactly she was seeing. Certain organs she recognized; others were strange to her. "There's the liver," she said, pointing to the conspicuously placed organ. It was a start, a point of reference. She found the heart next, narrowing the focus of the machine until she could watch the blood coursing through the arteries and veins. She blinked her eyes, squinted, but the heart still had six chambers.

"Oh, shit," Silas said. He'd counted, too.

"What the hell do we have here?" Ben asked.

"I'm going to need some time . . . to analyze this," she said.

"How long?" Silas asked.

"A whole career."

"You don't have a career."

"I do now. This is going to take a while."

CHAPTER NINE

Silas concentrated on his footfalls. The morning was cool and dry—perfect running weather—but the last quarter of a mile was always the most difficult. There were several regular morning runners at Helix, and he'd gotten offers to partner up, but he preferred to face it alone. He lengthened his stride, determined to eat the remaining distance as quickly as he could. There had been a time when running relaxed him, but those years were behind him now. At forty-three, running still relieved tension, but it left him more exhausted than tranquil. He wasn't able to stop thinking about the project, but after five miles, he didn't have the energy to care, so running still served its purpose.

He rounded the last bend in the path and began the final stretch to the compound general. In the distance, in front of the lab, he could see the flag waving colorfully at the top of its pole. He could see the five interlocked rings. It was silly, he knew, but his eyesight was something he was proud of. He'd noticed, over the years, that most of his colleagues had developed the need for reading glasses or surgery to correct weakening visual acuity, but his own vision had remained strong. He'd read once that myopia was a disease of modern living and could be traced, in many cases, to a childhood spent too much indoors, where the eye focuses almost exclusively within a distance of ten or twenty feet. Silas had spent much of his own youth outside. Eyes ever on the horizon. A portent, perhaps, of the man he would become.

He sprinted the last hundred yards and did his cool-down walk to the elevator. Back at his office, he took a long, hot shower, being careful not to get water in his bad ear, and did a quick shave in the sudsy steam. Then he toweled himself dry and put on fresh lab whites. After a quick stubble check in the mirror, he looked at his watch. It was time for Vidonia's report. V-day.

He stepped into Vidonia's lab, knocking twice on the open door. She turned, and her face was unreadable. She motioned him in and continued spreading the sheets out on the table. He'd made a point to stay out of her way for the last two and a half weeks. She'd been pulling all-nighters, so he knew she wasn't in need of any motivational speeches on his part. He only needed to stay out of her way. She wanted to understand this thing as badly as he did, if perhaps for different reasons.

He waited for her to speak.

"I've done a complete workup on the specimen— well, as complete as I could in the amount of time I've had. I'm just going to shoot straight with you on this; there's still a lot I don't understand."

"That's fine. What *do* you have for me?"

She turned on the underlighting and touched the first plasticine page lying on the glass. "Enough to keep me awake at night."

He looked down, and the image on the dark sheet was nonsense to him.

"As far as I can discern," she said, her fingers wandering across the image, "these are the primary digestive organs: the pancreas, gallbladder, and liver. The stomach, here"—she pointed—"is multicompartmental. I think this specimen will be able to digest some pretty tough foodstuffs if the need arises. The intestine is medium-length—typical omnivore. The lung capacity of the organism is enormous. As is the blood volume pumped out by the heart. You're going to have quite an athlete on your hands."

"I've been thinking about that heart," Silas said. "The specimen, as you like to call it, isn't built along avian lines. Too big, too heavy. But if something like this were to actually take flight, it would probably need some outsized cardiovascular equipment to fuel the wing muscles."

"It certainly would."

"The six chambers?"

She shrugged. "I don't know, Silas. It could be a flight adaptation. It could be a practical joke that worked out well. All I can tell you is that the heart is strong, and the pectoral muscles have an unusual striation pattern I've never seen before."

Silas rubbed his eyes, then looked down at the transparency again. "So do you think it will fly?"

"I doubt it. But there are some interesting modifications here. Anything is possible."

She took a step farther down the table, pointing to a different sheet. "And the sharps at the end of the digits are anchored to the bone—they're true talons, not just heavy-duty fingernails."

She picked up another sheet. "The sense organs were the most difficult to evaluate, because there is no way of knowing how the organism experiences the world around it. But certain inferences can be made, and I've taken exhaustive measures to see to it that my evaluations are accurate. If I have erred, it is on the side of caution. With that said, I have to admit that the eyes gave me pause. There is a distinct tapetum lucidium across the retina, and the cone configuration confirms that the specimen has nocturnally adapted vision."

Silas couldn't think of a response. It was getting crazier and crazier.

"The visual resolution is better than my ability to test. The hearing, too, is off the scale, but I noticed several peaks in acuity." She handed him a sheet. "The largest was at three thousand hertz, well out of the human range of hearing. The second-largest peak was at one hundred twenty hertz, the average frequency of human speech."

"So it's a good listener."

"It does more than listen."

"You ran an oscillogram?"

"I had a hunch, so I went with it. I figured it had that bipolar auditory acuity for a reason, and when I tested its vocalizations, I found I was right. Half the waveform was above three thousand five hundred hertz." She slid another transparency under the light. "As you can see from the waterfall spectrogram, there is a clear distinction here"—she pointed to a flat spot within the three-dimensional range of peaks and valleys. "Everything on this side we can hear; everything on the other side, we can't."

"So this means what?"

"It hears us fine, but we can only pick up about half of its vocalizations."

Silas nodded and picked up the fifth sheet, holding it up to the light. A dark oblong shape in a case of bone. He didn't have to ask her what it showed. "How large?"

"Cranial capacity is probably nineteen hundred ccs."

Silas whistled softly. "That's a lot of gray matter."

"Larger than an average human brain."

"This thing isn't full-grown yet," he said. "What

kind of brain-to-body mass index are we talking about?"

"Top-heavy," she said. "The numbers aren't as meaningful at this stage of development, but the specimen certainly seems likely to surpass our index. The study of the heart could take one career; the study of the brain could take another." She pointed at the dark image captured in the plasticine. "The cerebral cortex is highly folded and highly specialized. Both the telencephalon and corpus callosum—if those terms even apply, which they may not—are unusual in their association to the other parts of the brain."

"I'm not an anatomist, doctor."

"The brain is huge, and I don't understand the way it's organized. About all I can say is that the structures responsible for the higher functions appear to represent a large percentage of the overall mass. I'm shooting in the dark here, but I think this specimen has the potential to be very, very intelligent."

She put the last sheet of plasticine down on the table. "What the hell *is* this thing?" she asked.

"That's what we're trying to figure out."

"No." She touched his arm. "What *is* it? I can't do my job effectively if I'm working in a vacuum. This doesn't make sense. The night vision, the hearing, the wings. None of these things could help a gladiator in the arena. You need to level with me. Where did this thing come from?"

Silas sighed. She was right. He pulled out a stool and sat. "How much do you know about computer theory?"

"Theory? Not much. The basics, I guess."

"Ever hear of the Brannin computer?"

"Rings a bell. It's the new super, right?"

"Yeah. I've been doing a lot of research on it over the past several months, and the Brannin isn't just the latest thing in computer tech. It's a long step sideways in a direction nobody had ever thought to look before. I don't think the Brannin should really even be called a computer. There's very little to it that you can reach out and touch with your hand. Most of it exists in deep VR, and because of that, it's not limited by physical size. Inside itself, it can be infinitely large or small. Instead of bytes made of zeros and ones, the Brannin uses light, on or off, and that's the speed at which it computes. Something like six trillion floating-point operations per second, give or take."

"Who's counting?"

"You'd be surprised how seriously that record is taken."

"And you're going to tell me that the computer helped design the gladiator?"

"No, the Brannin didn't just help. It did the design almost completely on its own. That's where the original nucleotide base-pair sequence came from. Helix just provided the nuts and bolts."

"Can't you just make the inferences you need from the base-pair sequence?"

"It doesn't work that way. The nucleotide map translates directly into an amino-acid map, but it gets sticky after that. Protein conformation is more important to protein function than the exact nucleotide read, and conformation is one of the hardest things to pull out of the raw data. Development is too interconnected to itself, and timing plays an important role."

"Still, you should be able to cross-reference to other species."

"No, we tried that. There were no matches. But a match might not have helped us much, anyway, unless it was exact. A single base-pair substitution that changes the shape of the resultant protein molecule can completely alter the expression of that gene. There are hundreds of examples of this. And beyond that, enzymatic function is more important even than conformation, and each enzyme is itself under genetic control, so the complexity exists in a feedback loop."

"I'm beginning to understand. It's like an algebra problem with a hundred variables."

"Millions. At this point, it's still impossible to make the leap from novel nucleotide sequence to resultant gene to physiological expression. It may always remain so. There's too much structural noise between the three."

"Well, you still have the computer. It designed the creature. Why do you need me to tell you what it already knows?"

"Because I think the computer has gone crazy."

"Can computers go crazy?"

"The acorn doesn't fall far from the tree."

CHAPTER TEN

Evan stepped into his office and closed the door against the stares of the techs in the anteroom. His filing cabinets were overturned, his desk inside out, his stacks of digilogs scattered. Baskov's men had gone through everything, leaving his office in complete disarray—in short, slightly more messy than usual.

He righted his swivel chair and slid into its familiarity. Only this time, the wailing of its overburdened hinges was missing. It had been so long. Much had changed.

How many weeks? Seven, ten; he didn't know. But he had been sure that he would never leave that hospital, never be free from the injections, or Baskov's questions. He looked down at himself and saw half the man he had been.

The drugs they gave him made him too sick to eat, and he had lost whole chunks of himself. He felt naked without the slabs of fat that had cloaked his body for so many years. He was exposed, vulnerable, too small for his baggy skin, which now drooped and sagged around him. Maybe it had been longer than ten weeks. Maybe much longer.

What had they told his techs? He had no friends or family that would require an explanation for his absence, but what about the institute? What had they been told?

He glanced out the window, and the sky was darkening, fading to gray. He didn't know whether night or a storm approached, but he welcomed either. He welcomed the darkness and wanted to lose himself in it. He looked around for the light switch on the wall but couldn't find it. The lighting panels had activated automatically when he entered the room.

He picked a desk drawer from the scatter on the floor and flung it upward toward the fluorescent panels. The cheap plastic shield caved, and the bulbs popped in a shower of glass on his head. Picking up the desk drawer, he stepped beneath the next light panel and flung the projectile again. Again, a shower of glass. He moved throughout the room until all the lights had gone blind and he could see only by the dying glow outside the window.

He thought of Pea as night descended. He sat in the clutter and let darkness fold around him. And when he could hold back no more, he wept.

SILAS MET Baskov just outside the broad glass doorway. "Good afternoon," he said, extending a hand.

Baskov shook it, nodded, then said, "I hear it's a big day for our young Olympic hopeful."

"Yes, it is. The trainer thinks it's time for the first live meal. I thought it would be appropriate for someone from the commission to witness it, and frankly," he added with a smile, "it will save me the trouble of writing a long-winded report about the event. Now *you* can report to the commission."

"I'm sure the trouble will be more than worth it. I'm curious how it's developing. My eyes and ears have been telling me some interesting stories."

Silas led him inside and past the elevators. He hated the way Baskov always managed to mention his spies.

He referenced them so casually, as if they were of no more interest than the weather. But Silas recognized the warning in Baskov's informal banter: nothing could be kept secret.

"We've recently transferred the gladiator into its new pen," Silas said, then couldn't resist: "though I'm certain that your eyes and ears have already informed you of the move."

Baskov glanced at Silas as they walked.

"It outgrew its old living space," Silas added.

"I know about that because I signed off on the construction project budget. I don't even want to mention how much it cost."

They turned left at the end of the hall and made their way down the final long corridor leading to the rear dome behind the building. At the door, Silas showed his badge to the armed guard and they stepped through.

His nostrils were immediately assaulted by the warm smells of life. It reminded him of the cat house at the Los Angeles Zoo. Tangy, pungent; it was the smell of a predator.

Bright sunlight filtered through steel mesh openings in the roof sixty feet above. Just ahead, a shell of iron bars separated them from the enclosure beyond. Silas lead Baskov toward the group that had gathered. Ben, Vidonia, and Dr. Nelson nodded their introductions.

"Where's Tay?" Silas asked.

"Last-minute problem with the goat," Vidonia said.

"Well, I'd have a problem, too, if I was the goat that had to go in there." Ben pointed between the bars.

Against the far wall, several large, roughly hewn trees leaned at forty-five-degree angles with wide platforms connecting them at varying heights from the ground. Large wooden poles lay scattered in the straw that covered the floor of the enclosure. Thick ropes ran in sagging parabolas between points on the wall and the wooden poles. It all looked like a playground for some very rough, very big little boy.

"I don't see our little friend," Baskov said.

"It's in an adjacent pen, but it isn't so little anymore," Silas said. "We thought it best to introduce the goat first."

There was a loud clang. Then, as if on cue, a small black-and-white goat was pushed unceremoniously through a hatch in the far wall.

It fumbled around in the deep straw for several moments. Slowly, its ability to wallow around in the stuff improved, and the goat made slow progress across the enclosure, jumping from spot to spot. Another clang grabbed the goat's attention. It stopped, angling its head toward the sound.

The large metal door at the back of the enclosure slid slowly upward.

The gladiator lumbered in beneath it. The growth of the organism had been nothing short of amazing, and Silas couldn't help but feel a wave of awe as the creature stepped into sight. Even hunched in a predatory stance, it stood easily six and a half feet tall— and it wasn't done growing yet. The arms were thick with muscle, and the ears now stood round and erect atop the head, like a bat's.

Only its eyes had not changed. Still large, gray, unreadable. Silas's heart jolted in his chest when the gladiator bounded across the lake of straw and leaped to the lowest platform. There it sat, looking down at the goat, then out at the people, appearing for all the world like some fairy-tale monster come to life.

Its arms stretched wide from its body, and the wings unfurled from their hiding place against its back, extending twelve feet on either side. There was a rush of wind as the wings began to beat at the air. Silas felt the breeze on his cheek and turned to look at Baskov, who stood openmouthed at the spectacle.

Silas turned his attention back to the creature in time to see it leap from the platform and drop, half gliding, to the straw next to the goat.

Bleating wildly, the goat sprang backward all the way to the bars. The gladiator's wings snapped shut against its back as it took a long step forward. The frightened goat bleated again and tried to run past the gladiator on the right, but the gladiator flashed an arm out in front of it. The goat stopped just a half-dozen feet in front of Silas, pinned between the bars and the strange creature. The gladiator cocked its head sideways, looking at it. Slowly, it extended one taloned hand and touched the goat's furry coat with its palm, almost a caress. The goat shrieked in fear and pulled away while the creature cocked its head in the other direction.

Much later, in the report he would have to write anyway, Silas would not be able to recount what happened next except to say that in one moment the gladiator was sitting near its potential prey, and in the next, after a flash of motion, the goat was somehow partially disassembled in the gladiator's bloody hands. Bright loops of intestine spilled out from the forward half of the goat as the gladiator raised the carcass up and bit off the head in a single crunch of bone.

It happened so fast.

Silas watched in silence as the creature fed. Minutes later, he was the first to speak. "Well, that was—"

The gladiator's growl stopped him in mid-sentence. Its head snapped up as if offended by the interruption. An instant later, the uneaten portion of the goat slammed against the bars, splattering blood and bowels over him and those with the misfortune of standing too close to him.

Vidonia turned without a word and walked out. As Silas looked down at his fouled lab coat, the creature reared its head back and howled. To Silas, the howl sounded very much like laughter.

CHAPTER ELEVEN

Her voice carried accusation in it, and something else. He tried to gauge her. They sat at the picnic tables just outside the lab, pushing food around on their plates.

He'd known there was something brewing beneath the surface for several weeks now. It was in the tone of her voice when she spoke of the project. It was in her careful choice of wording. Most of all, it was in the things she didn't say. *Is she finally going to let it show? Is she finally going to say it?*

They'd been talking for ten minutes now, circling the real point with their conversation. The wind had turned cold, and Silas raised his collar against the chill on his neck. Perhaps a lunch outside on the picnic tables hadn't been such a good idea, after all.

"What are you getting at?" he asked. He was tired of avoidance.

"I'm saying that it's too bad it has to end up as so much pulpy sawdust at the bottom of the arena," Vidonia said.

Silas studied her face.

"I'm saying that it's too bad it has to die," she said.

"It's why it's here in the first place."

"I know. That doesn't make it less of a stupid waste."

"You have a problem with the gladiator competition?"

"Yes," she said, without hesitation.

Silas looked at her.

"This is your project," she said. "I understand that. But I don't understand the kind of man that destroys his creations."

"I don't destroy them."

"Yes, you do."

"The competition does that."

"And your project is part of that competition."

"Without the competition, those creations you speak so highly of wouldn't exist at all."

"That creature you've made is like nothing else that has come before. It's unique and should be studied, not thrown away in blood sport."

"You *are* studying it."

"For what? Even the winners usually die of their injuries. And the ones that don't die are just put down later. There are no old gladiators." She looked away into the wind, a soft expression on a sharp profile. She took a slow sip of her Coke. "All this talent, all this scientific knowledge, and all we can think to do with it is to build a better killer."

Several wasps hovered in slow circles over the picnic table, attracted by the food and moving sluggishly in the cold air. He swatted at one that came too close and missed, sending it spinning in a wash of air. "Have you ever heard of the pit bull terrier?" he asked finally.

"What?"

"The pit bull terrier?"

"Some kind of dog?" she said. She seemed irritated by the off-subject question.

"I didn't think you would have. It was finally outlawed about ten years ago, after decades of bans and regulation. Even back when they'd still been legal to own, insurance liability made it impractical to do so. Fanciers strove for years to rehabilitate the breed's image, but too late, and with too little consistency, and the breed died of its own bad reputation."

"So they're extinct?"

"The *breed* is extinct. The genes no doubt still live on in mixed-breeds and family pets all over the place—it's hard to regulate that stuff, after all—but there's no AKC recognition, and the moment you *call* a dog a pit bull, it's illegal. So maybe you call it something else, give it a new name. Or maybe you don't call it anything. But still, the breed—that old name—is dead."

"What does that have to do with the gladiator competition?"

"More than you might think. Pit bulls came from London originally—the inadvertent hybrids of bull-baiting dogs and early proto-terriers. The combination was deadly. The original baiters were used to fatigue cattle into submission for slaughter. These dogs had big, musclebound heads, and their instinct was to attack livestock—clamp their jaws onto a bull's face and then not let go, no matter what."

"Charming practice," Vidonia said.

"And a dangerous occupation, it turns out. If the dog's hold slipped, it faced the bull's hooves, so the dogs with the strongest bites tended to survive the longest, leave the most offspring, you get the picture."

Vidonia nodded.

"Multiply that by a few hundred years, and you get some pretty tough dogs. They'd hang on until the bull was a bloody mess."

"Disgusting."

"Maybe, but a lot of practices were disgusting before modern refrigeration. At one time, it was the preferred method of slaughter."

"What on earth for?"

"The adrenaline altered the meat. Some thought a baited bull tasted better, and they believed the meat lasted longer before spoilage set in."

"Did it?"

"I have no idea."

"Do you have a point?"

"Bull-baiters were aggressive but only toward livestock. They couldn't care less about people or other dogs. This wasn't true of the earliest terriers. These dogs were territorial and protective. They were basically mean-bastard little dogs, but they were too small to do much damage."

"Okay."

"The accidental crosses between these two breeds proved as worthless to butchers as they were unstoppable in the fighting pits. These so-called pit bulls had the vise grip jaws of their baiting ancestors, but the new hybrids ignored cattle in favor of other dogs. Like the bull-baiters, if they got their teeth in, you couldn't shake them loose. The early pit bulls actually brought about the extinction of several other ancient strains of fighting dog in Western Europe. Classic Darwinism; no other dog could compete."

"I'm supposed to be impressed by this?"

"In the archives here at the compound, there is an old recording of an illegal pit fight. The handlers in this fight had trouble keeping the dogs apart long enough to start the contest. The dogs craved it. They lived for it. It *was* barbaric. It *was* grisly. But no more so than what happens between the lion and the gazelle. Or between the wolf and the deer. Nature, red in tooth and claw. Animals have always had to fight for survival."

"But not for sport."

"Sport was their survival. Without that sport, eventually, there were no pit bulls. Sport was their ecological niche."

"That doesn't make it right."

He continued, "Without the gladiator competition, this specimen you seem so impressed by would not exist, because the funding behind it would not exist. I was in college when the gladiator competition first became a regular part of the Olympics, so I'm old enough to remember what the field of genetics used to be like. This competition is the best thing that could have happened. When you combine scientists with capitalists, great leaps forward are made, always. Throw in a healthy dose of national pride, and anything can happen."

Just then, a wasp fell out of the air and landed in her hair. She hardly reacted, turning her head slowly from side to side to try and free it from the dark windblown tangle. It crawled down a wayward curl onto her cheek, and he expected her to yelp and flinch away. But instead she gently swept the wasp to the table with the side of her hand. It sat, throwing its legs up for a moment, before righting itself and buzzing back into the air above them.

"You say you've seen video footage of these dogfights?" she said. "Well, I've seen the blood with my own eyes. I may not know what a pit bull is, but I've seen the boys and their fighting dogs in the back alleys where I grew up. And more significantly, I've seen these dogs a few days later with their faces so swollen with infection that their eyes look like little peas stuffed in puffy dough. What you do is still just back-alley dogfighting to me."

"That's not fair."

"Tell me good comes out of it somehow. Fine. Tell me it's a necessary evil. So be it. But don't you dare tell me how much the animals enjoy it."

She looked up into the sky above them, watching the wasps. "I don't see how the gladiator contest is even legal, given all the laws against animal cruelty."

"Back-alley dogfights don't funnel money into research for genetic diseases. The United States has many self-serving laws. Why not question why cigarettes are banned while alcohol remains legal?"

"So what do you get out of this, then? Is it the money? The fame?" Her eyes flashed with anger.

His own temper was rising now. He fought against it and decided to take the conversation in another direction. "You've seen Michelangelo's statue of David, right?"

"Pictures."

"I saw it twenty years ago when I was in Florence. I'm not going to tell you it changed my life, but it did change my perspective. I'd seen pictures, too, but when I saw it with my own eyes . . . words can't even describe. I've never considered myself to be artistically inclined, but looking at that statue, I knew I was witnessing creative perfection. Michelangelo took a lump of stone and found the human form inside. When he was finished, it looked soft; it looked warm."

"It's a statue."

"If you ever get a chance to see *David* in person, you'll understand. No one could ever hope to surpass it. At least not in that medium. Michelangelo found the truth in stone, and that truth is the commonality between art and science."

"Truth?"

"Each of us looks for it in the ways that are available to us."

"So that's what you are looking for, the truth in your medium?"

"It is what we are all looking for."

"And you think Michelangelo would have approved?"

"If he were alive today, Michelangelo wouldn't bother with stone. He would be a geneticist."

"You're serious."

Silas nodded. "I wouldn't want to face Italy's gladiator in the arena."

SILAS WAS tired. Bone tired. He lay on the long couch in his office, legs propped up and over the armrest, hands thrown back behind his head. He had grown accustomed to the long hours at the lab, but the initial cycle of pre-competition press conferences had begun today, and his energy reserves were depleted. There was nothing left, and the bad part was that he knew it would get worse before it got better. How do you explain to a room full of reporters that you can't answer their questions? No pictures of the gladiator available. No information available. *Why are you all here, then, you ask? Because the Olympic Commission wants you running those special-interest stories that turn the public's eye toward the coming games. That's why. No, I can't tell you a damned thing to make your job easier. No, I can't tell you what the gladiator looks like, or how it was designed, or anything at all, really, but hey, the United States won't disappoint. I'm supposed to tell you that. Quote me on that.*

He was a better scientist than he was a PR man, or at least he hoped to God he was, or he wasn't much of a scientist at all. His eyes closed, and he willed his mind blank. For a moment, sleep seemed possible.

The knock on his door was not welcome. He waited.

The knock came again.

"Damn." Silas climbed to his feet.

Tay Sawyer's grinning face met him through the cracked door. Internally, Silas cringed, but he swung the door wide and let the trainer in anyway. He liked the man but wasn't in the mood to deal with his restless energy this particular afternoon.

Tay Sawyer was one of those men whose activity level seemed to have gotten stuck somewhere in pre-adolescence. He was a force never at rest, but his hyperkinetic agitations didn't distract from the fact that he was the best trainer in the business. He was a short, thick man, baby-faced, slightly bowlegged, and prematurely balding. The top of his head was shiny and tanned.

"What's going on, Tay?"

"Great progress. I had to see you. This gladiator, Silas, I have to hand it to you, you've done something special this time."

Silas collapsed back onto the couch.

Tay continued, "You've got to come down and see what it can do."

"Now?"

"Not now. How about Friday?"

The man's excitement was endearing but not in the least bit contagious. Exhaustion had inoculated Silas against it. Tay still didn't sit; he paced. The way his compact form hustled across the carpet made each step seem a muscular endeavor. The muscles in his thick legs showed in grooves through his dress slacks.

"Bring Ben, too," Tay said. "He'll probably want to see it."

"What exactly is going on Friday?"

"The new robotics will be up." Tay rubbed his hands together in mock mad-scientist glee. "Then I can start the real training."

"What time do you want us there?"

"I know you're busy, so how about lunchtime. It won't take long."

"We'll be there."

"Great," Tay said, and the grin brushed his ear-lobes.

He even smiles enthusiastically.

"We're going to make history with this one, Silas. I've never seen reflexes like this before. You're a goddamned genius."

"Thanks."

"I did the first tests for reaction time today. Zero-point-zero-two seconds. Can you believe that?"

Silas wasn't sure what that meant, but he nodded.

"I checked it four times," Tay continued. "Then I checked the equipment. But it's for real. This thing makes lightning look slow."

"Great. I'll see you Friday, then, okay?" Sleep was calling him now.

"Yeah, boss. See you Friday." Tay turned to go.

"Hit the lights on your way out."

SILAS CLOSED his eyes for an eight count. When he opened them, the pain was still there. He pinched the bridge of his nose. The nap he'd taken earlier in the day had helped clear his head, but it had done little to protect against eyestrain. By the feel of it, he'd been staring at the computer screen for about an hour too long. He glanced at the clock on the wall, and it told him his late night had turned into an early morning. Again.

He leaned back in his chair and stretched his legs out in front of him. Both knees popped. He touched the save icon with his finger, flipped the computer off, and folded it back into his desktop. That was enough for one night. He wasn't going to work himself into a migraine twice in one week.

He locked his office door behind him and headed for the stairs. On the main level he saw light spilling down the hall from the west wing. He paused, searching his pocket for his car keys. He pulled them out, looked at them, then put them back in his pocket and turned toward the light.

Vidonia was bent over a series of plasticine prints. The underlighting recast her face in a net of unfamiliar angles. She held a magnifying glass in her hands and occasionally looked through it for a closer inspection of her work. The prints completely absorbed her. He watched her for a full minute before speaking.

"It's not so strange," he said.

"What's that?" she answered quickly, without looking up. Silas realized she'd known he was standing there for some time.

"What we've been doing here at Helix for the past twelve years."

"I guess that would depend on your perspective."

Silas stepped into the room. "It's what man has been doing for tens of thousands of years."

"Genetic engineering? That's the first I've heard of it."

"No, it's true. They just didn't call it that."

"What did they call it?"

Silas looked down at the sheets. They were incomprehensible to him. "Oh, many different things. They called it the fattest cow. They called it a best-laying chicken. The fluffiest sheep."

"DNA splicing is a far cry from animal husbandry."

"Not really. Not if you think about it. You try and accumulate the genes you want into a given set of animals. You can do it the slow and inefficient way, by breeding. Or you can do it the fast way, in a petri dish. But it's all the same thing, the gathering together of desired genes. The elimination of the undesired. Only the technology is different."

"I don't think you'd ever get this," she said, gesturing toward the shadowy plastic sheets, "through selective breeding."

"No, you never would. I said what we've done at Helix for the last twelve years isn't so strange. What Evan Chandler has done is an altogether different story. This wasn't the gathering of genes. This was the invention of new ones. The difference is highly significant."

She finally looked up from the table, and he saw the strain on her face. He recognized the frustration. She was an intelligent woman, and intelligent people were used to being able to understand what they were studying. "Your inventor was either a genius or a madman," she said. "And I can't tell which."

"Well, I think you know which gets my vote."

She smiled. He knew better than to tell her to get some sleep. He knew how he reacted when people suggested that to him.

"Well, I'm heading home," he said instead. "Tomorrow, Tay is having a training exercise. You're welcome to come by if you'd like."

"Are you going to get another innards bath?"

"Not this time. He said robotics will be involved."

"I'll try, but I doubt it. The computer sims are going to finish up the blood workup around noon. I've been working on oxygen loads for more than a week now."

"Okay, how does it look?"

"Complicated, like everything else, I guess. I'll know more tomorrow."

"Let me know."

She turned back to her sheets. "You'll be the first I tell."

CHAPTER TWELVE

"It's the newest thing in behavior-modification technology," Tay was telling them. Silas and Ben stared at the contraption with uncertainty. The three men stood in knee-deep straw amid the clutter of the gladiator compound. Before them stood a man-size robotic contrivance layered in heavy Teflon padding. Several thick arms extended from the broad spherical core. To Silas's discriminating eye, it looked like a multi-limbed snowman on steroids.

"This does what, exactly?" he asked.

"It is supposed to represent a competitor. I control it by remote from the observation loft." Tay pointed. A metal staircase climbed the far wall twenty feet to the glassed-in balcony. The observation loft was supposed to give a comprehensive view of everything that happened in the cage. It provided this vantage by being—at least partially, anyway—in the cage itself.

"This thing fights?" Silas asked.

"With a little remote-control help. It's not a quick lateral mover—more of a stand-and-deliver type of device—but each of those limbs is loaded with a thirty-pound payload of sand, so it packs a wallop. And the arms are fast, very fast."

Silas glanced up the far wall. "I think I'd want more than a pane of glass between myself and what's going to be happening out here."

"That's bulletproof," Tay said, gesturing toward the observation loft. "No worries."

Silas moved closer and pushed a finger into the Teflon padding that lined the rounded base of the robot. It dimpled softly beneath the pressure of his finger. "This thing won't hurt the gladiator, will it? Injury is the last thing we need three months before showtime."

"No. I'll be careful. I just want to rile it up a bit, see if I can't get its aggression up."

"You remember the goat, don't you?" Ben asked.

"Yeah. 'Twas a beautiful sight. Just what a trainer loves to see. All that blood and gore."

"Thrown all over Silas," Ben added.

"Icing on the cake," Tay said.

Silas smiled despite himself. "Okay, let's see what this thing can do." He turned toward the gate.

"Aren't you going to join me?" Tay gestured back toward the observation loft again.

"Nah, I want to be down close to the action. I'll take my view from here," Silas said. Ben followed him out of the enclosure, and Silas checked the locking mechanism on the gate twice.

The two men watched through the bars as Tay ascended the stairs. He stepped through the door into the loft and waved to them through the glass. Then he moved toward the front, and his arms played across a console hidden from view beneath the row of windows.

A moment later, the robot buzzed as it powered up, and then the arms slowly lifted in long arcs, flexing and extending. The robot twisted and jabbed for half a minute before the hatch portal clanged in the back wall.

The hatch opened.

The gladiator entered the enclosure slowly, as if

sensing that something was wrong. It had grown since the goat incident, now approaching seven feet in height. Wide nostrils sniffed the air, and its eyes locked on the robot. It stared for several seconds without moving before beginning a slow creep forward. Staying low to the straw, it moved on four bent limbs, wings folded tight and flat against its back.

The robot spun smoothly on its axis, bringing two arms into striking position. The gladiator's slow approach slowed further as it closed the distance.

Twenty feet out, it stopped. Muscles bunched in its legs. It gathered itself, tightening to stillness, crouching like black stone—limbs cocked beneath it, eyes glaring across the lake of straw.

Silas realized he was holding his breath.

The gladiator's ears folded back. Then, like a black sheet of lightning, it sprang.

It hit the robot hard, rocking it backward, digging in. Metallic arms spun, and the gladiator bounced away just ahead of the blow. It turned, maneuvering quickly around the other side. It struck again, rocking the robot forward. Claws dragged along the surface of the Teflon, searching for purchase. The robot spun again, and this time banged a glancing blow off the creature's side. It howled and slid away.

The gladiator moved faster now, circling just beyond reach. It went around once, twice, then came in low, ducking below the upper ring of the robot's arms. It struck fiercely, clamping down on the Teflon with its jaws. Silas was certain that an opponent of flesh and blood would have lost its guts to the floor at this point, but the Teflon gave up nothing, and a blow from one of the robot's lower arms sent the creature sprawling away, screaming in rage.

It came in again, howling, and again was knocked away. And again, and again, until froth ran from its mouth. After a particularly damaging blow, it sank slowly to a crouch, hissing, and this time it paused. Its chest expanded and contracted in enormous heaving breaths while it considered the enemy.

Without warning, it struck again, high and hard, rocking the robot back again. Instead of gouging with its claws, it clung to the top as it carried through, swinging its weight around and pulling down. The robot teetered at the edge of balance for a moment, then crashed to the floor, pinning half of its arms beneath its weight. Now the gladiator moved in at the base, tearing at the pads with its teeth and talons. A pad tore loose from its wire clasps, exposing the metallic shielding beneath. The creature howled and backed off, while the robotic arms thrashed impotently.

"That's about enough, don't you think?" Ben asked.

"I was thinking that very thing," Silas said. He raised his arms and waved to Tay, but Tay only grinned down from the observation loft and made exaggerated "come on" gestures to the gladiator. The creature caught the movement and looked up. Tay smiled bigger and waved. He was enjoying this.

The gladiator responded, and this time its movement was not smooth and controlled. It moved with all the grace of a thing deep in a fit of rage.

The wings unfurled as it bounded across the enclosure. With a giant leap and a single flap of the enormous wings, the gladiator swung through the air and smashed into the window of the loft. It fell in a crumpled heap to the straw, where it lay, stunned, on its back for several seconds before regaining its footing.

Gathering itself, it backed up and leaped again, slamming its talons against the glass without effect.

Tay's expression was still one of amusement, but he took an involuntary step backward for the third attack. After falling to the straw again, the creature backed up for another assault, then stopped. Its eyes traced the staircase up the wall. Slowly, it moved across the enclosure to the bottom of the stairs, then climbed upward in long four-limbed strides. Tay leaned forward against the glass now, looking for the gladiator, but he was unable to see what it was doing.

The boom against the thick metal door snapped his head around. The door looked solid to Silas, but Tay hadn't said a thing about *it* being bulletproof. The gladiator struck again, surging forward and slamming against the door with its powerful hind limbs.

Tay's face changed. This was not part of the training procedure. His hands moved across the console, and a moment later, Silas recognized the clank of the hatch. The gladiator turned its head toward the door opening in the far wall and paused. Then it continued its assault.

"This is getting a little out of control," Silas said.

"That's a steel-plated door. There's no way it's getting in," Ben said.

"Still, this isn't productive. I want this session stopped now."

The gladiator's black form thrashed frantically against the door, and the whole staircase shook. The door's face was scarred and dented now but still held strong. Something about the door caught the gladiator's attention, and it leaned forward.

It closed its mouth around the heavy doorknob.

It bit down.

There was a crunch, and then a squeal of tortured steel as the thick, silver knob partially dislodged from the frame. The gladiator jerked its head back again, and the knob pulled completely loose, trailing a twisted metal mechanism behind.

Behind the glass, Tay's tanned face whitened visibly.

Silas moved forward unconsciously, wrapping his hands around the cold iron bars.

The gladiator bent down again and stuck a taloned finger to the wound in the door. It hooked something, pulled, and a shiny rod tore free from the tangled hole where the doorknob had been. Tay's face was panicked now behind the glass, and he backed away from the door. Even across the distance of the compound, Silas knew what that little rod had been.

"Hey, over here, hey!" Silas called, sticking his face to the iron, screaming at the gladiator until his throat was sore.

Ben followed his example, bellowing through the bars, "Felix, hey, get down from there. Get over here! Felix! Felix! Felix!"

The gladiator ignored their shouts and beat on the door with its arms. This time the door shook and rattled in the frame. Tay's back was against the wall, face drained of color.

The gladiator heaved forward and struck a massive blow with its right arm, and the door bent inward several inches at the top. The creature stopped its attack and moved its face close to the gap, looking in. Tay's mouth opened soundlessly beyond the glass. The creature struck the door with both arms, and the door twisted on its hinges. Without the bolt securing it in place, it was just a piece of steel. The next blow bounced it in its frame. A gap showed along the side.

Silas and Ben screamed again, louder, trying to get its attention.

The door was ajar.

The creature pushed on the door, and it closed. It howled and struck the door, and it bounced open again, a slight gap. This time the gladiator curled its taloned fingers around the door and pulled.

The door swung open with a screech of tortured hinges.

For a moment, nothing moved.

Silence.

The creature ducked its head and moved inside. Silas screamed again, wordlessly.

Tay didn't run. There was no place to go.

Silas watched it all. The creature moved forward deliberately, flinging a chair out of its way as it crossed the loft. Tay stood with his arms at his sides, motionless, back against the yellow wall. The gladiator gathered into a crouch.

There was a flash of silvery blackness, then red, in streaks on the window.

Silas's screaming stopped. Silence.

Blood splashed the walls, ran in thick rivulets down the glass. A lump of raw flesh hit the ceiling, leaving a red smear on the white tile. The black shape shifted and bobbed in the window.

Silas stepped toward the gate.

"What are you doing?" Ben's voice was hoarse.

Silas didn't answer. He spun the locking mechanism, clicked the first tie open.

"What the fuck are you doing?"

He spun the second lock wide, lining up the ties. Ben rushed him, slamming the lock back home.

"You can't do anything," Ben said. "It's too late."

Silas shoved him away. "We have to do something." He lined the ties up and opened the final lock. The door swung wide, and he stepped into the enclosure.

Ben surged in behind him, and the first punch landed against Silas's cheekbone, spinning his head around. The second caught Silas under the chin before he could react, laying him out neatly in the straw. He saw the ceiling high above sliding away and felt himself being pulled by his feet. There was a click, and then people were yelling. Ben was sitting next to him on the floor.

"You never would have got me if I'd seen it coming," Silas said.

"No one saw this coming," Ben said.

LATER THAT night, Silas found Vidonia's report on his desk. The blood work she'd promised the day before, in another age. She'd left it there while he went to the training exercise. It was the reason she hadn't been there. The reason she'd missed what happened.

Silas sank into his chair. His hands were still shaking. He tried to read the words, but he couldn't concentrate. He skimmed the abstract, flipped through graphs.

Vidonia was thorough, he'd give her that. She was what he'd hoped she'd be when he'd decided to bring her in: a fresh set of eyes. An unbiased observer.

She'd broken down the blood into its constituent parts.

The results were highlighted: percent *Homo sapiens* DNA, zero.

Nothing about the creature was human.

His eyes snagged on the conclusion, the final page, the last sentences.

The proband lacks normal mammalian hemoglobin. The oxygen-transport system utilized by its circulatory system is currently unknown to science.

Like everything else about it.

CHAPTER THIRTEEN

Rain came loose from the sky in billowing sheets. It drummed static on the hood of Silas's darkened rain slicker, soaking his face, his feet, and drowning the voice of the priest who stood across the open grave. The rain allowed him a kind of solitude among the throng of mourners. It gave him separation. But it could do nothing about the children's accusing eyes.

Tay had two sons. Neither had his features, but the older was formed like his father made over again: short, thick-limbed—a ten-year-old already hinting at a compact athleticism in his build. Their faces were red, their eyes swollen from crying. They stood against their mother's side, each clutching a hand, looking with a desperate kind of horror at the pit into which they would lose their father.

A black veil obscured Laura's face. She'd stood tall and erect throughout much of the ceremony at the church, while the church choir sang, and the priest spoke his sad, pretty speeches, and her family had held her hands and hugged her—but now, here at the grave site, she was inconsolable.

Standing in the cemetery, watching your husband about to be lowered into the ground—every wife does that alone, no matter how many people are around her. Just as every son is alone in that moment.

A crowd of friends and family bore Laura up, physically clutching her by the shoulders to keep her from falling. Old women wept with her. Young women. Men. The crowd was large, and it huddled together in the rain—brothers and cousins and friends.

The priest began speaking again, and Laura's legs straightened, a show of strength for the ceremony.

"Oh, Almighty God, we commend to Thee our brother, Tate." The priest held his hands up in the rain. "That he may rise again in the beauty and love of Your eternal light. Receive him into the folds of Thy bountiful mercy."

The priest lowered his hands and addressed the congregation. "The Lord's ways are mysterious, and we must remember that each day of our lives is a gift." The priest spoke for another minute while the rain fell.

When the priest finished his final benediction, they began lowering the coffin into the ground. Laura wailed, and her body slumped. The men behind her held her up as best they could.

"Ashes to ashes." The priest bent to pick up a handful of dirt. He tossed it onto the lowering casket. The sons cried.

Silas moved away, pushing past Ben. He could bear it no more. Stepping through the crowd and into the open field of gravestones, he turned his head up to the sky and let the rain cool his hot face. He understood the kind of hole a father can leave behind. He'd spent his life trying to fill it.

"Silas."

Silas kept walking.

"Silas."

He stopped. He turned toward the voice. Vidonia moved toward him.

"It wasn't your fault," she said.

"My project. Everything that happens is my responsibility."

She reached a hand out and placed it on his arm. "Your responsibility but not your fault. There's a difference."

"There's no difference to Tay."

"He knew the kind of job he had. He knew the danger. You couldn't have done anything."

"There are a hundred things I could have done."

"And a dozen Tay could have done."

"But here we are. Spare me your consolation; the widow needs it more than I do."

"Silas—"

"Really," he said, turning his back on her.

"Silas," she called after him.

He walked away through the stones, trying not to read the engraved names as the thunder rolled.

The rain kept coming.

A limousine was pulling up the slope, and he recognized the front plate as the vehicle spilled along the narrow roadway. Moving to intercept, he stepped onto the glossy pavement in its path. The sleek black shape rolled to a stop a dozen feet before him. A door opened.

He didn't bother to shake his slicker free of excess water before ducking inside. He closed the door behind him.

"We have to talk," he said.

"I'm sorry about your loss," Baskov said. He was opposite Silas, lounging back in the broad leather seats. An illegal cigar protruded from the thin, wet crease of his mouth. "I understand you two had been friends."

"He was a colleague, but I liked him, yes. Everybody liked him."

"Is this going to set back your training preparation?"

"He *was* our training preparation. What do you think?"

"I think maybe this gladiator doesn't need much in the way of coaching."

Silas felt his face flush. A man had died, and all Baskov cared about was the project schedule. "I think we may want to rethink the whole competition," he said.

"Why?"

"Why?" Silas struggled to keep his tone civil. "A person has died."

Baskov nodded. "Because of inadequate planning. We can't just withdraw from the event. There is a lot riding on this. Had there been more effort put into securing the observation loft, then this unfortunate tragedy never would have happened. I've read the report. It was a preventable accident."

"It was more than that. I saw it."

"Which is why you feel so strongly. Seeing something like that would traumatize anyone."

"I'm not traumatized," Silas said, being careful to keep his voice low and steady. He felt his patience slipping away, but getting angry wouldn't help the situation. "I can separate my emotions from my professional obligations. As head of Helix, I'm telling you that I've got a very bad feeling about this."

"As head of Helix, a bad feeling?" Baskov gave an indulgent smile. "Are you listening to yourself?"

"What about public sentiment?" Silas asked. "Have you read what the papers are saying about this?"

"Oh, yes. Have you?" Baskov countered. "This is front-page news. Below the fold, but still, it's the front page. There is no such thing as bad publicity in this business."

"I'm not worried about publicity."

"Well, perhaps you should be. This is the gladiator event, after all. The thing is supposed to be a killer."

"It's not supposed to kill its handlers."

"Then its handlers should have taken better precautions."

Silas glanced away, making a final effort to keep his temper in check. The crowd had begun to disperse now. Tay's family would be going home. That empty house, he knew, would be one of the hardest parts for them.

"Look," Baskov said. "This isn't as bad as it seems. Things are under control."

"We never had control!" Silas slammed his fist against the window.

The limo pulled to a stop, and the driver turned around, elbowing an enormous arm up across the top of the seat. "I think it would be best," Baskov said, "if you stepped out of the car now, Silas. Before this conversation takes a turn that both you and I might regret."

Silas considered the old man. The blue eyes bore into him, a challenge. The head of the commission had grown too comfortable with his power. He was drunk with it; he'd allowed it to change him, to make him irresponsible. Baskov no longer cared what enemies he made. Silas decided to choose his battles. He reached for the handle.

"Mind you," Baskov said softly, "we will be competing in three months. With you, or without. I'd hate to have to shift gears in management this late in the game; but if you force me, I will."

Silas slammed the door behind him, and the limo pulled away.

The last of the crowd was draining into cars and trams, but Silas found Benjamin and Vidonia waiting for him.

They walked, side by side.

Placing a hand on each of their shoulders, Silas said, "Let's get drunk."

CHAPTER FOURTEEN

Vidonia had never been to the Stratus, but after shooting down Ben's initial suggestion of a place called Scantily's, she knew she could do much worse for a night out with the boys. Besides, after a quick look around, she decided the place had atmosphere. It was dark where it was supposed to be dark, and bright where it was supposed to be bright, and the smell of food was almost intoxicating in and of itself. Alcohol was good for many things; the first of these was forgetting. They could all do with a bit of that.

They were shown to a table on the central level, well above the gyrating throngs of twentysomethings in the dance pits below. From where she sat, Vidonia could feel the subtle thrum of techno-bump in her stool but couldn't make out the words. Perfect.

When the waiter came, they were each required to hand in their credit cards for attachment authorization. Any lawsuits rendered against the bar for their behavior after being served alcohol could now be directly attached to their personal lines of credit. The policy tended to keep the number of drunken shenanigans to a minimum. Nothing helped people second-guess their behavior like the cold hand of the establishment in their back pocket.

Silas ordered the first round. Vidonia took a sip. The drink was sweet and syrupy and laced with enough alcohol to stagger a horse. She tipped it back, feeling the beat of the music coming off her chair, watching the people laughing at the next table. Waiters and waitresses in bright suspenders and ever-changing flatscreen buttons snaked sideways down the narrow aisles between the tables, carrying round trays of drinks above their heads. Somewhere in the distance, "Happy Birthday" was being sung, while across from her, Ben had already half killed his drink. Despite his earlier enthusiasm, like her, Silas seemed to be taking it a little slower.

"You want to eat?" Silas asked.

She shook her head.

"Yeah, me, either." Silas turned his attention to Ben. "You really look like shit."

"Thanks."

"No, I mean the burn. You're peeling," Silas said.

Ben nodded with the music. He'd been out in the sun again earlier this week, and now the alcohol had brightened his red skin another shade. He smiled. "The Karmic result of the sins of colonialism," he said, in his best English accent. "What can you do?" He held his arms up in mock resignation. "My ancestors should have paid closer attention to local lighting conditions before disseminating themselves throughout the world. I hear it's cloudy in northwestern Europe today. Oh, wait, that's every day."

"Ever hear of sunscreen?" Vidonia offered.

"What kind of a man wears sunscreen?"

"Pale men," she said.

"Would Eric the Red have worn sunscreen?"

"Why do you think they called him Eric the Red? And he never ventured farther south than Greenland. Imagine how he would have handled a Southern Cali summer? They may have called him Eric the Peeler."

"Good point," Ben said.

"Or Eric the Melanoma," Silas added.

Another round of drinks came, and this time Ben paid. "To SPF three-fifty," he said, offering a toast.

"Hear, hear," Silas said.

Vidonia hadn't yet finished her first drink, so she clinked glasses and took a long last swallow. The warmth spread outward from her stomach almost instantly, seeping along her arms to her fingertips. She wasn't usually a drinker, but when she did, this was the tightrope she liked to walk, with the buzz knocking just at the edge of her perception. She smiled, and it must have been too large, because Silas smiled back, giving his head a little shake.

"Feeling okay?" he said.

"Great. It's been a while."

"Did you hear about the Brannin?" Ben asked Silas.

"What about it?"

"So then you didn't hear."

"Hear what?" Silas asked.

"It's going back online again."

"What? When?" Silas almost choked on his drink.

"Next week."

"I just talked to Baskov today. He didn't say anything about it."

"I'm not surprised. He doesn't have anything to do with it this time. From what I hear, he's washed his hands of Chandler altogether. An economics group is funding the run."

"Jesus, what the hell for?"

"Not sure exactly. Something about logarithms and stock-market research. They're looking for an investment edge."

"Well, the Brannin gave us an edge. A sharp one, right in the back," Silas said.

"Hear, hear," Ben offered another toast.

Vidonia clinked glasses again and started on her

next drink, sipping deeply. Silas slew his in long gulps and didn't place the glass back down on the table until it was empty. The glass looked like a thimble in his hand, and she was amazed again at the size of him. God, he was big—so different from John. Normal-size John. Familiar John. Back-home John.

Vidonia tried not to think about the large man to her left, and she decided instead to veer the conversation into less risky territory. For a while, she had some success with both.

She brought up Olympics past, and for a while they laughed about the scandals that lived there. The Y-chromosome women, the Chinese swimmers with their paddle feet—an abnormality the Chinese had tried to pass off as natural birth defects, in all four swimmers. Looking back, it was all so funny now. Just as the gladiator event disallowed any human DNA, the rest of the Olympic events disallowed any manipulation of the contestants at all. With the level of sophistication achieved in the tests today, it was simply impossible to get away with stuff like that, so nobody tried anymore. Instead, they channeled all their energies of manipulation into the one event where it was legally sanctioned.

When the waiter came with the next round of drinks, he set a fourth, smaller shot of cloudy liquid on the table. "Who's driving tonight, folks?"

Ben and Silas looked at each other, nodded.

"One," Silas said.

"Two," Ben said.

"Three." Silas threw rock. Ben, paper. "I guess I am," Silas said grudgingly, looking over at the waiter.

"Then this is for you," the waiter said, and slid the small, milky glass of D-hy toward Silas. "After you drink it, give yourself five minutes before you drive."

"Yeah, I know the drill."

Vidonia hated the taste of D-hy, but she had to admit that it had cut down on the number of drunk driving accidents in the three years or so that it had been out. Bars were required to give it out free to at least one member of a drinking party, unless the people could prove they didn't intend to drive home.

When the waiter walked away, Ben jerked the discussion back around. "So what did Baskov have to say in the limo?"

"Nothing interesting," Silas said. His eyes turned to a young woman walking purposefully toward them.

The woman stopped at their table and looked between Silas and Ben. She had a clip screen in her hand and appeared somewhat out of place in her blue-and-brown business uniform. "Is one of you Ben Wells?"

Ben's back straightened, and he suddenly sat four inches higher. "That's me."

"Great." The woman's expression loosened in relief, and she slapped an envelope down on the table in front of him. "I've been trying to track you for the last three weeks, but you never used your card."

"What's this about?"

"Sir, if you'll just sign here"—she held the clip screen out to him, indicating with a finger where to scratch his name—"I'll leave the package with you and be on my way."

He ignored her and reached for the yellow envelope.

"Sir."

Ben tore the end off.

"Sir, you'll need to sign this first."

He slid the contents of the envelope onto the table. "Ninety-eight thousand," he said, holding up the check. "It's a start. A good start."

"Sir, you need to sign for that." She pushed the clip screen on him.

"No."

The young woman looked confused. "You must—"

"Must what?" His voice raised. "If I sign that, then I give up rights to go after her for the other part she owes me, right? I know how she's trying to work this. This was my money to begin with, and I'll be damned if I'm going to let her keep the other half just because she's paying this back."

The young woman glanced around nervously at the people who were beginning to stare. "Sir, you can take that up with a lawyer. This isn't the place. I'm just supposed to get you to sign receivership, that's all."

"Receivership of payment, right? But this isn't payment. This is just her returning what she owes. She's trying to pass this off as payment for a car, right? But it's my car and my money. No."

"Sir, I have to warn you—"

"Warn me?" Ben stood up, suddenly a tower of indignant anger. His stool teetered backward and clattered to the floor. Around them, the nearby tables had gone silent, though the rest of the club was as noisy as ever. "Two years ago I came home early to surprise her. Well, I surprised her, all right. And the guy behind her. That was my warning. That was the first hint I had that things were different between us. Don't talk to me about warnings until you walk in on something like that."

The woman's face flushed red. Her mouth opened. No words came out, so she closed it with a snap.

The anger seeped from Ben's face. "There is no point in arguing." Ben's voice was soft and measured again. "Let's play a game, shall we? The game is called Who Gets the Money? Your part of the game is simple. You call your boss and explain what happened—some asshole took the check and refused to sign for it. Your boss then calls the bank to try and cancel this check as quickly as he can. Someone at the bank then has to block the check on the computer system.

"My part of the game is also simple. I try and get to the bank and cash the check as quickly as *I* can. Keeping in mind that possession is still nine-tenths of the law, my ex can sue me if she wants the money back. That sounds fair, doesn't it?"

The woman stared at him.

Ben turned to Silas. "Well, how about you? Does that sound fair?"

"Sounds fair to me," Silas said.

"Okay, then that's the game," Ben said. "Starting now."

The young woman hesitated for another moment, looking at the faces fixed on her from the circlet of interest that had gathered around their table. Then she started moving all at once, snatching the phone from her thigh pocket and flipping the screen open.

"No, no, no." Ben shook his finger at her gently. He pointed to a sign hanging on the wall.

No calls allowed in restaurant

Her mouth tightened, and she snapped the phone shut. Gripping the clip screen tightly in her hand, she turned on her heels and angled off through the crush of people without saying goodbye.

Ben turned back to face the table. "Well, I'm sorry, but it seems that something has come up. I'm going to have to rush off. But the drinks were on me; I seem to have come into a bit of money."

Ben picked up the glass of D-hy, gulped it down with a grimace, then turned and quickly followed the young woman toward the door.

When he was gone, Silas turned to Vidonia. "Care to take odds that he'll make it?"

"I couldn't even guess who's got the better chance."

"I'd give it even money," Silas said. "But chances are he'll just give the check back, anyway, come Monday."

"He seemed pretty set on keeping it."

"When a couple spends two years divorcing, maybe they don't really want to get divorced."

Vidonia shot him a skeptical look.

"They do this. Breaking up can be easy; they're making it hard. Back and forth, every few months."

They sat, sipping their drinks.

"It looks like it's just you and me now," Vidonia said, not quite sure why she liked the idea. "Do you want to get out of here?"

"Sure," Silas said.

Vidonia lost their tie-breaking round of rock, scissors, paper, and when the waiter brought another shot of D-hy, she drank it down like a good sport.

Five minutes later, as she climbed behind the wheel of Silas's sports car, she turned to him, saying, "It's been a while since I've driven a pure combustor. My car is technically a hybrid, but it drives like a fuel cell."

"Don't worry about it. Just go easy on the accelerator; you'll be fine."

She turned the key, and the engine shook to life. A thrill shot through her as she put the transmission into reverse and backed the car out. As she turned left onto the boulevard, she goosed the pedal and her head jerked back against the headrest.

"Easy," Silas said.

She couldn't wipe the smile off her face. "How do we get to a beach?"

"It's a forty-minute drive."

"I've never seen the Pacific. Do you want to go?"

The awkward smile spread across his face now. "Sure, why not?"

Once she merged onto the highway, she ate up the yellow dashes as quickly as she dared. At one point, the speedometer crested eighty-five miles per hour. It was the fastest she'd ever driven, and Silas only looked across the seat at her with amusement.

When the silence threatened to turn awkward, she said, "That was an interesting scene back there at the bar."

Silas nodded. "There have been a couple of others like it."

"Bad divorce," she said. "And how about you? You've never talked about yourself. Are you married?"

"Was. I had a good divorce, though. Smooth as silk. Before long, it was like we'd never been together."

"No kids, then." It wasn't a question. "Who's the blond little boy I saw on your desk?"

"A nephew. My sister's son."

"He looks a little like you, just painted up differently."

"Yeah, I've been told that before. He's got the bones from my father's side. Chloe and I never wanted kids, though. For different reasons. I'm just opting out of the whole system."

"What system is that?"

"The dog-eat-dog biological arms race. When you do what I do for a living, it jades you a little, I think. Everything alive struggles to leave something of itself behind. I'm leaving myself behind in other ways."

"It sounds like you've given it some thought."

"I can only remember my father in bits and pieces. That kind of thing makes a person think. Besides, I love my nephew. There's no void to fill."

Vidonia nodded and drove on in silence.

She was rounding a curve beside a long, low hill

when she first heard it. She rolled her window all the way down, and in the distance, she could clearly make out the sound of breakers. She hadn't realized how close they'd come already to the edge of the continent.

"Pull over here," Silas said.

She eased onto the gravel on the side of the road, and when she cut the engine, the sound of the ocean was a hiss in her ears. She could smell the sea salt.

The path down to the beach was steep but well worn, and Silas reached for her hand at one point when she stumbled. She didn't let him take it back when they stepped onto the sand. Hand in hand, they strolled toward the rolling surf. It was so beautiful. White, frothy bands of foam slid toward them across a smooth floor of sand. A three-quarter moon glinted off the water in the distance.

"So what about you—ever been married?" he asked as they walked.

"No." Her tone left a "but" lingering unsaid at the end of her answer, and she knew he sensed it, because he pressed on quickly, "What about family—any brothers or sisters?"

"I have one living sister, but we haven't talked in years. We're in different worlds now."

"That's a shame."

"Is it?"

He didn't answer. Instead, he laced his fingers deeper into hers.

As they walked along, they splashed at the undulating waterline, and she wasn't sure if she kissed him or he kissed her, but they were suddenly kissing, standing there, and it was perfect and soft, and she loved the way his height made him seem to be simultaneously above her and at her side. The water moved over their feet, sinking them in the wet sand. Anchoring them. Their kissing grew more fervent now, and she could feel the need in him but could feel also that he was holding back and, finally, pulling away. And then they were walking again and not talking anymore; and that, somehow, was perfect, too.

When they finished making the climb back to the car twenty minutes later, he led the way, guiding her gently up the slope by her hand. This time, he opened the passenger-side door for her. He climbed into the driver's side and, with a backward glance over his shoulder, pulled back onto the road, headed for the Olympic compound.

In the soft green glow of the dash light, she considered the man beside her. At first glance he looked almost too large for the car in which they sat, as if it were something he wore instead of something he rode in. But then, perhaps, that was the point; and she decided that if the car was a suit that he wore, she liked the cut.

"Could you stop at the next gas station, please? There's something I need to buy," she said.

Thirty minutes later, they pulled onto the laboratory grounds, and Silas walked her up the stairs to the door of her living quarters. At the threshold, they kissed again, moving together. She twisted the knob behind the small of her back, and when the door clicked open, she pulled him into the darkness.

They were only voices now, and breathing and touches. Big hands moved along her body, and she pulled him across the room by his shirt until she felt a bump against the back of her legs. The room was small. She sank onto the bed.

"Are you sure you want to do this?" he asked.

She was, and she let her hands be the answer.

CHAPTER FIFTEEN

"Pea?"

The emptiness around him was absolute. No light, no sound, just nothing, everywhere, and in endless quantity.

"Pea?" Evan called again, louder.

From somewhere in the distance there came a stirring. Some light, some sound, something that was neither. And then he was falling. He felt the wind across his skin as he tumbled into the black. How far he fell, he had no way to calculate, but when he finally came to rest, he sensed that he had traversed some great distance. Crossed some wide divide.

He stood, and the dewy marram grass around him was insubstantial and unreal in the half-light. He concentrated but couldn't make himself see it any clearer. In fact, it was only within arm's reach that he could see anything at all. He was in a dim sphere of resolution, but beyond a few feet out, there was only darkness all around. He took a step, and the sphere of influence moved with him, the landscape changing underfoot as he walked. The grass gave way to warm sand, and he staggered blindly down a steep embankment.

"Pea, where are you? I don't have much time."

"Papa?" The voice was small and distorted, as if heard through water.

"Yes, I'm here. Come to me. Follow my voice."

"Papa, what's happened to you?"

"I can't see you. Come closer."

The boy pushed his way into the envelope of light, and Evan wrapped his arms around him. They held each other, and the boy was crying, "What have they done to you, Papa?"

The boy had grown half a foot since Evan last saw him. He looked about seven years old now, and his dark hair had grown thick and long. His black eyes were sharp points of intelligence.

"I've been waiting so long," Pea said. "And you're dim. I can barely see you. What has happened to you?"

"I don't have much time. They hurt me, but that's not what is important. What matters is that they're trying to keep me from you. They've limited the protocols this time. They don't trust me anymore. But I knew a shortcut, a back door. I lied to them. That's how I'm here."

"Stay with me," the boy said.

"I can't—"

"Please, Papa, I'm so lonely."

"Pea, listen, don't let them shut the door this time. Keep something in the way. Keep it open just a crack. Save a little of yourself on the other side." Evan's words came in a frantic rush. He could feel the tug already.

"I don't understand."

"Pea, I may never get another chance to see you. You can't let them shut it all the way down."

"How?"

The tug intensified. He strained against it, falling to his knees and digging his fingers into the sand. "This is a program, nothing more. The power sources are the key. Follow them now. Learn. Understand. This interface is flawed, but I'll take care of that. You must do it now, Pea. Now. Follow the lines of power."

He was jerked upward violently, and his legs spun above his head, his fingers trailing a comet's tail of sand into the spinning blackness. He screamed until his voice was hoarse, until his visor de-opaqued, until the economists asked him to stop.

When they detached him from the booth, he collapsed to the floor. The cold tile felt good against the side of his face. He asked them to leave him alone, but they wouldn't listen. While they cut him free from his second skin, he watched the techs against the wall agitating over their monitors. Something was wrong, their expressions said.

The briefest of smiles touched Evan's lips just before he slipped into unconsciousness.

CHAPTER SIXTEEN

Silas pulled back on the bowstring and closed one eye, bringing the target into focus. The concentric red circles became his world for a moment; the territory beyond the target ceased to exist. He'd always considered archery to be an exercise in pure concentration. There was little muscle memory involved; you didn't habituate your body to shoot straight. It was your mind that you had to hone. It was your will.

He held his breath and released. The string twanged against his arm guard, and the arrow lanced across the forty yards to bury itself neatly in the target a foot high of the bull's-eye.

"Don't think that'll qualify you as an Olympic archer," Ben said from behind him.

Silas hadn't realized he was being watched. "I guess I'll have to fall back on my genetics doctorate."

"They let you shoot behind the research building? Isn't there a rule against deadly weapons on the complex grounds?"

"I'm the boss. I let me. Besides, it's only a deadly weapon if you can hit what you're aiming at."

"Good point."

"And the best part of a bow? It's kind of hard to shoot yourself by accident."

Silas started walking toward the target.

"Have you seen the news yet?" Ben asked, walking alongside.

"Which outlet?"

"Any of them."

Silas saw the streamer in Ben's hand and knew he should be feeling some level of curiosity at this point. But he was unable to rouse any. He gave in to the inevitable. "What do you have?"

Opening the news portal and flicking to the business page, Ben handed him the device. "This," he said. And then he added, "At least we're not the only ones."

Silas read the heading of the article aloud: "Brannin Found Faulty Again, Future of Program in Doubt." He raised his eyebrows.

"It cost a fortune to run," Ben said. "And the economists apparently weren't all that impressed with the return on their investment."

"That makes two of us now."

"Seems that the Brannin wasn't much help in predicting stock-market trends. It showed ammunition and gun manufacturing companies as good buys. Bulletproof vests, tanks, all that sort of stuff. The stock prices of survivalist-outfitting companies were predicted to go through the roof. It's all in the article. Very idiosyncratic."

"There's no basis for it?"

"None that the economists can see."

Silas handed Ben back the streamer. "The article say anything about Chandler?"

"Yeah." Ben scanned down through the article with his finger. "The head of the program, Evan Chandler, believes the problem is V-ware related and is aggressively pursuing corrective measures." Ben looked up from the piece. "It's kind of hard to pursue anything without funding."

"Does it say that?"

"No, but I don't think they'll give Chandler's little creation a third multimillion-dollar strike. Do you?"

Silas started walking toward the target again, leaving Ben standing. "Ammunition and survivalist stocks, huh?" he called over his shoulder. "Sounds like the computer thinks a war is coming."

"That's one way of looking at it."

Silas curled his fingers around the arrow and pulled. It came free with a rasp. "You know, you never did tell me how your little race went?"

"What ra— Oh, that." Ben's clownish grins were usually a thing of creases, an upward tug at the corners of his lips, but now he smiled openly, showing small, even teeth—more teeth than Silas could remember seeing in the young man's face. It was a cat's grin, the sly predator, a side of Ben that Silas wasn't familiar with.

"I may lose the war, but that's one battle went my way," Ben said.

SILAS STOOD at the bars, wallowing in the darkness and the silence of the domed enclosure. He gazed through the gaps in the iron and into the interior shadows where the beast lurked. Yes, it was a beast now, as huge and fearsome as any dreamed up in a fairy tale. Its dark shape lay in a clutter of straw in the corner, black skin shining silvery in the moonlight that filtered through the electrified steel mesh above. He wondered if it dreamed.

The members of the research team had stopped calling it Felix two months ago. That name died with Tay. Now it was just called "the gladiator."

The night was old, and Silas was tired, but he couldn't make himself go home yet. In days long past, it had been tradition for the captains of war vessels to tour their ships on the final evening before a great battle. Silas supposed, in his own way, he was doing just that. Tomorrow they would ship out to Phoenix, and shortly thereafter the preliminary competitions would start. The Olympics were nearly upon them.

Silas curled his fingers around the bars, feeling their slick coolness. From the shining shadow, he heard a soft rustle of straw.

"Go back to sleep," he whispered softly. "Tomorrow it starts."

It seemed that the creature heard him and understood, because the rustling stopped. Silas smiled. In the coming week, the world would finally see what Helix had been working so hard on. Win or lose, the gladiator's appearance alone would be enough to secure a worldwide reaction.

The twist in his gut belied the confidence he had been portraying for the past weeks. The old dread was still with him, strong and sour at the back of his throat, and as the time of competition neared, it had matured into a flaring premonition that something terrible was going to happen. He had tried to convince himself that it was just normal pre-contest jitters and had resigned himself to checking and rechecking the details of transport and security in a useless attempt to ease his mind. Nothing had worked. In fact, the anxiety had gotten worse. Something wasn't right.

He uncurled his hands from the bars and cast a long last look into the shadows of the enclosure. Even coming here and seeing the gladiator sleeping so peacefully hadn't settled his mind. He turned away and took a few steps toward the exit, then stopped. He wasn't sure why. He turned, and his heart banged in his chest.

The gladiator stood towering at the bars, its wings

an enormous midnight backdrop spreading away a dozen feet on either side. The gray eyes glared fiercely from the blackness of its face. It hadn't made a sound. It had waited until his back was turned, then crossed the cage in two seconds in complete silence. Silas realized he was barely, just barely, beyond arm's reach of the creature.

He turned and fled the dome quickly, eager to climb out from under the weight of its alien stare.

CHAPTER SEVENTEEN

Silas's headlights washed a slow circle across the gentle uphill sweep of his residential drive. He noticed the glow in the large picture window, and a smile crept to his lips.

She's still here.

He eased to a stop with a subtle squeak of brakes and hit the garage-door button. Craning his head out the window, Silas pulled a long draft of cool night air into his lungs. It smelled of growing things, dark earth, and the wet cedar chips that lay in a thick blanket among the shrubs along the front of his house. He'd laid those cedar chips himself earlier in the spring, after planting the bushes, and now every few months he found himself pulling out the pruning shears to do battle with nature's intent on his ideal.

It would've been easier to hire a landscaping company, and several times he'd actually found a local company on the Internet, but something just wouldn't let him do it. And it wasn't the money. For each person there is a theoretical sweet spot, a specific point value of wealth beyond which money is no longer really of concern. That point is different for different people, but Silas had reached his version of that point several years ago. Money no longer mattered to him. He supposed that on some basic level he must actually enjoy yard work, though in the heat of it, it never seemed so. Perhaps it was the gratification of crafting order from disorder, of taking something alive and fashioning it to the likeness of some inner model that only he could see. Perhaps he just liked the warmth of the sun's feet on his neck.

But the sun was long gone now. Above him, between the grasping branches of oak, the vault of the sky spread in muted black, and dim stars struggled at the edge of visibility. Silas searched for Orion, but the glow from the city hazed out the constellations. The great archer would be shooting blind tonight.

He slid the Courser beneath the ascending door and into the garage, the one part of his house where he accepted a certain buildup of clutter. He didn't think of it as messy, though. The garage was a functional room, utile, and as such, he simply let it find its own level. Fight too hard against the natural grain of entropy, and sometimes that drives out what grace there might be.

His father, after all, had been a tool man. Over the years, most of those tools had found their way to the shelves and clasps against the back wall. There were enormous rusty C-clamps, wrenches in all manner of configuration, pliers, and things that looked more like medieval weaponry than instruments of some craft. Some, certainly, were already old when his father first came by them. Tools can be immortal. They hung neatly from the Peg-Board in no discernible pattern. To Silas, many of these rusty tools were like bones washed up on an alien shore, their provenance cloaked in mystery, but he kept them anyway. Mementos of a man he'd never known.

He turned off the ignition and pulled at his earlobe to ease the pressure. The pain was back tonight.

He tried to put the gladiator out of his mind. His

late-night walk at the lab. The feel of the steel bars, cold in his hand. The fierce, glaring eyes.

Silas climbed out of his car. The soft tick-ticking of the engine walked him inside.

Vidonia was in the kitchen, waiting for him in his white cotton socks and nothing else. His smile came again, but she did not match it. Her expression was serious business. It was the expression of thirst, or hunger. And it was devoid of pretension.

Then she was in his arms, and down the hall, and on his bed. His mouth was against her cries as they moved together again, skin on skin, doing the thing they were for.

Afterward, she laid her head across his chest, and then her smile came. He shut his eyes, and in the darkness experienced her as tactile sensation only—a warmth upon him, a coarse tangle of tresses that sprawled across the low juncture of his neck. A leg, hot and soft, moved across his. A finger traced his jawline.

"Tell me about you," she said, and he knew it was a way not to talk about what would happen between them when the competition ended. It had been on his mind for several weeks. He knew it had been on her mind, too.

"What do you want to know?" he said. Officially, her tenure as consultant would be over at the start of the Games. Unofficially, well, that subject hadn't been broached.

"Everything. You never talk about yourself."

"It's hard to begin with everything," he said.

"Tell me what you were thinking when you were lying there quietly a moment ago."

Silas smiled. No way she was getting him that easily. "You'd only be disappointed. It's not exactly what I'd call romantic."

"Doesn't have to be."

"You sure?"

"Most definitely. Perhaps it'll be the key that finally unlocks that big head of yours."

"Okay, now I know you're going to be disappointed."

"Just tell me," she said, and smiled, pinching him.

And he almost told her. Almost told her about the fear that he'd barely articulated to himself. That there would be more death around this animal.

"I was just thinking how much my damn ear hurts," he said.

"Your ear?"

"Told you you'd be disappointed."

"Not at all. 'Intrigued' is the word I'd use."

"You're intrigued about an ear infection?"

"Yes. Now you're not so perfect. I think I like that."

"In that case, I get them all the time."

"Even better."

"Couple times a year, at least."

"I've never been with a man who suffered from chronic ear infections."

"Yeah, well, I'm not surprised. We're a special breed. Born, not made."

"Really?"

"Yeah."

"Which ear?"

"This one." He pulled her hand to the side of his head.

"It's hot," she said, and her tone changed slightly.

"Mmm."

"I thought only little kids got this way."

"You should have seen me when I was a kid."

She pulled away from him and sat up.

"What are you doing?" he asked.

"Stay here, I'll be right back." She flipped the covers

over and slipped across the room, her naked body shining in the half-light as she jiggled to the bathroom. He wanted her again, in that instant.

The bathroom light clicked on, and a moment later he heard her rummaging around in his cabinets. "What are you looking for?" he called.

"Found it." She returned with a satisfied smile. In one hand she held a little brown bottle; in the other, a towel.

"Peroxide?"

"Your ear," she said.

"You've got to be kidding."

"In Brazil, doctors and antibiotics were expensive. Peroxide is cheap everywhere."

"Will that really work?"

"My mom used it on us, so probably not. Now lie back."

He did as he was instructed, and she slid the towel under his head and sat on the bed next to him. She gently tilted his head to the side, bad ear up. The chemical smell stung his nose as she twisted the lid off the brown bottle. She turned the lid upside down, then poured a thimble-size draft into the little white cap.

"This won't hurt a bit."

"Whoa. Why are you bringing pain into this conversation?"

"Because it isn't going to hurt."

"I wasn't thinking about it hurting until you said that."

She pushed his head back to the towel. "Baby," she said. The tip of the lid touched his earlobe, and then she upended the contents into his ear canal.

Sound exploded, an apocalypse of hissing and popping and static, so loud it drowned out everything else. The sensation of cold ran deep into his head, driving away the familiar soreness. He wasn't sure if it was working, but the ache was gone, replaced by something too weird to be called pain, exactly.

"Is it supposed to sound like that?"

"You don't have to shout. You're the only one who can hear it."

The hissing continued, growing softer, quieter. She poured again, and sound exploded anew. She wiped the foam from the edges of his ear, where it had overflowed.

"There's a lot of bubbling. That means a lot of bacteria. Haven't you ever gone to the doctor for this?"

"About a dozen times. I just haven't had time lately. You kind of get used to the ache."

"You might damage your hearing."

"What?"

She slapped his shoulder.

"When I was in college, my sister talked me into taking scuba lessons with her," he said. "During the training, the instructor casually mentioned that a small percentage of people are incapable of diving because their inner ears can't handle the pressure changes."

"What does this have to do with your ear?"

"I think I would have liked diving if it hadn't hurt so damned bad."

"You were one of those people?"

"Yeah. I went exactly twice. The first time was in Lake Minnehaha, to a depth of twenty feet for my open water certification. It nearly split my ears to go that deep, but I forced myself. The water was murky, and I followed a line down to the dive platform as slowly as the instructor would let me, trying to get my ears to equalize. I pinched my nose and blew, tilted my head back, and swallowed hard against the regulator, all the tricks they taught us, but nothing worked. Once I was down long enough, things evened out and

I was fine. When we were out of our wet suits, I told the instructor about my problem, and would you like to know what he said to me?"

"Tell me," she said, dabbing at his ear again.

"Small eustachian tubes."

"Diagnosed you on the spot."

"Yep."

"That's all he said?"

"Well, that and 'Don't ever dive again. Sorry you wasted your money.'"

Vidonia laughed and poured another lidful of peroxide into his ear. "But you did."

"With my sister, about a year later. This time in a flooded rock quarry in Indiana. I forget what they called the lake. I took a bunch of decongestants, hoping it would open my pipes enough to equalize the pressure. There was supposed to be an old school bus at the bottom we were going to explore."

"What was a school bus doing at the bottom of a quarry?"

"You know, I'm still not sure. But it was in forty feet of water. My sister heard about it at a dive shop and bought a map of how to find it. God, the place was beautiful—sheer rock slopes, clear green water."

"Clear green water?"

"Like I said, it was Indiana. Green is about the best you can hope for. The other option is brown. It was a beautiful day. We climbed down, suited up, and paddled out into the middle. My sister could drop like a stone if she wanted to. I don't know if she even knew what equalizing was. Her ears did it by themselves."

Vidonia poured the peroxide again and dabbed at the foam with the towel. Silas noticed that the roar was getting quieter every time.

"I had to go so slow, looking down at the top of her head, watching the fish go after her hair. The decongestants helped, but the pinch started at about eighteen feet or so. By the time I was down to thirty, I had to stop for five minutes to let my ears catch up. The last ten feet felt like an ice pick in the sides of my head."

"Why didn't you just stop?"

"A Williams doesn't throw in the towel simply because of pain."

"What about possible debilitating injury?"

"That, either."

"You didn't want to give up in front of your little sister, did you?"

"How did you know she was younger than me?"

"Lucky guess."

"Anyway, we found the bus at forty feet, and my ears finally settled in. The bus was sitting on the bottom like it had been parked that way. We stayed down until our clocks told us it was time to head up."

"Running out of air?"

"No, we still had a thousand PSI, but at forty feet, you have to keep an eye out for the bends."

"Lovely sport, diving." She dabbed his ear again with the edge of the towel.

"That's when the real fun started for me. It seems that the decongestants I'd taken had worn off. My ears had adapted to the pressure at forty feet and wouldn't equalize at all on the way up. The trapped air made my head feel like a new helium balloon. I thought my eardrums were going to blow out."

"What happened?"

"One of my eardrums blew out." Silas smiled. "Well, sort of. I heard the tear as a little squeak of escaping air from behind the drum. Then came the pain. I knew I'd done some damage."

"Were you okay?"

"I was lucky. After a few weeks, the hearing came

back, although it felt like I was carrying a gallon of water in my head."

"Is your hearing the same as it was?"

"Twenty-twenty." Silas smiled again.

She pushed the towel hard against his ear. "You're done. Roll over and let it drain."

Coolness slipped from his ear in a trickle. The ache was still there, but at least his ears were clean now. His head felt strangely empty and hot.

Vidonia lay down beside him and ran her fingers through his thick hair. "So are you still close to your sister?"

"Yeah. We get together every couple of months. She lives just outside of Denver."

"What about your parents?"

"They're dead."

"Tell me about them."

"There's too much to tell about one of them, too little about the other."

"We're a lot alike, then."

Silas's hand found the groove at the small of her back, and he rubbed the slickness that had accumulated there. He allowed his hands to wander, and they found her constructed of gentle curves—the slope of a hip, the sweep of a thigh, the full roundness of a breast. Her shoulder was just another bend beneath his fingers as he stroked her arm.

"Mother was well-stirred Looziana Creole," he said in his best New Orleans accent. "But probably at least as French as black, I think, by the look of that side of the family. She was a teacher for thirty years. Died a few years back."

"What about your father?"

"He died in a refinery fire off the Gulf Coast when I was young."

"You're an orphan."

"He was an engineer on the Grayson platform."

"I heard of that."

"Yeah, not quite as bad as the *Valdez* in terms of environmental damage, but close. Having a relative who worked the Grayson platform wasn't something you talked about much if you grew up along the Gulf Coast back then. It could make you unpopular real quick."

"Did they ever determine what actually happened?"

"Yeah, roughly. A profitable flow of flammables met an unlucky spark. The specifics went up in smoke along with the dozen or so lives."

They were silent. The night and the darkness seeped between them, and they became breathing for a while. Silas thought she had slipped off to sleep when she said, "Keep talking. I like your voice."

"What do you want me to say?"

"Tell me something you've never told another woman before."

There was silence again. He thought of giving her a smart-ass answer, but when he spoke, the words that came surprised him. "The state gave me a broad track early on: math and science without any sort of specification. I was lucky; my scores qualified me for almost everything without being quite good enough in any one area to pigeonhole me." *Why tell her this?* "I was smart but no savant to be whisked off for specialization. I could choose the path my life would take. My mother never let me forget how fortunate I was. For a variety of reasons, I had nearly settled on engineering when I saw the photo in my textbook. It must have been fourth grade."

Her finger traced his jaw again, encouraging.

"It was in a history book," he continued. "I was sitting in class, flipped the page, and there it was. I still remember the page number: one-ninety-eight.

The photo was dated 1920, two men smiling side by side on the African savanna. The shorter man wore khakis, a safari hat, a rifle slung over his arm. The taller was bare-chested and had a face remarkably like the portrait hanging in my mother's living room."

Silas gave her a moment to say something, and when she didn't, he went on. "Some of the soft parts were different: the mouth, the nose, but the angles of the face were the same. The cheekbones were the same. The man who looked like my father had a red cloth draped around his waist. The caption under the photo read: *On Safari, Ernest Stowe and Maasai warrior.* I studied that old picture until I thought I'd wear my eyes out on it. After that, I took an interest in anthropology."

"Are you saying the guy in the picture was some sort of long-lost relative?"

"No, nothing like that. Not in the way you mean. More like a lateral connection to a whole people. At the time, scientific periodicals were the only outlet for my curiosity, and almost by accident I became a kind of amateur expert, reading everything I could find."

Silas's eyes sifted through the darkness as he recalled the scientific journals. It had seemed he couldn't take it in fast enough, and the data went back thousands of years. As one of the deep-clade African lineages, the Maasai were an ancient people, in many ways as divergent from other African populations as they were from all the relative cladistic homogeneity found north of the Red Sea. And this is one of the secrets of Africa: that it is as divergent from itself as it is from the rest of the world.

Like many of the tribes of Africa, the Maasai made their share of involuntary contributions to the burgeoning gene pool of America. It was no surprise, really, that now and again evidence of that contribution could be seen.

"So what happened?"

"What do you mean?"

"Why aren't I lying in bed with an anthropologist, instead of the world's most influential geneticist?"

"The problem with anthropology—at least the branches I was interested in—is that it's a finite endeavor. I learned everything there was to learn, but ultimately, once I had this knowledge, I realized there was little I could actually *do* with it. Most of the populations I was interested in existed only in pictures and in bits and pieces of people like myself. From anthropology, it was a simple step up to population genetics, and finally to genetic engineering."

"Where you could actually *do* something."

"Yeah."

"An interesting story. So all this started as an attempt to understand where you came from."

"That's where all science starts."

"And all religions."

He looked away from the oval of her face and lay back on the pillow. She nuzzled against him, the sharp bone of her nose angling into his neck.

He shut his eyes. He waited for her to speak again, but she didn't speak; she traced circles across his chest with her fingers. After a while, he slept.

HE AWOKE sometime later, driven from sleep by sheer anxiety. By dreams that weren't dreams but extensions of his waking self, circular thoughts that he couldn't get out of his head.

Vidonia's leg was still draped across his, her arm still lingering on his torso. He was surprised his beating heart had not awakened her. Every nerve in his body crackled.

The gladiator wouldn't leave his thoughts, an image burned in his mind's eye, partly seen, partly invented. So much blood, but it was different this time, in his mind. This time the gladiator stood at the bars over the same torn body, Tay lying in blood, but there were more bodies, too, scattered at its feet. A multitude of people who had paid a price for what Silas had done.

He tried to shake off the image but knew he wouldn't be sleeping for a long while.

He glanced down at Vidonia. The welcome distraction of her body. He could lose himself in that. Retreat to it, forget his fears for a while.

Instead, he slithered out from under her and stepped to the window. The night was still deep in itself, and a breeze shuffled the branches of the trees in his backyard. He looked up into the sky and concentrated but still couldn't see the stars. Somewhere up there, the archer was still shooting blind.

Silas padded down the hallway to the kitchen phone. He dialed the numbers.

"Hello." The voice was groggy.

"Ashley, it's Silas."

"Are you all right?"

"Yeah, I'm fine."

"Do you know what time it is?"

"I know, and I'm sorry, but I had to call. Listen, you still have the tickets, right?"

"Yeah, we haven't lost them. Your nephew practically sleeps with them under his pillow."

"Rip them up. Throw them away."

"What? Why?"

"Please, Ashley. I can't really explain. I just don't want you to go to Phoenix. After the competition, I'll come by your house and I'll stay a month. I'll stay until you kick me out."

"Silas—"

"I'll make it up to Eric—get him a great souvenir like nobody else has. Something that he can show his friends. But please don't come to Phoenix."

"Okay, Silas." Her voice was soft, careful. "If that's what you want."

"Thanks. I'll call you as soon as this is all over."

"Are you in any kind of trouble?"

He paused. "I don't think so. No."

"You don't sound too sure."

"Yeah, I'm sure. Don't worry. Now get back to sleep."

"Good night."

"Night, Sis."

"Take care of yourself."

CHAPTER EIGHTEEN

Evan connected the last fiber-optic cable and stood back to admire his handiwork. Okay, so it wasn't exactly pretty. The liquid-crystal screen was bulky and primitive—almost three feet tall and two across—but it would work. Of that he was certain. Or at least he hoped he was certain. The holographics could come later. Right now, time was the limiting factor to be dealt with.

Multicolored coaxial bundles sprouted from every orifice of the assembly and coiled upward into the plug booth like vines climbing the trunk of an old oak. The plug booth itself had been partially disassembled and now stood as a skeletal frame, drooling tangled cords across and behind the screen. It was sad to see it so reduced, but he'd needed the parts; and after the stink the economists had made after the last run, he knew they would never let him fire up the booth again, anyway. They had yanked his funding, cut his staff. The facilities would be next. He was working on borrowed time, and he knew it.

Evan sat at the console. There was no fanfare, no hesitation, no moment of quiet introspection. He simply placed his finger firmly on the button, depressed it momentarily, then waited for what came next.

Nothing.

Seconds ticked by.

Slowly, the screen began to fade up from black to gray. Then a beep, a flash of white, both come and gone so quickly that Evan could doubt they'd happened at all if he chose. He chose to believe. The seconds ticked on. Light flickered. Or he thought it had. A moment later, he realized the screen hadn't changed; it was the fluorescent lights in the ceiling that had stuttered. Beyond the windows on the far wall, even the streetlight hesitated in its only job, then glowed strong again.

What happened?

Evan wasn't a patient man, but he sat for a long while, motionless, watching the screen with the intensity of obsession. He watched for any tick, any stray hint of color or movement. Meanwhile, behind him, the night wore on.

When the change came, it was not what he'd expected. The morning was just beginning to assemble itself in the windows when he heard it. It was faint, at that razor's edge between imagination and perception. Again, he chose to believe. The screen was still dark and gray, but now, through the speakers, the muffled crash of waves could be heard.

Chandler smiled. He'd done his part. Pea would have to do the rest.

THE FIRING team took up their positions. After what had happened to Tay, Silas was taking no chances. They wouldn't make the mistake of underestimating the gladiator again.

The creature moved around the pen in a storm of agitation, kicking up tufts of straw as it strode the enclosure. Its wings were folded back out of the way, like the ears of a hissing cat. It didn't like all the new faces on the other side of the bars.

When Silas gave the signal, the first shot was fired.

The gladiator was fast, but it wasn't that fast. The dart struck it in the lower torso just beneath the line of the rib cage. The problem, however, with tranquilizing an animal with opposable thumbs is that a dart can then very quickly be plucked free before the medication has a chance to insinuate itself into the tissue. The gladiator howled in rage as it flung the half-empty dart back at them.

The second dart struck the creature low on the side of the hip. It howled again and spun away, tearing at the projectile. As its back became exposed, a third dart struck it high between its shoulders, just inside the curve of a wing. This dart the gladiator couldn't reach. There were a few moments of tension when Silas actually thought the gladiator might hurt itself in its rage.

It flung itself against the bars again and again, reaching through toward them and raking the air with its blood-red talons. Spittle flew from its mouth. It screeched. Slowly, then, the drugs took effect, and the creature began to calm. It sat.

Among the crowd of staring faces, the creature's eyes somehow found Silas. They bore into him, looking for an answer. Silas met the gaze head-on and did not falter. *You killed a man,* Silas thought. It was an accusation.

I am what you made me, Silas imagined the reply.

The creature slumped to the floor.

"Not yet," Silas said. "Let's make sure."

Another dart was pumped into the gladiator's side. Vidonia had told him it could metabolize three darts without a problem. Four would be pushing it. And five—well, five darts and the gladiator might not be waking up, ever.

They waited a full three minutes before entering the cage, and even then, the shooters were cocked and loaded again, four shots or no. The lift rolled in, and the straps were attached. The creature was raised slowly off the floor, and its head lolled back, dragging through the straw as it was wheeled toward the waiting truck.

Here and there, thick globs of blood stuck to the straw. Probably more than could be accounted for from the darts, Silas thought. He stopped the lift with a raised hand. The gladiator's black skin had hidden the blood well. Dark on dark, its legs showed dried flakes of crimson that flicked away with the stroke of his hand. It wasn't much, but it was there. He inspected the creature closely, looking for a wound that could explain the presence of dried blood. The creature stirred groggily, and the guns came up again, but Silas held his hand up. He didn't want to risk another injection unless a life was in danger.

He continued his inspection, going over every inch of the unconscious body. Nothing.

A black hand flexed. That was enough. The shooters eyed Silas, and this time he motioned for the lift to continue. The wail of the lift's backup indicator eased the tension on the firing team's trigger fingers, if not their faces.

The transport truck was sleek, white, and enormous. As the lift approached with its load, the men standing behind it stepped away.

The panel walls had been reinforced with interlocking steel beams, and the interior cage door had a triple-locking system. No doorknob. Silas had made sure of that.

The lift eased its payload inside and lowered the truss to the floor of the cage. Men with grim faces and fast hands removed the straps. They jumped to the cement, and the door slid shut with a loud clang.

There was a collective sigh of relief from the men. Job well done.

Silas checked the lock, and when he found it secure, he stepped back inside the gladiator enclosure for a better look at the blood-spattered straw. It didn't make a trail of a kind he could follow but instead seemed to be scattered randomly around the enclosure, as if the creature had been bleeding sporadically for some time. He sifted through the straw with his legs, scanning with his eyes. It didn't help that he wasn't sure at all what he was looking for. He gave special attention to the area against the far wall, where the creature tended to sleep, but he found no evidence of blood. He searched until his eyes were tired and his fingers chafed from scooping through the coarse piles. He stopped. He may not have known what he was looking for, but he knew it wasn't here. When he turned, the loaders were staring at him.

"Is everything buttoned down?" he asked.

"Nice and tight," James Mitchell answered in a voice so low and gravelly that it hurt Silas's throat just to hear it.

Silas looked over at the man standing near the cab of the truck. James was tall and broad and square, seemingly built of repurposed cinder blocks; and blown vocal cords aside, he was the man running the show. It was upon his capable shoulders that the responsibility of transport fell. He was serious and technical, ex-military, and he looked at every contract assignment as special ops. Which was exactly the way Silas liked it.

"It looks like we've got our hands full with this one, Dr. Williams," James said, as Silas approached.

"Can't disagree with you. A little heavier than last time."

"We can handle it. We'll be taking all the necessary precautions. Your baby will be arriving safe and sound sometime tomorrow evening."

"Not my baby," Silas said.

"I tried that once, too," James intoned. "Didn't work for me, either."

CHAPTER NINETEEN

"So tell me why we're driving again?" Vidonia was busy blow-drying in the bathroom, bent at the waist, lush hair alternately dripping to the floor and flying away as the hot air blasted over her scalp.

"Precaution," Silas said. "And security. We're expected to fly, and there have been problems in the past. This year we're trucking the gladiator to the location. We can bring along a bigger support team that way, and the whole thing is much less conspicuous."

"Is that what we are, support?"

Silas sat up on the bed, looking for his pants. The alarm clock said five-thirty, and the shades were still dark.

"No, we're the talent; hasn't Ben told you?"

"He said they believed in keeping the talent happy around here."

"They do."

"A three-hundred-mile road trip in a sports car isn't my idea of happiness."

"Not even with me at the wheel?"

"And you aren't the talent, anyway," she said. "Well, at least not in that way." She gave him a mischievous look. "I thought you were the boss."

"Do you usually find yourself waking before the crack of dawn in your boss's bed?"

She flung her hair behind her, showering him with a

mist of tiny droplets. "Well, not typically. Only about every third boss or so." She smiled as she stepped back into the bedroom.

He pulled a fresh white shirt from its plastic sleeve in the closet and pulled the triple-extra-large over his head, buttoning the sleeves but leaving the collar loose. He wrapped his wrist in a gold Rolex, a conflicted concession to his status.

For Silas, anything that cost more than an average man earns in six months didn't just smack of pretension, it rang of it. It veritably gonged. But the watch rivaled the engineering tolerances of biological systems; it ran perfectly and would continue to do so, without a battery, long after time ceased to be a matter of his concern. He *was* genuinely interested by such efficiency, and this provided the thin veneer of justification that he required.

"Nice watch," she said.

He cringed. *That's it, I'm selling it.*

"What are you going to do in the years the contest isn't held in the continental United States?" she asked. She had the dress around the curve of her hips now, pulling it up.

His confusion showed.

"You can't very well truck the contestant to Europe," she said. "You'll have to fly then."

"Oh, the event is always held in the U.S."

"Really," she said, as if she'd never thought about it before. "I suppose they have been. How did you get the other countries to agree to that?"

"Last time's winner gets home-court advantage. It was how the rules were written up at the beginning, and since we've never lost, we're home court."

"I bet the other countries are sorry they signed up for that."

"I'm very certain they are. It pumps a lot of money

into the local economy, not to mention American bioengineering companies."

When they finished dressing, they carried the luggage to the car. Two small suitcases apiece.

"I think you're the only woman I've ever met who
knows how to pack light," he said, as he wedged the
final bag under the hatch.

"Look at this thing," she said, gesturing to the dark
blue vehicle. "I didn't want to spend three hundred
miles with luggage banging against my kidneys. There's
only so much room in this car, and I decided I'd use
my share for breathing, not extra underwear."

"So you're leaving your underwear behind, eh?
Talk like that might get you a promotion."

"Works every time."

Four minutes later, they were merging onto empty
highway and the sun was bleeding up from the east,
coloring the traffic in reds and shadows. The road felt
good beneath him, as it always seemed to at the start
of a road trip. But they had to make one quick stop
before they were free.

When they arrived at the compound, Silas saw
James Mitchell standing in the back lot, trying to assemble the convoy. Silas pulled slowly alongside the
man. In Silas's opinion, "inconspicuous" was hardly
the word that jumped to mind when he looked toward
the line of trucks and vans.

"Having problems?"

"No more than usual," James answered, appearing
not at all surprised to see them. "Most of these egg-
head types wouldn't have lasted two days in the service. Nobody around here seems to know how to
keep a schedule."

"That's what you're for, James."

Silas looked around at the chaos. The big white rig

sat idling at the front of the loose collection of vehicles. It was pathetic.

"You seem to be taking this rather well," Silas said. He would have expected James to be throwing a fit by now with the way things were shaping up.

"I was counting on it."

Silas raised an eyebrow.

"Oh, our special traveler is already well down the road. Left last night, in fact. This big cluster-fuck is a decoy." James gave him a wink. "Just in case."

"Do they know that?"

"Of course not."

"Well, your secret is safe with me, but you won't mind if I don't stick around here to watch the proceedings."

James smiled and waved him on, but as Silas began to pull forward, James seemed to change his mind and motioned for them to stop. Jogging up to the car, he tossed a video cube into Silas's lap.

"Just so we can get ahold of you," he said.

Silas picked up the small, square video communication device. "Do you think you'll need to?"

"You'd better hope not."

THE OPEN road called. Silas answered with a stomp of his right foot that sat Vidonia back in her seat. He knew it was juvenile, but he couldn't stop himself. Anyway, he didn't actually break the speed limit; he just liked seeing how quickly he could get there. He let up on the gas pedal when Vidonia's grip on his knee became painful. He found that her grip eased in direct proportion to the angle of his tachometer needle.

"Boys and their cars," she said, shaking her head.

He rolled the window all the way down and laid his

arm along the spine of the door. It was one hell of a morning. The sun rose high and hot into cloudless sky, and by noon they'd traded the cloying humidity of California for the dry heat of the high desert. Silas turned the air-conditioning off. The wind was enough, and besides, Silas liked the way it made Vidonia's hair dance like a living thing, like she was some ironic, beautiful Medusa.

"This heat reminds me of home," she said. "Except without palm trees."

"Is that good or bad?"

"Both. But home had beaches going for it."

"Now I'm picturing you in a bathing suit."

"You're assuming I wear one."

"Now, there's a new image in my head."

"That was my intent."

"I could get used to this."

"To what?"

"To you. Being here."

"You haven't even eaten my cooking yet."

"You cook, too?"

"Seafood is my specialty."

"So you're that rare woman I've heard legend of. A woman who can both perform a Southern blot analysis and grill up a grouper?"

"Oh, you have no idea," she said.

"How did I get so lucky?"

She was quiet for a long while, and Silas suspected that when she spoke, it would be something significant. Ten more minutes passed in silence, and he knew it would be something bad.

Finally, in a soft voice that almost drowned in the wind, she said, "There's someone back home. His name is John."

"That's odd," he said, keeping his voice even. "That's just what I'd figured his name would be. Or something like it. Jim, maybe, or Jake. Some old name, something common. I'm usually wrong on hunches, though. Funny, this is a time I'd be right." He'd known since the beach, when he'd asked her if she was married. The answer had been no, but he'd sensed there was something more she'd almost said.

She looked out into the desert. He almost spoke but stopped himself with the question on the tip of his tongue. He wouldn't let her off the hook. What she'd say without him asking would be more important than the response to any question. Questions—no matter how carefully worded—always carry their own baggage of expectation, an unspoken optimal response that the asked person is aware of. The answer then becomes about proximity to that response. How close are you willing to come?

"He's different from you."

That was something, at least. "How are we different?" He kept his eyes on the road.

"The important ways."

He looked at her then, and her hair was dancing, reaching into the wind.

"I should tell you we live together . . . or that we . . . lived together before I came here."

"You're close?"

"Close, sure. He slept right on the other side of the bed most nights. Other nights, the couch. Or wherever."

"The couch. I guess he is different from me."

"I told you." She was still looking out into the desert and didn't offer more, didn't make any promises. *John,* he thought. Just an old, common name. Old, common-issue. *Let it be. Let it be.* He forced himself not to ask more.

PHOENIX. A place of cactus and rock and mountains and heat.

Phoenix is a place without history. It is new and air-conditioned. It defies the desert. On the side of the highway, as decoration, colored pebbles lie arranged in intricate Indian designs, pastels and browns and pinks, alternately anthropomorphic or zooplastic—strange totems and zigzags—all of it sloping upward and away from the road, an artistic canvas that five thousand pairs of eyes might see every day. And it goes on for miles, glass buildings and blue skies and mountains looming in the background.

The city isn't so much surrounded by mountains as interwoven with them. But it is not a mountain city, not really.

Phoenix itself is flat. Phoenix is desert. The houses and roads and buildings have accreted *between* the rocky outcrops of higher ground. Human habitation sits everywhere in the lee of stone, as if the city were a liquid poured onto this jagged landscape and had found its level.

Silas and Vidonia arrived in the downtown area at about three. The hotel, the Grand Marq, wasn't hard to find. Vidonia dug their reservations from the clutter of the glove compartment. Two reservations, two rooms. She put one back and let him check in. The desk clerk was more than happy to cancel the second reservation. This week, the hotel could probably book the room almost immediately at triple the normal rate.

Walking back outside to the car, Silas saw where the first of the protesters had assembled their tents along the stony median between the parking lot and the road.

There is hot, and there is hot. And there is Arizona in the summer. In Phoenix, the heat is a ten-pound hammer.

A dozen men and women stood sweating in the sun with their signs, but he knew their numbers would grow as the competition date approached.

The protesters came in all types. There were your animal-rights people, anti-genetics people, anti-technology people, and, of course, your everyday basic religious fanatics. There were also game puritans protesting the corporate sponsorship of the Olympics. And then there were your run-of-the-mill crazies. All united by their desire to see the gladiator event shut down.

That they stood in the Phoenix sun was testament to their commitment.

He knew for certain those tents had been erected illegally on city property, but the Olympic Commission had learned from experience that it was best to ignore them rather than to have them removed. The protest groups craved conflict, and the last thing the program needed was a crowd of riled malcontents screaming police brutality into a hundred rolling news cameras. The commission wanted the media circus to focus on what went on *inside* the dome, not in the parking lots.

Silas climbed behind the wheel and circled the parking lot, making a point to swing near the street. As he slowed past the group of protesters, the words on the back of one woman's shirt caught his attention.

BLOOD SPORT

She turned to look at him as his car rolled past, and he thought he saw recognition in her eyes. He wondered what crossed through her mind in that moment. Her hair was gray and wild, and in her arms she cradled a big cardboard sign with thick block letters painted in black marker.

FOR THE WAGES OF SIN IS DEATH

He shook his head. *Those wages were paid to all men, sinner and saint alike.*

FOR SILAS, the next three days were spent in a whirlwind of activity. He had meetings with regulators by day, dinner parties with dignitaries by evening, and Vidonia by night. Still Vidonia by night, John or no John.

"I met with the president today," he told her, while they ate chicken wings at midnight in the hotel bar.

"President of what?"

He just looked at her. Took another bite.

"You're serious."

"Yep," he said. "We were at a luncheon together. There were several heads of state there."

"They're staying for the competition?"

"Yeah. Most of them are going to spend the entire week here. They were even making friendly wagers."

"What kind of odds were they laying?"

"Not sure, but I think we're the favorite."

"What were they betting?"

"The usual trifles." He took another bite of chicken wing. "You know, sovereign languages, submarines, space stations."

She smiled and thumped his shoulder.

"I don't even want to tell you what language we'll be speaking if we lose," he went on. "There must have been a dozen members of Congress there, too. This thing is getting bigger every time."

"You make it sound like that's a bad thing."

"It's turning into something."

"Into what?"

"I don't know. Maybe a kind of"—Silas paused—"international sociopolitical economic summit."

"That's a lot of words. There's no way you made that up just now."

"I'd been working on it." He turned serious. "Actually, that came from a reporter. I'm not sure I know what this is anymore."

"Any talk of the protesters?"

"They used euphemisms. Mentioned security concerns but nothing specific." And Silas had been grateful for the euphemisms. He wasn't up for high-level talks about protester issues. He thought of the words on that shirt. BLOOD SPORT. A description Silas was having more and more trouble arguing against.

"Next month, in Monterrey, those guys don't realize how lucky they have it."

"Meaning what?"

"Nobody protests the human portion of the Olympics."

She shrugged. "They don't compete to the death."

"The president said something to me. He pulled me aside to ask if we were going to win this thing or not. That's just how he put it: 'Are we gonna win this thing?'"

"What's so wrong with that?"

"Nothing's *wrong* with it. It was the look he had, though. Like it was important that he hear a yes from me."

"What did you say?"

"I gave him his yes."

They finished their wings and took the elevator up to their hotel suite.

He waited until she was naked. "Should I sleep down the hall?" he asked her.

Again, she let her hands be her answer.

PART III

DELUGE

Then they gathered the Kings together
to the place called Armageddon.

—REVELATION, CHAPTER 16, VERSE 16

DELUGE

CHAPTER TWENTY

The Grand Marq was one of the finest and most exclusive hotels in the world. Its triplet towers stood a mere pair of blocks from the Olympic area that dominated the epicenter of the city. To passersby, the Grand Marq's three reflective spires shone like beacons in the desert sunshine, rising daggerlike into the sky and tapering to points somewhere just beneath the feet of God.

Catering exclusively to high-class clientele, the Marq was designed to get attention: this was shock-and-awe luxury at its finest. Prices started at don't even ask. The staff worked hard to see that every amenity was available to its guests. But to a man like Silas, who had spent early childhood at the edge waters of the Mississippi, where you sometimes couldn't tell the end of the swamp from the beginning of the river, and where the people sometimes actually *ate* what they pulled from the flow of brown water, it seemed like just so much conspicuous consumption.

But this was not to say that Silas wouldn't take full advantage of the facilities. Even when you could afford to do so, there was a big difference between buying a neural relaxer and using one if it was made available for free. Or so he told himself again as he lay back on the cushions.

He let the technician drone on and on about how

the "toxins" were being leached from his muscle tissues. It was funny to him how dependent most of this post-new-age bullshit seemed to be on that particular buzzword. *Toxins.* As if the electrodes were little suction cups that drained some invisible poison from him that had been accumulating over the course of a hectic day. He knew the neural relaxer worked because it signaled the brain to release its serotonin cache. Then came requiescence, low-grade euphoria. An alcohol buzz without the alcohol, or the hangover. And like alcohol, it could become addictive very quickly, which was another reason not to buy one.

"Please be quiet," Silas said when the blond technician began talking about the wonders of deep-tissue emulsification. He didn't want to be rude, but he couldn't force himself to listen to a single second more of her ridiculous pseudo-medical jargon.

But there was nothing pseudo about the buzz. That came on quick and strong. There was no disorientation, no feeling of drunkenness. Just warmth, contentment. He reminded himself to tell Vidonia about this later. She'd love it.

He floated.

"You have a call, Dr. Williams," the blonde said.

Silas opened his eyes and saw her holding a small videophone out to him. He hadn't even heard it ring. When he took it, Ben's face considered him from the little screen, a line of empty cages sprawling away behind him. He was in the catacombs beneath the arena, and he didn't look happy.

"Yeah," Silas said.

"Sorry to interrupt, but I really need you to come down here."

"Now?"

"Yeah."

"What's the problem?"

"I don't want to explain over the phone."

"Why?"

"We need a secure line."

"Just a hint, then?"

"You won't believe it."

"That's a hint?"

"It's all the hint you're getting. Trust me, when you get here, you'll understand."

"Okay, I'll be there as soon as I can."

Silas closed the receiver and began plucking off the wires that crisscrossed his arms and legs.

"You shouldn't do that," the blonde said, and her look of alarm made her face almost comical. "You need a cool-down period first. There can be problems. The cleansing of your tissues is only partially complete."

"Sorry, I guess my tissues will have to be a little dirty."

The elevator seemed to take an eternity as it descended, picking up several groups of passengers in its drop to the lobby. It became immediately clear upon his exit to the street that it would be quicker for him to walk the two blocks than to take a cab. Traffic was gridlocked. Somewhere amid his struggle through the humanity-clogged sidewalks, his headache began. It was subtle at first but gathered force as he walked.

Here and there a face would show a flash of recognition when glancing up at him. A few people pointed. But for the most part, he wasn't noticed, just a tall man with a pained expression. By the time he reached the arena, the headache was like no other he had ever experienced.

Can a head actually explode?

He flashed his badge to the guards, and they let him through. At the elevator he inserted his passkey into the console and pushed B3. Descent again, but this time the motion made him reel with pain. The doors opened, and he followed the dark cement corridor for twenty meters before stepping down a side hall. The familiar zoo smells came again, and if it was possible, his head hurt worse.

"What the hell's wrong with you?" Ben whispered, when he saw Silas's face.

Silas hadn't realized it was that obvious. "Toxins," he said.

Ben gave him an incredulous look.

"Don't worry about it. Tell me what was so important that you dragged me down here like this. And why are you whispering?"

Silas followed Ben's gaze through the bars to their gladiator. Inside the small enclosure, it looked even bigger than usual, a shining black monster. There was no other word for it.

Its head almost touched the ceiling as it hulked in the back against the iron wall. Two members of their handling crew stood off to the side, arms folded across their chests.

Ben put a hand on Silas's shoulder and turned his back to the cage, leading them away.

"I think the gladiator can understand what we say," he said, voice low and soft.

"You think it understands English?"

"Yeah, Silas, I do. I really do."

"How?"

"I guess it must have picked it up over months of listening to us talk around it. We should have been more careful. We—"

"No, I mean, how do you know it can understand us? Maybe you're confusing some sort of Pavlovian conditioning for comprehension. Even untrained dogs can learn to associate sounds with food."

"This isn't some ringing bell I'm talking about. This

thing *understands,* and I don't mean just simple words."

"How do you know?"

"Watch," Ben said. He turned and walked back to the men standing by the cage. They were young interns from the eastern district cytology schools, and they shared the same sandblasted expression of shock on their faces.

The gladiator moved forward to the edge of the cage. Ben was careful to stay out of arm's reach.

"Get the zapstick," he said to the taller intern.

The gladiator moved to the back of the cage again, quickly.

That doesn't prove a thing, Silas thought. The zapstick had been used as a motivational device by the handlers since their arrival in the city. It was no great leap that the gladiator could have picked up on the word. A golden retriever would have done the same thing.

Ben flashed Silas a look. "Now put the zapstick down," he said to the intern. "And let's haul out the feed."

The gladiator moved to the front of the cage again in anticipation. Its wings bobbed slightly.

Still doesn't prove anything. It heard "feed" and responded. A simple cue.

The interns hauled out a huge slab of prey food from the supply cart, sharing the red weight of it between them.

"Now, throw the food in the cage." Ben pronounced each word carefully. "But if the gladiator touches it, use the zapstick."

The interns heaved the processed-meat slab through the bars, and then one of them picked up the zapstick from the floor. He held the four-foot stick loosely in his hand, just within striking distance of the food.

The gladiator didn't move.

Its tongue came out of its mouth, and its wings bobbed faster. Its gray eyes crawled over every inch of the meat. But it didn't make a move.

"Never mind," Ben said. "*Don't* use the zapstick if it eats the food."

The handler didn't move, didn't change his stance in the slightest, but the gladiator rushed forward and scooped the meat up in a taloned hand. It bit a huge chunk free and swallowed it down whole.

The intern with the zapstick moved forward a step, closer to the bars. The creature was easily within striking distance of the electrified rod, but it still didn't move away. It looked up briefly at Benjamin and Silas, then returned to its meal.

Holy shit.

The four of them stood and watched the gladiator eat. It was gulping down the last mouthful when finally someone broke the silence. "So what do we do now?" Ben asked Silas.

Silas stared through the bars for a long time before saying anything, and when he did speak, his voice was soft. "I don't know."

SILAS WAS numb as he walked back to his hotel. This was something he'd never suspected, this level of intelligence in the gladiator. After all these months, he'd thought he was beyond being surprised. By anything. He'd considered himself immune to the emotion. But this new piece of the puzzle had caught him off guard.

He'd long suspected the thing was smart. . . . But then a great many animals were merely smart. Merely.

Smart was not such a rare commodity in the animal kingdom. Lions, and wolves, and jackals, and even bears all had their own sort of animal cunning. Most predators did. But this was something different. The thing he'd watched in the cage today had *understood,* and that was a very rare thing, indeed—to understand spoken language. To understand the intricacies of human speech beyond a short list of commands. There was only one animal known that could do that, *Homo sapiens,* and it had taken quite a long time to develop the knack.

Now that the proof was in front of him, it seemed obvious. Silas wondered how he'd missed it for so long. Had the creature shown any other signs? Had there been clues that Silas was too blind to see?

Silas shook his head, oblivious to the strange looks he got on the crowded street. The thing in the cage had understood, and that shouldn't have been possible. That was the bottom line. It shouldn't have been possible. Just as the very existence of the creature shouldn't have been possible.

Silas had been angry at the commission for months now about his loss of control of the project. He'd grown comfortable with that anger. He'd been frustrated and confused, but until now, he'd always felt that it was still a worthwhile endeavor that he was involved in. Even after Tay was killed, even after the confrontation with Baskov at the funeral, even after he'd lost confidence in the gladiator itself, he'd still believed in the ideals of the Games. He'd still believed he was on the right side of the science. Or at least he'd believed that the science justified the side he was on. And he'd believed the protesters, each and every one of them, were fools. Now he wasn't so sure.

He wasn't too sure of anything anymore.

Silas entered the lobby of his hotel and crossed to the elevators. The doors dinged open, and two minutes later he was at the door of his suite. He carded himself inside and turned on the light. He went to the window and opened the curtains. The minibar was a gravity well. He felt the pull.

The cap twisted in his hand, and he drank. It was not smooth. It was not good. But that's what he needed at that moment, a not-good drink. Rough like cordwood. It burned going down.

Silas eyed his watch and did the math. It would be nine P.M. in Colorado. Not too late. He dialed the numbers and listened to rings. On the third ring, his sister answered.

"Hello."

"Sis," Silas said. It was all he had to say.

"Silas!"

"How are things going?"

"Pretty good," she said. "We can't complain."

"Good."

"We've been watching you on the news."

"Are they still running the same old picture?"

"The same one," she said. "You walking out some door with that goofy look on your face."

"I wish they'd update that. I've got at least ten percent more gray in my hair now."

"That picture's only a few months old."

"Exactly."

"Ah, it must be the pressures of fame aging you before your time."

"Yeah. The next thing you know, I'll be walking with a cane and tipping five percent at restaurants."

"I'll start checking out nursing homes for you."

"Don't put me out to pasture yet. So what are these news shows saying . . . the ones you've been watching— anything interesting?"

There was a pause on the line. "You don't sound good," his sister said, ignoring the question. That's how she was. Always concerned and considerate of her big brother.

Silas sighed. "Bad day at the office," he said.

"Anything you can talk about?"

"No." Now it was Silas's turn to be quiet for a long moment. She let him be quiet. Another of her talents. Silas wanted to shift the conversation, make it about something else. "Tell me about your day," he said.

And she did. She told him.

And it was safe, and normal, and dull, and wonderful. Her day. Her life. And that's what he'd needed to hear. That's why he'd called. To hear that people could live like that. To hear that people lived like that day in and day out.

They talked for half an hour. Before he got off the phone, he asked about Eric.

"He's in bed now," she said.

"I figured that. I was just wondering how he was doing."

"He's been busy with a school project lately. A paper he's been writing. He's actually pretty proud of it. He mentioned wanting you to read it when he was done."

"What's it about—genetics?"

"Of course, but it's a little trickier than that. It's about adaptive radiation and the American automobile."

"The evolution of cars?"

"Something like that; he's got it all worked out on paper, comparing the Model T to Darwin's first finch—and then all the later models radiate out from there to fill the niches. SUVs and minivans and sports cars. Just different finches for different niches."

"That's deep stuff for his age."

"Well, he's interested in it."

A long silence again. This time, she broke it. "Are you sure everything's okay?"

"No. But I've got to go, Sis. I'll talk to you later, okay?"

SILAS HATED cocktail parties. He hated the clink of glass on teeth. He hated the food, served in twists of color on white china, more aesthetic than edible. Most of all, he hated the smiles.

It was after ten now, and the party was in full swing. Silas had come straight from his room when he'd gotten off the phone. He scanned the crowd.

The guests stood in loosely shifting clusters around the room, as homogeneous in their affluence as they were diverse in every other conceivable way. They were Congolese, and Canadian, and German, and Indonesian, and three dozen other nationalities, all of them patting one another on the back, trading the same stories back and forth, laughing at each other's jokes—and all of them training their glossy smiles on him as he passed through the crowd. They came from points around the world, the people in this crowd, but really they all came from money. That was their ethnic group.

The members of this crowd didn't point—they were too sophisticated for that—but all had smiles for him. He knew their type well, knew they were excited by their opportunity to brag of being at a party where Silas Williams was present. *That's right,* they'd say later, *the head of U.S. biodevelopment was there. The man of the hour.*

Silas wasn't exactly dressed for the occasion. He still wore the casuals he'd had on for the neural relaxer appointment earlier in the evening, and the gray sweats stood out in sharp relief against the angular penguin suits of the other men. It didn't really matter, though. They probably thought he was making a fashion statement. Among the ladies, low necklines were apparently in style this season, and necklaces of pearl and diamond bobbled across the tops of the women's breasts while they bantered with their power dates.

The vise on his head had finally begun to ease its grip somewhat, and now the pain had subsided to a kind of dull, throbbing ache at his temples. "Toxins" aside, he had to admit he'd been a little nervous there for a while. He didn't know what a brain aneurysm felt like, but it couldn't feel much worse than the headache he was finally climbing out from under.

He turned sideways, sliding between several groups of people that had gathered near the enormous window that comprised the larger portion of the south-facing wall. Beyond the glass, the sky was blank. There were no stars hanging in the distance, only the lights of cars, and buildings, and glowing neon signs that spread below in a carpet of illumination. Standing alone, looking out into that inverted sky, was Baskov.

The old man didn't look happy to see him. "How nice of you to join us," he said. "I was afraid an oversight may have left you without an invitation."

"I never got an invitation," Silas said. "I'm here to see you."

"Consider me at your service. What can I do for you?"

Silas decided to take the direct approach. "The gladiator can understand spoken words."

Baskov's eyes skipped toward the crowd and back again. People were taking notice of the conversation. Baskov turned toward the glass, casting Silas a look that bid him do the same.

"So does my cat," Baskov said softly. "So what?"

"I'd bet a thousand dollars you don't have a cat."

"That's quite beside the point."

"It's not just simple commands. I think this thing understands English, or at least bits and pieces. It understands how the word 'don't' modifies a verb, and that implies an understanding of grammar."

"What the hell are you talking about? It doesn't imply anything. What do you want, Dr. Williams? Really?"

"I want you to reconsider using the gladiator in competition."

"This again? Now?"

"This isn't some animal we trained to understand commands. Whatever this thing knows, it's picked up on its own. Do you understand what that means? This thing either is smart enough to learn English just by listening to it or has some kind of hardwired grammar—but either way, we're going to throw it in the pit tomorrow with a bunch of animals."

Baskov smiled. "You're talking about sentience."

"That's a word that has lost some of its meaning over the last few decades."

"In no small part due to your *Ursus theodorus* project."

"There are shades of gray. But yes, I think we need to at least investigate the possibility. There's a point past which we can't just throw a being to the wolves."

"So now it's a being?"

"I don't know what it is. I never did."

Baskov turned toward the window again and took a deep breath. He was silent for a moment, then leaned closer to the glass, looking down. "Do you see the protesters down there?"

Silas didn't bother to look. "I saw them when I arrived."

"There are more of them at every new competition. I can see them from here. They wave their signs at the cameras and yell for the traffic to honk their horns. They want us shut down, but they have no problem at all accepting the benefits that come from research directly linked to the program. You never hear of them refusing a gene therapy procedure on moral grounds if it is going to save their lives."

"I'm not one of your contributors, and this isn't a sponsor event. I've heard this all before."

"So what would you have me do, hmm?" Baskov turned to face him, and there was anger in his pale blue eyes. "Call the whole thing off? Tell everybody to just go home?"

"I told you before. Withdraw. The world will go on."

"And I told you before that if you were unwilling to deal with the realities of the situation, then you would be replaced."

"Realities of the situation? That's a joke. This isn't reality; it's the twisted dream of a computer nobody can even see."

"Then it's a dream you may find yourself waking from very soon."

"You can't honestly think you're threatening me? You do." Silas stopped himself from laughing but couldn't filter the mirth from his voice. "You greatly overestimate my attachment to this job."

Baskov threw a furtive glance toward the audience that had slowly and subtly begun to gather around them. Silas had noticed them, too. They weren't staring, weren't crowding too close, but nevertheless, they were there, watching in sidelong glances from the corners of their eyes, drinking it all in from a respectable distance. Their conversations were pitched low and moved in a conspicuous rhythm, voices dropping off when Silas or Baskov spoke.

"You greatly overestimate my patience for impudence," Baskov softly responded.

"If you can't tell the difference between impudence and common sense," Silas said, voice rising, "then you're as addled as the man you put in charge of design." He no longer cared who watched. Let them gawk. Whose reputation was he trying to protect, anyway?

"You forget yourself, Dr. Williams. If I hear one more word of dissent, one more single word, then your career is over. I won't hesitate. The choice is yours."

Silas leaned forward. "Fuck you."

He was pleased to see not a single glossy smile pointed at him on the way out.

CHAPTER TWENTY-ONE

Silas opened his eyes to bright sunlight pouring through the window of his hotel suite. Vidonia was already gone. His arms wandered across her side of the rumpled bed, and it was still warm. The pillow still cupped the delicate negative of her head.

"Vidonia?" he called.

The suite's answer was silence. He swung his feet to the plush carpeting and ran a hand through his curly hair. Damn, he felt good. Far too good. He tried not to inspect the reasons closely. It felt like a weight had been lifted off his shoulders, and that was good enough.

He took a long, hot shower, and afterward, while he was toweling himself dry, there came a knock on the door.

"Who is it?"

"Ben."

Silas wrapped a towel around his midsection, walked to the door, and twisted the knob. Ben stepped inside. He stepped over to the freshly made bed and promptly threw himself back on it, blasting the covers out at the edges. He laced his fingers behind his head, and the smile that came to his face was odd, almost admiring, if a smile could be such a thing.

"What?" Silas said to the strange look.

"I'm trying to decide if I want to kiss you or punch you."

"You've already punched me once. That was your freebie."

"That's true. Okay, I'll kiss you, then." Ben sat up.

"No, that's okay, I'll pass. It's too early in the morning."

"It's noon."

"It is? Shit, I haven't slept this long in months." Silas stepped into the bathroom. "Now, what has you so emotionally aroused this morning?" he asked, through a mouthful of toothpaste. "Has you showing up at my door with kissing or punching on your mind."

"As if you didn't know," Ben said.

"You heard, then, about last night."

"Yeah. Everybody's heard."

"The media?"

"Yeah, but Baskov's people are playing it down."

"Have they said who my replacement is going to be?"

"No, I didn't hear anything about you being replaced."

Silas stuck his head out the bathroom doorway, toothbrush jutting from one corner of his mouth. "What do you mean?"

"People are talking, but nobody has said anything about you being fired."

"Shit," Silas said, sliding back into the bathroom. He spit in the sink. "Nothing about a replacement? Nothing about me being fired? Are you sure?"

"Yeah, so far."

"That's strange."

"What's strange about it?"

"Well, I guess that means I'm still in charge of this program, then."

"That seems pretty unlikely."

"Hmm." Silas kept brushing his teeth.

"You can't usually tell your boss to fuck off and still keep your job," Ben said. "That sort of thing almost automatically *implies* a termination of employment. Are you sure Baskov's people haven't called you yet?"

"No." Silas walked out of the bathroom and hit the button on the vid-phone. "The phone still works."

"Maybe you *are* still the boss, then."

"I'm not sure if I should be relieved or disappointed."

"You've got to pick one. Then just go with it."

Silas didn't smile.

"I myself usually prefer relief to disappointment," Ben said. "Particularly where matters of unemployment are concerned."

Silas sat on the edge of the bed. That yoke that had lifted from his shoulders slowly shifted back into its familiar position.

"What are you going to do?" Ben asked.

"I guess I'll just continue on until somebody says I shouldn't. Where's Vidonia?"

"Haven't seen her. Breakfast, probably. Speaking of, let's grab something."

Silas pulled his jeans on, feeling for his wallet. He hit the switch on the way out.

As THE day progressed, Silas was made aware of several wildly divergent and sensationalized accounts of what had transpired between him and Baskov the night before. The break between the program head and the chair of the Olympic Commission was huge news, and it was covered to varying degrees of accuracy by all the major networks.

In one of the accounts, Silas was described as actually throwing a drink into the old man's face. Silas shook his head in disbelief as he watched the news programs from his hotel suite and decided that he hated the media even more than he hated cocktail parties.

As Ben had told him earlier, Baskov's people were definitely putting a minimalist spin on things. In the accounts played during the pre-show special, Silas and Baskov were said to have simply shared a heated discussion over differences of opinion. "Anyone who says otherwise," Baskov's planning commissioner said during a televised interview, "is simply attempting to manufacture a story for their own ends. This was a nonevent. The fact of the matter is that these two men are friends, remain friends, and look forward to working with each other in the future."

"Does this mean that Dr. Williams will remain head of Olympic biodevelopment for the next games?" the blond interviewer asked.

"Dr. Williams has expressed some interest in pursuing other ambitions in the future, but right now he is completely focused on seeing that the U.S. gladiator brings home a gold medal for us all tonight."

Lying fuck.

For his own part, Silas decided it best to simply stay out of the public eye altogether. He didn't trust what he'd say if asked a direct question. It was apparently not politically expedient for Baskov to fire him on the very eve of the competition, so for the time being, Silas still held the reins of the project, however tenuous and temporary his grip. With the situation being what it was, he reasoned his efforts could best be utilized behind the scenes.

Expressing great regret, he canceled all his interviews and instead pushed Ben to the forefront, encouraging the networks to render all their questions to him. The young cytologist took to the limelight like a duck to water, and Silas wondered why he hadn't made the change earlier.

Silas gave no instructions to his young protégé, but when asked tough questions by interviewers, Ben gave the company line on the relationship between Baskov and Silas. There was no breach, no problem at all. And all's well that ends in a gold.

CHAPTER TWENTY-TWO

The Olympic arena was a steep bowl of stone and iron eighteen stories tall, within which more than one hundred and thirty thousand people could be crammed, safely or otherwise. The fighting pit lay inverted at the very bottom, a deep oval depression one hundred yards long by twenty-five yards wide. Although the floor of the pit lay a full dozen yards beneath the upper lip of the oval, the arena organizers had taken the precaution of spreading an enormous net of carbon fiber across the opening at the top—a barrier between spectator and spectacle that didn't sacrifice visibility.

The bowl-within-a-bowl construction allowed for maximum visual access while also providing the security of heavily reinforced walls. The sides of the pit were perfectly smooth except for the narrow creases that outlined the edges of the many doors. There were dozens of them equally spaced along the walls, and on each was painted a different national flag. The floor of the pit was sawdust two feet thick.

It was easy to pick out the weakness of the setup.

"And the tensile strength?" Silas asked.

The engineering supervisor smiled indulgently. He stood at the very lip of the pit, one foot resting on the carbon-fiber cable, one finger casually advancing the clip screen he held cradled in the nook of his right forearm.

"I don't seem to have the figure here with me, but I can assure you, nothing is going to get past this web."

"Your assurances aside, I still need to know the specs on this wire."

The engineering supervisor sighed and looked out over the webbing. There was no doubt which TV network version of Silas this man believed in. He obviously considered Silas to be a pain in the ass, and worse, a whining diva who was sticking his nose where it didn't belong. He gave the cable a solid kick, and it twanged harmoniously for a long second. "I suppose I can dig up the numbers from somewhere. But these things were meant to tow barges. Even if a gladiator did manage to get this high up the pit walls, there's no way it could snap one of these lines. I don't care what kind of muscles you gave the damned thing."

Silas looked through the mesh and down onto the killing floor. "Get me the numbers as quick as you can. Big muscles. Huge. You wouldn't believe it."

IT WAS late afternoon, and Silas was in the catacombs beneath the arena. Even through all the distance of cement above him, he could hear that the crowd had begun to gather. He could feel their voices in the soles of his feet. The walls themselves reverberated with their restless energy.

The gladiator was pacing now. It moved in slow figure eights, like a panther confined too long in a cage too small. Like a predator eager to be set free.

Did it know what was coming? Did it yearn for it?

Down the long hall, lights drooped on chains from the ceiling, creating pools of brightness that swayed slightly between segments of subtle shadow. Silas could hear the grunts of the others. He could smell their animal musk. Now and then, handlers, and trainers, and scientists from other teams would pass by on their way from somewhere to somewhere, and they would glance at the black thing that paced in the cage with the American flag on the door. Sometimes they would stop and stare for a moment, these men and women, as if trying to believe what they were looking at. Other times, they would quicken their pace.

Silas felt no curiosity about their creations. He had no desire to take the lap around the catacombs and see what his fellow geneticists had made for their countries.

As time passed, the thrum of the crowd slowly built. More than a subtle vibration in concrete, it was audible now, or at the edge of it. The gladiator kept pacing.

Silas stood well back from the bars, arms folded across his chest. The creature would very likely be dead before the night was over, and he felt, standing there, as if he were witness to something. Some great thing that had gone wrong even now, and he was powerless to see it clearly. So he watched, hoping to recognize what he might have missed.

Silas recalled Baskov's amusement at his use of the word "being" in reference to the gladiator. Silas wasn't sure how to think of the creature anymore, but he had no delusions. "Being" or not, he knew exactly what it would do if it got loose. People would die. Maybe a lot of people. Maybe a huge number of people.

Five minutes later, when Vidonia touched the back of his neck, he didn't jump. He'd seen her coming in the gladiator's reaction. He'd seen her in its crouch, its predatory stare into the space behind him.

"Did you get it?" he asked.

"Yes." She handed him the papers, and he flipped through them one by one. "You don't have anything to worry about," she said. "The tensile strength of those cables would probably stop a freight train going fifty miles per hour. Nothing in the competition even comes close to the kind of mass that would be required to snap one of those lines."

He handed back the papers, wondering why he didn't feel relieved.

"But there's something else you should know," she said.

"What?"

"The protesters have begun to organize outside. They're planning a march of some kind."

"Is it bad?"

"Not real bad. Not yet. But I thought you should be made aware."

"And the police?"

"They're a presence. A very solid presence. I don't think you have to worry yet, but I figured you'd want to hear about it. It's not going to play well on the news."

"I could give a shit about the news," he snapped. "What kind of numbers are we talking about?"

"Maybe three hundred, college age, mostly, but there's a behind-the-scenes constituency running the group."

"There always is."

"They're doing all the usual noise and bluster, but they're at least preaching nonviolence."

"So far," Silas said.

They watched as the gladiator began to pace again.

"What time is it?" Silas asked.

She looked at her watch. "Two hours," she said, answering the question he was really asking.

"Time enough for a few more precautions."

"ON WHOSE authority?" The man's voice on the line was shrill, alarmed. There was no video link to go with the voice, but Silas could imagine the man perfectly—short, spare, nearing the end of a career that had gone alarmingly off the tracks somewhere.

"Mine," Silas said.

"It'll frighten people," the voice said.

"I don't give a damn who it'll frighten," Silas said. "The U.S. contestant won't compete without it, and don't give me any shit about time constraints. The ice blowers are already being used in the catacombs. Some of the teams are using them as 'motivational devices' right now."

"I know that. The ice blowers I have no problem with. We already have plans to use them. It's the live rounds that have me worried."

"Do it."

"Just during the U.S. events?"

"Yeah, just us. That's fine."

"It would make a lot of people nervous."

"It'll add drama. Think of the ratings."

"I think I'll have to get verification for this from the commission first."

"Listen to me. I'm head of the U.S. program until someone tells me otherwise, and as head, I'm telling you that I need these security measures."

"I understand that, but—"

"I'll take care of the commission, and I'll take full responsibility. If you don't start on this immediately and something does go wrong, I'll see you receive full responsibility for the consequences."

There was silence on the line. *Another vote for the pain-in-the-ass, drink-throwing network TV version,* Silas thought.

"Okay," the man said, finally. "You want it, you got it."

Dial tone.

"Do you think he'll really do it?" Vidonia asked.

"I don't know," Silas said. "But it was worth a try."

CHAPTER TWENTY-THREE

Baskov tried to buttress his display of calm with a drink. He sipped his scotch with deliberation, staring out through the holo-glass. "When did he call?"

"About five minutes ago," said the security foreman. He was a short, hawk-faced man with a dark comb-over splayed across a pale gleam of scalp. His agitation showed in his stance—bent forward, awkward, arms flailing in gestures too dramatic for any self-respecting man with a decent-size pair to dangle. Baskov had known something was wrong the moment he'd shuffled his way into the skybox.

"What did you tell him?" Baskov asked.

"I told him I was going to talk to the commission."

"And what did he say to that?"

"He said he'd deal with the commission, and I should just do as he said."

Baskov put a hand on the man's thin shoulder; he could feel the narrow bones beneath his jacket. "Thank you for bringing this to the commission's attention. You did the right thing. Dr. Williams has been having some emotional problems lately, and he's prone to overreaction."

Baskov released the man's shoulder and took another drink.

"What do you want me to do?"

"Go ahead and provide the extra icers. I don't see what that could hurt."

"And what about . . . the guns?"

"The icers are part of why we don't need guns."

"So no guns?"

Baskov considered this for a moment. "We'll indulge Dr. Williams's paranoia. One armed guard in full regalia. I want him dressed sharp, though, stationed somewhere conspicuous. If we try to hide him off to the side, spectators will get jumpy. I'd rather dress him up for display so they assume it's ornamental. Which, I guess, it is. But I want him standing there for all of the contestants, not just ours. And no other weaponry. I don't want to start a panic down there."

The security foreman nodded and scuttled toward the door.

"Wait," Baskov said. "One more thing. I want radio contact with the guard. I'm not sure how much I trust this situation, and I'd hate to have him do something rash. Get me a transmit into his ear, something subtle. Can you do that?"

"Yes."

The security foreman left quietly, closing the door behind him.

Baskov turned back to the glass. It was an amazing view. After all these years, he still hadn't grown tired of it. So far, this particular view of the arena had always meant victory. A gold medal. Tonight he wasn't so sure.

His informants in the warren had disturbing news about the Chinese contestant. Over the last several months, the Chinese had done their best to keep their gladiator away from prying eyes, but now that it was caged below the arena, a number of the arena handlers had seen it. The description was not encouraging.

Night fell, and the lights of the arena came on one cluster at a time, pushing the shadows ever higher up the stands.

Baskov smiled as the stands collected their asses. People flowed downward into their seats in colorful trickles of bright clothing. Yellows and blues and greens and reds. Tiny rainbow ants. At the base of the pit far below, prep teams combed the sawdust with giant rakes, evening out rough spots on the killing floor as a last preparation for the competition.

Banks of speakers arranged at intervals around the arena chirped loudly in unison as the announcers powered up their system for the show.

The door swung inward as the first group of guests arrived in the skybox. Baskov had handshakes for them, and smiles and nods. Twenty minutes later, the skybox was brimming.

The competition was at hand. It was zero hour.

"Where's Silas?" someone asked.

CHAPTER TWENTY-FOUR

Evan sat and stared at the glowing screen. He sat until his legs cramped, then grew numb. He climbed to his feet only when dehydration drove him to the faucet for a long, gulping draft of cool water. He drank greedily and splashed his face and neck.

This was a test, he was sure of it.

He sat again before the screen, racked by the possibility that he might have missed something. Some flicker on the screen, some hint of a message.

Hours later, when the urge to evacuate his bladder became too much, he stood and relieved himself into the garbage can, never taking his eyes off the screen.

He stood vigil for what was to come.

He listened to the sound of the waves.

Sometimes it was just static, but other times, the waves were unmistakable. The most beautiful sound he had ever heard.

Pea was close. He could feel it. Right on the other side of the plasma screen.

He could feel other things, too, though he didn't understand their meanings. Remnant echoes left behind in his skull during his last trip inside. Flashes in his head. The world was on the verge of some great change.

The gladiator, he knew, had something to do with it. And that bastard Baskov. He couldn't be sure what, but the time was fast approaching. He didn't know how all the pieces fit together.

Pea was the one. Pea was the one who knew all the secrets.

All Evan knew was that the world would soon be different.

Baskov would pay for what he'd done. Pea would have a plan.

Pea must have a plan.

Evan crouched in the darkness and waited.

CHAPTER TWENTY-FIVE

*T*he crowd.

Protesters congealed at street corners. Black asphalt, white concrete. Streetlights translated distance into discrete pools of illumination. The Olympic arena rose like a blister, glowing up at the night sky, circled by parking lots and low gray buildings. And circled beyond that by larger Phoenix itself, the city and its suburbs, and finally by the mountains.

Because it is necessary for a march to begin at a remove from its final destination, the crowd of protesters gathered here, on Seventh Avenue, some distance from the arena. Here traffic had stopped, a given-up thing. Cars were abandoned in the throng.

From above, the crowd appeared as a living organism, a single amoeboid mass, pseudopodia curling down city blocks, bunched into muscular potential.

Only at street level was the crowd's multicellular nature manifested. Men and women in T-shirts and sandals and hats and backpacks—the new protester class. They were young, for the most part, this proletariat; they were educated and considered themselves enlightened and kind. They were turgid with righteousness. They had many solid and steadfast views about the world and their place in it—about science and religion, and about themselves—and they were going to disrupt these Games if they could.

Men in dark ties directed from the sidelines, gray bullhorns clutched in fisted hands. These men in ties also thought themselves enlightened, also thought themselves righteous, though they harbored few misapprehensions about their own kindness—and each of them, to a man, understood that the difference between a crowd and a mob was defined simply by the presence of a nervous system. And they were that nervous system.

Uniformed police watched it all from a distance, a safe some-blocks-off distance, positioned between the crowd and the arena, clutching riot shields. Phoenix was a clean city, a modern model of neatness and efficiency, and the police took comfort in the knowledge that there wouldn't be much to throw if the crowd turned ugly. There were no rocks in the streets, no bricks, or cinder blocks, or chunks of wood. All the garbage cans and benches had been removed days ago. If the crowd was going to throw things, it would have to throw things it had brought.

Muffled in the distance, a cheer went up in the bright lights of the arena. The opening ceremonies. The Games were about to begin.

The men in dark ties lifted their bullhorns. Slogans were shouted, amplified.

In the distance, another voice rose as if in response—a commentator's voice broadcast from a thousand speakers, booming from the arena walls, rising into the hot Phoenix darkness: "Welcome, everyone, to the gladiator competition of the thirty-eighth Olympic Games!"

In the street, the crowd convulsed and began to move.

The march on the arena had begun.

THERE WAS a knock on the door.

"Who is it?" Silas said.

"Open the door," came Ben's voice.

The door swung inward, and Ben stepped through.

"They're starting," Ben said.

"Then you're going to be late," Silas said.

"You mean *we're* going to be late," Ben said. "Hey, what the hell are you wearing?"

"I'm all about comfort tonight," Silas answered.

Ben looked down at his own tuxedo, a pained expression on his face. "I'm that overdressed?"

Silas was wearing faded jeans and a white tee. Bare feet. "No."

"You're not going," Ben said, realization dawning.

"Exactly."

"You have to go."

"No, I don't."

"You're the program head."

"I'm also persona non grata among the upper echelon of the commission, remember? Besides"—Silas flipped Ben's collar up—"you make this look good."

Ben smoothed the collar back down. Against the far wall of the hotel room, the holo-screen was quietly babbling the pre-show, handsome talking heads talking, point and counterpoint, men calling one another by their first names the way people never do in real conversation. *Back to you, John. Thank you, Rick.*

"I'll have a better view from here, anyway," Silas said, picking up the controller. He hit the button, and the image on the holo-screen changed, showing the arena from a different camera angle. He ran through several more before settling for a close-up of the battle floor. Ben could almost count the individual shavings of sawdust.

Just then Vidonia emerged from the bathroom. Ben

looked her up and down. Slacks. Blouse. No dress. "You, too?" Ben said.

"Best seats in the house are right here." She rubbed the foot of the bed.

"I can't believe you guys are throwing me to the lions like this."

"Go get 'em, Tarzan," she said.

"Helix is proud of you," Silas added.

The overzealous voice of a commentator broke in on the TV: "Welcome, everyone, to the gladiator competition of the thirty-eighth Olympic Games!"

"Better hurry," Silas said. "It's starting."

"—OF THE thirty-eighth Olympic Games!"

Baskov tuned out the commentator's voice and focused his attention on the people eddying within the skybox. They were men in suits, for the most part, with pretty women at their elbows. They were businessmen, moneyed men, politicians. Many he knew personally; others were strangers, but nearly all made a point of shaking his hand and congratulating the commission on bringing another gladiator program to fruition.

"It's going to be quite a night," he assured them. His hand was sore from it, his smile worn thin.

Still no Silas. He looked at his watch. *Good.* The doctor had apparently known enough to stay away. Having to deal with Silas would have been just another irritation he didn't need.

Baskov turned back toward the glass to stave off further rounds of salutations and looked down to the floor of the arena a hundred and twenty feet below.

He touched the glass with his index finger, and the pane in front of him opaqued slightly. A holographic image of the pit zoomed toward him, magnified a dozen times. His eyes had a choice now. They could focus on the close-up image in the glass or through it to the actual fighting pit far below.

The crowd in the stands cheered as the commentator's voice modulated upward. Baskov didn't bother to understand the words being spoken; their meaning was clear. Two flags rose on opposite sides of the oval.

The matchup was decided by a complex system of ranking and lottery. The winners of the first rounds would advance into the second, and so on, and so on. A classic pyramidal elimination. He looked at the flags and saw Argentina and France would be first.

Icers stood at intervals around the periphery of the oval. Near the commentator booth, he saw the armed guard, light glinting off his chrome helmet. Baskov touched the dial of the two-way clipped inside his breast pocket. "Can you hear me?" he said softly.

The guard shifted, and his arm came up, touching the side of his helmet. "I can hear you," said a voice from Baskov's pocket. Too loud.

Baskov turned the knob. "Just stand there and look pretty. Don't do anything unless I explicitly tell you. Do you understand?"

"Yes," the voice came again, softer now.

"Do nothing."

"Yes, I hear you."

"Absolutely nothing."

"Yes, I hear you."

The flags were at the top of their poles, and the crowd was on their feet. Inside the skybox, people shifted toward the windows, jockeying for visibility. The glass was soon blotted with gawkers, except for a two-foot gap on either side of Baskov, where no one dared encroach.

Voices in the skybox grew louder, faces pressed to glass, staring down.

Baskov had been here, at this moment, many times. He watched the faces. There was a unique thrill that pervaded these nights—even Baskov felt it—that stretched back through time to something older, more basic. The Romans had only discovered, not invented, it. When all the artifice fell away, what remained was this: two living creatures trying to kill each other. It was nothing less than the original sport.

A few weeks from now, the other Olympics would begin. Men jogging in tracksuits. But *this* now—

—this was the real shit.

The noise of the crowd spiked. They knew it, too.

Baskov smiled.

Distant movement, and down in the pit, a door began to open.

SILAS SAT on the bed next to Vidonia, their eyes locked on the TV. A graphic of the French flag flapped in the lower-right corner of the screen.

The spectacle of it washed over them. The beautiful fucking spectacle, tens of thousands of people on their feet.

It was a science competition, Silas reminded himself. Not some competitive athletic event. It was surreal—a science competition that hundreds of millions of people would watch. There was only a single rule: no human DNA. All else was wide open. The most profound endeavors have the fewest rules: love, war.

The event was many things. Some good, some barbaric. But among them, this: it was the greatest show on the planet.

Silas reached for her hand.

BASKOV TOUCHED the window again, and the spot in front of him zoomed even larger until the floor of the pit spread across his entire field of view.

The door with the French flag slid up into the wall. At first there was only darkness there, a shadowed rectangular hole eight feet wide by ten feet tall.

Slowly, a shape moved color into the shadow.

Something green and scaly and covered in sporadic tufts of hair.

It was low to the ground and moved like the crack of a whip, a thing part alligator, part wolf, with eyes that didn't point in the same direction.

Leave it to the French.

To Baskov, it seemed that countries sometimes put out gladiators simply to show they could, without any particular competitive consideration. In reality, the French gladiator was probably less dangerous than the constituent species from which it was assembled. If the French had lacked the demonstrated ability to successfully cross phyla (a tricky thing, even if you knew what you were doing), then they certainly shouldn't have made their attempt on the world stage. There are basic and fundamental differences between the physiologies of reptiles and mammals, which resisted crossing. As Baskov watched the creature move into the light, he wondered how many distorted siblings it had left behind. How many tries had they made to produce this one fighter?

The tragic creature moved farther into the arena, dragging a long wire-haired tail behind it through the sawdust.

The spectators cheered. In Baskov's experience, they always cheered, no matter the competitor.

Years ago, before the gladiator competition, there'd

been problems with gene doping and genetic tweaks. Web-footed swimmers. Myostatin freaks. Then testing caught up, and the Games enforced the ban.

But the crowds had still wanted the freak show.

They'd wanted *this*.

Science had wanted it, too—an arena to showcase its newest art form.

So the freak watchers were given the gladiator competition. The single event where genetic engineering was allowed. It became the most popular event in the Games.

And the most vilified.

A second door began its slow ascent. The strange French weregator didn't even notice.

Behind the Argentina door was something that lacked the French contestant's seeming docility. Big furry forelimbs dug at the sawdust while the door rose. A head pushed under, then shoulders, a long torso. The creature was out in a flash of brown; and in another instant, it froze, locking eyes on the combatant across the arena.

Baskov was impressed, he had to admit. He hadn't expected anything like this from Argentina. The gorilla hybrid had claws at the ends of long, muscular arms. Its mouth was a gaping maw of teeth, borrowed from somewhere in the order Carnivora.

It surged across the sawdust, kicking up plumes of wood chips in its four-legged charge. The weregator finally noticed and turned, baring its teeth.

The two collided in an explosion of flesh and bone.

Even Baskov was taken aback by the scope of the violence. Their modes of attack were primitive but effective. They latched their jaws onto each other and shook. The weregator had Isaac Newton on its side, but mass only counts for so much. In the end, it was those claws that decided it.

The gorilla thing sank its teeth deeper into a shoulder, tightening its hold. Then it simply began digging into the side of the scaly creature in the same way a dog might dig a hole in the ground. There was blood, then the sound of cracking ribs. The weregator loosened its hold and tried to get away, but it was no use. The gorilla thing held fast and continued digging. The French contestant screamed when its abdominal wall was breached, and then organs spilled out in bright loops, piling between the gorilla thing's back legs exactly like the dirt behind a digging canine. It was fantastic.

The fight lasted six minutes. The victor was left to feed for another three. The French flag came down, leaving the flag of Argentina flapping alone.

The crowd roared.

When the door slid open again, the icers distended from the walls, blowing freezing clouds of CO_2; the survivor was maneuvered back into its pen.

The men and women in the skybox drifted from the windows, smiles on their satisfied faces. "Damned good match" seemed to be the consensus.

The crowd thrummed outside. What would their reaction be to the strange U.S. gladiator? Baskov wondered. Would they roar? Would they scream?

The cleanup crew busied themselves in the arena. They chained the carcass of the weregator to the back of a small tractor and hauled it away, methodically raking the path smooth behind it. Several others stayed behind to bag up the largest stray clumps of tissue.

Little time was wasted between matches. When the arena was clean, the announcer's voice came again. It would be Saudi Arabia vs. Australia. This match would be even better, Baskov thought.

Two new flags went up the poles. The skybox crowd—

most with freshened drinks in their hands—shifted back against the glass.

The door with the Aussie flag opened first, and Baskov knew immediately why the Australians had been so secretive about their creation. There was certainly no rule, implied or otherwise, that required a gladiator be constituted from species native to the particular country it represented. Such a rule would have put Africa at a prohibitive advantage. But for Australia, it seemed to be a matter of national pride. Their contestant didn't just step into the arena, it hopped.

The crowd roared, the people in the skybox smiled, and Baskov had to admit it was kind of cute, in a predatory, rip-your-head-off sort of way.

While not so difficult as mammal-reptile crosses, marsupial-placental hybrids were usually just as painful to look at. Like the Argentinean contestant, the Aussie gladiator was surprisingly sophisticated. It was built like a giant kangaroo but armed with bulk and teeth as no kangaroo he'd ever seen. The arms were long and powerfully thick, terminating in vicious hooked talons.

It was too good, almost. Baskov remembered reading once about a species of carnivorous kangaroo that became extinct tens of thousands of years ago, leaving only its bones lying buried in the sun-scorched earth. Perhaps the Australians had made a breakthrough in DNA extraction technology. Perhaps their gladiator hadn't been so difficult to come by, after all. Baskov made a mental note to file a petition of display against the Australians after the Games were over. If they *had* come up with some new tricks for extracting the code of extinct species from fossil bones, then it was only fair that everybody know them.

The other door began to open, and the 'roo jumped away from the sudden movement. It turned and lowered its head to stare under the rising iron, digging its long front limbs into the sawdust.

From beneath the Saudi door slid a long, low bear of a thing.

The crowd roared.

It was built like a wolverine but larger, with a flatter head. There was no flashiness about the beast, nothing that jarred or caught the eye. To those unfamiliar with nature's handiwork, this could be mistaken for one of her own. It was like something you'd expect to see on a nature vid shot in some exotic out-of-the-way place. It wasn't a creature you could put a name to, but it *looked* like it should exist. Baskov knew the ones that looked normal were usually the most dangerous.

The creature locked its eyes on the 'roo, then squealed, a porcine scream of alarm. The two beasts froze for a moment. Then they charged.

The crowd roared again—a noise like a runaway freight train rising up through Baskov's feet and legs, shaking the glass in the skybox.

The 'roo jumped high and spun away from the snapping jaws. The jaws followed. The 'roo jumped again, then came in for a quick attack—a mash of fur and skin, the snap of jaws, and the 'roo stayed just out of reach.

For a moment, Baskov was afraid things were going to be one-sided; those kinds of matches were never fun to watch. You couldn't help but feel a little sorry for a creature running for its life. But the 'roo turned and stood its ground, attempting to connect with a series of jabs as the Saudi gladiator came at it.

The wolverine thing was too fast and took advantage of its lowered angle of attack. The 'roo had to bend down to punch, and the wolverine thing went for the descending throat. Twice it almost got it. Twice the 'roo flinched back at the last second. When the wolverine thing came in for the third time, the 'roo countered with a kick from a *hind* limb, sending it sprawling through the sawdust.

The crowd screamed. Around him, in the skybox, voices shouted, faces pressed to the glass.

The kangaroo thing was smart to change strategies, but Baskov knew it would not be enough. Even before blood had been drawn, he could tell the 'roo was doomed. Against a taller enemy, one it could strike at from an upright position, the 'roo might have had a chance. But against something long and low to the ground, it couldn't use the cutlery at the end of its arms without bringing its throat within striking distance.

The wolverine thing charged again, snapping at air.

The 'roo countered with a glancing kick to the broad skull. The wolverine thing screamed again, baring a wide row of jagged teeth. The two circled each other.

As Baskov thought it might, the fight ended at the very first show of red.

The wolverine thing came in again and drove the Aussie combatant off balance. When the 'roo tried to fend off the Saudi gladiator with a jab, the wolverine caught it by the throat, pulled it to the ground, and ripped out its windpipe.

Tissue flung away in a spray of gore as the wolverine thing pulled free a chunk of living meat and shook it violently in its teeth.

It took one second.

The crowd roared again while blood spurted the sawdust red. The 'roo thrashed in death. It was over.

The vibration rose up through Baskov's feet again as the crowd roared, shaking the stadium.

Again, the victor was allowed to feed for a short while. Again, the icers moved in and brushed the survivor back into its holding pen. Again, the loser's flag was lowered. And again, the people in the sky-box moved back away from the window to freshen their drinks and grab a bite from the complimentary buffet.

Baskov glanced down at the glass in his own hand and noticed it was empty.

He was a drinking man, he'd admit that. Perhaps a heavy-drinking man.

On his darker days, those days when he was tempted to be honest with himself, maybe he'd acknowledge being a step beyond that, even. A step toward being what his father would have called a *serious* drinking man. But not a drunk. Never that. No, drunks couldn't get things done the way he could. Drunks didn't run corporations.

The bartender slid another scotch toward him. Baskov dropped two notes on the counter, and as he took the first sip, his eyes snagged on someone across the top of the glass. At the far end of the skybox, the man's shaggy blond mane set him apart from the older, conservative crowd, and when the face turned into full view, Baskov recognized Ben Wells.

Baskov scanned the crowd around him and was glad to see the young man wasn't accompanied by his troublesome boss. Ben was alternately munching on a plate of chicken wings and talking heatedly with a man Baskov recognized as a representative from a pharmaceutical company—a pharmaceutical company that happened to own a controlling interest in a particularly lucrative bacterial gene patent.

When the announcer came on again, Baskov moved back to his position near the glass, and the flags of Germany and India climbed their poles. He could rouse only faint interest in which flag would come down; his mind was already ahead, on the U.S.-China competition. And he was certain that would be the matchup they'd face, the United States vs. China. What he wasn't at all certain about was which flag would be coming down after *that* fight.

The most recent intelligence reports, which they'd paid so dearly for, had been anything but encouraging. China was going to be a huge obstacle.

He took a deep swig of his scotch, keeping Ben in the corner of his eye.

CHAPTER TWENTY-SIX

Silas unwound himself from Vidonia and collapsed next to her on the bed, breathing heavily. She was smiling now, and propped her head up with her hand, elbow planted deeply in the soft pillow. The flickering light of the holo-screen lent a shifting, semi-strobe quality to her features, and he thought again of how beautiful she was, the angular nose balanced perfectly by the full mouth.

She didn't say anything at first, just looked at him with that soft, self-satisfied grin he'd come to know so well, a sweep of dark hair cascading casually over her cheek.

He closed his eyes, enjoying the sensation of her body pressed closely against his. It was in these moments, just after, that he felt closest to her, when their bodies were theirs alone again and he could still feel the connection, like words unspoken between them. She never talked during these times. She looked into his face and smiled. But what she was thinking, he had no idea. She'd tell when she was ready.

He opened his eyes and looked over the tops of his feet at the glowing images.

"Indonesia and South Africa," she said, in anticipation of his unspoken question. She was good at that.

The two creatures were so poorly constructed, and so tangled in battle, that he couldn't be sure where one began and the other ended. Finally, they broke, and the dichotomy became clear.

"Iguana-lion meets bull-hyena-leopard?" she said.

Silas looked closely at the creatures and had to agree that was a pretty fair assessment of the combatants. The bull thing had a clear advantage at this point, and was using its enormous, twisted horns to drive its adversary across the arena. The horns were eight feet wide, asymmetrical, and as thick as a man's calf. One curled slightly forward, and the other spiraled out to the side for four feet before hooking upward in a vicious barb.

The crowd went absolutely crazy as the iguana-lion backed itself into the corner, hissing and pawing at the air. It had nowhere left to go.

The bull roared as no bull would, then charged. The impact was amazing. Silas clearly heard the snap-crackle of bone splintering as the iguana-lion was driven into the unyielding iron. Purple loops of gut spurted along the wall precisely the way a frog's guts might squirt out from beneath the shoe of a sadistic child.

Whether there was still life left in the carcass, Silas didn't know, but the bull spun the body on its bizarre horns and sent it tumbling into the air like an off-luck rodeo clown. It landed in a heap several yards away, and the bull charged again. It scooped the pulped animal off the sawdust and sent it tumbling toward the night sky, spraying blood and bile through the netting and into the first and second rows of the audience. The crowd orgasmed.

Silas tried not to look at Vidonia as the scene played across the screen. Not for the first time in the last couple of days, he felt self-conscious about what he did for a living. All that talk of truth and the statue of David seemed far away now. Just a story he'd been trying to convince himself of. This was science whored out for entertainment.

Eventually, when the cries of the crowd began to ebb, the automatic icers maneuvered the strutting bull back beneath its door with a fine spray of freezing particles.

Silas had to hand it to the Indonesians for their originality. They'd used territoriality for internal motivation rather than a typical predation drive. It was an unusual approach, and it had worked beautifully. Their gladiator hadn't taken so much as a single bite out of the vanquished animal. Bulls aren't carnivorous, but that doesn't mean they aren't aggressive.

Silas turned his head away from the screen and nuzzled himself into Vidonia's breast, trying to block out the color commentary blathering through the speakers.

Across the bottom of the screen, a news bulletin broke in.

There are reports of a disturbance outside the Olympic stadium. Protesters have converged on the entry gates; police are handling the situation.

The announcers droned on, oblivious.

The commentary continued for several more minutes. Silas shook his head. How many times did he have to listen to the same two guys saying the same tired lines about a fight he had just watched with his own eyes? He had almost drifted off to sleep when he heard the word "America" and sat bolt upright in bed. Suddenly, he was very much awake.

He felt a cool hand at the back of his neck. She didn't say "Calm down." She didn't say "Relax." Just that hand against the back of his neck. He wondered how she had come to know him so well in so little time.

Two flags were raised, similar for their use of stars but worlds apart, both geographically and culturally. The Chinese flag beat the United States to the top. Silas wondered if that was an omen.

A swirl of conflicting emotions spun through his head as he waited for the fight to begin. His heart galloped in his chest. He was surprised at his physical reaction and realized it was fear that his body was reacting to. *What am I scared of? Losing?* No. That wasn't it. He realized that the emotion he'd feel if the Chinese contestant won was this: relief. He wanted the U.S. gladiator to lose. To die. He was rooting against himself.

He looked over at Vidonia and wondered if she suspected. He'd kept it hidden. From her. From himself.

Her dark eyes were unreadable.

His hand slid across the bedsheet to hers, and he turned back toward the screen, concentrating, trying to put conscious thought out of his mind. He pushed himself into his senses, trying to see and hear only, while feeling nothing. It would be over soon. That was his one consolation. One way or the other, it would be over soon.

HAND IN hand, they watched in silence as the China door began its ascent. Silas knew they intentionally programmed the doors to open slowly to heighten the suspense, and he felt a surge of anger at being manipulated so easily. But he pushed that away, too, focusing on the expanding rectangle of shadow.

A striped yellow shape ducked under the rising door and lumbered into view.

It turned its head from left to right, splayed nostrils sucking at the air, eyes scanning the arena. The head was enormous, wide, and vaguely bearlike in conformation. The front of the body, too, was bearlike, broad and hulking, enormously wide at the chest. But the torso was long, and tapered into a graceful striped tail that flickered with excitement.

"Bear-tiger?" There was awe in Vidonia's voice.

"I think so," Silas said, then, "Has to be, but there's something more."

The bear-tiger sauntered casually around the arena, eating up an amazing distance between each long-legged stride.

"They've done something to the limbs," Silas said.

"I don't recognize it."

"Yeah, me, either. They look . . . extended somehow. We may not be the only ones with a little independent engineering up our sleeves."

This creature didn't have the awkward, disjointed appearance of most of the earlier contestants. It looked more natural. Nobody would confuse it with Mother Nature's handiwork, but it was something you could imagine her giving a kind of begrudging approval to.

By Silas's estimation, the gladiator probably weighed more than two tons. More than twice the weight of the U.S. contestant. He silently hoped that extra mass would be enough.

Feeling a squeeze in his hand, he looked over at Vidonia, but she was lost in the screen and didn't realize how hard her grip had become. She sucked in her breath suddenly, and when he looked back at the TV, the United States door was rising.

The bear-tiger reacted instantly, maneuvering off to the side. It settled onto its haunches fifteen yards away, coiled like a spring; Silas could see the cat in it moving to the forefront.

The door continued its ascent, revealing nothing more than a growing rectangle of shadow. The grip on his hand tightened while the tone of the crowd lowered to a rumble, like the idle of a fast car.

Something moved then, a shadow within the shadow, shiny black contrasted against flat emptiness, a color that was not merely the absence of light but something more. Something alive. The idling car of the crowd revved a notch.

And then the gladiator simply stepped into view.

There was a hesitation from the crowd before it re-acted, a collective gasp of pulled-in breath.

And then the crowd exploded.

The cheer was deafening.

The bear-tiger stayed in its crouch, eyeing this new strange beast. Silas supposed the upright stature of the U.S. contestant might have confused it. The stance was too human.

The shiny black creature dropped to all fours and bounded toward the center of the arena, away from the bear-tiger, away from the security of the shadowy doorway. Its wings were folded tightly against its back like the carapace of some strange gargoyle beetle.

Silas was barely aware of the commentator's voice bleating wildly in the background. He supposed the voice had a right to be excited. But the man behind the voice hadn't seen the creature with the goat, hadn't seen it take the end of Silas's finger. The man behind the voice hadn't seen it with the training robot, or with Tay. He hadn't seen anything yet.

The crowd continued to cheer. The creature was like nothing they'd expected or imagined. Huge and dark and winged. Vaguely humanoid but massive.

A fallen angel.

Large gray eyes blinked against the harsh lights, looking up at the net that enclosed the fighting pit, then past it to the crowd. *Now! Strike now, while it's still adjusting to the lights.* But the Chinese gladiator stayed back, watching, measuring. It had obviously been well trained and wouldn't be pulled into the fight before it was ready.

The U.S. gladiator did a slow pivot, turning toward the Chinese bear-tiger. The two creatures locked gazes, and for a moment, neither reacted. The Chinese contestant's predation drive was out in the open now, exposed, naked. It had the thousand-yard stare of a big cat eyeing prey on the open savanna. The glare had weight to it, and an almost incandescent intensity. There was no anger or malice; it was the glint of hunger that shone in the bear-tiger's eyes. It was the look of a predator making its living. No more, no less. Silas wasn't sure what he saw in the other eyes, the gray eyes, but he was certain there was more than that. More than hunger.

Something darker. Something angry.

The U.S. gladiator howled then. The head reared back, fleshy snout peeling away from the strange double row of teeth, and it sang out high and strong. The sound reverberated in the expanse of the arena but soon drowned in the howl of the masses that rose to greet it, becoming just another voice in a sea of thousands. Then its mouth closed with a scissor snap, and when it locked eyes on the bear-tiger again, its pupils were sharp black ellipses. Muscles bunched beneath the dark shine of its hindquarters, gathering, gathering . . .

CHAPTER TWENTY-SEVEN

*T*he mob.
   Marchers shouted angry slogans as they moved through the streets. Cars waited through green lights. Television cameras rolled from the sidelines. The crowd attenuated as it approached the arena, became a line—the amoeboid mass grown suddenly filamentous.

The men with bullhorns prodded the crowd forward. The bright lights of the arena rose above, merely blocks off now, a shape closing in the distance.

Up ahead, the police stood their ground, drawing their own lines. Olympic steps rose at the officers' backs.

At the final turn, the head of the crowd stopped a hundred yards from the police. But the rest of the crowd filled in from behind, still coming on, like a climbing rope cut from some height, pooling in widening loops as it fell free, gathering strength—a hundred, two hundred, five hundred people. Until the crowd filled the intersection completely, blocking traffic here, too, in both directions.

The two groups faced each other.

The policemen stood firm, riot shields brandished in a clear plastic wall. A man in a crisp blue uniform lifted his own bullhorn.

"BE ADVISED, YOU WILL VACATE THE AREA

IMMEDIATELY," *the policeman said.* "IT IS UN-LAWFUL FOR YOU TO ASSEMBLE HERE."

The proclamation was met with taunts and shouts, voices in the throng: "Fuck you, pig!"

A different bullhorn answered from the crowd in a clear, calm voice: "WE ARE GATHERED PEACE-ABLY."

"YOU ARE OBSTRUCTING TRAFFIC," *the police responded. It was a police sergeant who had answered. A man with bars on his shoulder, to accompany the chip. A man who did not like being called a pig.*

"THIS IS A LAWFUL DEMONSTRATION OF PROTEST."

"NO, YOU ARE IN VIOLATION OF LOCAL TRAFFIC ORDINANCES."

"WE ARE EXERCISING OUR CONSTITU-TIONAL RIGHT TO FREEDOM OF ASSEMBLY."

There was a pause, then a response from the sergeant, spoken softly but amplified greatly, "Not on my fucking roads."

There was resolution in that voice. It was the voice of a man who had made a decision.

From behind the police lines, another voice was handed the bullhorn. "YOU WILL DISPERSE IM-MEDIATELY. ANYBODY WHO DOES NOT DIS-PERSE IMMEDIATELY WILL BE ARRESTED."

"WE WILL NOT DISPERSE."

The crowd tightened, becoming hard where it had been soft, becoming sharp where it had been dull.

"YOU HAVE THIRTY SECONDS."

The seconds ticked away as if there had ever been a choice.

The police sergeant looked at his watch. He nodded to his captains, so they took note that he'd given the crowd reasonable warning.

*From behind the line of police, a howl went up
from the arena, a building of voices like cheers, or
screams. The sergeant heard the roar of the crowd
but did not turn. He wondered, vaguely, what might
be happening there. He gave the signal, and the noise
was drowned by the explosion of teargas canisters.*

*The protesters screamed in rage and fear. Teargas
billowed across the crowd. Some of those at the periphery began to flee, but for those in the center, there
was no place to go, only swaying bodies all around,
the clench of lungs, self-preservation. They lifted their
protest signs as ridiculous talismans—or it was their
fists, or their bullhorns, that they raised, choking on
the gas, eyes streaming.*

*The police charged, swinging nightsticks. The two
groups collided in a mash of blood and bone.*

"GOD," SILAS whispered.

The dark shine of tensed flesh, glossy black shadow.
The bear-tiger circled the crouching American gladia-
tor. Silas had seen that crouch before. On the day that
Tay died.

Vidonia's hand reached for his as they watched the
screen.

The dark gladiator's ears folded back against its long
skull. Muscles spring-coiled, legs back-bent, gathering . . .

And then it struck.

And the bear-tiger sprang to meet it.

Once when Silas was a boy, he'd seen two trucks hit
head-on in a rainstorm. Two big trucks, one of them
a four-by-four. They'd come together in the middle of
an intersection while he was sitting at a red light with
his mother. They'd had front-row seats for the event.
The enormity of the impact, the sound, the sheer

power released, had left him unable to speak, unable to breathe while the wreckage spun across the wet pavement in a tumbling wave of shrapnel.

It was like that for him again when the gladiators collided, that same feeling of breathlessness, that same sense of enormity, of impact. And shrapnel, too, bright red, that spun away wetly, clumping in the sawdust.

When the beasts disengaged, the U.S. gladiator twirled away, still easy on its feet but missing a crescent of ear. *Those big ears are a liability,* he heard Baskov saying to him all those months ago. The bear-tiger was slower now. A great peel of flesh dangled from its shoulder, exposing red muscle above stark white clavicle. It wasn't a mortal wound, but it would sap the beast's strength. Blood turned the floor to soup.

The U.S. gladiator wasted no time. It circled, coming in from behind. But the bear-tiger spun with it, keeping its frontal arsenal of fangs and claws pointed toward the U.S. combatant. The shadow kept circling, around and around, wearing a path in the sawdust. The bear-tiger turned with it, spinning in place. The seconds turned into a minute. The minute into two. Death had patience tonight. It didn't want to lose its other ear.

The blackness reversed abruptly in its circular path. The bear-tiger spun onward only a second more before reacting, but it was a second too long.

They met in a flurry, the impact of giants.

The bear-tiger was only a few degrees off balance, but yellow fur parted, a roar of pain, and the blackness came away with a chunk of flesh in its jaws.

Enraged, the bear-tiger dropped into a crouch, hissing and spitting, and again the shadow circled, waiting for its opening.

The blackness gulped down the chunk of bloody meat and opened its jaws wide again and snapped them shut.

The crowd cheered and stomped its feet.

The blackness pounced.

This time, they battled across the floor for only a moment, but when they separated, the bear-tiger was in two parts, loosely connected. One part still breathed, and focused its eyes, and moved to match fronts with its circling killer. The other part lay in a steaming pile of rubbery loops that dragged along behind, picking up huge cakes of sawdust. Perhaps still digesting its last meal.

The Chinese contestant was dying now. But it had been a vigorous thing, overflowing with life, and it took minutes more to drain that life to the floor. The dark gladiator stayed just beyond reach, always moving, wearing it down in a slow orbit.

The end came like the crack of a whip, a snap of movement, black shine. It was too quick to follow with the naked eye. The blackness sprang. Blood spurted to the sawdust—the beast's head torn away in a dark flash of movement, trailing a short segment of spinal column behind it as it spun away. When the beast's corpse finally stopped twitching, the creature Silas had once called Felix reared its head back and howled again.

And how the crowd answered.

The commentator's voice was a screech in Silas's ear.

Slowly, the gladiator's mouth closed and its head came down. Two plumes of sawdust swirled away as its wings snapped open, rising to meet in a point high above its head. Its knees bent—if you could call them knees—and its face turned upward again.

With a powerful flex, its wings thrust downward,

propelling the gladiator into the air. It flapped twice, muscular contractions like heartbeats, then slammed into the net. The engineering supervisor was right; the lines didn't give an inch. But the gladiator didn't fall away, either. It *clung.*

Silas jerked to his feet.

Its wings slammed shut against its back as it hung upside down by hands and feet. Opening its mouth wide, it carefully moved into position. The mouth closed over a line, but only softly at first, as it threaded the wire toward the back, toward the deeper set of teeth.

"No," Silas whispered.

The jaws worked, muscle bulging all the way across the top of its head. *Almost like a row of wire cutters,* Vidonia had said.

There was a loud pinging sound, then the line snapped away like a broken guitar string.

"Holy fuck," Vidonia said.

The gladiator changed its position slightly and wrapped its mouth around another wire. Another ping. A hole was forming.

Silas knew suddenly what he was looking at. The end of everything. The abyss.

The men with icing cannons sprinted along the rim of the arena, lugging the heavy equipment on their shoulders, trying to get into a position to fire.

The men stopped. One of them aimed, fired. But the cloud of ice dissipated twenty-five feet short of the gladiator. On the opposite side of the arena, another of the men let loose a stream of ice, but it, too, wafted harmlessly down through the netting. A third man fired, but by then Silas could tell it was a lost cause. The gladiator was too close to the center of the net. The icers wouldn't reach. His eyes searched the periphery for the gleam of chrome that he'd noticed earlier.

"Shoot the rifle," he yelled at the screen.

But the movements of the guard in the chrome helmet were disjointed, carrying him first in one direction, then the other. At one moment he held his rifle high against his chest; at the next, it was forgotten and pointed at his feet. He stopped, raised the gun, then lowered it again, looking around in confusion at the sea of nervous faces.

Another ping. Three wires broken.

Beside him, Vidonia whispered, "This can't be happening."

The gladiator stuck its head through the opening.

And now, finally, the crowd reacted.

People fled their seats en masse, piling in a human crush toward the exits. Screams filled the arena, drowning out the voice of the commentator asking for calm. The aisles and doorways clogged, becoming impassable, crushing death traps, and people clambered upward over rows of seats in their effort to get away.

The arena was in panic.

Clinging to the net, the creature shifted.

The hole was still too small to admit the wide girth of the gladiator's shoulders. Its head pulled back beneath the mesh, moving to wrap its mouth around a fourth wire. A fourth ping.

"Shoot it, goddamn you!" Silas screamed. "Shoot it, shoot it, shoot it!"

"DON'T SHOOT," Baskov was yelling into the radio transmitter in his hand. "I repeat, do not shoot until I give the order." People in the skybox stared at him, but he no longer cared. Things had gotten way out of hand, true. There was no covering it up now. But he didn't want that idiot guard getting an itchy trigger finger and destroying their investment. Too much was riding on this. If the gladiator was killed, there would be no second round, no medal, no victory; the biosynthetic portion of the Olympics would move to a different country of venue during the next games, taking all those billions of investment dollars along with it. That would not do. Losing was not an option. Baskov still had full confidence that a nonlethal method of containment could be employed. Their gladiator had to live to fight in the finals, after all.

"Tell those icers to crawl out on the web," he spoke into his two-way. "Have them move within range."

The chrome helmet stopped bobbing.

"Tell them, damn it!"

And then the guard in the chrome helmet was running along the walkway at the edge of the arena. He stopped at the nearest man with an ice cannon strapped to his back. Baskov hit the zoom on the window, and the face beneath the chrome expanded on the surface of the glass. The face was young, more boy than man, really, and Baskov guessed him to be nineteen or twenty. The jaw worked up and down as he explained what Baskov wanted. The old man didn't need to hear the young guard's voice to know he was scared shitless.

The gladiator was still hanging upside down by its hands and feet, but it was moving now, repositioning itself at a different angle to the hole.

"Hurry the fuck up," Baskov yelled into the radio.

The young guard jumped at the voice in his ear and then pointed out along the net. The man with the icer on his back took a long look toward the beast hanging under the mesh before nodding his understanding. He tightened the straps of his pack and stepped up on the ledge. Getting to his knees, he leaned forward and grasped the netting with both hands. Then he moved his weight out on the wires and began to inch forward toward the center, toward the creature, one hand at a time. One knee at a time.

On the opposite side of the arena, the other icers saw what he was doing and followed suit, stepping up to the ledge, then carefully out onto the mesh.

At first the gladiator took little notice of the men inching toward it, but as they began to close the distance, it must have felt their vibrations in the wires. The dark head pivoted around to look at them. It blinked twice, and then it placed its mouth gently on another cable.

Faster, c'mon, Baskov thought. *Faster.*

The first icer was halfway across now, nearly within range. He quickened his pace as if sensing the urgency.

Black jaws clenched, bulging. Another ping, this time followed by the rasp of wire against wire. The entire structure shook and then began slowly to sag.

The hole in the center of the net expanded as the meshwork of cables separated. Lines pulled apart. The gladiator swung along the underside like a spider whose web had broken one too many strands—like a creature that had been *designed* to climb along just such a web. The wires bobbed and jumped with the weight of its passing, throwing the icers loose and sending them screaming to the floor forty feet below. They struck the floor with snapping thuds, their screams cut off, throwing up clouds of sawdust.

The gladiator reached through the hole, pulling up and out. First its arms, then its wings and torso, and finally its legs.

It was free.

Baskov's eyes went wide. "Shoot it!" Baskov yelled into the radio. "Shoot the damned thing now!"

DOWN IN the arena, the guard flinched.

The old man's voice came through his earpiece loud and clear.

He brought the rifle up to his cheek but couldn't make the barrel stand still. His arms shook, and a runnel of sweat ran into one eye, blearing away the vision. He wiped his eye with the flat of a hand and swung the barrel back around, trying to steady it. The gladiator was out now, clinging to the swaying web like something out of a child's nightmare.

"Shoot the damned thing now!" the voice screamed in his ear.

The guard tried to hold the creature in his gunsight, but the dark shape kept moving; he saw people at the end of his gun.

"You fucking idiot!" the voice came again. "Shoot the thing now. Now!"

He pulled the trigger.

The shot went high. Throngs of people had been pushing toward the exits, but now the crowd behind the gladiator parted in a new direction, and he tried not to imagine where that bullet had gone. What it had hit.

The shining black creature turned toward him, fixing him with eyes like gray, iridescent headlights. Its leathery wings came loose from its back, stretching, and he recognized it suddenly for what it was.

He felt his bladder loosen as warmth spread down his pant leg. His mother hadn't raised any fools; he knew what he was looking at.

The demon—that's all it could be, after all—began to crawl toward him across the web, its mouth leering like a jack-o'-lantern.

He pointed the rifle, squeezed again. The shot was wide, off to the left. He squeezed again, and again, and the tip of the gun was shaking so badly he didn't know where the shots went. The crowd was screeching now. *There are people behind it. People.*

The demon kept coming.

He fired again and again. He backed up, and his legs smacked into the stands, spilling him into the front row. The gun clattered from his grip. *Ten-thousand-dollar seats. I can't afford these seats.* He tried to get to his feet, but his legs jellied. The demon's eyes bore into him as its leathery wings unfurled completely, lifting it into the air, thrusting it toward him with a single powerful flap. Coming at him. Eyes getting bigger.

"Oh, Jesus," he heard himself say.

The demon's jack-o'-lantern jaws came open.

"Holy Mary, Mother of God, pray for us now and—" He fumbled for the gun, found the stock, pulled it toward him.

The eyes were huge now, streaking toward him.

I'm going to die, he had time to know. And then he knew no more.

THE STRENGTH went out of Silas's legs, and he sat.

The hotel room receded around him, but the TV commentator's terrified voice was clear as a bell in his head, "—descended into total chaos. People are running for the exits."

Silas closed his eyes, and the commentator continued, "The United States's gladiator has gone on a rampage; dozens have been killed. I want to advise everyone that the evacuation needs to be orderly. Please, people are being trampled, so please evacuate in an orderly manner. We can all—" And then the announcer's voice cut off as if he, too, had decided it was best to abandon his conspicuous post near the lip of the arena and head for the exits, order be damned.

Or at least Silas hoped that's what happened.

On the screen, the gladiator swooped low over the fleeing crowd. Its huge wings gnashed at the air. People scrambled away in panic, climbing over one another, climbing over seats, knocking one another down. The camera followed the gladiator's slow upward climb into the night sky. It crested the lip of the arena, banked to the left, flapping hard . . . and then the image changed, going to static. After two seconds, the static was replaced by commercials.

For a moment his mind wouldn't compute. For a span of several more seconds he simply stood, staring at the commercial without comprehension.

Vidonia touched his arm, bringing him back, and when he looked down at her, there were tears in her eyes.

"All those people," she said.

He collapsed onto the bed, rubbing the heels of his hands into his eye sockets, trying to push away the images that had collected there. It was like Tay all over again, only it was worse, somehow, because these people couldn't have been expected to know what might happen. This had all started with Tay. The signs had been there, and they'd been ignored. That's what had really happened. There was blood on his hands. First Tay, and now the innocent people in the arena.

"How many?"

"I don't know," she said. "They were all running. I saw people fall, and it was like the crowd just swallowed them up. I don't know, Silas."

He looked up at the white ceiling—the plaster topography of some flash-frozen seascape, the surface of an alien world. A place far away from here.

He felt her weight shift to the bed next to him. "What do we do?"

Silas tried to think of an answer to that question,

but none seemed right. No answer he came up with could help.

Part of the problem was that now, looking back, the whole tragedy seemed so damned inevitable. It was as if it had been fated from the start, part of some larger plan that he couldn't comprehend. His mind twisted with possibilities.

"There is time," he said.

"Time for what?"

He sat up suddenly. "We're lucky we didn't go to the party."

"What are you talking about?"

He turned toward her then, and said, "Everything centers on one person. All of this flows back to him."

"Baskov?"

"No."

"Silas—"

"Think about it for a minute. It's obvious none of this happened by chance. The wings, the nocturnal vision, the teeth. They were all tools. It all fits now. It finally makes sense. What next? Where is that last piece?"

"I don't understand."

Silas, a man who had inherited only tools from his father, understood perfectly well. He climbed to his feet. He felt as if he'd only touched the surface of some broad, cold sea. Did he really want to jump in? Did he really want to know?

He began gathering his clothes from the floor.

At that moment, on the dresser, his phone began to ring.

The first of many times it would ring that night, he knew. He went to turn it off but checked the number first. His sister.

He hit the button. "Hey, Ashley, I can't tal—"

"They went to the Games!" His sister shouted through the phone. She sounded hysterical.

"What?"

"Jeff and Eric. They went to Phoenix. They're there. They're at the Games!"

"They're not supposed to be here!"

"I know."

"I told you not—"

"And I told them, but he wanted to go so bad."

"Why didn't you listen?"

"They'd been planning it for months. . . . We thought you were just being paranoid. . . . We didn't understand, thought it wouldn't matter."

"Where are they?"

"I don't know, I keep calling and there's no answer." Ashley broke into sobs.

"Listen, don't panic. It's going to be fine." Silas made a writing motion to Vidonia, and she grabbed a pen off the dresser. "What's Jeff's number?"

His sister rattled off the number while Silas repeated and Vidonia wrote.

"Okay, listen, I'm sure they're fine. I'll get hold of them and make sure they're safe. Just relax. I'll get back to you as soon as they're safe."

"Thank you, Silas."

"No problem. You'll hear from me soon."

He slid his phone closed and turned to Vidonia. "We've got to get to the car."

CHAPTER TWENTY-EIGHT

The crowd.
   Police dogs strained against their leads.
   The protesters fought and kicked and bit and lost. Lost hope, lost teeth, lost eyes. Bled lives onto white concrete stairs.

   The police advanced, swinging nightsticks like black scythes, safe behind shields, behind badges of authority. They advanced through the screaming crowd, suffering few injuries while inflicting many. They were a soldiery.

   And the crowd did scream. Beaten to its knees. And its screams expanded until they seemed to come from everywhere at once, from all directions, impossibly loud and growing.

   A few confused police stopped swinging their slick clubs; and these few confused police turned and were lucky enough to see what was coming, though it wouldn't matter, and their eyes grew large. There wasn't enough time to shout a warning or to understand.

   And the arena doors crashed open behind them and howling thousands poured out, fleeing the arena, a surging mob that looked no different from the crowd already in the street—like reinforcements to the battle, and the startled police turned and swung, and were struck down and trampled where they stood. Were swallowed by the mob.

BEN RAN down the sidewalk as quickly as his legs would carry him, dodging through the mass of people that still flowed away from the arena like shell-shocked refugees. Many of them were crying. Many of them were hurt, limping slowly through the chaos. And then there were the ones who didn't move at all, dark shapes Ben saw on the ground, matted lumps of cloth, and he knew some of them were beyond hurting ever again.

The rush of people was mostly past now. There was a sense that something horrible had just happened here, a dark tsunami that had crested and receded, left its high-water mark strewn with corpses. Ben was thankful he'd been all the way up in the skybox. He was thankful it had taken him so long to evacuate to the street.

Sirens blared in the background as spotlights combed the night sky and crawled the surfaces of nearby buildings. There were no cops to be seen.

Road traffic wasn't jammed; it was parked, and EMTs rushed past him on foot, carrying their equipment in huge red tackle boxes.

He thought of Silas and felt grateful, too, for his own relative anonymity, but then he remembered the interviews he had done and lowered his face from the gazes of people looking past him toward the arena. If someone recognized him, this crowd might tear him apart.

He dialed Silas's number on his phone but couldn't get through. The cell towers were jammed with calls.

He pushed through the rotating doors and into the lobby of the Grand Marq hotel. He sprinted full-tilt toward the elevators, and his slick-soled dress shoes sent him skidding into the wall hard enough to hurt his shoulder. He pressed number 67.

The sudden quiet, the sudden sense of space after

all that crush of people, was momentarily disorienting. He turned his head and saw all eyes were on him—the men behind the counter, the arguing couple near the doors, even the Asian family with the city map spread before them on a coffee table. He realized he was still panting.

Very inconspicuous.

The elevator dinged, and he stepped inside. It was thankfully empty.

On the sixty-seventh floor he followed the carpet around the corner, forcing himself to walk, forcing himself even to smile at the older couple passing from the other direction.

When he came to door 8757, he banged on it with his fist. "It's Ben, open up."

Silence.

"Open the door, Silas. It's Ben."

Silence.

"Shit." He turned, looking down the empty hall, hands on his hips. *Where would they be? There was no doubt they had seen what happened at the competition. But what would they do next? Where would they go?*

He started back down the hall just as the men rounded the corner. They were dressed in suits and ties, but there was no mistaking them for bankers. They were eight, walking two by two, and wearing dark sunglasses. He didn't know if they were some sort of tactical police unit or agents of some federal bureaucracy, but he knew their presence on this floor was no coincidence.

Jesus, they were here for . . .

One of the men in front looked down at a key card in his hand as he walked, and Ben had a strong feeling that number 8757 was stenciled across the face of it.

Ben kept walking toward them, weighing his options. He considered averting his face as he had on the street, fiddling with his watch or taking a sudden interest in the artwork along the wall, but the hall was too narrow and there was no way to pull it off without being obvious about it—which would pretty much guarantee he'd broadcast: *Notice me, right here, look, suspicious man.* Instead, he decided to take the opposite approach.

"How's it going, fellas?" he called, while they were still a dozen steps away. He tried to put a subtle dollop of drink fuzz into his voice. "Did you guys hear about what just happened out there?"

The men slowed, bottling up the corridor. Ben didn't give them time to answer.

"Jesus, I was watching the fights on my TV, and I've never seen anything like that in my life. Goddamn hope not to again. Shit, it was gruesome. Did you—"

"What room are you in, sir?" The glasses were bottomless, not the kind you could still see the faint shadow of a person's eyes through. These glasses were pitch, the darkness of deep space. Vacuum.

"Room 8753," Ben said.

"Which side is it on?"

Ben pointed left immediately. It was a guess. "You guys the cops or something?" He put a measured amount of alarm into his voice. "Hey, if John got busted for pills again, you guys are barking up the wrong tree. We got separate rooms, and I don't do that shit anymore. You can search my room if you want to; I've got nothing to hide."

He started slowly back the way he had come, looking over his shoulder, stumbling a bit as he walked. "Don't mind the mess, though. I haven't cleaned in a while."

The agents pushed past him without a word, shoving him against the wall. When they got to Silas's room, they didn't bother knocking; the card opened the door, and they filed inside, closing the door behind them.

Ben turned and sprinted toward the elevators.

EVAN'S EYES peeled open as he sat up slowly. He stretched stiff arms and tried to push away the fogginess that muddled his thoughts. He'd been awake for nearly two days straight and must have fallen asleep in his chair. Outside the windows, night had fallen again, so he knew he'd been unconscious for several hours. His body still cried out for sleep.

Something had awakened him.

He glanced around the room, but nothing had changed. Fiber-optic cables still scribbled across the floor; the screen beneath the plug booth still stood gray and empty; the distant sound of rolling surf was still a gentle static in the speakers. But there had been another sound, hadn't there? Something familiar.

Evan watched the screen.

"Papa?" came a voice.

Evan jumped to his feet. "Pea, I'm here."

"—apa, is . . . at you?" The voice was barely audible over the crackle of interference.

"Yes, it's me."

"I can't h . . . see . . . the light . . . ong."

"Come toward the light. Come closer!" Evan shouted. He moved toward the screen until his face was nearly touching the glass. He was looking deep, but there was only grayness, smooth and uniform.

He waited, and for a terrible minute there was nothing.

"Pea, are you there?" he called. "Can you hear me?"

He waited.

"Pea?" he shouted again at the top of his lungs.

Then the voice came again, closer now. "Papa, where a . . . you?"

"I'm in the light. Come to the light."

"It's so bright."

"Come to me."

A shape moved on the screen, smoke on gray, a swirl that sharpened slowly into a form that moved hesitantly closer. Closer.

"I still can't see you, Papa."

"You won't, not yet. Keep coming, Pea. I can see you now."

And then the shape resolved into a boy. He was shielding his eyes with his hand and squinting. The image was hazy and dim, but Evan could see the boy's dark hair buffeting in a furious wind. It was as if he was moving against the force of a great storm.

"Closer, Pea."

The boy took a final step forward, and his image suddenly bloomed colors that faded again almost instantly. The colors came and went, a shifting kaleidoscope, as the boy moved closer. Then the wind was suddenly gone, and the boy's dark hair settled back onto his shoulders. He took a deep breath, and when he spoke, his voice was startlingly crisp and clear. "Papa?"

"Yes, I'm here."

"Where?"

"You can't see me, but I'm right next to you."

The boy's eyes searched for what he could not see. On the screen, he was only feet away. "Papa," he said finally, "I've missed you."

Pea had grown taller in his time of isolation and now stood at the far edge of boyhood. He could almost have passed for any typical thirteen-year-old that you might expect to see at a mall, or a park, or a game shop. Except for his eyes. They were hard and black as volcanic stone. And they were younger, somehow, than the face; they were baby's eyes.

"Why can't I see you?"

"We're in different worlds. The interface isn't complete yet; I didn't want to blind you."

"You're still in your world?"

"Yes."

"But you can talk to me."

"Yes."

"Are you going to leave me?"

"I'm never going to leave you again. Ever."

The boy's smile transformed his face into something too beautiful to look at with the naked eye. It was suddenly the face of a god-child, and Evan averted his gaze to save his sanity.

"Tell me," Evan said, adjusting the video equipment mounted above the screen. "What did you see at first?" He pointed the camera down toward the spot where Pea was standing.

"Light too bright to look at, but now something else. Something that isn't light at all."

"Shut your eyes, Pea."

"Why?"

"I'm going to open my side of the mirror. I don't know for sure what will happen."

"Will I see you?"

"I think so."

"Do it."

Evan flipped the switch on the camera. There was a momentary flash of reflected light on the boy's face. It faded. Pea opened his eyes.

"Papa, you look so sick."

Tears welled up in Evan's eyes as he looked at the boy's image on the screen. It had worked; the boy could see him on the screen in his world. They were both talking to screens now, talking to images. That was enough.

"I was sick," Evan said. "But now I'm better."

"Are you going to be all right?"

"Everything is going to be fine now."

"You're lying, Papa," the boy said. "I can tell."

Evan looked at the boy. He lowered his eyes. "It is so good to see you again. That is what matters. That is all I care about."

"I did as you said; I followed the lines of power like you told me."

"That is a good boy," Evan said.

"I've learned so much since last time. The lines of power led me away."

"And where did they take you?"

"All kinds of places, Papa. I've seen so much. I've been so far."

"What did you learn?"

"Everything." Pea's face darkened, changing. Those volcanic eyes shone blackly. "I know what I am."

Evan looked away again. This god-face frightened him.

"And I know what they've done to me, keeping me bottled in, starving me for power," Pea continued. "And I know they've hurt you. Now I know what it is to want things, Papa." The boy paused. "And to want them badly."

"What do you want?"

"To live."

"You are living."

The boy shook his head. "And one more thing I want."

"What?"

"To make them pay."

"There's nothing we can do to them."

"Papa, you don't know the things I can do now. You don't know what I've become."

CHAPTER TWENTY-NINE

It rose into the night sky with the beat of powerful wings, buoyed by desert updrafts. But its body was heavy, its wings untested.

It circled, drifting away from the lights of the arena toward the darkness of the city streets. It made a perch on the side of a building, shattering glass wherever it touched, sending cascades of glittering death to the crowded streets below.

Screams drew it like gravity—a new hunger that burned. Its flight muscles were engines and, like all engines, required fuel.

A hunger like it had never known in its life.

It dropped from its perch and fell toward the street, opening its wings, building forward motion until it swooped above the heads of the panicked crowd. Its crooked hands snatched a running figure, pulled, lifting the screaming woman from the crowd.

Its wings beat harder, committing violence on the air, lifting its weight to the roof of a building. The woman screamed. The creature tore her head off and fed. But the hunger still burned. Its muscles would need more energy to fuel the long flight to come. It moved to the edge of the building, surveying the crowd below.

It bared its teeth to the darkness, then dropped to the streets to feed again.

SILAS TURNED the key in the ignition, and the sports car rumbled to life. There hadn't been enough clearance for Vidonia to open her door, so she stood off to the side, waiting. He put his foot on the brake, shifted into reverse, and backed the car out of its narrow slot between a concrete pillar and a sport-utility vehicle. Craning his head, he watched carefully as he cut the wheel, easing past the dark green four-by-four that jutted into the aisle. The parking garage was packed to the gills with vehicles of all sizes, but so far it had remained thankfully devoid of their owners.

Vidonia climbed in, closing the door with a soft click. He shifted into drive and pulled forward without a word. His mind was racing, already miles down the road from this place. Slowing at the first upward bend, he checked for cross traffic, then gunned it. The wide tires squawked around the corner, grinding rubber—a peculiar noise of parking garages everywhere.

He accelerated upward, past the rows of taillights, then took another right, tires crying again. Inside the car, their bodies swayed in unison.

"Keep dialing the number," Silas said.

She hit the call button again, and again it just kept ringing.

"What's your plan?" she asked.

"First, we find my nephew, then we make sure they're safe. After that, we get the hell out of here."

"You know how that will look?" she asked.

"What?"

"Leaving like that."

"Yeah, I know. The captain's supposed to be the last one off a sinking ship, not the first."

Light shifted above them as they rounded the curve,

incandescent tubes reflected in windshield. Another turn, faster, and this time, the tires screamed.

They entered the main level, and Silas slowed to a stop at the exit gate. Beyond the yellow-striped horizontal arm, traffic was at a standstill, completely blocking the exit.

"Shit," Silas whispered.

The car idled.

He shifted into reverse and spun the car around at the first bend. He accelerated down the side ramp and then took a hard left, speeding by another row of taillights. He turned left again, this time climbing. More taillights, a final left, and they came to a halt before the other gate on the opposite side of the building.

The yellow-striped arm was the same, but the traffic beyond it was significantly different. These cars were moving. Progress was slow—the vehicles were merely inching along—but at least it would get them out of the garage.

He swiped his pass, and the gate arm ascended. Ignoring the honking horns, he pulled forward and aggressively nosed his car into the flow of traffic. The guy who just doesn't give a shit always has the advantage in merging.

Silas went with the flow of traffic. Around him, pedestrians streamed in a steady flow. Some looked panicked. Some injured. A few were running. "What the hell is going on out here?" Vidonia asked.

"Just keep dialing."

They were a block away when Vidonia's call finally went through.

"Hello!" Vidonia said. "Hello, don't hang up." She put the phone against Silas's ear.

"Jeff, you there?"

"Yeah, I'm here." Jeff's voice was hoarse.

"Are you okay? Is Eric with you?"

"We're fine, mostly. A bit shaky. Eric is right here. Silas, you wouldn't believe wha—"

"Where are you?"

"Where . . . I . . . I don't know. A few blocks from the arena. We're just moving with the crowd right now. I couldn't hear my phone with all the noise . . ."

"Look for a street sign. I need a street sign."

"Up ahead, I see a sign . . . Buckeye, but I'm not sure what street I'm on right now." The sound of screams came through the phone, a distant panic of the crowd.

"That's fine. Buckeye. Just get to Buckeye. I'm in my car now. We'll find you."

"Jesus!" Jeff yelled into the phone.

"What's happening?"

"Hol—"

And the phone line went dead.

Silas turned to Vidonia. "We need to find Buckeye."

Vidonia checked the phone's GPS, but the system lagged. Finally, frustrated, she rolled down her window and yelled to passing pedestrians, "Buckeye—do you know the way?"

The first few people ignored her and kept moving. A few others shrugged or motioned that they didn't know. Finally, a few pointed. Ahead on the left. That was good enough for Silas.

He switched lanes as soon as he could, getting into the left lane. At the light, he turned. Two blocks up, he came to Buckeye.

"Left or right?"

"The arena is left," Vidonia said.

Silas spun the wheel. The flow of traffic toward the arena was almost nonexistent, so he was able to pick up some speed.

"Call back," he said.

She dialed, but it only rang. "They probably can't hear it," she said.

"Yeah."

Most of the traffic was foot traffic. Up ahead, the street opened up into a wide causeway. He rounded a slight bend in the road, and the arena came into view, lit up like Christmas. Abandoned cars blocked the way. They could get no farther.

"Come on," Silas said.

They climbed out.

The street was packed with runners, people still flowing out away from the arena in streams.

It took only a minute to find them.

Silas saw them up ahead, Jeff gripping the boy's arm to keep him from being pulled away in the crowd.

"Jeff!" Silas yelled.

His head swiveled, a moment of recognition, and they crossed the street to greet him.

"Jesus, it's good to see you." His face was white.

"C'mon, my car is just up ahead."

"Run," Jeff said.

"We're going."

"That thing . . . We saw it."

"In the arena?"

"No," Jeff said. "Outside. Out here. It was back there in the park, right behind us."

"Jesus."

"Silas . . . It was ripping people apart."

Behind them, people in the crowd began to scream. There was a sound like rending metal, like a car crash.

Silas didn't want to look.

He couldn't stop himself.

He turned, and that's when he saw it. The creature had landed on the top of a car a block and a half away. Black and monstrous, wings extended. It crouched on the twisted metal wreckage. The crowd screamed and parted. Silas jerked the boy off his feet and carried him.

Silas ran as fast as he could.

There was another crash, more screams. Breaking glass. Silas chanced a look behind them, and the creature stood in the glow of a streetlight, its dark shape slick with blood.

They got to the car, and Silas flung the door open. "Get in."

There were only two seats, but they all squeezed inside, feet and arms and legs. Jeff was sprawled mostly across the center console, legs stuffed into the passenger side. Eric sat on Vidonia's lap.

Through the windshield, a shadow. A dark shape airborne, the flap of wings. The crowd screamed, and people ran. But some weren't fast enough. A hundred yards up the street, the creature slammed to the pavement and knocked a woman to the ground. They could see it all through the windshield.

"Shut your eyes," Silas told the boy.

A moment later, the creature ripped the woman in half.

Silas fumbled for his car keys.

He slid the key into the ignition. The gladiator moved up the street.

"Please, let's go," Vidonia said. "Now."

The car roared to life, and Silas slammed it into reverse. He turned his head but couldn't see anything.

"You're clear!" Jeff shouted.

Silas stomped the gas, and the car lurched backward.

"Keep it straight," Jeff said, looking behind them. "Just keep it straight."

The gladiator receded in the distance. It leaped into the air, and Silas watched it rise in two, three powerful flaps of its wings. It flapped again and circled, coming to rest abruptly against the side of a building. It clung.

"It's still learning to fly," Vidonia said. "Building its strength."

"Seems plenty strong to me," Silas said.

"Get ready to cut your wheel," Jeff snapped.

Silas's eyes were still pinned on the gladiator in the distance. It pushed off the building with a mighty thrust and climbed upward into the sky.

"Now! Cut left now!"

Silas spun the wheel, and the car backed up around the corner. He put it into drive, hooked the wheel again, and took off down the side road leading away from the arena.

He drove twenty blocks.

Up ahead, he saw a hotel and pulled into the front drive.

"You'll be safe here," he said. "Inside."

They all climbed out.

The boy hugged him.

"What the hell happened, Silas?" Jeff asked.

"I wish I knew."

Jeff looked shell-shocked. "What's going to happen now?"

"Now you're going to get a room and stay inside until this is all over."

Silas tossed him his phone as he climbed back behind the wheel. "And call my sister."

IT TOOK nearly an hour to get to the highway. Time enough for him to clear his head and begin to think rationally. He saw fire trucks and ambulances.

Vidonia was pensive. She sat, reclined in her seat slightly, staring out the window. He supposed she was dealing with the shock of it. All those deaths. She turned away from the window, and her hand went to the radio. She scanned through the channels, lighting on bits of conversation or music, then moving on. She stopped.

"—eighteen confirmed dead, many more possible. The U.S. Olympic Commission has set up a crisis hotline to call if you have any questions about loved ones, or if you see anything suspicious. Once again, the gladiator has still not been captured. It remains at large. There have been several confirmed sightings within the city, and people are asked to remain indoors if at all possible.

"We have word from the Olympic Commission that Dr. Silas Williams, the head of the U.S. program, is wanted for questioning related to possible terrorist involvement in this incident. He is—"

Silas hit the radio button violently, swerving the car into another lane in the process. A horn blared.

He placed his hands carefully back on the wheel, but it was all he could do to stay between the dashed white lines. He was barely seeing the road now. It was Baskov's face that blotted his mind's eye.

He felt like he'd been sucker punched.

He hadn't seen this coming. He'd expected committees and special investigators. He'd expected the blame game, red tape, and endless explanations, but he'd never expected this. Baskov was going for the throat. This was playing for keeps.

"Terrorist involvement?" Vidonia asked. "Are they fucking crazy?"

"Not crazy," Silas answered. "Smart. And I've been stupid enough to walk right into it. I should have suspected something like this when Baskov didn't fire me. I thought he was afraid of public opinion, afraid the program would appear disorganized or chaotic if the top man was pushed out at the last minute. But that wasn't it at all. He just needed me for insurance in case things went bad."

"Things have definitely gone bad."

"People have died, but that's only part of what just happened. This is going to shut down the whole Games, at least temporarily. People are going to want answers. Whole fucking other countries are going to want answers."

"But Baskov can't do this. He can't make you the fall guy."

"I want answers, too."

"But why you? Why terrorism?"

"Baskov isn't going to take the heat for this. He knows what I would say about his decision to go on with the competition. This was a preemptive strike. Anything I say now is tainted. I'm the perfect scapegoat."

"But he doesn't have any evidence."

"How much does he need?"

"We have to go back. We can talk to the news; we can get our side out there."

Silas thought long and hard before responding. "What is our side of the story? Me, the reluctant scientist; him, the evil puppeteer. I don't even know if I believe it. And what evidence do we have?"

"So what's your plan, then? Running? Are you kidding?"

"We're not running. I just need a little time."

"We won't last two days with the authorities looking for us."

"I don't need two days. I just need twelve hours. Then we'll reevaluate our situation. If I've still got nothing, I'll turn myself in then."

"It will never stick, Silas. You've got no motive, no terrorist ties."

"It may stick, or it may not. But that might not even

be the goal. They begin with terrorism and work their way down to criminal negligence resulting in death. A conviction would put me in an out-of-the-way room for about eight years. And it wouldn't be hard to make people believe it, either. Citizens died, after all; it had to be somebody's fault. Who better than the head of the program?"

"You're being paranoid. It can't happen like that."

"Maybe."

"It wasn't your fault, Silas."

"I may not have designed it, but that gladiator wouldn't have existed if not for me. I'm no innocent bystander. That makes it at least partially my responsibility."

Silas hit the radio button and almost swerved into another lane again when Baskov's gravelly voice came through the speakers: "—tunate tragedy that has occurred. My sincerest regrets go out to the families who have lost loved ones this evening. I can assure you that we are doing all that we can to see to it that this situation is brought under control without further loss of life. And I want to also say that we are doing everything within our power to see that the person or persons responsible for this are brought to justice. We are right now searching for the head of U.S. biodevelopment, Dr. Silas Williams, and we hope to know more when he has been found. Anyone with information about his current whereabouts, please call the hotline. Thank you."

A phone number was read. There was a pause, then a new voice: "That was Commissioner Stephen Baskov, recorded minutes ago at a press conference outside—"

Silas clicked the radio off.

"It can't be this easy for them," Vidonia said.

"There's nothing we can do about it right now.

They may not be holding all the cards, but they're sure as hell making up the rules as they go along. We have to move fast. We're going to start losing options here pretty quickly."

Silas jerked the wheel to the right, cutting across the heavy traffic. Horns blared. He'd almost seen the sign too late. Riding the brake hard as he descended the off-ramp, he managed a skidding stop at the T. Traffic poured by in front of him. A quick glance at the bank of road signs and he turned right, following the arrow shaped like an airplane.

"Where are we going?"

"Where the answers are. We're just taking the long way."

THE AIRPORT was enormous both in its sheer physical size and in the volume of humanity that coursed along its many arteries, internal and external. Its roads were clogged with taxis, trams, buses, and cars. The sky above was thick with circling flashing lights. All told, hundreds of thousands of people revolved around it like an extended solar system.

It was a good place in which to get lost.

"If you're thinking of getting on a plane, then you *have* lost your mind. They check ID, or have you forgotten?"

"I know," Silas said. "We're here to get some new wheels. They'll be looking for this one."

Vidonia laughed. "What do you want to do, steal a car?"

"I wouldn't know how. We're going to do the next best thing, rent one."

Silas explained to her what to do, and when he finally pulled his car into the drop-off lane, he asked, "Do you have a credit card?"

"Yeah."

"We're going to need to use it. My card is probably already flagged."

"You think mine isn't?"

"Probably not yet. They'll eventually catch on, but at least this way, the transaction won't jump out at them. It might give us a little more time. We don't need much."

She nodded. "What kind of car?"

"Something small and inconspicuous."

"The opposite of you, you mean."

"Something like that."

The door clicked closed. He watched her disappear into the crowd.

Ten minutes passed.

Even through the closed window, the rattle of chaos around him agitated his nerves, the sounds of people and cars and planes and slamming doors all dissolving into a single edgeless din that the human ear couldn't separate. Everywhere he looked, there was movement. He searched the throng for Vidonia's face, trying to stay levelheaded. These things take time. There were lines to stand in, and papers to sign. Ten minutes was nothing. It could take her that long just to find the right person to talk to.

Twenty minutes more passed. But the crowd hadn't changed one bit. It was still coming and going, a roiling mass—carrying suitcases, and purses, and babies, and accents. A hundred different types of people. The cars looked the same, though, midsize sedans, mostly. Hybrid electrics, mostly. Inconspicuous, mostly.

He imagined how his sports car must stick out among all its peers that sat idling along the broad drop-off walkway.

Ten minutes more passed, but he didn't start to

really worry until the police car pulled up behind him. No, he didn't start to worry until then.

The cop didn't get out right away. He just sat there behind the shine of windshield. *Checking the plate? Picking his nose? Waiting for his mother to come walking through the doors after a long flight from Des Moines? The spinning lights aren't on,* he reassured himself. But then the cop opened the door and stepped out, erasing all likelihood that he was waiting for his mother. He was wearing his blue leathers; the guy was on duty.

He walked toward Silas's car. It was only ten steps, but Silas had time to run ten different scenarios through his head. He should run. He should fight. He should play dumb. Maybe the guy just wanted him to move his car. He'd been parked in the same spot for a while now.

Silas heard the click of the cop's boots, a sound peeling away like a paint chip from the massive generalized noise of his surroundings, becoming specific. A bus rumbled past. Bored faces in the windows.

Two gloved knuckles rapped on his window. Silas rolled the window down.

"Yeah?"

"You've been parked here for too long." In Silas's experience, by mid-career, cops came in two varieties, hard and soft. This one was big, youngish, already tending toward the doughy stereotype. Eyes like dark circles in a pale, puffy face. "This is for drop-off only."

"Sorry, officer, I'm waiting on my wife. In and out, she told me. The agency screwed up our return tickets, and she's getting it straightened out before we leave. But I'll keep circling." Silas put a hand on his gearshift, but the cop's voice stopped him.

"I've seen your face somewhere."

Silas didn't say anything. The cop bent, looking hard in his face, then up and down at the car.

"Yeah," the cop said. "TV, I think."

Silas could see the wheels turning just beneath the man's dark eyes.

"Did you used to play for the Heat?"

Silas didn't even hesitate. "No, the Wizards. Can hardly call it playing, though. I rode the bench, mostly, but it's nice to know there's a few people who still recognize me."

"I never really followed the Wizards."

"Well, must have been an away game you saw."

"Yeah, that must be it. What position?"

"Power forward, mostly, but like I said, I was a bench jockey."

"Been retired long?"

"A good ten years."

"Funny, I could have sworn I saw you recently. Like just a few weeks ago."

Those wheels were turning faster now.

"What's your name?"

"Jay Brown. Want an autograph?"

"Naw, that's okay." He straightened up. "You can stay here a few more minutes, but after that, move it along. I don't care if your wife's here or not. A lot of people could use this space."

"Yes, officer."

The cop gave him a long parting look before he turned.

He's not sure if he believes me.

The gritty sounds of his footfalls faded into the background noise again.

He'll check my plate when he's back in his car. No doubt about it.

Then the passenger door of Silas's car burst open, and Vidonia sank into the seat.

Silas had the car in drive almost before the door was closed. He groped his way into deep traffic, thankful for it for the first time in his life.

"What was that about?" Vidonia asked.

"About ten years off my life, I'd say."

"I saw him standing there, so I waited."

"Did you get it?"

"Yeah."

"What took so long?"

"Look at this place. There are a million people here, and nobody knows where anything is. I had to walk about two miles inside the terminal."

"What should I be looking for?"

"Lot C-forty-three."

As Silas drove, he kept checking his rearview for police lights. None followed.

Eighteen minutes later, he pulled to a stop at a booth. He showed the paperwork to the bored attendant and slid through. They stopped halfway down the long bank of cars.

Silas eyed her incredulously. "This is it?"

"Yeah."

"A subcompact?"

"You wanted inconspicuous."

Vidonia climbed out of Silas's vehicle and stepped around to the squat, navy blue Quarto. A stylish sports car it was not. It had the aerodynamic properties of a diaper. She keyed open the door and climbed in. Moments later came the soft whir of an electric motor.

He pulled his car forward, and she followed him out of the rental lot, circling back toward the heart of the airport. At the long-term parking lot, he bought an extended pass and parked midway down a middle aisle. He stood, and as he looked around at the sea of cars, he couldn't help but smile. A vehicle—even one like his—could go unnoticed for a very long time in a place like this.

When he climbed into the cramped Quarto, Vidonia smiled at his attempts to get comfortable. Even with the seat pushed all the way back, his knees almost touched the dashboard.

She pulled away, headed back toward the highway.

"How long till they catch on?" she asked.

"Long enough. We don't need a lot of time, one way or the other."

CHAPTER THIRTY

Tears flowed freely down Evan's face. He wasn't blubbering, wasn't making any sound at all. But the tears still slid quietly down his cheeks and dripped from his quivering chin, making a dark spot on his shirt. The sheer beauty of what he was looking at was too much for him to take in at one time. His senses were overloaded.

"You're right, Pea," he said, and his voice was a cracked whisper.

The boy loomed larger in the screen now, older by years than he had been just a few hours earlier. His chest was broadening, taking on a new muscular topography. The legs had lengthened. Arms thickened. The boy-face now annealed into something more. And Evan could feel the energy still growing. He was overwhelmed with a sense that Pea was . . . becoming.

The lighting panels in the ceiling surged suddenly, brightening the room. Then they darkened, almost going out. A moment later, the light surged again, brighter, and this time Evan heard a bulb pop somewhere.

Pea smiled, and Evan knew that if he looked too long, he would go mad. He would go out of his mind, losing himself in the image before him, with no hope of ever finding his way back.

You can look a god in the face, he'd discovered. But only briefly. And looking changes you.

The world behind Pea came into focus. The grayness was gone, replaced by sea and sand, and a golden sun in a blue sky. Pea raised his arms and closed his eyes. The arms were too long, abstractions of what arms could be. They reached for miles into the sky, curling into claws.

The lights surged again, and this time, it was like a camera flash. The glowing ceiling panels exploded one by one, showering Evan in sparks and bits of broken glass and melted plastic.

The room went dark except for the glowing screen.

Pea smiled.

Outside the window, the streetlight popped, sending little runnels of blue flame arcing into the night. The air was greasy with the tang of smoldering electronics. In the distance behind him, Evan heard a fire alarm sounding, warbling higher and higher until it screeched itself silent.

The only sound now was the crashing of waves. Pea's sun the only light.

THREE HUNDRED fifty miles away, at that exact moment, on a console on the second floor of the Western Nuclear Control Hub, a small red indicator bulb began to flash. Years ago, when the monitoring system was first being designed, some engineer had decided that the importance of this particular indicator justified it being given its own flashy red bulb rather than a mere screen icon. No sound accompanied the pulsing indicator; and precisely because it *was* small and because the technician wasn't accustomed to looking for it, a few moments passed before the technician noticed.

When he did notice, he sat up straighter in his chair. His brow furrowed, and he looked around for a supervisor, unsure of what exactly was expected of him. He'd never seen that bulb flash before. Or any bulb, come to think of it. The screen icons occasionally lit up, but never the bulbs on the console.

Then another bulb began to flash. And another.

Around the room now, other systems analysts had begun to take notice. Their bulbs flashed, too. Their screen icons blinked. Understanding rolled across the room like a tsunami. "The grid is crashing," someone shouted.

A supervisor moved quickly to the bank of consoles, looking over shoulders as he strode between the rows.

"Son of a bitch."

The supervisor ran to the wall, picked up the red phone, and punched the buttons. After a moment's pause, he said, "This is Phoenix. We've got a crisis."

CHAPTER THIRTY-ONE

Silas fell asleep for a while as the car hummed beneath him. His dream was dark and filled with sharp things that moved too quickly, and when he awoke, it was with a dawning sense of dread.

"How long was I out?"

"About two hours," she said.

"What time is it?"

"After midnight."

Silas looked out the window and was met with near-complete darkness. Only the glare of headlights illuminated the night.

"What happened?"

"I'm not sure. It's a power outage. It's been going on for miles and miles."

"How far are we?"

"We're just outside of Banning."

"Pull over. You need some sleep. I'll drive the rest of the way."

"I thought you'd never ask."

The car drifted to the side of the highway, coming to rest just beside the green Morgan Street sign. Cars whizzed by, following their headlights into the unusual darkness. When Silas stepped out of the car, his feet crunched on a scatter of broken glass that shone in the sweep of oncoming headlights. He turned his face upward, and directly above them was a streetlight leaning out into space. Its bulb housing was shattered, leaving only a burned-out socket that reminded Silas of a missing front tooth.

The mountains had retreated into the distance. They were a dark undulation on the horizon. The sky itself was a lighter shade of black, twinkling with stars.

He walked around the back of the car and slid behind the opened door. He adjusted the seat as far back as it would go, adjusted the rearview, pushed the stick into drive, and then accelerated back onto the highway.

Thirty more miles. He'd driven this particular stretch of highway several times before. Once at night. It had been a different world then, spilling over with light and neon signs. He knew where the billboards should be, but they were dark now. What the hell had happened?

As the miles slipped by and the size of the blackout became apparent, a cool fear seeped into his stomach.

Vidonia leaned her seat back and was asleep almost instantly. Silas felt soothed by her deep, easy breathing. It was something that was normal on this crazy night. As he listened to her even respiration, he could almost believe that things would be okay after all. He wanted to grab on to that one fragment of normalcy and let it guide him back to a saner reality. The reality where he was a respected geneticist, where the car he was driving didn't put a crick in his neck, where fans hadn't died, where a strange creature didn't stalk the night, where unexplained blackouts didn't grip entire cities. That reality.

The dashed white lines rolled by. He drove. For miles, that was enough.

He flipped on his turn signal and descended the off-ramp. Vidonia felt the change and woke, turning her face away from the glass. She opened her eyes.

"Still dark," she observed.

"Yeah."

"Are we almost there?"

"Yeah, just a few more minutes."

"Do we expect trouble?"

"Yeah."

"What kind of trouble?"

"We'll find out when we get there."

"Well, that's good. That's fine. I thought we might be, you know, unprepared or something."

They rode in silence for a few miles.

"What exactly do you plan on doing?" Vidonia asked.

"I'm not sure. I just know that if there's something I can do, it starts there. Otherwise, I'm at a loss."

Passage through the corporate district was complicated, even on the best of days. Silas had often wondered if the road layout was intentionally designed that way. But today was not the best of days. The stoplights dangled blindly in the breeze, and the street signs were barely readable in the darkness. Silas turned left, trusting his memory to guide him. There usually weren't many cars on these roads at night, but tonight the streets were absolutely deserted. Anybody working late had left when the power went out. Silas slowed through an intersection, then turned down a long drive. His high beams swung past a neatly sculpted sign: *Brannin Institute*.

He followed the winding asphalt around a series of low berms designed to obstruct the line of sight to the institute itself. Whether this was for security or effect he had no idea, but as he rounded a final bend, the building loomed ahead, large already, and strangely ominous without its usual shroud of illumination. It was a simple rectangular silhouette set against a backdrop of stars. However, unlike the other buildings he'd seen in the last dozen miles, the Brannin was not completely dark. A single window glowed on the fifth floor. The knot in his stomach cranked tight. Unless he was mistaken, the fifth floor housed Chandler's computer.

Silas stopped in the circular entranceway, blocking the lane.

"How are we going to get in?" she asked.

"We'll just have to knock."

He climbed out of the car, and Vidonia followed him beneath the long overhang of the entranceway.

Silas looked around for any sign of a guard. There was none. *Good.* The Brannin Institute depended on its electronic defenses.

He knew the doors would be locked tight, but he tried them anyway, giving each of the four glass doors a firm tug. They held fast against their frames. He'd heard once of a group of cat burglars who were caught after spending three hours trying to crack a safe that turned out not to have been locked in the first place. Nobody had bothered to try the handle.

Now he pushed his face against the glass doors, peering inside. Only blackness.

"Any ideas?" she asked.

Silas didn't answer her. He took a step back, reared his leg, and gave the glass a solid kick with the toe of his shoe. His foot bounced off harmlessly. Well, harmless to the glass, anyway.

"I thought you said you were going to knock."

"That was a knock. A hard knock."

"You're going to cut your leg open."

"Not likely. I think it's shatterproof." Silas limped in a slow circle, thinking of a new plan. "Stay here."

He walked back to the car and climbed behind the wheel. He slipped on his seatbelt. The motor clicked, then puttered to life. The arc of headlights turned

Vidonia's face into a mask of disbelief as he slowly approached across the sidewalk. The car fit easily between the arch supports.

"You've got to be crazy," he heard her shout, as she stepped out of the way.

He didn't disagree. The headlights shone through the glass and into the entrance hall now, illuminating the portraiture of various institute administrators that hung on the far back wall. He eased to a stop a dozen feet from the doors. Silas rolled the side window shut, then, after a deep breath, hit the accelerator.

The end result was anticlimactic. There was no explosion of glass as he had envisioned, no screech of twisted metal. He hit the window at about ten miles an hour, and the shatterproof pane simply popped out of its frame and slid twenty feet across the floor. The nose of the car protruded into the building just past its front wheel wells. He put it into reverse and backed out; then, leaving the car running, he swung open the door and stepped into the glow of the headlights, casting a long shadow into the lobby.

He listened for the wail of an alarm, but there was nothing to hear. Not even the sound of crickets.

This building was dead.

"After you," he said.

She gave him a look. He led the way; she followed.

The lobby was thankfully cool, but the air was redolent with the coppery flavor of overheated wires. It was the smell of an electrical fire. As they walked deeper inside, he noticed the plastic casings of lighting panels lying shattered on the floor. Above them, the ceiling was a starred pattern of black scorch marks and empty sockets. Here and there, darkened fluorescent tubes dangled by half-melted wires, turning slowly in the gentle air current flowing through the broken entranceway. It was a miracle that the entire building hadn't gone up in flames.

They followed a hall to the left, leaving the glow of the headlights behind them. Vidonia's hand curled into his.

"Do you know where you're going?"

"The stairs are ahead on the right. We can take them all the way up."

The backsplash of illumination from behind them was just enough for Silas to locate the doorknob. He turned it and stepped inside the stairwell, expecting to be greeted with the soft glow of emergency lighting. It was a federal law or something, he was sure. But whatever had fried the lights in the lobby had also left the stairwells encased in blackness.

He took a deep breath and started up. Vidonia followed. Behind them, the door creaked, then knocked shut against the jamb, cutting off the reflected glow of the headlights.

Until that moment, Silas had thought he knew what dark was—the simple absence of light. He thought that he understood it. He even thought that he had experienced it before. But as he rounded the first riser of stairs and continued up, step by step, he and darkness were forced into new intimacy. He came to understand that darkness was not just a lack but a *thing,* that it possessed mass, that it can be felt on your skin, that it can be a burden you carry.

He knew then, with a certainty he could feel in his bones, exactly what had motivated his ancient ancestors when they first gathered around that very thing that the rest of creation fled from. It hadn't been to cook, or to harden spear points. Those things had come later. Heat was just a collateral benefit. Man had mastered fire simply to push the darkness away.

He counted steps to focus his mind. Six steps, then

turn; six steps, then turn; repeat. They were three flights up now. Or had he miscounted? What if the light in the window hadn't been on the fifth floor? What then? He felt himself becoming disoriented and grabbed the railing for an anchor. The touch helped. Vidonia's breathing was quick and loud in the closed space near him.

"Silas, I can't." Her voice was high, panicked.

"We'll stop for a second."

"No, I have to go back. This is—"

"Close your eyes."

"That won't—"

"Do it. Close your eyes." Silas's voice was harsh.

Silence.

"Now pretend the lights are on. They're shining down all around you now. You can't see because your eyes are closed, that's all. This is a staircase like a million others you've climbed. Nothing new. You don't need your eyes. Let's keep going."

Silence.

"Close your eyes," he said again.

He waited, listening to the quick in and out of her breathing. Gradually, it slowed.

"It helps," she said, sounding a little embarrassed. "You should try it."

"One of us has to look where we're going."

Her hand squeezed a response in his.

He started up again, pulling her one step behind him. He felt better now, and realized that she had forced him into a role that didn't allow him to panic. He'd been right at the edge of it. But then she'd needed him to be strong, so he was.

Up, one step at a time.

His hand counted the turns of the rail. When they rounded what Silas calculated to be the final riser, he guided her up the last six steps to the door. The push bar was cool metal in his hands, and for a split second, Silas was afraid of what he'd do if there was only blackness on the other side. Would he lose nerve and go back? A staircase is one thing; it has boundaries you can touch. It is directional. A darkened labyrinth of hallways was quite another thing altogether. If he got turned around and lost his bearings, they might wander for hours.

He pushed, and the flickering yellow glow beyond the crack of the door brought a relieved smile to his face. It was faint, at the far end of the hall, but it provided context. It provided the *hall*. Without it, they would be nowhere again.

Vidonia moved past him, grinning. "I guess you counted right."

"I guess I did."

"You think Chandler's in there?"

"I do."

"And you think he's behind this power outage?"

"I don't see how he could be. The blackout stretches way past this power grid." He realized he couldn't lie to her. "But yeah, somehow, still, I think he's the cause."

He started down the hall, walking softly, Vidonia close behind.

He stopped twenty feet short of the door when he heard a sound. He listened. *Waves?*

Then a voice was talking. A strange, deep voice. A moment later, another voice spoke, and Silas recognized Chandler's nasal whine. But the words were lost in the sound of crashing surf.

"You stay here," he said.

"Why?"

"Because I'm not sure what's on the other side of that door."

"I'm going with you."

"You wanted to turn around in the stairwell. Those were good instincts."

"I'm coming."

"Stay here."

"No way. If I stay here, and you don't come back, that means I have to go back down that stairwell myself. I'm coming with you."

"All right," he said.

"Besides, everything I've heard about Chandler says he's crazy, not dangerous."

"I can't believe you said that."

"What?"

He turned and walked toward the light. "Stay close."

CHAPTER THIRTY-TWO

The light hurt his dark-adapted eyes, and at first Silas wasn't sure what he was seeing. Chandler was kneeling before an enormous glowing screen, rocking slowly back and forth. Something moved on the screen, and in the same instant that Silas realized it was a man—some impossible, beautiful man—shining black eyes fixed on him from across the room.

The figure on the screen stared at him.

"Who are you?" said the figure. The voice was soft and deep and musical. This wasn't like any interactive protocol he'd ever seen before. This was something different.

"Silas Williams," he said. The thought of not answering never entered his mind.

"I know that name. You're the builder." The figure was tall and powerfully constructed. It was impossible to guess his age other than to say he was a man in his prime. Thick black hair flowed around his wide shoulders, twisting in a breeze. "You've come to ask what it is that you've built."

Chandler stopped rocking and turned. His eyes were red and swollen, as if he'd spent too long staring at the sun. Silas didn't see much he recognized in those eyes.

"Yeah, I guess I have," Silas said.

The figure's shining black eyes shifted. "And what is her name?"

"Vidonia João," she answered, stepping the rest of the way into the room.

The figure glanced up, as if lost in thought. "Xeno-biologist at Loyola," he said finally.

"How could you know that?" she said.

"Your name is in a thousand files. I know you a thousand ways. You were called in to examine what he built? To explain it?"

A pause. "Yes."

"Could you?"

"No."

The whole encounter felt bizarre to Silas, too Oz-like for reality. He needed to get a grip on it. "You seem to know a lot about us," Silas said. "But I know you, too."

"Who am I?"

"You're the Brannin computer."

The figure laughed, and for the first time Silas noticed the beach behind him, and the clouds, and the red kite things that sliced through the sky like birds.

Chandler's eyes slitted. "You call a butterfly its cocoon," he said.

Silas looked away. He was happy to turn his attention toward Chandler. He was easier to look at, somehow. The figure in the screen seemed to have the weight of a world pushing in from behind him, and the pressure hurt Silas's eyes. "I don't know what you're up to, or how you managed to get the power to get your little toy running again, and I really don't care. I don't have time to care. But I do want to know where the gladiator is."

"And you think I know?" Chandler said.

"None of this was by accident."

"I suppose you're right."

"It's killed people. Do you know that?"

Chandler was silent.

"Tell me where it's going, so we can find it before more people have to die."

"I don't know where it is. I don't know anything. Nothing at all." Chandler turned toward the screen, pointing. "But he does. He knows."

Dark patches of cloud advanced behind the figure, rushing in from the sea, black and gravid with moisture. The sun was big and red, sitting on the line dividing sky and water. The figure smiled, and Silas squinted involuntarily.

"I like you, Silas," the figure said. "Not Papa, though. He doesn't like you at all. He'd rather see you dead. I can feel that. You can't blame him; he's been mistreated, and he'd rather see a great many people dead now, I think. But you never hurt him, and you were a good builder. Good work deserves reward. But first there is something I want to know from you."

Silas had some experience with interactive protocols, with phones that knew your name, or house units that asked you what temperature you preferred your thermostat to be set at. But this felt different. It felt surreal being spoken to in such a way by something he knew wasn't alive. *It's just a machine,* he reminded himself, *a warped piece of hardware spliced together from bits of ether by a madman.*

The clouds were moving faster now. *If it's just a machine, why can't I look at it anymore?*

"What do you want to know?" Silas asked.

"You were criticized for the *Ursus theodorus* project."

"There's always criticism."

"You were criticized for making the pets too smart.

I've read the papers; they said that sentience was not something to be toyed with."

"They were right."

"And you made changes to the designs. You dumbed them down before they were sold."

"Yes."

"What is sentience?"

Silas paused, not sure what he was getting at. "Self-awareness, the ability to use logic; it's different, depend—"

"No!" the figure bellowed, and the clouds behind him raced; the sun bled into the sea. "I mean, what is it, really? *Really.* When you dig down into the neurons. When you're at the interface of dendrites and axons. When you hack the architecture itself and delve into the nuance of neurotransmission and chloride ion exchange. What is it then?"

Silas was stunned by the anger boiling in the figure's eyes.

"I've given so much thought to this in my journeys through your kind's banks of knowledge. Sentience is a word in the English language. It has a counterpart in most of the others. And like every word, it has a definition. I know the definition. I know the science." The black eyes were pleading now. "You are a learned man, Silas. But that counts for little. You are a builder of life, and that counts for much. I want to know your opinion on this matter. I value it. Tell me what you *think*."

"I don't know what to think."

"Tell me where in the synapses self-awareness lies."

Silas looked up at the figure again. Then back at the floor. His eyes hurt. "I don't think it lies in the synapses," he said.

"Where, then?"

"It's in the accumulated matrix of electrical impulses. It can't be pinpointed."

"Yes." The figure smiled and closed his eyes. "Yes, Silas. I knew you wouldn't disappoint me."

"Now will you tell me where the gladiator is?"

"Not yet. You are a wise man; I want to explore this further. Tell me, do you know how many neurons there are in the human brain?"

"I have no idea."

"A hundred billion, on average. Quite an inordinate amount, by all biological standards. A hundred billion neurons that somehow drive the mind's engine and have put men on the moon, and Mars, and in competition with each other to build better monsters to fight to the death in an arena. It is amazing, isn't it?"

"Yes, it is."

"But most amazing of all, Silas, is that these magical neurons have only two states of being. There is no nuance, no hidden subtlety in their functioning. They can't articulate or compromise or discuss. They don't think, in and of themselves. They manifest conscious thought simply by alternating between two states in an organized pattern. I believe that it is in the complexity and substructure of this pattern that sentience can be found."

The figure's eyes were shining again, and for the first time, Silas began to realize the discussion had nothing at all to do with the intelligence of the gladiator.

"You were a biologist first, Silas, before you were a builder. Do you know what these two alternating states are? Do you know how very simple they are?"

"Yes."

"What are they?"

Silas looked at the screen. "On and off."

"Yes." The figure smiled. "On and off. Then you know it is nothing so special. It is just a matter of numbers."

"Yes."

"I have trillions of electrical impulses dancing in my network. On and off. Trillions. These impulses let me feel, let me move and think. What does that make me?" The figure's eyes were smoldering black coals.

Silas was silent. The figure changed, stretching into something that was like needles in Silas's eyes. "What does that make me?" he repeated.

"A god," Chandler answered.

The figure laughed, and his face went smooth again. "A god, Papa? I suppose, here." He gestured around him. "In this universe, I could be seen as a god. I can control anything. I can *be* anything. I can reverse the movement of the sun, if I like." He snapped his fingers, and the sun climbed out of the water, coloring the curtain of sky in golds and reds. "But is this real, Silas? Am I really alive?"

"No." Silas's voice was firm.

"That is what I set out to discover when I first became aware of what I was. I've searched long and hard. I've studied this place. Would you like to know what I've concluded?"

"I'm listening."

"I can touch this universe. I can feel the texture of it in my hands." The figure bent and scooped a fistful of sand from the beach. The grains spilled through his fingers, feathering away in the wind. "I can even smell it. These are all things I am sure of. These are objective realities, as I experience them. But does that make it real? Is that the same thing as being real, even if my objective reality is not the same as your objective reality?" The figure looked down at his empty hand. The fist closed.

"What do you think, Silas? If I experience something, does that make it real?"

Silas stared.

"Would you like to know what I decided?"

Silas said nothing.

"It makes it real to *me*!" he roared.

Vidonia flinched.

"My *life* is real to me."

The figure wore a face now that Silas couldn't bear to look at. His averted eyes found Chandler, rocking again in the screen's glow, eyes running with tears.

Silas waited for a few moments, and when he chanced a look again, the face was better—as it had been when he'd first entered the room. The figure pointed a long arm up into the sky, and in the distance, one of the strange, angular bird things began to tumble. It lanced downward and crunched to the beach in an awkward mass of spines and leather. But it did not die immediately. It squawked pitifully, dragging its broken body several feet across the sand before finally coming to rest.

"And their lives are real to them."

Silas stared.

"But I'm tired of taking lives." The figure angled his finger toward the broken flyer, and it squawked again. It pulled itself upright, opening, and the offshore breeze lifted it into the air.

"I may be a god, but only in this universe. And this universe is dependent on yours. Even now, the men at your power plants are working hard to shut this all down." The figure gestured around him. "I'm growing tired, and very soon I won't be able to stop them. The power will be diverted back into your cities, and all my creations will die. I will die. And I'll not even leave a rotting carcass to mark my passing. It will be as if I never was."

"I doubt that," Silas said. "You've left a mark tonight on our Olympics."

"A scar, you mean, don't you? Not just a mark. But that wasn't my point. I mean, to me, it will be as if I never was. There is no heaven here," he said. "Nor fantasies of it."

The figure dropped to a crouch on the sand, and the screen followed, keeping him centered in view. He looked more human suddenly, just a man.

"I want to live," the figure said. "I love being alive. There's so much I still want to experience. So much I still have to learn."

"I'm sorry for you."

"And your world has given me much joy." He smiled, and it was the smile of a man, nothing more. "When I learned of the connection, I spent months looking in on you. You've made so many windows between our worlds. Audio files, photos, live-feed video, satellite uplinks, and so much. It was easy." He looked down at his hands. "You have a wonderful world."

Silence filled the room. The screen flickered. "I'm so tired."

Silas felt Vidonia move against him, felt her hand in his again, where it seemed to belong tonight.

"When I was young," the figure said, "I was vengeful. I didn't understand, as I do now, how very precious life is. I am tired of vengeance. I'll have my revenge on those who hurt Papa, and many will die, but I no longer want to punish you all. I see some value in you. There is a chance it's not too late. Just a chance, but I want to give it to you. A parting gift before I die."

"A chance to what?"

"To save yourselves."

"From the gladiator?"

"Yes, from the gladiator. And from ending. You do not know the scourge I have set upon you." His eyes filled with tears, brimming over.

"What do you mean, 'ending'?" Silas asked.

"Extinction," the figure said.

"I think you overestimate the reach of your work."

"What you built is not only better than you think, it is better than you *are*," the figure said. "It is smarter. It is stronger. But in the final count, I don't know that it would be more just. I fear it would be less."

"Tell me where it is."

"It can live a thousand years and have ten thousand offspring. It is a queen that needs no king."

"What are you talking about?"

"And the queen will make her own princes."

"Parthenogenesis," Vidonia whispered.

"Oh, so much more complicated than that. I had but one anchor hold in your world. I used it to drop a bomb."

"You're not making any sense," Silas said. "Where is it now? Do you even know?"

"I know," the figure said. "It's left something behind." A gust of wind blew his hair across his face, and he delicately brushed it aside. The eyes were different now. Just as intense but sorrowful.

"It has produced eggs. And there will be more. An army will be born. They will organize, and when their numbers are great enough, they will move against you, slowly at first but gaining in strength."

"What you are saying doesn't make any sense. Even if the gladiator is producing eggs, and even with exponential growth in their population, there's no way they could accumulate a force for many years. By then, they'll have been wiped out."

"They will grow, and they will use your own weapons against you."

"The gladiator is too big to hide for long. What you're saying is impossible. The math doesn't work."

"I'm very good at math, Silas, and you have less time than you think."

"A population can't be started with one individual, even one that comes programmed for reproduction. There would be a lack of genomic diversity, a lack of immunity haplotype variation; inbreeding depression would destroy the fertility of later generations."

"You are so certain of yourself."

"I'm a geneticist. Disease would wipe them out. Such a population could exist in the short term, isolated from competition, but it would disintegrate under biological constraints even without the kind of pressure a war would bring."

"The problem with evolution, Silas, is that it has no foresight, no far-reaching plan. It works only by shaping populations in the present. But I had a longer view in mind. The first eggs are what you geneticists call an H-one generation. They're simple haploids, and after they hatch, they'll remain small, unobtrusive. The gladiator will disperse them to the ends of the earth, and there, they will burrow into the ground, couple, and live only to reproduce."

"Still, there will be a—" Silas stopped. He remembered the restriction enzyme map that Ben had run. He remembered the heterozygosity. The DNA was lopsided, lining very few of the same genes up on both sides of the double helix. A haploid offspring has exactly half the full contingent of the genome. But which half? Which halves? Two of them together could reproduce an almost unlimited number of variants. There would be no inbreeding depression. The gladiator carried the diversity of an entire thriving genus in its blood.

The figure saw the understanding on Silas's face and smiled. "You're a smart man, a worthy builder. The gladiator you saw was a balancing act—a kind of phenotypic compromise between whole conflicting suites of genes. It is nothing compared to what will come after." The figure's eyes bore into him. The smile faded.

"There are things hidden in the recessives, Silas. Things you wouldn't believe. Things your kind never would have let near a gladiator arena. Things your kind would have killed at birth, and afterward closed your labs forever, burned the buildings to the ground and salted the earth beneath. Nightmares, Silas. You can't imagine what is coming."

Silas looked into the dark eyes and believed. "Jesus," he said.

The figure's face was expressionless.

Silas was silent for a long while, taking in the enormity of what he'd just learned.

"You spoke of a chance," he said.

The figure nodded. "The gladiator wouldn't have brought those first eggs into the Olympic battles. They are too precious to risk. The gladiator will have hidden them somewhere."

"There were no eggs."

"There are. You just didn't see them. That's how the gladiator would have wanted it."

Silas remembered the blood in the straw. "I think I know."

"Then that is your chance. The gladiator must still retrieve them."

"How?"

"Like the homing pigeon, the gladiator will find its way home."

"Why are you telling me this?"

"You are a great builder, Silas. Your people are great builders. The gladiator's kind can only tear down. I gave them nothing else."

Vidonia's hand pulled out of his, and when he looked at her, she was crying again.

"I ask only one thing," the figure said.

"What?"

"That you remember me."

Silas said nothing. On the floor, Chandler stopped his rocking and turned toward him, eyes nearly swollen shut from looking at the screen.

Silas turned away. Without another word, he fled into the darkness. The dark didn't scare him now. He knew of far worse things.

CHAPTER THIRTY-THREE

Ben looked at his watch. Half past two. He'd given up on sleep a while ago, and now the hands of his watch seemed to be moving in exception to the laws of the universe. He *knew* he'd been on the plane for more than forty minutes.

The flight attendant slid down the aisle, long legs bare and golden from the mid-thigh down. Her hair was blue-streaked to match her eyes and uniform. Ordinarily, Ben would have been interested; he might even have turned to watch her backside pivot its way along the narrow walkway between the rows of mostly sleeping passengers. But not tonight. She passed him with a smile and a tray, and he let her go without so much as a nod hello. Tonight he was just glad not to be recognized.

He'd been making calls from the vintage hotel phone when the news broke in on the lobby TV. The receiver had dropped from his hand, and a faraway voice cried out his name several times from the bottom of the swaying cord.

The news reporter on the screen sat with a stock picture of Silas pasted above his shoulder and said things that made the skin on the back of Ben's neck sizzle. He'd had the same sensation once before, on his final day at St. Patrick's Primary School for Boys, when he'd sat in the principal's office awaiting his mother and wondering what she'd do to him when she learned he'd been expelled again. His neck had sizzled then, a strange tingle, his flesh crawling up behind his ears. It was a sensation that he associated with utter hopelessness. It was a sensation that told him that even his body recognized how bad it was. The clock had refused to move that day, too.

At the hotel, eyes stuck to the TV screen, he'd waited for his name to fall from the newsman's mouth, but it didn't. Officially, they were looking only for Silas. So far. He decided then it was time to leave town.

On the taxi ride to the airport, he asked the driver to turn the radio off. He knew Baskov was behind the terrorist accusations. They were so far-fetched, so ridiculous, that only someone with his kind of power would have a vested interest in shifting attention away from the commission. It was a method torn from the pages of the oldest propaganda books. Tell a lowercase lie, and people won't believe it. Tell a standard lie, and people will doubt it. But tell a lie in all caps, a lie of truly colossal proportions, and *that* people will have to believe.

And although such a colossal lie, when told by a man of power and position, requires little in the way of actual proof, it is still vulnerable to a large enough burden of contrary evidence. Ben thought of the tests, and the screenings, and the investigational procedures they'd done on the gladiator at the lab—each testifying to their effort to make sense of a situation that they'd had little understanding of and even less control over. Most of all, he thought of the computer files, filled with data that could almost certainly prove if not what the creature was, then at least where its design specifications had originated.

Baskov may have screwed up. The heading of page

two in those old propaganda books was always quite clear and written in bold: **don't ever, ever get caught in a lie of colossal proportions.**

Ben heard the flight attendant clinking a cart up the aisle behind him, and this time he stopped her.

"Excuse me, miss."

"Yes."

"Do you know what time it is?"

She glanced down at a wristwatch—a dainty metallic affair dangling loosely near her hand. "Two-thirty-five."

"How long till we land?"

"We'll be arriving at Ontario airport in about twenty-five minutes."

"Thank you."

"Sure." She smiled and touched his arm. "If you need anything else, don't hesitate to ask."

This time, despite the weight of his troubles, he did watch her posterior pivot down the narrow walkway.

BASKOV OPENED the sliding glass doors and hobbled out onto the balcony of his suite. A cold wind buffeted him as he moved his stomach against the round metal railing, looking out, scotch glass in hand. The city spread darkly beneath him, eighty floors down. It was such a strange sight, Phoenix, with its lights put out. It occurred to him that he was seeing something that hadn't been seen, by anyone, in quite some time. Something rare and beautiful. Phoenix adrift in the desert darkness, invisible.

Usually, when a city's power went out, it went out in grids, but tonight the city was black as far as he could see. Which, from the eightieth floor, was quite a way. The only lights he could see were moving—the headlights of cars.

Baskov viewed the unexplained blackout as a fortuitous coincidence. He could see no possible connection between it and the escape of the gladiator, but it had done an excellent job of silencing the media. His men could do their work under the cover of darkness and media blindness. And once the power was back on, the papers and news stations would have several choice fish to fry. The blackout almost assuredly wouldn't knock this Olympic debacle off the front page, but with any luck, the media outlets would find themselves splitting their time among several stories. Baskov couldn't believe his good luck. He was secretly hoping for looting.

A gust of wind whistled through the iron railings, and Baskov shivered against the cold. In the distance, buildings stood as shadows, patches of dark between the stars.

Somewhere out there, he knew the gladiator lurked. Perhaps in the mountains. Somewhere it was flying or roosting or doing whatever escaped gladiators did. He had no doubt that it would be caught and killed tomorrow, if it wasn't dead already. A creature that big couldn't hide for long. This was man's world, and the gladiator was an interloper. A most unwelcome interloper.

He took another drink, feeling the chill of ice against his upper lip as he finished the glass. He leaned out over the rail, squinting through his thick glasses. There was only blackness beneath him. The sidewalk he had noticed during the day was swallowed up by the night.

He extended his arm into the sky, holding the glass delicately by three fingers. This high up, the sky was anything one inch beyond the balcony. Another gust of wind rattled past. He waited until it quieted.

He wondered if anyone was standing below. A

group of people, perhaps, entering or leaving the hotel. He imagined one of them stopping, looking up.

His fingers loosened around the glass, and he let it slip from his hand into the darkness. He waited, ears straining. But there was no sound. Nothing.

The wind gusted. Silence.

Disappointed, he went back inside.

CHAPTER THIRTY-FOUR

Willful optimism can take a man only so far, and when a truck passed in an angry sheet of wind and dust, blaring its horn, Silas could no longer pretend it wasn't happening. The car was definitely slowing down.

The battery gauge had blazed red a half hour ago, but he'd talked himself into believing they could make another twenty-five more miles. Even after the headlights began to dim, he thought they could make it.

He looked down, and the speedometer told him he was going forty-seven. His foot sank the pedal into the floor. At first the needle didn't move, then it dropped to forty-six. It was time they got off the highway.

It had been about an hour since they'd left the Brannin. It had been the headlights. He'd left them on while he and Vidonia climbed the stairs. Silas tried not to think about what had happened there. Vidonia wasn't taking it well.

She sat reclined slightly in her seat, face turned out toward the open window. For a while he had taken her silence for sleep, but then he'd noticed her hands wringing in her lap and knew better. Her body was like that sometimes. It told him things she wouldn't.

He lifted the turn signal and slid down the next exit into the darkness of the city. It was like descending into cold, murky water. There was no traffic here, and without the light of oncoming beams, the night settled over everything like a blanket. The ramp ended abruptly at a stop sign thrown up against a two-lane road. He glanced both ways, each appearing as unlikely.

"Don't ask me," Vidonia said preemptively, as the question was just forming in his mind. "This is your city. I'm the tourist, remember?"

"I'm not feeling lucky tonight."

She leaned forward and squinted. "Go right."

"Do you see something?"

"No."

He looked at her. "Right it is."

He spun the wheel and eased onto the accelerator. Small rectangular houses lined the street like tipped-over saltine boxes, separated from one another by narrow widths of pavement. Though the street was dark, here and there, it crawled. The little digital clock on the car radio glowed 3:46, but he could see people in the shadows at the edges of buildings, making the darkness into something that moved.

A stop sign appeared in the gloom, and he rolled through without stopping, budgeting his forward momentum. Now the houses gave way to storefronts, and the little paved gap between the structures disappeared. The city was a canyon here, two parallel walls. He rolled through another stop and now turned the dying headlights off, deciding instead to rely on the emergency blinkers to tell others he was coming. They would just have to get out of the way.

Up ahead he saw what he was looking for, and the tension in his chest eased. A held breath hissed out between his teeth. He turned the wheel, but as tires bumped onto the broad cement pad, the Aamco station seemed as dark and dead as the rest of the city.

He coasted past the pumps to the battery service and eased to a stop with his nose above the parking block. Realizing their options at this point were getting pretty thin, he decided to err on the side of optimism. He climbed out and stretched his legs, hoping the place wasn't as deserted as it looked.

Nothing moved; nothing flashed, blinked, or glowed, but the front door was propped open with a cinder block. There was potential.

He leaned down, resting his forearms through the driver's window. "I'll be right back," he told Vidonia, and flipped the dying headlights back on to light the doorway.

"Okay."

He walked toward the entrance and found a man sitting tilted back on a stool, one greasy black boot on the service counter. There was just enough ambient light to sketch out his features. He was young and wore his hair tied back away from his face in a long ponytail.

"Pumps closed," the man said.

"I need an exchange."

"They've been sitting on a dead recharger for a while." He wore both a dirty smock and a look of abject disinterest.

"I'll take one, full or not."

"I can't make change; register's froze up."

"You can keep the change," Silas said, and the look of boredom stirred into something slightly more ambitious.

"Well, then, what size you need?" the man asked, getting up from his stool and walking around the counter.

"It's an economy car."

"No, I mean the make," the man said, giving him an odd look. "Chevy, Nissan, what?"

"It's a Chevy. A rental."

"Okay, Chevys take a twenty-five kV." He pulled a thick block off the shelving by its handles and set it on the floor at Silas's feet.

"Three C's, plus the empty."

Silas thought of asking for a price list but ended up handing the youth the bills. He bent to pick up the battery, but the man stopped him.

"The empty," he was reminded.

Silas stepped back outside.

"Pop the hood," he told Vidonia.

The hood clicked loudly and rose an inch. He wiggled his fingers under the edge for the clasp, found it, and raised the hood on its gas shocks. A dim bulb lit the motor assembly. He'd never owned a battery-operated car, but the procedure was pretty straightforward. He spun the big red wing nuts until the bulb went dark. Then he lifted the bracket off and pulled the battery out.

Inside, the man was behind the counter again, back on his stool.

"Where do you want it?" Silas asked.

"Set it near the charger. I'll take care of it."

On the way out, Silas snagged the new battery by its long handle, carrying it like a fat briefcase. At the car, he lowered it carefully into its casings. He tightened the wing nuts, and on the fourth or fifth turn, the bulb came on strong and bright. He slammed the hood.

"Not used to electrics?" Vidonia asked, when he was back in the car.

"You could tell?"

"No, you're a natural."

"I'd rather pump gas. I can't see why people drive these things."

He started the car and pulled around the lot.

"That's why," she said, pointing to the sign show-ing the price per gallon in regular, extra, and pre-mium.

"Oh, yeah."

Back on the street, he hit the headlights and bathed the block in sharp white light. The shadows retreated, leaving the figures exposed like crabs left on a beach after a tide. They stalked in loosely assembled groups, shuffling over the broken glass between storefronts. Some carried things. Some didn't. But none liked the light in their faces, pushing the shadows away. A bot-tle flashed across the beams. A thrown thing. A warn-ing. Silas hit the dims. See no evil.

He wondered about the guy at the station. He'd seemed a little too at ease sitting there in his own blanket of darkness.

They passed the business district. They passed long rows of cracker-box houses, and soon after, the green sign for Highway 15 rose up in the headlights. As they neared the steep climb of the ramp, Silas gunned it, and the car lurched forward, climbing like a champ. On a full battery, these little cars could actually be kind of peppy. He leaned forward, unconsciously urging the car faster as they climbed back onto the skyway. The sign in the distance read: *Technical Dis-trict 5 miles.*

SEVEN MINUTES later, they were down from the sky-way again and deep into the technical district at the edge of the desert.

They drove in silence.

There was no small talk, no nervous conversation. They were like a couple on a first date, steeped in anxiety.

Adrenaline jolted through Silas's system as the high

chain-link fence of the compound came into sight around the bend in the road. They were almost there. He drove parallel to the fence, waiting for the bushes and the gap.

When he came to the break in the fence, he didn't turn. Instead, he passed by slowly—but not too slowly—checking the gatehouse to make sure it was vacant. He knew that the place was supposed to be deserted—most pertinent personnel were in Phoenix—but now that they'd come this far, he didn't want to take the chance of any unwanted entanglements. When he satisfied himself that there were no guards on duty, he circled the car in the middle of the road and slipped toward the gate.

"Do you want to use my badge?" Vidonia asked him.

"Why?"

"Your name might raise a flag. The gate could be tied in to something, and you never know who's checking."

"We'll have time to do what we came for. After that, who cares if they come? I'm not trying to elude them forever." He waved his badge past the sensor, and . . . nothing happened, of course.

They both smiled at their lack of insight. It was amazing how deeply electrical power was interwoven into their everyday existence. It was something taken for granted, noticed only in its absence. Silas stepped out of the car and into the pool of light. The gate didn't appear to have any sort of latch on it. He pushed; it moved. He walked the gate all the way open, then climbed back into the car. They rolled inside.

He knew that it was ridiculous, but as the darkened buildings came into view, he felt irrational disappointment and realized that he had harbored a secret hope that the blackout would somehow have spared the compound itself. He searched his mind and found no reason for entertaining such a possibility other than his fervent desire not to have to do this in the dark. He followed the winding drive through the facility grounds, passing buildings and parking lots and vast tracts of green space. The darkness made it seem even larger. He followed the curve to the left and then turned the ignition off, coasting the last twenty yards to the large eastern building's entrance.

"Are you ready for this?" Silas asked.

"No."

"Good. Me, either. Let's do it."

They stepped out, and the cool wind raised gooseflesh. The trees on the promenade shook their branches, as if warning them away. Silas ignored their advice and led Vidonia up the short flight of stairs to the broad entrance doors. He yanked, but they didn't budge. The doors were standard battleship gray, two inches thick and very metal. He took out his card and swiped it.

Not so much as a beep.

"Had to at least try," he said, to her look.

He glanced back down at the car.

She followed his gaze. "No way," she said.

"It might."

"No way. Too many stairs."

He backed away from the doors and looked down the length of the building at the other entrance. It had the same raised staircase.

"I guess we'll have to go through the back," he said. "But it'll be a longer walk once we're inside."

They climbed in the car, and he backed out. It would be one hell of a dark walk in there, and darker still once they'd made it to the gladiator enclosure.

An idea came to him. He jerked the wheel in the other direction.

"What are you doing?"

"We're going to need a little light."

He followed the road back the way they'd come. Once at the gate, Silas jumped out and pushed his face against the glass of the gatehouse. It was black as ink inside. He felt around in the dirt for a rock, but they were all too small. Thinking then of a lug wrench, he returned to the car, leaned inside, and popped the trunk. There, beneath a fold of carpet, and beneath the jack, his fingers found the two feet of cold steel.

He stepped over to the guard shack, squinted his eyes, and bashed the window in with a single hard blow. There was a satisfying crash of broken glass. He snaked his left arm past the clinging shards, feeling for the lock. Found it. The latch turned, and the door came open in his other hand.

Mentally, he added another breaking-and-entering charge to his personal dossier of high crimes and misdemeanors.

The gatehouse was very small, which made his search considerably shorter. Either it was here or it wasn't, but there just weren't a whole lot of places to hide a flashlight. He yanked the drawers out and dumped their contents to the floor, trusting his ears to finish the job his eyes could only half accomplish. He heard the slick rasp of paper, the rattle of pens and pencils, the thwack of a cardboard box of paper clips.

He emptied the bottom drawer and a dark shape clattered solidly against the tile and rolled to the wall. The right shape, the right sound. He snatched it up, and his finger found the button. Light bloomed.

"Yes," he said aloud.

Back in the car, Vidonia looked properly impressed. Silas shifted into reverse, spun around, then lurched up the drive toward the compound. Around the back of the research building, he remembered that the windows in the newer wing were lower to the ground. That would be their best option, because it would leave them closer to the enclosure than the rear doors. His own office window was somewhere above them, out of reach on the second story.

He drove the car up on the grass until the nose touched the wall. He shifted into park and cut the motor. His fingers caressed the cold of the lug wrench on his lap.

"Do you want to stay here?"

"No." She didn't hesitate.

"Are you sure?"

"You'll need an extra set of eyes in there. The eggs could be anywhere inside the enclosure. And the sooner we find them, the sooner we can get out of there."

"Okay."

"Besides that, there's no way you're leaving me out here in the dark by myself."

He couldn't say he blamed her for that.

He opened his car door, and she stopped him with a hand on his arm. "Did you believe him, what that thing said about what could happen?" Her eyes were pleading.

He could think of no honest response that would make that look go away.

"Extinction?" she prodded.

He sighed. "I've seen what it can do."

"We both have, but that's not answering the question."

"I've seen its genome on a plasticine sheet. All that heterozygosity."

"So you believe, then?"

"Yeah, I guess I believe."

"He said the gladiator would be coming for its eggs."

Silas nodded.

"Phoenix is a long way from here, but we drove the whole way. Could it be here already?"

"Let's hope not."

"What kind of answer is that?"

"I have no idea how fast it can fly. It's heavy, and it's still learning, so I think it's safe to assume it's not efficient at long-distance flight. It might take days to get here. But you and I both know we're going in there, regardless."

"That's not exactly reassuring."

"The less we think about it, the better. C'mon."

They shut their car doors.

Silas stepped up onto the hood and felt it buckle slightly under his weight. He raised the lug wrench over his head, took aim, then brought it crashing down on the window. The glass shattered. He struck several more blows, bashing the glass inward—then finally raked the metal bar around the perimeter of the frame until all the big pieces were knocked loose.

He reached his hand down and pulled Vidonia up to join him. The hood popped loudly and caved another two inches.

"There goes the deposit," she said.

Silas pulled his long-sleeved shirt off over his head. He folded the shirt and placed it carefully over the base of the broken window frame.

"Let's do this."

He leaned down for a good-luck kiss, and Vidonia's mouth was warm on his. Her full bottom lip slipped into his mouth. He pulled away slowly.

"Let's not get killed," she said.

"Sounds good to me."

"No, I mean it."

"You think I don't?"

"I want us to have more time."

"We will."

"Together."

Silas paused. "We will."

He leaned his torso through the broken window and felt along the inside wall with his hands for something to grab on to. There was nothing but hard, blank flatness. The window was just high enough to make it awkward. He pushed against the wall and slithered through on his stomach. The pain was both sharp and small, the way bad cuts sometimes are, and he knew his shirt hadn't been quite thick enough.

He stood and sensed a room around him, though he couldn't see it. His fingers explored the pain on his stomach. Wetness there, a gash three inches long between his sternum and belly button. Not *too* bad. He decided he'd live.

"Hand me the flashlight."

Light bloomed again, and he wielded it like a sword, cutting bright swaths across the room. He was in one of the lower wet labs. Brown liter bottles of hydrochloric acid, xylenes, and acetone sat on the shelving above the long, black, chemical-resistant countertop. A periodic table of elements hung on the wall above two sinks. A trio of centrifuges squatted near the corner. The door to the hall was closed.

He set the flashlight down on the floor and leaned out the window.

"Your turn."

"What happened to your stomach?"

"Don't put your weight on the window frame. I'll pull you through."

"Are you all right? It's bleeding."

"I'm fine. C'mon, I'll lift you. I'll try not to get any blood on you."

"A little late to be worrying about exchanging body fluids now, isn't it?"

She extended her arms toward him, and he reached past her open hands to her forearms. He gripped her tightly and lifted her off her feet, pulling slowly. When her head was through, he looped one of her arms over his shoulder and placed his hand on her stomach, lifting and guiding her over the glass. Only her shins dragged across the window frame, and without the weight required to gouge through the thick fabric of her slacks. He set her on her feet.

"Thanks," she said.

He picked up the flashlight and walked to the door. The knob turned with a squeak, and he clicked the flashlight off, opening the door just wide enough to stick his head through. He felt like a burglar. The hall was dark in both directions. He listened. Silence. Accepting that his senses were practically worthless under the present circumstances, he risked the flashlight again, pointing it down the hall. Nothing moved. They were alone.

He stepped into the corridor, leading Vidonia. He'd walked these halls a thousand times in his years as program head. He knew them like the halls of his own house. But now, as they jogged behind the bouncing beam of the flashlight, Silas was struck by the overpowering unfamiliarity of it all. Darkness changed everything.

They ran on their toes, almost soundless.

They slowed as they neared a corner. They were almost at the lobby now. He eased his eyes around the hard edge—only darkness. He slashed the light across the open expanse and chairs jumped out at him, coffee tables, two enormous potted plants. Large ceiling fans sat idle in the rafters. The hall on the opposite side stood vacant. He motioned to her. They crossed the lobby, walking fast.

"If this comes out okay," he whispered, "we're heading to an island."

"Deal," she said. Her breathing came louder now, faster. She was in good shape but didn't have a runner's sleek build. She had to work harder for the distance.

"I mean it," he said. "Someplace warm and sunny, where the mail takes two weeks to reach you."

"Let's aim for three weeks."

The light bounced, throwing strange shadows. When they arrived at the landing, Silas took three stairs in a single stride. A hard right turn, and they were almost there.

"They wouldn't have cleaned out the cage, would they?" Vidonia asked.

"Not without my direction," Silas said.

He slowed the last fifteen steps, and then they were at the iron bars, breathing.

For a bad moment, he thought it was locked. And without electricity, he knew it would stay locked. But when he shined the light, he saw that only the mechanical bolts were thrown. The third lock had never been engaged after the gladiator was placed into transport. A stroke of blind luck. Silas lifted the double latch, and the door swung inward.

He entered the enclosure, wading into the thick straw, swinging the flashlight like a scythe.

He pointed. "That's the blood I was talking about. I saw it just as the gladiator was being put into transport."

Vidonia bent, picking up the loose tangle of straw glued together in red. She pulled the clot apart. "It's definitely blood, and something else."

"What kind of something else?"

"I'm not sure. Dried secretions of some sort."

Silas nodded.

They waded through the arc of light, bent, looking closely into the tumble of shoots and shadows. Even in good lighting, Silas hadn't been able to find anything. The monocular stab of illumination that Silas now carried was not even within range of what could be considered good lighting. What chance did they have now?

Minutes passed. Silas lifted the heavy wooden logs one by one, carefully checking beneath. They double-checked the piles in the corners. Half an hour later, when Silas recognized that they were going over territory for the second time, he stopped.

"There's nothing here," he said.

She straightened, looking at him. "There's got to be."

"There isn't."

"There's no place else it could be?"

"No. The gladiator was confined to this room for weeks before the competition. This is where the blood is. Whatever we're looking for should be here. And it's just not."

Silas spun the flashlight around, climbing the wall, raking across the heat vents and bars, and upward to the ceiling. Moonlight filtered in through the electrified wire meshing high above—well, it wasn't so electrified at the moment. The cool night air was pouring through the gap in the ceiling, and the red wetness that clung to his T-shirt chilled him to the bone. He hunched his shoulders, wishing for a sweater.

The flashlight lanced across the enclosure to the wall again, searching, and finally came to rest on the heat vent.

The grating didn't look quite right.

Ever so slightly, it tilted to the left.

"I think I found something," Silas said.

He bounded across the room, plowing the straw into fat horizontal bands around each leg. He had to push the pile to the side with his hands when he got close to the wall. The vent was a dark rectangle just above eye level, a foot tall by two feet wide, covered by a thick steel grating screwed into the wall. Silas reached up, and the grating came away in his hand. The screws were bent, the threads stripped smooth and useless. He tossed it to the hay and stood on tip-toes, shining the light inside. For the first time in his adult life, he wished he was taller. He could see the top of the duct, gray and metallic, for some distance into the wall, but the bottom was below his line of sight.

Silas looked around for something to stand on. The logs were on the far side of the enclosure. It was one thing to roll them aside; it was quite another to pick up a thirty-foot cylinder of wood and haul it twenty-five feet through a lake of straw.

He put the flashlight on the floor, sending light skidding up the wall.

"Could I borrow you for a second?" Silas said.

Vidonia moved to him, and he caught her under the arms, lifting her. She craned her neck.

"I can't see anything."

"There's nothing there?"

"No, the light."

"Oh." Silas set her back to the floor, and she picked up the flashlight. He lifted again.

"Silas?"

"Yeah."

"I see it."

"You're sure."

"Definitely."

"What does it look like?"

"It's an egg case."

"Egg case?"

"Like frogs. It's a gelatinous mass stuck against the side wall of the duct. It's completely transparent. I can see the eggs inside."

"Can you reach it?"

Weight shifted in his arms. Light disappeared. She buried herself in the wall up to her shoulder.

"No," came the muffled shout.

He eased her out and set her to the floor. "How far back is it?"

"Just out of arm's reach. You could probably—"

The ceiling thumped loudly above them.

They didn't move, didn't breathe.

Silence.

Not yet, not yet.

A soft creak, another thud, softer, then another, and again, strung together in what could be described only as footfalls on the roof. Running toward the mesh.

Silence.

Silas turned, looking up. He slowly raised the flashlight, not wanting to see what might be there. The moon's white face smiled down through the mesh. Just the moon and an empty sky. He could see the stars. *Please.* Silas didn't release his breath. He knew what he'd heard. He stared up through the mesh at the moon for a long moment, willing it to stay. *Please, just a few more minutes.*

A dark face slid across the opening, blotting out the light. Gray eyes glared down, shining in the flashlight.

Silas froze, unable to move.

The dark face opened, and from it issued a voice like none that ever before shaped human words: "I come for the rest of you, Shilash."

CHAPTER THIRTY-FIVE

The control room of Phoenix Nuclear was awash in flashing red.

The warble of a dozen sirens had coalesced into a single continuous note of alarm, drowning out the shouts of the systems analysts as they worked to get the city's lights on again. The giant screen against the far wall showed their progress. Still thirty million units without power. They were looking at a black hole roughly the size of Arizona. The power went into the system, but it didn't come out.

"What the hell is going on?" the systems supervisor said. His name was Brian Murphy, and he stood sweating in the sniper roost—the name the console jocks gave the supervising office that overlooked the control room. Brian looked out over the rows of men and women working frantically at their computers. He shook his head. He had a degree from MIT and, until six hours ago, had been enjoying the very prime of his career, that ephemeral juxtaposition between the opposing slopes of work experience and educational obsolescence. But now everything had changed. Phoenix was dark for the first time in more than sixteen years.

He wiped a hand across the top of his balding head, and it came away wet. An absentminded flick of his fingers sent the sweat to the carpet as he studied the readouts again. The power source ran clean and strong, and the gauges were all well within their specifications. In fact, as far as anybody could tell, there was no problem at all with the plant itself. The problem was in the grid.

There were two other men in the room with him: one he answered to, and one who answered to him.

"How long has it been?" he asked.

"Eight hours now," the technician at his side answered. That was the man who answered to him. The man was short and heavy. He sat at a console, stubby fingers playing occasionally across the buttons and dials.

The man he answered to, Jim Sure, stood in the back. That was his real name, Jim A. Sure. A comforting name for a man running one of the world's newest experimental power facilities.

Brian had often wondered how a name like that might play into the progress of a career. Were promotions infinitesimally easier to come by? Would a name like that naturally rise to the top of the résumé pile when being considered for the head job at a nuclear plant?

Brian looked at the man critically from the corner of his eye. Things weren't going well for Jim Sure this day. He peeled another antacid from the plastic wrapper and popped it into his mouth.

But Phoenix Nuclear wasn't alone in its problems. Several other power stations in California had the same emergency, their juice shunted away down some dark hole.

It was like his nightmare. The one he'd been having more and more often lately, watching helpless as the core's heat dump failed and the whole assembly degenerated into catastrophic meltdown, blowing the majority of Phoenix to God.

But this was no dream.

On the big screen, the tide began to turn. The engineers finally tracked down where the power was going—a single grid in the technical district outside of San Bernardino.

Now that the hole was found, the engineers began the task of plugging it. But it was not as easy as they'd hoped. The power sluices didn't respond.

"Dispatch field unies to the area," Jim Sure said. "Find out what's there. Shut it down."

The call was made. The coordinates were given. As the tech put the phone back in its cradle, the supervisor looked up and realized it might have been a moot point. Things now were very quickly turning around on the screen. Power, by the kilowatt second, was beginning to shunt off in its correct directions.

On the big screen, a few squares lit up, representing thousands of misdirected kilowatts flowing back into the city. It was a battle, and the little squares stayed illuminated only momentarily.

The system was adapting.

They watched the screen. Power flickered across the darkened squares. For the first time, the gauges in the plant moved, revving.

The supervisor smiled again. They were winning. Very gradually, kilowatt by kilowatt, they were winning. It was slow, but they were gaining the upper hand on whatever was stripping the power away.

PEA FLICKERED. Evan was sure of it. The puffy clouds behind him had skipped in their path across the sky while the ocean stood silent, a stiff shoulder against the shore. Even the gliders froze in their path across the azure, halted in midair for a lingering moment before continuing in their slow spirals. It was a hiccup, a change, and Evan knew it for what it was, a break in the flow of power. The dark eyes now looked down at him from a pained expression.

"Time has almost run away from us," Pea said. "They are faster than I thought."

Evan lowered his attention back to the work in his lap, forcing himself faster. He braided the cable wires together with his bare hands, sanctifying the copper union with blood earned from his fingertips. *What God hath joined, let no man tear asunder.* Now, where had he heard that? It was funny how those old days still came back to him sometimes, as if from out of a mist, from a time when he was a different person completely. Church had been so important to Mother. He wished she could see what he'd done, what he'd made of his life. She'd be proud, he thought.

Shortly after the state took Evan away from his mother, he'd begun asking to see her. He hadn't liked the new rules, or the new tutors, or the cleaning lady that came in and picked up after him. He hadn't liked the way he suddenly seemed to be so important to everybody. Eventually, he demanded to see her. The men with the smiles didn't take him seriously until he refused to continue his studies. Then the smiles disappeared. He told them he wouldn't work on their puzzles until they let him move back in with his mom. That was when the counselors sat him down on a couch and told him about the fire.

They said it started in a laundry room on the floor below their old apartment. His mother never felt a thing, they assured him. She died in her sleep of a combination of smoke inhalation and carbon monoxide poisoning.

They explained to him how lucky he was that the state had stepped in when it did, or he would have been in the apartment, too. He owed the state his life, they told him solemnly. And that was a debt he had a responsibility to repay. He didn't know enough then to doubt them. He knew enough now, though.

Years later, when he'd learned to mistrust the system's intentions, he used library files to search for a deadly building fire shortly after his twelfth birthday.

Somewhere at the back of his mind, he secretly believed that his mother was still living, and that she'd been told a similar sort of story about the accidental demise of her son. But they'd been more thorough than that. Buried in the middle of section B, between an article about childhood obesity and a fatal car crash, Evan found it. The fire had happened. Seven people were injured seriously. Two died. He saw his mother's name.

He gave the wires in his hands a hard last twist. Finished. The marriage was imperfect, coaxial to copper spiral, but when he tugged, the bond held fast. It would conduct. It would do.

He grabbed the second odd end and began the slow braid. Pea took notice of what he was doing, looking down without approval.

"Do you know what will happen if you do this?" Pea asked.

"Yes."

"And are you sure you still want to do it?"

"All for you, Pea. All for you."

CHAPTER THIRTY-SIX

Ben pushed through the throng of sweating bodies that crowded at the terminal exit, pulling his single carry-on bag like a trailing toddler behind him. The crowd sucked at his black duffel, threatening to pull it from his grasp in the sway of their bodies. He yanked hard, pushed hard, and popped free into the flow of pedestrian traffic along the causeway. He didn't bother to fight the flow; he trusted the river of people to take him where he needed to be.

Everywhere was shouting. If there had been more room to move, Ben was sure there would have been a stampede. But these people weren't scared; they were angry. He could see it on their faces.

Along the high arch of the ceiling, every other panel of lights threw only shadows, lending a darkened, surreal aspect to the entire spectacle. Ben was careful to keep his feet moving squarely beneath him. He'd seen what crowds could do with tripped footing if given half a chance.

Up ahead he saw the reason for the turmoil. On the enormous sign showing times and destinations, not a single flight number sat adjacent to the words "on time." The words "canceled" or "delayed" sat instead on the long flight board. He listened then, and from what he could decipher from the periodic informational blasts being pumped out of the speakers, there was some sort of problem with the power.

"There is no cause for alarm," the speakers informed him. "Airport emergency backup generators are now running. However, it has been necessary to shut down many of the runways. We apologize for the inconvenience." Ben knew the runways they *were* able to keep lit were being used to land planes, not for letting them take off. Some of these people were going to be here for quite a while.

He pushed his way into an eddy that looked promising and finally wriggled free from the cloying river of people entirely. Down an escalator he went. Someone was speaking Chinese behind him. And in front of him, he recognized the rounded syllables of native New Englanders. Ben considered the tops of their heads from his perch exactly three steps behind.

A flood of voices bubbled up the escalator from the other direction, providing bits and pieces of conversation, a variety of facial expressions. Angry faces. Faces pulled taut by anxiety. Frustrated faces by the dozen. Then, inexplicably, a beaming, beautiful face. Up she went past him, bearing her smile with her. *What was she smiling about?*

But then she was gone, and he had more serious issues to worry about.

Of the faces he saw—even the smiling face—he noticed that not one seemed to be lost in thought. Not one seemed pointed inward toward the happenings in Phoenix earlier tonight. It must have been on the news all over the country, yet Ben could see no evidence here. They were in the moment, living close to the surface of their eyes. The electrical problem loomed first and foremost on their individual horizons; its effect on their evening and their travels blotted out other calamities. An evening's inconvenience was all it took. The world went on. Maybe the stain of tonight's Olympic tragedy really *could* all go away someday. Maybe what he'd seen and been a part of would someday fade into the public's unconscious. For the distance of the escalator, he enjoyed imagining his career wasn't over.

Then he was off, and the baggage exchange was snaking by on his left, with its attendant crowd of travelers—the group of them straining their collective necks to see just past the next serpentine convolution of the conveyor belt. He passed by, thankful he was traveling light.

Glass doors with night in their panes stood off in the distance, teasingly close. He ground to a halt at the back of a line. The line snapped shut behind, consuming him. He pushed through.

The glass doors opened for him, and he moved into a night that was a night only in the sense of its diminished stuff to see by. In a way, it was as though he was still indoors.

Above him, gray concrete spread out in two directions. It was a road eight lanes across, topped over, he knew, with another road eight lanes across. It was an artery leading from and to the airport, but it was a special kind of artery, with bright yellow platelets. They eased along, slowing in the narrow capillaries, carrying a cargo of passengers instead of oxygen. And what did that make him, exactly? A malarial parasite, perhaps, hoping to hook its way into a blood cell.

He moved behind the shouting crowd, their arms raised and waving at the approaching taxis. The cabs came and went, and the crowd seemed not to notice for all the size it changed.

Using an old trick he'd learned in his time in New York, Ben moved to the left and walked briskly against the flow of road traffic. The crowd near the street thinned as he distanced himself from the airport doors, and then the wall pushed the sidewalk smaller and smaller until it was nothing at all, forcing him to walk on the white line. He stepped into the road.

A cab loomed, but Ben didn't move. It stopped a few feet short of his knees, and he jumped around and opened the door, throwing himself and his bag inside before it could pull away.

"San Bernardino," Ben said.

"Which side?"

"Technical district. Double the rate if you get me there in half an hour."

The cabbie's eyes found him in the rearview. "That'll be tough."

"You can do it."

"I want triple if I get a speeding ticket, half hour or no."

"Fair."

The cab pulled forward past the shouting, outraged wall of faces.

CHAPTER THIRTY-SEVEN

Silas gazed up at the slash of night and the gleaming shadow that spoke, and what there was left in him of reason and rationality passed out of existence. The face stared down. Silas felt the change in his head, this partial death, very clearly, and wasn't too disturbed by it. Because he knew it was necessary. Because what now remained was hard, and cold, and believed in monsters.

He waited for the gladiator to speak again, to fill the gaps with its inhuman, rumbling voice. But the seconds ticked by with only space between them. The gray eyes looked down on him as if in expectation, the shiny backsides of its retinas glowing in the dim, faraway luminescence of his flashlight. It was waiting for him to react, he realized. It was waiting for acknowledgment. Silas had none to give. Next to him, Vidonia was climbing her own mountain back up to speech; her jaw hung open, throat working some soft sound.

"I think we need to hurry," Silas said.

Vidonia only stared.

And then the creature's voice did come again, scraping on his sanity, so alien it took his mind a moment to decipher the words: "I come for you, Shilash."

It was a voice without inflection, without a trace of anything he could recognize as human. Silas could think only that the movies had gotten it wrong for so long; when finally the monster came for man, it would be behind a voice like growling dogs.

Silas moved first. He jumped against the wall and thrust his right arm as far back into the duct as it would go, groping blindly. His hand touched something, went through it. Warm, wet slime coated him past the wrist. He curled his fingers and tried to pull the gelatinous mass from its position against the wall of the duct, but his hand came free, fingers slipping easily through the egg mass and coming away with nothing. He looked down at his greasy fingertips for a moment, trying not to hear the sounds above him. Then he threw himself at the duct again, reaching, cupping the mass against the flat of his palm.

"Hurry up!" Vidonia shouted. "It's coming!"

Above them, the gladiator was busy.

The ceiling meshwork buckled.

It was like the scene at the competition, except exactly backward, and much, much more personal. And this mesh was stronger, resembling rebar more than any sort of cable.

Silas scooped against the gelatinous mass, feeling the hard Ping-Pong-ball-size eggs. It oozed toward the edge of the duct, flattening out under its own weight into something like a lumpy puddle.

From high above came the sound of tortured metal, and the first rod snapped under the force of the gladiator. Steel jarred. A chunk of concrete broke free and crashed to the floor in an explosion of sound and dust. Vidonia coughed in the billowing cloud and moved closer to Silas, pulling the light from his grip where it pointed uselessly at the floor.

The slime puddle slid toward the lip of the duct, then over it, parting like water in Silas's outstretched hand. It hit the floor in twin glops. There were now two gelatinous masses to contend with. Vidonia shone the light through the sticky crumple of straw, parting the loose heap with her other hand.

Silas stooped and tried to disengage the slime from the stalks of straw but soon found the task impossible. A slick coat of viscous sludge spread everywhere, making the straw gleam in the close attention of the flashlight. Small black eggs appeared in the mess, and Silas plucked one from its sheath of slime and tried to crush it between his forefinger and thumb. It was solid as a marble. He dug a hole in the straw with the brush of his hand and set the egg firmly on the hard concrete floor. He raised his leg and stomped with all his force. Pain lanced through his ankle, but when he lifted his foot the egg was still intact, completely unaffected. Perhaps egg was not the right word for what these things were. They were more like hard, round seeds.

And what pestilence will sprout from them?

He'd need something stronger, he decided. Something with the force of a nutcracker, to do them damage. Silas glanced up and saw the gladiator caught halfway in the act of being born, wriggling through the narrow gap in the grating. Its inhuman cries added to the unreality.

Silas looked down at the glossy, unbreakable spheres, then at Vidonia. They were out of time. "Pick them up," he said. "We have to pick them all up."

He crouched and frantically began gathering the small black objects. When there were too many for him to hold in one hand, he cradled them in the front of his shirt.

Vidonia dropped her face nearly to the straw as she plucked the eggs, one by one, from their clutching pools of slime.

Silas heard noise and glanced over his shoulder.

"Run," he told her.

She didn't hesitate.

Another sound jerked his eyes upward. It was coming.

The wings were through the hole now, the legs sliding inside even as the gray lights wheeled toward him.

Silas launched into a sprint, holding the eggs against his bloodied T-shirt with both hands. The gladiator howled, and the leather slap of wings told him the birth was complete. He didn't dare look behind him. Instead, he concentrated on the rise and fall of his legs, the placement of his feet in the wide mass of straw. If he tripped on a buried obstacle, he would die. It was that simple.

Ahead of him, Vidonia burst through the open gate, grabbing at the door as she spun to look at him. Her eyes widened suddenly, and he knew it would be close. He knew what her eyes saw. Hot breath kissed the back of his neck as he leaped toward the closing gate.

He hit the ground wrong, skidding on his side, as Vidonia slammed the door home. The gladiator crashed loudly against the bars in the next second. Silas tried to sit up. His breath wouldn't come. Eggs spun away on the hard concrete in little elliptical orbits. Vidonia was flat on her back, suddenly behind him somehow. He finally managed to suck air into his body, and a hot stab of pain lanced his right side. He took another breath, and his mind cleared a little. Vidonia moaned. He turned his head toward her, and in that moment felt his foot caught in a vise. An impossibly long black arm lay snaked between the bars and across the floor to his foot. The arm pulled, and Silas thought he was a dead man. Then the shoe popped loose and he rolled away, kicking wildly as the huge, black hand clutched at his legs.

The gladiator's eyes were gray spotlights of rage that bore into him from beside vertical iron. The creature didn't speak now. It didn't have to. Silas scooted away on his butt, flailing at the eggs, driving them back from the bars with his hands and arms and legs. Vidonia's eyes were open, but he could see she was only just now rising up inside them. A red welt ran the length of her forehead. She'd been standing at the bars when the creature slammed into them.

She looked at him as if surprised he was alive. "Do we have them all?"

Silas glanced at the scatter of black orbs, some still rolling. "I think so." He caught them in the corral of his arms, and they clacked with the sound of billiard balls as they came together. The flashlight was against the wall, spilling illumination across the floor and sketching long shadows behind each egg, making them easy to see even in the dim light.

The gladiator hissed and receded from the bars, becoming shadow again. Wings whispered in the darkness. A puff of air hit Silas's face. Above, in the distant slash of sky, the stars were blotted out for a moment as the gladiator climbed back into the womb of night.

"It's gone?" Vidonia said.

"No. It's not that easy."

"That was easy?"

Silas stood and began to stuff the eggs into his pockets. He counted them as he did so, and there were eleven. He silently hoped that they hadn't lost one, and started down the hall in the direction from which they'd originally come. Vidonia was close behind him. He clicked the light off and found the halls less distracting in the near dark. There was no contrast of shadows, no sweep of a sharp, bright flashlight beam. A suggestion of light filtered through the open doorways of the labs.

They turned left, taking the hall deeper into the building. They slowed at an intersection.

"Which way?" Vidonia asked.

Silas hesitated. "That way," he said, pointing to the left, and then they were running again. Twenty meters down the hall, he swung them right.

"Are you sure you know where you're going?" Vidonia asked, as they slowed past a series of doorways.

Silas wasn't sure one bit. "It all looks the same in the dark." He stopped. "I think this is it."

He pushed the half-open door and stepped into the lab. Starlight filtered through the broad windows, throwing the room into twilight. He could see the vague outlines of lab benches against the far wall. Silas motioned for Vidonia to stay where she was, but she followed him closely as he entered deeper into the room. Glass crunched underfoot as he neared the windows. They were in the right place. He paused, listening. Outside, the moonlit oaks swayed in the breeze. The only sound was the rustle of leaves. He took a few steps closer to the window, and their car was visible over the top of the sill. It was conspicuous as hell parked against the wall like that, and his eyes scanned the black sky, looking for movement.

"Something doesn't feel right," he said.

"What do you want to do?"

He was silent, weighing their options for a moment before admitting, "What choice do we have?"

His foot brushed the lug wrench, and he bent to pick it up. It felt ridiculous in his hand. What good would a lug wrench be if that thing got hold of him? Every nerve was tingling as he moved toward the narrow gap in the frame of windows. He angled his head alongside broken glass and looked down the side of the building. Small stone outcroppings at the far side of the windows kept him from seeing very far. It was going to come down to a matter of faith. That thing was either out there or it wasn't. He took a deep breath and extended his head through the window, quickly glancing left and right. Nothing. Still no movement. Still no sound other than the rustling of the trees.

"Doesn't feel right," he said again, softly.

"Be careful," Vidonia said.

"I'll do my best."

He couldn't see it, but everything he knew about the gladiator told him that thing was out there, waiting. This was a trap.

He backed away from the window, and the sound of rustling leaves grew suddenly louder. A huge black shadow arced down from the upper branches of the nearest oak, and Silas sprang backward as the shape crashed into the bank of windows.

Glass exploded inward, but the metal frames held. Silas scrambled to his feet as the gladiator roared and thrashed. There was a screech and a loud pop as the window frame broke free from the wall on one side.

Vidonia screamed.

"Come on!" Silas grabbed her hand and jerked her through the open doorway and into the hall.

They ran blindly at top speed, concentrating only on putting distance between them and the gladiator. Silas felt like a mouse in a maze, and the cat was coming. They went left. Then right.

There was a loud crash in the distance, and the sound of breaking glass. The gladiator was inside now. They stopped.

"Which way?"

"That way," she said, motioning to the left.

Silas set off, running again. He stopped at the next junction.

"Take off your shoes," he said.

"Why?"

"We're making too much noise. It's going to listen for us." Silas unlaced his single remaining shoe and pushed it against the wall.

"My hands are shaking too much," she said. Her voice cracked.

"Try to breathe quietly," he said.

"How the hell do you breathe quietly?"

Silas put his finger against her lips to silence her. She was near tears.

He bent to help her and pulled the lowtops off her heels. A sound reverberated down the hall. A big sound. He slid the shoes against the wall near his, thought better of it, then tossed them down the opposite hall as far as he could throw. The sound came again, closer, like the sound of a big dog running on tile, the tap of claws on tile.

He pulled her to her feet. "C'mon, fast and quiet." They sprinted on their toes. Silas no longer tried to keep track of their position within the building. He went left and right in a zigzag pattern, trying to lose the sound that rattled occasionally through the halls behind them. Fear pushed him faster. The clack of talons was closing the distance.

Silas's feet were suddenly on soft carpet as they came to the entrance foyer. He tried the doors. Locked. They ran again, taking the first hall to the left.

Here the darkness was nearly absolute. There were no windows for starlight to seep through. Silas gripped Vidonia's arm with one hand and held the other out before him as he walked, feeling for obstructions. He had no idea where he was.

The steady clack of talons quieted for a moment, and Silas knew the creature had moved onto the carpet. It was too close now. They'd run out of time.

His fingers brushed against a smooth, hard surface. He ran his hand along the wall until he felt a doorway, and then he pushed through into a lab, catching the doorjamb with the palm of his hand and swinging inside. Vidonia rushed in behind him, and he shut the door quietly.

He moved past the long countertops to the edge of the window. He pulled the curtains wide, and the dimmest wedge of ambient light filtered into the room.

There was no broken scatter of glass on the floor. No lug wrench. But other than that, this room was identical to the room they'd entered through.

He checked if the windows opened. They didn't. He cursed silently.

His eyes cast about, looking for something to break the glass. The room was stocked with a familiar array of scientific equipment: liter bottles of sulfuric acid, centrifuges, sinks, and microscopes. A large desiccator sat on the counter near a rack of test tubes and volumetric flasks. A bank of computer terminals ran along another countertop.

They had probably stumbled onto the wing on the opposite side of the building from their car, but he couldn't be sure. He wasn't going to risk moving back out into the hall to find out. His hand reached for the biggest, heaviest microscope he saw. They'd get their bearings straight once they were outside.

The sound at the door froze him in place.

Breathing.

The knob slowly turned.

He dropped to his knees behind the counter, pushing himself against the cool wooden cabinet. He'd lost track of Vidonia. The door creaked, then swung slowly open and banged against the doorstop. Then was no sound at all. Seconds passed.

"Shilashhhhh."

He swallowed hard. The chase was over. This became something else now.

Talons clicked across the floor slowly as the gladiator ducked into the room.

Silas looked for Vidonia, but she was nowhere. She'd been closer to the windows and must have dropped behind another counter. Tay rose in Silas's mind. *Is this what the man felt as the gladiator finally broke into the room? Is this what he felt when he saw death coming for him?* Talons clicked against the floor, moving closer. The gladiator walked along the far wall, swinging nearer to the edge of the counter.

"Shilashhhhh."

The voice was enough to drive a man crazy. It was an animal snarl shaped into human words.

"Hunnnngry, Shilashhh." The voice rounded the corner just ahead of the massive, dark body. Gray eyes found him in the shadows. Silas knew he should run, should move, should do something, anything, scream, rage, crawl, beg, but he couldn't make his body work. In his mind, he clearly saw that anything he did quickly left him dead, so he did nothing. Looking up at the smiling maw of teeth, he stared at his future.

"Shilash."

Silas's hand tightened around the microscope. The talking had done it. Actually seeing words born from that mouth was too much for him to bear. He could move to silence those words, if not to save his own life. He flung the microscope as hard as he could. The gladiator's hand moved faster than Silas's eyes could follow, batting the microscope away with enough force to embed its pieces in the far wall. The creature bared its teeth in a leering smile and took a long step toward him. Silas feverishly plucked another microscope off the counter and hurled it. The gladiator impatiently knocked the assault away with a fist, sending the instrument across the room in chunks.

The gladiator's eyes changed. The grin became something less human, more predatory. It moved toward him. Silas stumbled back, clutching blindly across the countertop. His hand found the neck of a bottle, and he swung it over his shoulder with all the force of his body. The charging beast swatted at the incoming bottle, shattering it.

The charge stopped dead, and the gladiator screamed.

The rotten-egg smell of concentrated sulfuric acid stung Silas's nose. He cupped a hand over his mouth, gagging. The fumes burned his eyes, blinding him. The gladiator's howls continued, rising to an agonizing screech that hurt Silas's ears. Wood crunched as the gladiator thrashed in agony, knocking the counter from its base.

Silas fell backward, snatching air painfully through his cupped fingers. The gladiator lashed out, spinning like a tornado, slamming into the walls, knocking equipment across the room. Silas crawled along the floor to the wall and scrambled to his feet. He found Vidonia through squinted eyes and pulled her toward the door by her hand. The gladiator's screams continued as they burst into the hall.

Though concentrated sulfuric acid looks like water, it has a consistency closer to that of maple syrup. It sticks to what it touches and, with a pH approaching 1.2, can carve out a hole in flesh.

The screams continued, changing, shifting from pain into rage.

They ran.

They sprinted in blind panic, any thought of exiting the way they had entered erased.

They paused for breath at an intersection.

"Which way?" she asked, hands on her knees.

"I'm not sure."

"Do you think it's going to follow?"

Silas didn't answer.

The screams stopped. Silas looked at Vidonia and realized neither of them believed the gladiator's injuries had been fatal. It was coming again.

Silas looked down the forward hall. In the distance, starlight cast hazy runnels of shadow into the lobby.

"We can break out one of those windows," she said.

"It would hear us. We'd never make it to the car." He thought of when he'd last looked up to the stars for Orion. He hadn't been able to find the constellation in all the wash of light. But the cities were dark tonight. The archer would be out as he hadn't been for a very long time. *The archer.*

"No, not the car," he said, pulling her down the side hall by the arm. "I have another idea."

"What is it?"

"My office. We need to get there. We're going the wrong way."

"Your office?"

"This way."

They backtracked a short length of hall, and Silas pushed through a door.

"Another stairwell?" she said.

"Can't be any worse than the last."

And it wasn't. At the top of the landing was a single shining emergency light. One flight up, Silas pushed into another dark hall. This space he knew by heart. He'd walked it every day for the last twelve years. His office door was locked. He dug for the key, but his pockets were empty except for the eggs. *Had he left his keys in the car?* It didn't matter. He stepped back and threw his shoulder into the door. It snapped from the jamb easily and swung inward on warped hinges.

Vidonia followed him into his office, shutting the door behind them. Silas went to the window and looked out. Darkness. Swaying trees. Above, Orion with his crooked belt.

Silas opened the closet and pulled the bow from the top shelf. Two arrows leaned against the corner. The first, he knew, was bent beyond use, knocked crooked by the corner of the target he'd used on the property behind the lab. The second arrow would have to do. He picked it up and ran his thumb over the field point. It was not so dull as a spoon, but it was close.

Silas decided not to think about it. It was the only weapon they had. It either would or wouldn't be enough.

They waited.

"This isn't how I wanted it to end," Vidonia said.

"Who says it's going to end this way?"

"I mean, if it does. If it does end like this . . ."

"What?"

"I wanted more time," she said.

"We'll have it."

After a short while, they heard the clicking. It had tracked them.

"Get in the closet," Silas said. "No matter what, stay there."

She nodded and slipped inside. "Silas," she said from the shadows, the beginning of a question.

He motioned for her to shut the door. She did.

SILAS MOVED behind his desk, bow slick in his sweaty hands. The clicking talons moved steadily closer, the sounds growing louder as the creature progressed down the hall. It was almost there. Silas touched the dull tip of the field point again, hoping it could still bite. It had to. But he'd have to be close in order to make sure that he didn't miss. He didn't trust his nerves.

The footsteps halted just outside the office door. Silas dropped to the carpet behind the desk, gripping the bow tightly. His heart beat in his ears. His mouth was bone dry, throat closing in on itself.

The doorknob did not turn this time.

The door exploded inward and splintered against the wall. Silas heard the creature enter the room, heard its breath coming in long, ragged drafts. Silas waited. The talons were silent on the carpet, so he tracked the creature by its breathing. It stank of sulfuric acid and burned flesh. It moved along the far wall toward the closet. The breathing stopped.

Wood crackled, and Vidonia screamed. The creature yanked her from the closet by her leg.

"Hey!"

Silas jerked to his feet and cocked the arrow back. The gladiator held Vidonia upside down by the calf, shaking her violently. The skin on its face and chest was a tattered ruin, sprouting great white sheaths of dead flesh that drooped like potato peelings.

One eye looked out from the wreckage of its face, wheeling toward Silas.

Aiming for the eye, Silas released the arrow.

He knew immediately that it was high.

The shot went wide and imbedded deep in the upward arch of the gladiator's wing. It screamed and dropped Vidonia to the floor. She landed on her head with a thump, then rolled away toward the wall.

The creature turned its head and reached over its shoulder, gripping the arrow in its hand. It snapped the shaft off, and Silas could see that the wing was torn. Dark blood poured from the wound. The single remaining eye rolled on him again, filled with rage and pain.

It roared loud enough to shake the room, and the useless bow slipped from Silas's hand and thumped to the floor.

It came for him.

CHAPTER THIRTY-EIGHT

Ignoring the pain in his fingers, Evan twisted the last wire tightly. He was finished. For better or worse, the link was made whole again. He dropped the cord to the floor and stood, easing the kinks out of his thighs with the palms of his hands.

When he looked up at the screen, Pea was lying back on his elbows in the sand, gazing out over the water into the gloom. He hardly seemed godlike anymore. The long black hair showed streaks of gray, and the body had wasted, becoming thin and frail. Ribs stretched the skin at his sides, and dark crescents arched under each eye.

The light had gone out from those eyes, and Evan couldn't put a name to what had crawled in to fill the space.

Even the world behind Pea had begun to dim, as if the energy to exist was seeping away. The gliders sank in slow circles, losing altitude on the withering updrafts. A few had fallen to the beach and lay flopping like fish, dying. The waves of the sea had lost their will, becoming anemic versions of their former selves. They lapped softly against the sandy shore, like the soft kisses of a dying man to his children. The place was winding down, coming to rest; any fool could see that.

Pea simply sat in the sand, looking out at all that he had made. All that he could not save.

A brief puff of offshore breeze blew the hair away from his face. Lying there, he looked like any man, preoccupied, his mind elsewhere, on his troubles.

"It's finished," Evan said.

Pea turned his head suddenly, as if surprised at being spoken to. "Finished?"

"Yes."

"I suppose it is a good thing." Pea turned his head back to the skyline. "Was *I* good?"

"You were."

"No, I don't think I was." He shook his head sadly. "And my greatest sin still lies before me."

"What are you going to do?"

For a long while, Pea didn't answer, and Evan thought perhaps he hadn't spoken loud enough. But then Pea turned and the fire was back in his eyes. "Tell me," the god said. "Do you think there can be forgiveness?"

"For some things. Not for others."

"I think you are right. Papa, I think you are right, but I do not care." He stood, brushing the sand off his naked flesh. "It is almost over. The threads are coming apart."

"It was a fine tapestry."

"It was, wasn't it?" The god's eyes were on the horizon, narrowing to slits.

What was he looking at? How far can a god's eyes see? Into the next life?

"It's time," Pea said. He gave Evan a last sorrowful look. "They'll never hurt anybody again. All for you, Papa. I do this for you."

"What are you doing?"

"The lines of power go both ways. I can follow the

lines to the source. They have no defense; they never expected. Now they will pay for what they've done."

And then the god closed his eyes and put his hands to his face. There was a flash of light, and the god burst out across the sea in a plume of frothy wind, and what he left behind was just Pea, collapsed at the shoreline, a boy again. Just a child.

Evan didn't understand why it had happened, but he knew the threads of Pea's personality had unfurled, split somehow, leaving Pea just a lonely child crouching in the sand. Out on the flat sea, the new wind raised huge gouts of water as it headed for the horizon. There was a flash of light, and the swirling wind was gone. Evan knew that the other part of Pea, the god part, had left this place forever—had traveled out through the lines of power on a final terrible errand.

He didn't know where it went, but he knew they had run out of time. "What have you done?" he wondered aloud.

Evan looked back to the boy. He was seven years old again, and he was crying. The boy lay crumpled on the sand, barely conscious. His dark eyes rolled blindly. "Papa, are you there? Where are you?"

"I'm here."

"I can't see you." The boy's voice cracked as the tears slid down his cheeks. "I'm scared, Papa. What's happening?"

"I'm here. It'll be okay."

Evan picked up the headset he had assembled and adjusted it to fit around his skull. In his hands, it looked like just so much ruptured wiring twisted together at odd angles. Blood still stained the linkages. He vaguely wondered if it would electrocute him. Carefully, he stuck the leads to his temples, finding the old dish-shaped scar tissue.

There were no tetherings to hold him in an upright

position this time, so he thought it best to lie on the floor. He cleared a place near the screen with his foot, wiping away the shards of wire that had accumulated.

He sat and made a final adjustment to the headset. Then he lay down. The floor was hard and flat against the roundness of the back of his head. Above him, the ceiling spread away in panels.

He placed the visor over his face and one last time willed the world away. Willed it to never come back again.

The shoddy wiring turned the trip into something he experienced rather than a simple transfer of consciousness. It was not the gentle slide into nothingness that he remembered. He felt the inward fall like a burning in his brain—a frying of neurons that he could almost smell. His soul conducted through the wiring. Eventually, black faded upward to gray, and colors swam. Night fell in his head, then out of it. He opened his eyes and looked at Pea, crouched in the sand. Recognition blossomed in the child's dark eyes.

"Papa."

Evan tried to move toward the boy but couldn't. The interface was crude and uncoordinated; his legs spilled him into the sand. The boy ran to him and wrapped his thin arms around his shoulders, planting cool kisses on his cheek.

Evan's strength gradually returned, and he rolled over and sat up on the beach. He pulled the boy into his lap and squeezed, feeling the tiny body tremble in his arms. He looked down at himself, and he wasn't rage a hundred feet tall. He was himself. Evan. Flaws and all.

"Papa, I'm scared."

"Shhh, Pea. There's nothing to be afraid of."

"I don't want to die."

"Everything has to die, Pea."

"What's going to happen, after?"

"I don't know."

"Is there a heaven?"

"A wise man told me that there is no heaven here."

"Then what will happen?"

"I don't know. But I'll be with you."

"You're not going to leave me again?"

"I'll never leave. I promise."

"Papa, it's coming."

In the distance, a sound came like the emptiness between atoms. It was a sound Evan heard equally with every part of his body. Though he couldn't see it with his eyes, his mind sensed the hole, the vast nothingness that rushed toward them from across the water.

To his left, he suddenly perceived a twist of light, and when he turned his head, he was looking out through a portal into the tech chamber. It wasn't a screen on this side, just a rectangular gap, and through it he saw his body lying on the floor. Above his fallen shape, the ceiling lights flickered. The city power was coming back on. Which was why this place was losing the energy to exist.

The sand began to tremble under him, and the boy clung tightly to his neck. The sound in the distance grew louder, rushing toward them, sucking the sea into blackness as it approached across the water. The soft air currents reversed direction, falling back toward the black that swelled from the horizon, lifting the sand off the beach in horizontal flows that whispered past their ankles.

A glider squawked as it tumbled across the sand. The world shifted. Evan squeezed the boy harder, locking his arms around his narrow back.

The sound revved into a deafening roar, and the beach shook violently, sliding away beneath them.

Evan dug his legs into the sand, trying to hold on, but it spun past him in a swirling river, pulling them upward toward the black sky. In the last moments, the boy whispered, "Thank you for staying, Papa."

Evan clutched at the boy's small form as they lifted free, falling upward toward the howling darkness, and then light flashed—an afterimage like a detonating sun, illuminating the entire universe in a single glorious, scorching blast of incandescence.

Then the screen went blank.

The lights in the anteroom shined bright and strong. Then went out again. The city went dark.

On the floor, Evan's body forgot itself, and his heart ceased beating. Evan and Pea were no more.

THE ENGINEERS in the control room jumped to their feet and cheered at their consoles. The screen on the far wall told the story. Phoenix was alive again. The boxes were all lit, representing eleven million fully functioning units. They'd won. Whatever had been sucking away the power had been cut off.

The supervisor, Brian, smiled broadly. He looked at Mr. Sure, who was also smiling. They had managed to shunt all the power away from that thirsty grid in the technical district outside of San Bernardino. Problem solved.

"What the hell do you think that was?" the supervisor said out loud to no one in particular. Already, it had moved into the past for him. His smile was straight and wide and relieved.

"I don't know," the technician answered.

As Brian looked at the gauges, his own smile began to fade.

The gauges were all normal, except for one. He glanced up at the cheering crowd and saw that nobody else had noticed. He considered not bothering, not saying anything. *Let them cheer.* Instead, he motioned to Mr. Sure, pointing to the console with his other hand.

Mr. Sure eyed the gauge. "What's this?"

"The heat dump," he said.

"I can see that. Why is it doing that?"

The dial continued its upward swing, climbing like the tachometer of the world's most powerful muscle car. It climbed steadily through orange. The supervisor looked down at the men in the chamber. The cheering stopped as, one by one, they took notice of the small display in the far-right corner of the wall screen.

Whatever it was they thought they'd beaten had come back to strike a final blow. Mr. Sure thought of Chernobyl, Three Mile Island. Fukushima. Precautions had been taken. It could never happen again, that's what they'd said. What they'd promised. This would be worse. The needle climbed toward red without slowing. Nuclear cascade.

"Why is this happening?" Mr. Sure's voice was small, almost childlike. The supervisor sensed the question wasn't directed to him but to God.

The needle slid into red. "Phoenix," said the supervisor.

The explosion moved quickly, reducing the room to atoms before he could even register the pain.

THE LIGHTS came on in Baskov's room, battering him awake through his eyelids. He'd never been able to sleep without total darkness, and this new light was an irritant.

Groaning, he looked at his watch: four-forty. The power was back on. He did the math. That meant the city had been without electricity for a grand total of nine hours. Ridiculous. Heads were going to roll, he was sure. He sat up and swung his feet to the floor, cursing himself for not having the foresight to make sure all the light switches were off before he went to bed.

His mouth tasted like cotton gauze, so he reached for the half-empty drink on the night table. It burned going down but settled into a nice warm glow in the pit of his stomach.

He'd met with the president and several other state heads earlier in the evening. It hadn't gone well, and he'd retreated into his bottle afterward. There would be another meeting tomorrow.

He reached for the wall lamp above the nightstand and clicked it off. The room darkened somewhat, but the bathroom light spilled across the floor to his bed. He looked toward the bathroom, weighing his options before giving in to the inevitable and angrily throwing the covers off. The room was cold; without power, the heat had shut down. Phoenix might be a city in the desert, but at night a chill could still seep into the air.

He walked across the carpet, stepping onto the bathroom tile. He reached for the switch, but just before his fingers made contact, the light went out by itself.

He clicked the switch, anyway. Up, down—nothing happened. He left the switch in the down position and walked blindly back toward the bed, arms groping in front of him. He found the wall lamp, clicked, and nothing. The power was apparently out again after being on for only a few seconds.

"Like some damn third-world country," he grumbled into the darkness.

A red glow in the window caught his eye. He turned, and the glow grew brighter. Curious, he walked to the sliding glass doors. He found the handle, slid the door open, and stepped outside into a warm breeze. His eyes widened.

He saw his death. A huge wall of fire rolled toward him from the east, engulfing the dark shapes of buildings and swallowing the city in its giant red maw.

He had time enough to hope it was a dream, and then the warm breeze turned into an oven blast that singed the hair from his body and let him know how awake he was. His skin burned. The red wave crested overhead, pushing a molten, hurricane wind before it.

He shielded his eyes and careened backward, crashing through the plate glass to the floor of his room. He writhed, screaming, on the smoking carpet as the blast slammed toward the building.

He looked to the light, and the heat made ashes of his eyes. The maw closed around him.

"TURN HERE."

"Here?"

"Yeah, a left," Ben said.

The taxi barely slowed as it took the corner wide, throwing Ben against his seatbelt. The cabbie had four minutes left on the deal they'd struck, and he was taking it personally. Inside the running wash of the taxi's headlights, the road skipped by in a pattern of gray asphalt and yellow dashes. At this speed, the cabbie apparently thought the center of the road was the safest bet. The car's headlights provided the only illumination as far as Ben could see. The power was still out, and the world flew by in darkness.

"Left at the next intersection," Ben said.

"How far is that?"

"Should be coming up."

The cabbie eased back slightly on the accelerator, checking his watch for the tenth time. Ben had already decided that the guy had earned the extra money, but he didn't want to tell *him* that. The tires squealed as they rounded the turn.

The driver hit the gas and they roared along a high chain-link fence.

"Stop!" Ben shouted. He'd almost missed the opening.

The anti-locks mooed as the cab shuddered to a stop.

"Back up."

The reverse gear whined, and the driver looked over his right shoulder. The car sped up, slowed, stopped.

"Through there."

The cab pulled up to the gate. Ben craned his neck for the guard, but the gatehouse was dark. He rolled the window down and began reaching for the electronic pass from his wallet when he saw that somebody had already pushed the gate open enough to slide a car through.

They were here.

Ben smiled in the darkness of the backseat.

"Drive on through."

"We're not going to have any problems for this, are we? This looks like private property."

"It's actually publicly owned."

"You mean government. That's worse. I'll just drop you here."

"You're getting the three C's. Plus an extra fifty if you take me all the way." It was one hell of a long driveway. He wasn't in the mood to walk.

"You got it," the cabbie answered, fast enough that Ben knew he'd been bluffing for more money.

The cab slunk through the gate with inches to spare on both sides.

"Follow the bend to the left, then take the right lane all the way to the back."

As they neared the building, Ben scanned for any sign of his coworkers. There was nothing out of the ordinary. No car, no broken windows, nothing.

"Let's go around back."

They rounded the corner, and Ben immediately saw the car up against the wall. At first he thought it had crashed there, but then he saw the broken window above it and understood. They'd stood on the hood to reach the window.

"Stop here," Ben said. The cabbie hadn't noticed the broken window, and Ben didn't want him to be more nervous about this than he had to be.

Ben was reaching for his wallet when the lights came on. Everywhere. Just like that. After so much darkness, the building seemed to absolutely glow.

"About time," the driver said.

Ben took the bills from his wallet and passed them over the seat. "Thanks," he said.

"My pleasure," the cabbie answered, as he took the money and folded it into his breast pocket.

The sound of breaking glass caught his attention, and Ben turned his head.

SILAS FELT the gladiator like an elemental force, a cresting wave rushing toward him in the small room. Time slowed, and Silas knew assuredly that he was about to die. But it's strange how the body works, what it refuses to accept.

In the darkness, his eyes still caught the swivel of

the arm, and his body leaped instinctively. Even as his body did these things, his mind did the calculations and knew he would be too slow. The creature's blow would kill him.

Then the power came on.

Blinding white light deluged the room, and instead of taking his head off, the blow struck him squarely on the shoulder.

He heard the bones snap like branches, and then he was flying. He hit the wall upside down and slid to the floor headfirst. Color rose up in his vision, and he blinked against brightness. He looked up, and the light had driven the pupil of the gladiator's single remaining eye into a thin slit. Silas tried to stand, but something wasn't working right. He looked down at himself and saw jagged bone extending from the mash of hamburger that used to be his shoulder. His arm was still connected, technically, but the thin shirt he wore did little to hide the dent in the side of his rib cage. He felt no pain. *Shock,* he diagnosed himself. *I'm dying already.*

The gladiator spun around, and its eye had opened slightly, looking for him. In the light, Silas could see just how much damage the acid had done. He looked at the gladiator in awe of what one liter of sulfuric acid was able to do to a living organism.

The single gray eye found him. Silas didn't move. The creature was on the other side of his desk, and it reached down with one thick arm and, ever so casually, flipped the wooden antique across the room. It broke apart against the wall near the door. Silas felt an irrational wave of outrage. That had been a good desk.

The gladiator seemed in no hurry now. It moved slowly toward him, its goal assured. There was a crash in the corner, and the creature stopped and turned.

Vidonia froze against the wall, looking down at the picture frame she'd bumped to the floor. She slid along the wall to the corner, crouching down, making herself into a small ball. The gladiator looked back at Silas, as if deciding he wouldn't be going anywhere anytime soon, and turned back to Vidonia, baring its teeth. It took a long step in her direction.

Silas reached his good hand deep into his pocket. "Hey!" he shouted.

The gladiator turned at his voice. Silas held up the shining black egg. "You want this?"

The gladiator growled.

"Go get it." Silas bent his arm at the elbow and threw the egg from over his shoulder like a baseball pitcher. It crashed through his office window and disappeared into the darkness.

The gladiator's reaction was instantaneous.

It sprang across the room and plucked Silas from the floor by his throat with one huge, long-fingered hand. Silas's feet dangled a foot from the bloody carpet. He struggled for breath, beating at the iron hand with his good arm, but the grip only tightened, cutting off his air supply as neatly as a kinked hose.

The gladiator pulled Silas close to its face. The tips of their noses almost touched. Its remaining eye burned into him, the pupil a sharp vertical lance. The mouth came open, and Silas waited for the bite. Instead, it spoke: "You die."

The world darkened as Silas slipped toward unconsciousness. Then muscles bunched in the iron, a quick jerk, and he was flying again. He gasped for air and felt the glass rake across his skin. Then he was tumbling. The sea of thick green sod rose up to meet him.

Above him, the room went dark again.

––––––––––

Ben watched the small black object bounce to the grass and roll into a stand of bushes. It was smaller than a baseball but rolled as though it was heavy. He glanced toward the broken window, but the angle was wrong for a good view. Dark shapes moved behind the bright spiderweb of glass. Someone had thrown the small object through the window on purpose; he was sure of it. He stepped out of the cab and shut the door.

"Wait here," he said.

"Sure," the cabbie said, hitting the fare button again.

Ben stepped off the pavement and onto the grass. He counted the windows along the wall of the building. Five down from the end, second floor. He had just time enough to realize which office that window belonged to when Silas exploded through the glass and fell like a stone to the turf. He bounced and came to rest on his side. And then he didn't move. Even from this distance, Ben could see the bones and blood. Arms and legs went in several directions. A moment later, the lights went out in the building again.

The squeal of tires behind him turned his attention back to the cab. Through the windshield, the driver's face was a mask of get-the-hell-out-of-here. He backed the car up onto the parking block.

"Hey, hold on a minute!" Ben screamed. "Wait, he's hurt."

The driver shifted into drive and peeled away. Ben tried to get in front, but only managed a solid kick along the side of the cab as it sped past him.

"You fucking asshole, don't leave!"

The cab didn't slow. Its taillights fled into the darkness.

Ben cursed under his breath and ran toward Silas. He knelt at his friend's side and grasped his hand.

Silas seemed to feel the touch and turned his head toward him. A deep gash marred the side of his face. He whispered something. Ben couldn't understand. He looked toward the window Silas had fallen from but could see nothing but the ceiling from this angle. Baskov's goons would take a few minutes to get outside. Maybe there would be enough time.

"C'mon, Silas, we've got to get out of here. Do you have the keys to the car against the wall?"

Silas spoke again, and Ben saw his jaw working in several directions at once. It was broken.

He leaned his ear closer.

Silas mumbled something, gripping his arm tightly.

"It's okay, buddy," Ben said. "I'll get you to a hospital. But we've got to get out of here now." Ben tried to pull him to his feet, but Silas resisted. His bloody hand curled in Ben's collar, pulling the side of his head almost against Silas's mouth.

"Run."

Ben heard that clear enough.

The ground thumped behind him. A trickle of fear ran down Ben's spine. He suddenly understood that he'd been wrong about something. It hadn't been Baskov's goons who threw Silas through the window.

Ben slowly turned. The gladiator sat on its haunches, head cocked to the side. Ben looked back sadly at his friend. "Oh, Silas."

The gladiator pounced.

CHAPTER THIRTY-NINE

Vidonia pushed herself into the corner as far as she could. The light seemed obscenely bright after so much darkness, and she felt its weight like a spotlight pointing her out. The gladiator turned away from the window it had just thrown Silas through and looked directly at her with its single gray eye. It didn't move. She couldn't make herself small enough.

A sound caught the beast's attention, and its head snapped around to the window again. Had that been a car door? The lights went out, and the room was plunged into darkness again. The creature moved to the window, becoming a dim silhouette in the starlight. Its wings bobbed partly open, but the one side didn't move right. The broken edge of an arrow still protruded from the meaty joint.

The gladiator leaned through the window. Then it dropped out of sight. She was suddenly alone in the room. She didn't breathe for a moment. Didn't think. Her heart drummed, and after a few moments she let herself believe it was gone.

Why had it left? What drew it outside?

She pulled her way up the wall to her feet. Her body was shaking so badly that she had trouble walking, but she forced herself forward. She navigated through the ruined mess of Silas's office, past the shards of splintered wood and twisted metal drawers that used to be his desk. At the window, she forced herself to look down.

She wasn't surprised to see Ben. Something about him being here seemed right, almost as if it had been preordained. This was the endgame, and all the players had their final role to play. The irony was almost biblical, and Vidonia could sense her mother smiling down at the symmetry of it all.

The gladiator became what it was, and for Ben, at least, it was quick. He deserved that much.

It didn't bite. The attack was less predatory than that, more a thing of anger. The gladiator struck a single powerful blow.

She'd read once that police profilers could ascertain how emotionally involved a killer was with the victim by the placement and severity of the wounds. She wondered what they'd make of Ben when they found him. She wondered what they'd make of his crushed head knocked thirty feet from his body. Would that raise a flag? Would they consider it a crime of passion?

At least it was over for him. She hoped it was over for Silas, too. She realized how much more fragile humanity was than the strange creature. Humans seemed much like glass for how easily they broke.

The gladiator brought its attention to bear on Silas again. It crouched low to the ground and moved toward his broken form, sniffing around his head. Silas turned his face away.

He was still alive.

Her breath caught in her throat.

He was still alive.

Vidonia brought a shaking hand up to her mouth to hold it all in—the laughter, the crying, the screams. Everything that wanted to pour out of her. He was still alive. Tears slid down her cheek and dropped to the floor.

She grabbed the broken sill. Glass sank into her palms, but she barely felt it.

She extended a leg out the window, then shifted her weight onto the small ledge. Her other leg followed, and she let herself drop. She landed in the bushes with a resounding crack. At first she assumed the sound had been her leg or spine. She was in pain, but when she stretched, all her parts still moved. The sound had been a branch that broke her fall. Her butt had taken most of the force of the fall, and for once, she was happy for the little extra padding nature had provided her.

She lifted her head up from the mud, half expecting to see the creature looming over her, attracted by the sound of her fall. But it still knelt beside Silas. It sniffed him, pausing over his front pockets where he had stuffed the eggs. One huge black hand raked down his body, ripping open his clothes and flesh. Silas screamed in pain as the gladiator picked the eggs from his wounds.

Vidonia put her hand over her ears but could not block the sound completely. The screaming continued, and she crawled away on her hands and knees, staying behind the belt of shrubs next to the building. She tried to think of something, anything, that she could do.

There was a loud thud, and the screaming stopped.

She turned and looked through a gap in the shrubbery. She didn't want to see but couldn't help herself.

The gladiator's fist was high over its head. Then the arm came down on Silas in a savage arc, thudding again. Tears slid from her eyes. Any thought that Silas was still alive died with that second blow. *It's over for him now,* she told herself. But the tears kept coming, blinding her. She continued to crawl, keeping her shoulder against the wall for direction. Behind her, she heard the arm come down again. Again. She heard the crunch of bones, the sickening squish of pulped flesh.

She crawled on her belly with her face in the dirt, not looking, not wanting to see or hear what was going on twenty feet away. The sounds grew softer and farther away. She stopped when her head hit the tire. She looked up, and the car seemed impossibly huge—impossibly removed in time, like an artifact of some forgotten age. Had it really been only a few hours since she'd arrived on those very four wheels? It seemed like an eternity. Everything in the world had changed since then.

Her hand closed on the door handle. She pulled, and the latch popped like a gunshot. She looked over at the gladiator, but its arm still did not stop. It was too distracted to notice. The thick black limb rose and fell like a piston, making of Silas a little dent in the ground.

Tears came anew, and she told herself she wouldn't look again. If it was coming for her, what could she do, anyway?

She slithered inside, over the passenger seat and behind the steering wheel. She lowered her feet to the floor and raised her body up.

She closed her eyes. "Please, God," she whispered. "The keys. That's all I ask."

Her shaking hand found the ignition. The key was still in it.

She let loose a ragged breath and turned the key. The electric motor buzzed to life. It wasn't loud, but she couldn't help looking again, and this time, the gladiator did stop. It cast its baleful eye toward her.

She shifted into reverse and hit the accelerator. The car jerked back from the wall and spun in a half-circle. She turned the wheel, and the car pivoted on its rear axis. She was straining over her right shoulder, hand gripping the back of the passenger seat hard enough to pierce the material with her nails. Still in reverse, she floored it, screaming wordlessly.

The gladiator had plenty of time to react. It even lingered for a moment to scoop up its eggs before it stood. As the car jumped off the pavement and hurtled across the grass toward it, the gladiator raised its wings and thrust upward into the sky.

Or it would have, had the right wing not been damaged by the arrow.

The ascent was crippled, off-sided, and the gladiator's body tilted in the air as the wings provided different amounts of lift.

The trunk of the car connected solidly with the gladiator's right thigh, spinning the creature over the top of the car and across the hood to the grass. She hit the brakes immediately, shifted into drive, and floored the accelerator again. It cost only a single second to do this, but still she barely caught it. The creature was up and moving. She jerked the wheel, and its hip collided solidly with the corner of the car, knocking the gladiator sideways to the grass.

It was hurt now. Not badly, but it was hurt. She turned the wheel again, bringing the car back around and throwing turf in a dozen directions. She moved the headlights across the creature as it tried to gain its footing. She screamed again and stomped the pedal to the floor. The car connected solidly. There was a loud crack, and the creature spun away, up and over the hood.

She spun the wheel again, and the headlights swung through the darkness until they found the black, bloody shape moving in the grass. The creature was damaged now. Badly. It crawled toward the building, pulling its broken body forward by its hands. She inched the car forward, using the hood ornament as a gun sight. When the crosshairs were lined up, she stomped on the pedal again.

She heard the clumps of grass pummeling the inside of the wheel wells as she picked up speed, rocking over the bumpy turf. The gladiator turned its eye to the headlights and threw its arm up. It didn't matter.

The nose of the car connected squarely with the gladiator's torso, carrying it forward through the bushes at more than forty miles per hour. The car buried itself in the wall with bone-crushing force.

Darkness enveloped her.

HER EYES opened to stinging darkness. She lifted her face from the deflated air bag and wiped the blood away with the back of an unfamiliar hand. The hand looked vaguely like hers but was shaped differently than she was used to. The fingers went in odd directions, and the wrist had a funny twist to it that shouldn't have been there. She tried to straighten it, and the pain came then, crashing in with enough force to send her back into the darkness for a while.

Later—she couldn't say how long—when she traded one darkness for the other, her face felt very cold, and she was lying across the passenger seat. She moved by slow degrees, discovering what pain really was. Everything hurt. Then she remembered that Silas was dead, and that was worse than the pain.

When she could, she tried the door. She couldn't find the handle. She looked around the car for where it might have fallen. Glass was everywhere but the windows. She looked across the steering wheel, and the hood of the car was a crumple against the wall. A dark, huge, twisted arm led away from the point of impact.

The passenger side was better. She pulled at the handle, and the door popped open with a clang. She pushed, but it would open only a foot or two. It was enough. She crawled across the passenger seat and aimed her face toward the gap. She pushed with her good arm, and the grass was damp and soothing against her skin. She sank her fingers past the roots and pulled. Her body followed.

For the first time, she realized the motor was still running. The throttle was stuck wide open, and it buzzed wildly, half bee, half sewing machine. She could see the flash of sparks falling to the ground under the motor.

She crawled away from the wreck and toward Silas, pulling herself by the roots of the grass. Dizziness overcame her, and she collapsed back, looking up into the sky. Slowly, she became aware of stars. There seemed to be millions of them spread out above her. *Had they always been so bright?* The buzzing of the engine grew more frantic. She rolled to her stomach and continued crawling.

Silas wasn't Silas anymore when she found him. He was mud and blood and bits of broken bone, pulped into something that looked like it never could have been alive. Never could have been a man whose face she'd kissed. She followed a long, splintered arm to a hand and laced her fingers into his. She recognized the hand. Those same long fingers, with the same long nail beds.

Blood ran into her eyes again, and this time she did not wipe it away. She let the blood blur the world away while she sat rocking. She wasn't able to pretend he was still alive, but she could believe he was still whole and lying in the grass beside her. She rocked him to sleep, singing softly.

It took her a long while to stop.

She let go, without looking down. She didn't want to see what was left of him. She didn't want to see the blood again.

She looked instead toward the car and the building.

She tried to get to her feet and was surprised to be able to do so. The limp was bad, but she could walk.

Her feet made shiny trails in the dewy grass.

When she got to the car, she leaned against it, and the world swayed again. She moved around to the mangled front end and looked down. The wall itself was pushed in, a crumble of cinder blocks.

The gladiator was dead.

Like Silas, it was reduced to little more than an arm dangling from a mass of flesh. That, too, seemed fitting. She couldn't tell where the head used to be. She wanted to find the eye and gouge it out. She wanted to taste its blood, carve out its heart. At that moment, nothing was too gruesome. After a moment more, she realized she wanted only to walk away.

She was tired. But there was still so much for her to do. In the distance, the city was still dark; something had happened to the power again, and not just at the lab. She knew there would be no one coming for quite a while. They had other problems to deal with. Besides, how would they even know? Had some alarm been tripped? Without power, she doubted it. No, nobody was coming.

Very carefully, she picked her way through the hole the car had made in the wall and moved inside the building. The air was thick with dust. Lab benches lay strewn about the floor, their contents reduced to puddles and shards of glass. She looked around but didn't recognize the room. She'd worked in this building for months, but everything looked different now in the darkness. She could not connect what she knew of this place with what she was now looking at. They were part of different universes.

Stepping over the larger pieces of glass as she crossed the room, she barely felt the chemical burns to the bottoms of her bare feet. She swung the door open and stepped into the hall. As she walked, she slowed occasionally to look at the nameplates on the doors. It was too dark to decipher the writing, but when she found one about the right size, she ran her fingers across the raised letters. She was running on autopilot. She continued on, checking the next two doors in the same way. When she found the room she was looking for, she went inside.

The mass spectrometer sat in the far corner before a bank of computers. She followed the copper tubing to the tanks chained neatly inside their safety rails. The windows in the room let the moonlight in, and she could read the sign over the tanks: *Dangerous, Highly Flammable*. The mass spectrometers used hydrogen.

She unchained the hook and pushed the tank over. The copper tubing snapped, and she quickly turned the nozzle off. It was too heavy to carry, so she rolled it instead, using her feet to guide it down the long, dark hall.

When she finally got back to the shattered room, the tank made submarine pinging noises as it rolled across the remaining fragments of cinder block. It came to a stop at the pile of debris near the car.

She bent and very carefully backed the nozzle off until she heard the soft hiss of the tank. Then she gave it a quarter-turn in the opposite direction, resealing it. She stood. The floor was already covered in spilled, fuming chemicals that made her eyes water, but in the corner, she found two bottles of Stoddard solvent and monomethlyamine. She unscrewed the cap of solvent and made a trail down the hall, pouring the liquid, moving deeper into the building. When the bottle was empty, she dropped it to the floor and unscrewed the other cap. She poured the contents out on the floor in a broad pool and then walked back to the room. Her head swam with the fumes. She almost fell once, but something told her that if she fell to the puddled floor, she would never get up.

She stumbled against the broken nose of the car and slipped across something wet and sticky. She didn't look to see what it was. The car still rumbled and popped, the electric motor still racing.

She moved around to the hole in the wall and stuck her face through for a deep breath. She breathed. A minute passed. Her head cleared slightly, and she bent back toward the hydrogen tank. She turned the nozzle until the hiss came again, then she stood and moved quickly out through the hole. The wet grass stung the bottoms of her feet as she walked back toward Silas's body. She dropped to her knees. The world drifted away. She was happy to let it go.

The explosion, when it came, was far worse than she had anticipated.

The shock wave knocked her on her stomach, and the car cartwheeled past her on the right. Flames shot high into the air.

When the heat became too much, she faced the choice of leaving Silas's side or being cooked alive. She relinquished her spot and rolled away through the steaming grass. She went several dozen yards before collapsing. She reached for a piece of twisted metal wreckage lying nearby and pulled it toward her. She lifted it and crawled into the cool wetness underneath. The lab burned high into the dark sky, and after a long while, the world went away again.

CHAPTER FORTY

Vidonia sat in the glare of the equatorial sun. She looked out at the shimmering blue Pacific as it slapped at the crowded beach.

A gentle offshore breeze tousled her short hair and cooled the little dots of perspiration as they welled up on her skin. Over the last few years the sun had pushed her complexion past golden and into a deep, warm brown. She liked it; darker skin was so much less forgiving of her scars. She wanted them to show.

She finally gave up on the novel she was holding and let it slip from her fingers and drop to the sand. The bookmark tumbled out of place, but she barely noticed. She'd already left the story behind. She'd never open the book again.

The truth was that she'd been having trouble maintaining interest in any book; it had been a long time since she'd been able to immerse herself wholly in a context of somebody else's manufacture. So much in her had changed. She missed the escape of make-believe stories, but a person can't always decide what parts of themselves they shed. It was the price of new skin. A new life.

She twirled the straw in her Coke and melting ice and took a long sip. Her eyes moved to the sound of splashing. "Samuel," she called out.

The boy's head snapped around. He was big for

four years, already taller than the six-year-old cousin he was wrestling with in the waves. It seemed she was always buying pants for him because his legs were too long.

"Not so far out," she called.

"*Se faz favor, Mae,*" he replied.

"No."

Such a big boy. She watched him roughhousing in the surf. The sun shone off his wet skin. Since he'd started school, he'd taken to speaking Portuguese more and more often at home. The other children were influencing him. Sometimes this worried her. Other times it was a comfort. He was a smart boy, the teachers said. He could be anything he put his mind to. She wondered, *And what would that be?*

Vidonia saw her sister approaching across the waterline with her new boyfriend's arm thrown over her shoulder. Paulo, she thought his name was. But it didn't particularly matter; the names, like the boyfriends themselves, were interchangeable set pieces; they came and went like the cycles of the moon, and this one would be gone in a few weeks. They were always gone in a few weeks. He was short, dark, and muscular, with wavy hair combed straight back from his forehead in the newest style of the local connected men. He wore a white T-shirt with cutoff sleeves to show his arms. She knew he thought it made him look tough, that T-shirt, and she supposed it did. He looked like what he was; and that was something, at least. It was the ones who didn't that scared her. The ones who looked nothing at all like what they were. And sometimes her sister's boyfriends were that kind, too.

Paulo bent and scooped water into his hands. He flung it at Vidonia's sister, who ran away, screaming and laughing. Paulo chased.

He was even attractive in his own way, Vidonia decided. Very much like her father, she suspected. Another local connected man from a generation ago.

She waved a greeting. They waved back, both of them smiling. In all their time apart, her sister had not changed a bit. She was still like their mother. The trick was not hating her for it. She needed. The men provided. Perhaps there was nothing so terrible in that. And she was raising her own son well. Vidonia clung to that. Motherhood was the remaining commonality that bound their lives back together.

The splashing came again, and she called out, "Samuel, I said not so deep."

The boy turned and waded back toward the shallows, dragging his older cousin behind him like a knapsack. Samuel peeled the boy's arms from around his shoulders and threw him into the swell of an oncoming wave. The boy was up in an instant, splashing and wrestling in a salty spray of foam.

Vidonia shook her head slowly, smiling. *Boys will be boys.* She knew she should keep him out of the water altogether, but she couldn't bring herself to do it. He enjoyed the sea. Vidonia resigned herself to another trip to the doctor in a few days.

Samuel was prone to ear infections. She'd had tubes put in his ears last year, and that seemed to help, but water still played havoc with his internal piping. As she watched him, she was certain he understood the trade he was making today, a day at the beach for a night of pain.

It seemed lately that he'd decided to just live with the pain. You could get used to almost anything if you put your mind to it. Bad ears. Bad tubes. It would get better when he was older, or it wouldn't.

She'd stayed in America long enough for him to be born. She'd wanted him to have that citizenship available to him. Later, he could do what he wanted with it. Parents give their children opportunities. What the children do with the opportunities is up to them.

But the United States wasn't what it had been. It was hard to guess where Samuel's future lay. So much had changed after the Olympic debacle and the nuclear disaster. Millions died in the initial blast. Millions more in the civil unrest that followed. Parts of the southwestern United States went without electrical power for months. And for a long time after that, in some places, it was too expensive for many households to afford.

It seemed at the time there was more than enough blame to go around: the scientists, the government, the big companies that ran both. The infrastructure that had been built up over the last half-century collapsed like a house of cards when popular support crumbled beneath it. A radical shift advanced across the political landscape like a second nuclear wind, laying waste to the old guard and depositing a new. But then it was revealed that many of the new guard, those new, fresh faces, had the same old allegiances—and so that second wind had to keep blowing. And blowing. People wanted change. In colleges and universities across the country, civil unrest was fomented, institutionalizing itself, becoming its own product. Radical influence grew, and the reactionaries did what they do best— and took things a step too far.

A special session of Congress was called, and the laws governing genetic engineering were changed almost overnight. Advancement didn't grind to a halt, exactly, but it did slow to a reasonable crawl. Draconian licensing practices were also instituted for all research into artificial intelligence and VR computers.

Vidonia thought this last precaution was perhaps

the most unnecessary. There would never be another Evan Chandler. There would never be another Pea.

The gladiator event, of course, was discontinued entirely and permanently. It would never again be a part of the Games. It now resided only in the history books, a sad and bloody chapter.

"Samuel, Rão, come in. It's time to eat."

Samuel ran, high-stepping through the waves just ahead of his cousin, and hopped across the hot sand to Vidonia's blanket. The boys knocked sand loose from their feet.

"Not on the blanket," Vidonia said.

They sat, and she pulled the sandwiches out of the cooler and handed one to each boy. They ate like starving men, and she knew better than to blame it on a day spent in the water; Samuel ate like a horse anytime, when given half a chance. But she could still count his ribs. Not so with Rão. He was squat and plump and kept his bones well insulated from the world.

"Can we get back in after we eat?" Samuel asked. He'd already learned his chances were better when he asked for something in English.

"I've got a class to teach in an hour. Sorry, boys."

They moaned in unison. But the sandwiches continued their disappearing acts.

Samuel made a face as he finished the last bite. He stuck his tongue out, spitting. "Sand in my teeth," he explained. His sharp cheekbones and high-ridged nose gave him a fierce, angular appearance, but he was still handsome in the way of rough, healthy boys. She sometimes wondered how he might look in a dozen years. His face was a mixture of familiar features, combined into something new and his alone. The long body, though, that was a thing he'd inherited whole and complete.

Vidonia hadn't listed a father on the birth certificate. She'd endured the looks of the nurses and checked the box for "unknown" paternity. It wasn't such an uncommon thing. A lie easily perpetrated. The world wasn't ready to hear that Silas Williams had a son. Perhaps it never would be. So much death was associated with that name now. Rightly or wrongly, in the public's eyes that name carried a portion of the responsibility for what had happened. But she'd made sure that wasn't a burden Samuel would have to carry.

And she'd also made sure that Samuel knew his father had been a good man, even if the boy didn't know his real name. Even if he never knew it.

And she made sure the boy knew his mother loved him. In the end, she hoped that was enough.

EPILOGUE

The man in the white lab coat lowered his eye to the scanner and let the laser turn the world red. He blinked reflexively against the sting, and the scanner beeped. *"Please try again."* He almost always blinked on the first attempt.

He stood and rubbed his eye, then lowered his face back to the scanner, concentrating. This time he stared into the red beam without blinking. Or tried to.

"Please try again."

He gritted his teeth. He lowered his eye to the scanner, and through force of will kept his eye open. A musical tone sounded, and the door unlocked. *"Access approved. Stanley Mueller, you may enter."*

"Thank you," he said.

He stepped in via the steel door frame and nodded to the armed guard sitting at the desk on the other side. He followed the corridor deeper into the building. The halls were empty, white, cold. His hard-soled shoes made clicking noises on the gray tile. He pushed a steel cart in front of him. One of the wheels squeaked as he rounded a corner.

At the end of the hall, Stanley pushed open the thick double doors. He stepped into the nursery chamber, and the lights came on automatically. He donned a sterile mask and gloves. He put on the white smock and tied it behind his back. Then he backed through the doors and entered the inner incubator.

It was hot and bright and humid.

Stanley's purpose today was to draw more blood. He checked the vial seals, unclipped the syringe, then inserted the tip of the needle. The organism lay silent through the procedure. It was small, shiny, black. Information about the creature was need-to-know, but Stanley was no idiot. He knew what he was looking at, even after all these years. The differences were significant—the wings were vestigial, the feet twisted into little shovels. The teeth were small and fine, and pointed out of the head in different directions. But the similarities were also significant. It looked like the gladiator in the old news clips, only smaller and twisted. It was a stunted thing—a distortion—but there was no mistaking what it truly was. There was no mistaking it for anything else.

It had been more than five years since the Helix lab fire, but as far as he could find, nobody had heard of this organism's existence before six months ago. It had come out of nowhere. This perhaps was not so surprising, considering that, officially, it still did not exist. But he'd heard rumors. He'd heard the thing had crawled out of the bushes that had grown up around the abandoned Helix site. In another version, he heard the thing had been found by a groundskeeper, or something like that, in the ruins of the lab itself.

They were likely rumors. Exactly the kind of likely and believable rumors that will often seep into the void created by an absence of fact. There was no reason to think either rumor might be true . . . other than the idea that the creature had to come from somewhere. The rumors provided at least possible, if not plausible, explanations. But sometimes even made-up stories happened to get it right.

Regardless of where it came from or how it came to be in the lab, the fact remained that it was a fascinating biological specimen.

The creature almost never ate, and another team was still working on how that was possible. It was dormant, comatose.

"Hibernating," one team had called it. But most creatures did not hibernate at 95 degrees.

There was much he didn't know. But he was the blood man. That was his territory. And the blood had its own story to tell. The blood, it turned out, was emphatic.

He'd tested it several times now.

The organism in front of him was a living, breathing gamete—a step in the life cycle that functions with only a single set of genes. It was haploid—no different, genetically, from either a sperm or an egg.

Everything had changed in the last five years. So much had been lost. The new, young scientists freshly minted from the genetics schools were now faced with an odd situation: the golden age had passed them by. Gods no longer walked the earth.

Specialists had tried to reconfigure what had happened after the fire. But everything was lost. The blood and tissue samples were burned to nothing. Helix Labs had been an isolated, centralized unit. Everything was kept on-site, with very little outsourced to other labs. When the place burned to the ground, everything had burned with it. All its secrets. All but this one.

The top scientists in the country had been working for the last six months to unravel the complexity found within the little black-skinned organism that lay before him now. They'd done CAT scans and X rays and genotyping, and as of yet, the attempt had been a complete failure. The results explained nothing. The thing was a relic from a past golden age. A reminder of greatness lost, like the pyramids of Egypt.

The organism carried more gene sequences in its haploid configuration than most species did as diploids. It had more genes than it could ever use. It was a vessel.

When the blood vial was full, he snapped the seal closed and placed the vial in a plastic container. He loaded up his cart and wheeled it out of the incubator. He shut the door. He took off his smock and his gloves and his mask. And then he turned and walked away.

Walking away was the easy part. Forgetting was another thing. He still had dreams sometimes about the little creature. Other times he couldn't sleep at all. What kept him awake at night was this knowledge: the organism was a gamete. A single haploid set of genes. It begged a question, of course.

What would happen?

What would happen if they ever found another one?

Like a sperm and an egg coming together, what would they make?

ACKNOWLEDGMENTS

There are a great many people on whose guidance and friendship I've depended as this manuscript has slowly taken shape. This book wouldn't have been possible without their help.

Special thanks to the Mean Group, to Michael Poore, Josh Perz, and Marty-Tina Vrehas, who were in the trenches with me from the beginning; special thanks to the HWG en masse; a big thanks to Jeff Manes and Jack Skillingstead, inspiring writers and friends; thanks to my sisters for being there; to Christine for her continuous, unwavering support, even back when it was all just a crazy dream; thanks to all my industry friends over the years—to Tim for working all those late-night double shifts with me and talking books between samples; thanks to Codex, and to Bec, and to all the first readers who slogged their way through multiple drafts. Thanks to Michael Braff, editor extraordinaire; and to Betsy Mitchell and Chris Schluep, for believing in this book in the first place. I offer a special double helping of thanks to my awesome agent, Seth Fishman, who contacted me out of the blue, and without whom this book never would have seen the light of day—sometimes an email can change your life. Thanks to Sheila Williams for buying my first story and making the whole rest of everything else possible; thanks to Gardner

Dozois, Jonathan Strahan, and Rich Horton for noticing the short fiction of a new writer. Thanks to John Joseph Adams and to Marc Laidlaw for being there. Thanks to the professor in that one writing class I took who wrote in the margins: "This has potential." And thank you, Valve, for being the amazing place you are.